"Evoking the luxurious and extravagant world of the Gilded Age, Newport heiress and feisty amateur sleuth Deanna Randolph is a force to be reckoned with in this lively mystery."

—Tessa Arlen, author of the Lady Montfort series

"Utterly captivating! Freydont skillfully combines the glittering excess of the Gilded Age and a believable upstairs-downstairs dynamic with a thrilling murder mystery. Readers will fall in love with this intrepid new sleuthing pair and the dashing young men they assist. A must read for fans of historical mystery."

—Anna Lee Huber, bestselling author of
the Lady Darby Mysteries

"A wealth of secrets lies beneath the surface as spunky heiress Deanna Randolph and her maid Elspeth navigate the glittering waters of Gilded Age Newport's high society while working to catch a murderer. Charming and colorful characters, a richly detailed setting, and a compelling mystery make *A Gilded Grave* a thoroughly captivating read."

—Ashley Weaver, Edgar® Award–nominated author of
Murder at the Brightwell

"This well-crafted mystery is an absolute delight. Freydont has brought Gilded Age Newport to life with the skill of a historian and the insight of the keenest social observer. Deanna Randolph is my favorite new sleuth."

—Tasha Alexander, *New York Times* bestselling author of
The Counterfeit Heiress

continued . . .

A
GILDED
GRAVE

Shelley
Freydont

BERKLEY PRIME CRIME, NEW YORK

BERKLEY
PRIME
CRIME

An imprint of Penguin Random House LLC
375 Hudson Street, New York, New York 10014

Library of Congress Cataloging-in-Publication Data

Freydont, Shelley.
A gilded grave / Shelley Freydont.—Berkley Prime Crime trade paperback edition.
pages ; cm
ISBN 978-0-425-27584-9
I. Title.
PS3556.R45G55 2015
813'.54—dc23
2015007911

PUBLISHING HISTORY
Berkley Prime Crime trade paperback edition / August 2015

PRINTED IN THE UNITED STATES OF AMERICA

10   9   8   7   6   5   4   3   2   1

Cover illustration by Aleta Rafton.
Cover design by Lesley Worrell.
Interior text design by Kelly Lipovich.

Penguin
Random
House

For Pearl Wolf, friend and colleague,
always up for a road trip and a good dinner

Chapter

1

Deanna Randolph eased away from the hairbrush that was scraping her scalp.

"Miss Deanna, would you please hold still? Everyone will be ready to go and you'll still be sitting here."

Deanna glanced up and smiled at the mirror image of her maid, Elspeth. The filigree that surrounded her dressing-table mirror framed them like a portrait. The seated figure, dark hair piled up on her head and clothed in a white dressing sacque, dark eyes peering out at the painter. The smaller figure standing behind, barely a head taller even with her mistress seated. Her fair complexion, made even rosier by the gaslight of the bedroom, almost luminescent above the black and white that was her daily uniform.

Deanna would like to paint them just this way. Not in the

style of the Pre-Raphaelites, with their vibrant colors and play of dramatic lighting. And not like the pen-and-ink covers of the dime novels featured in the windows of the Bellevue Avenue newsstand. Something less defined, their figures softened and made slightly hazy by the gaslight, like the brushstrokes of the Impressionists.

But all she was ever given were pears and vases and landscapes to dutifully reproduce.

Oh, to be like Mary Cassatt, painting and living in Paris. Or Nellie Bly, traveling around the world. Or even Kate Goelet, the dashing lady detective of the dime novels she and Elspeth secretly read each night as Deanna got ready for bed.

"Miss Deanna!"

"Sorry," Deanna said, falling back to earth. She was eighteen and about to make her second coming-out, the first in New York, and now tonight in Newport for the summer season. She glanced over her shoulder at Elspeth, only twenty-two but already in service for ten years, the last two as Deanna's maid.

They would both be going to the ball at Seacrest tonight, Elspeth to sit at the ready to answer Deanna's every little need and Deanna to impress the elite of Newport. She straightened her back and felt nerves flutter in her throat.

Elspeth tapped the brush on Deanna's shoulder. "You'll want to make a good impression tonight. So, hold still." She paused, the brush raised over Deanna's head. *Maid Slaying Her Mistress with Hairbrush.*

"And if you're worrying about seeing Mr. Joseph tonight, don't be. Orrin says he never attends any social events."

"Ugh." Deanna slumped again. "I wasn't thinking about Joe at all. Not until you reminded me."

"I'm sure no one will remember anything of what happened."
Elspeth tugged Deanna's shoulders back.

"You mean that I was jilted before I was even proposed to?"

"Orrin says—"

"I know. Your brother thinks Joe is a paragon of modern
society. Sometimes I'm sorry I suggested Joe take him on as an
apprentice."

That was before Joseph Ballard had shocked her, their families, and all of Newport at the end of last season by announc-
ing that he wouldn't be returning to New York but planned to
remain in Newport year-round to work on his inventions. To
add insult to injury, he was living and working in an old warehouse he'd rented in the working class Fifth Ward, when he
had a perfectly good mansion on Bellevue Avenue.

"Oh, miss, you don't mean that."

"No, of course I don't." Deanna sighed and pushed at a curl
that had sprung from her fringe of bangs. *Stupid things, bangs.*
"I'm sure Joe is a perfect master. Now, let's not talk about him
anymore."

Elspeth returned the brush to the dressing table, lifted a strand
of pearls and tiny white flowers, and pinned them to the knot of
hair that crowned Deanna's coiffure. Deanna hardly flinched
when the pins scratched her scalp. It wasn't that Elspeth was
ham-handed; she was quite gentle. It was just fashion that wasn't
comfortable. No wonder Deanna's sister, Adelaide, was always
succumbing to the migraine.

"I don't know why they're having a ball at Seacrest tonight.
They say that Mr. Woodruff has been acting right strange
ever since he came back from that heathen place."

"Barbados isn't heathen," Deanna said. "At least, I don't
think it is. And Cassie says her father always gets seasick."

Elspeth harrumphed. "Seasick? He's been back on land for almost a week and he's not getting any better. Daisy, she's chamber maid over there, says one minute he's all energetic and the next he looks like he's gonna kick it. She's had to light a fire in his bedroom every morning. I just hope he didn't bring home some unheard-of disease and give it to the whole household just so he can show off those guests of his."

"I'm sure Lord David Manchester is no heathen and is perfectly healthy, even if he does live in Barbados."

"Hmmph. They say he has a valet as black as the night and seven feet tall, who can pull coins out of thin air, but if you get in his way, he puts a curse on you."

"Sounds like a carney trick, if you ask me," Deanna said.

Elspeth shrugged. "Maybe. Or maybe it's really black magic."

"I think black magic only happens in novels, Elspeth."

"Maybe." Elspeth added another tiny spray of flowers to Deanna's hair.

"Are you finished?"

"Almost. They say that Lady Madeline—she's Lord David's sister—didn't even bring a lady's maid. Said her maid was afraid to get on the boat. Well, I don't blame her. My ma came on a boat from Ireland, said she nearly died. Anyways, Mrs. Woodruff offered her the use of her own maid, but that Lady Madeline points to Daisy, who was filling the water ewer in her bedroom, and says, 'That one.' Now Daisy is a chambermaid *and* a lady's maid, and she only came over from Ireland a year ago. What do you think about that?"

"I think Daisy is going to be very tired before the Manchesters leave for home."

"Well, I say, good for her."

"So do I."

Elspeth stepped back to regard her handiwork. "All done. You look like a princess." She helped Deanna out of her dressing sacque and disappeared into the next room.

Deanna stood before the full-length mirror wondering if she would be a success tonight or if people would whisper about her because she'd been jilted. But when Elspeth returned carrying Deanna's ball gown high above her head, she forgot about Joe, and what people would think, and even about Kate Goelet and her detectival adventures.

The dress was unbelievably beautiful, with the lightest jonquil bodice, trimmed in Valenciennes lace, and tapering to a fitted waist before flaring out in soft flounces of gold-embroidered gauze. Mama had spent time and money to ensure Deanna's success at her first Newport ball. Now it was up to Deanna to do her part.

She held on to Elspeth's shoulders for balance and stepped into her dress, then stood patiently while Elspeth closed the row of tiny buttons down the back of the bodice and shook out the flounces that trailed down the back of the skirt.

"There now, you're as pretty as a peach. You'll turn heads tonight, miss."

"Wonderful, just what I need." How could she feel excited and depressed at the same time? She was a minnow—no, a goldfish—swimming with the sharks. Smiling, bejeweled, and beautiful sharks, but deadly all the same. She might not have been out very long, but Deanna knew what was what.

"I don't mean the old snouts. If one of them looks at you funny, you just out-grand them."

Deanna nodded, but it was easier said than done.

"I meant the gentlemen what will be there tonight. And one gentleman in particular."

Deanna shivered, even though the room was oppressively close. "Not Joe."

"Not him, though I'm sure he's kicking himself for how he acted. I meant Lord David. Everyone says he is very charming— and handsome and rich—" Elspeth gave her a saucy smile. "And single. I bet he'll only have eyes for you."

There was a quiet tap at the door followed by the entrance of a diminutive parlor maid. "Miss, you're wanted downstairs."

Deanna sucked in her breath and pulled on her gloves. She waited impatiently for Elspeth to do up the buttons, took her fan and evening bag from the dressing table, and paused long enough for Elspeth to stand on tiptoe to give her headdress a final check.

"Oh, miss, you look beautiful," the parlor maid said before she stepped back to let Deanna pass through the doorway.

Elspeth draped Deanna's evening cape over her shoulders and followed her out of the room. "You'll do us all proud, Miss Deanna."

"Yes, I will." If she couldn't be a painter or catch villains, at least she could marry well. She'd have to be content reading about someone else's adventures. "Tell me again what you've heard about this Lord David Manchester."

—∞◦)◯(◦∞—

They were waiting for her in the foyer: Mama, Papa, and her older sister, Adelaide. Her father looked grumpy, an expression he'd been wearing too much lately. He was over-worked, poor dear, and he had never quite regained his vigor in the three years since her brother, Robert, had died during the influenza outbreak at Yale. That was why Adelaide was engaged to marry Charles Woodruff, to consolidate the two families' R and W Sugar Refineries, now that Bob was dead.

Deanna kissed her father's cheek and breathed in the lingering aroma of his pipe tobacco. That did more than anything to calm her nerves.

Her mother gave her an appraising look and nodded. She herself was dressed in deep green Chantilly lace with large puff sleeves and a diamond parure, and beside her, Adelaide was a vision in pastel pink. Her sister looked beautiful and very self-assured, and Deanna felt a tiny spark of envy. Adelaide had been out for three years and engaged for one. Deanna had only been out for six months; she was still feeling her way.

"Girls," her mother said. She didn't need to say more. The one word contained a lifetime of advice, commands, expectations, and warnings of how to behave. She turned, paused long enough for the footman, who had been staring unabashedly at Adelaide, to rush to open the door, then swept out of the house.

Adelaide followed immediately after. Her father gave Deanna a reassuring smile, offered her his arm, and the two of them went out together.

"Heavens, it's close tonight," Mrs. Randolph said as soon as they had all taken their places in the carriage. "Let's just hope it doesn't come on to pour before we arrive."

The sky was indeed overcast, the moon a vague halo behind the clouds. There was no breeze, and both the night and the carriage were dark and oppressive. Deanna could hardly make out her family in the shadowed depths of their seats as the carriage started out, moving slowly and stately down the street.

Deanna reached to open a window.

"Your gloves," her mother said. Deanna drew her hand away from the window.

"Deanna, please sit still," Adelaide said languidly. "You're mussing my skirts."

Deanna sat back. Beside her, Adelaide sat perfectly still. She could stay that way for hours. Nothing perturbed her. Deanna, on the other hand, tumbled from excitement to dread with each sway of the carriage.

"You know, my dear," her mother continued, "just because you had a successful New York season doesn't mean you will take in Newport. There are different requirements of a young lady here." She sighed heavily. "Especially after that embarrassing incident with Joseph Ballard last summer. I don't know how your father and Lionel Ballard could make such a muddle of something so simple. You'll just have to brave it out if the subject comes up."

"Yes, Mama."

Deanna concentrated on sitting still while her mind raced with all the instructions she must remember at the ball. All too soon, the carriage took its place in the long line of conveyances slowly progressing up the horseshoe drive to Seacrest, the Woodruff family's summer cottage.

Her mother gave her a penetrating look. "Remember that you are a lady born and bred, Deanna."

"Yes, Mama. I won't forget." How could she? Her mother had been molding both her daughters for as long as Deanna could remember. And over the last winter, she'd been well and truly finished. She was eager to take her place in society. Still, she'd miss leaving her girlhood behind. No more sneaking off to run down to the sea or swinging in the tire swing her brother, Bob, and Joe Ballard had made in the garden of Bonheur, the Ballards' cottage on Bellevue Avenue. No more lying in the grass watching the clouds pass or naming the constellations in the night sky.

She'd not been able to visit even one of her old haunts since arriving in Newport last week. There hadn't been a minute that wasn't filled with shopping, fittings, visiting, and afternoon drives. It was a different life; she'd looked forward to it, but now she wasn't certain she was going to like it.

Her mother stirred the air with a plumed ivory fan. "Seacrest is always stifling. Deanna, make sure you are breathing properly. And if you get overheated in a dance, retire immediately to the ladies withdrawing room and send for your maid before you start to perspire."

"I know, Mama."

A snort came from the corner of the carriage where her father sat.

"George, this is her first big night in Newport. It's a mother's duty to remind her of every little thing. Newport is not New York. And one little misstep here—"

"Oh, leave off, Jeannette. You'll make her so nervous that she'll fall out of the carriage, trip up the stairs, and knock over a tray of champagne."

"I won't, Papa."

"Of course you won't." He leaned forward to pat her knee. "And even if you did, you would carry it off with such panache, no one would dare snub you."

"Don't you dare," said Adelaide in her perfectly modulated voice.

Deanna glanced at her sister. Adelaide would never expend the energy to fall up the steps or knock over a tray of champagne. Sometimes Deanna was amazed she could stand upright.

The air in the carriage ruffled as her mother made use of

her fan. "I wonder how many people are invited? Seacrest won't accommodate a large number of guests, no more than two hundred at the most. Francis and Eleanor should have heeded our advice and used Hunt instead of this American architect no one has ever heard of."

The carriage inched ahead.

"I don't know what Lord David will think of us, with us missing dinner."

"I'm sure Francis will explain that the ferry was late. No doubt there will be other late arrivals."

"And Lionel not even bothering to make an appearance to the man's introduction to Newport society."

"As I explained to you, my dear, Ballard had business issues that couldn't wait."

"Ah, business," she said, dismissing the idea with a wave of her fan.

"Keeps you and the girls in finery, and I must say the three of you are looking exquisite tonight."

Deanna shot a smile across to her father. Her? Exquisite?

Mrs. Randolph nodded slightly and returned her attention to Deanna. "Lord David is the owner of a huge sugar plantation in Barbados, and from what I hear very handsome—and eligible. And a peer. I expect you to be on your best behavior tonight, Deanna, and please, please try not to scare this one away."

"But I—" A look from her mother hushed Deanna's tongue. She hadn't scared Joseph Ballard away, had she? It had all happened so suddenly. The families had decided the two of them would marry, and before Deanna had even assimilated the news, Joe had bolted. An unladylike word, but there it was.

It wasn't even as if she'd loved Joe. Or he, her. They had practically grown up together. When Bob died, Joe became a surrogate big brother. He'd always been solicitous to Adelaide, who was just four years younger than he, but Adelaide never wanted to do anything fun or interesting or energetic.

Joe called her Adelaide the Limpid.

Deanna, on the other hand, according to Joe, was a handful. He could be bossy and a little overprotective, like an older brother, but he could also be fun.

She erased the slight smile from her face. She wasn't going to think about Joe tonight.

The carriage moved forward and finally came to a stop at the front steps of Seacrest. The door was opened by a liveried footman, and a ripple of anticipation danced up Deanna's spine.

Jeannette Randolph looked quickly across at her daughters.

"Adelaide, pinch your cheeks. You're looking positively peaked."

Adelaide pinched her cheeks, and they all descended.

∞∞)Ҩ(∞∞

D eanna didn't fall out of the carriage or trip up the steps, but she did stop to take it all in. Deanna and Cassandra Woodruff were great friends, and she'd been to Seacrest hundreds of times. It was one of the many new "cottages" that lined Bellevue Avenue. Not as monumental as Marble House or Chateau-sur-Mer, not nearly as big as the new Vanderbilt "cottage," The Breakers, which had just been completed in time for the summer season.

Seacrest was a sprawling confection of towers and turrets and fairy-tale details with wonderful places to play hide-and-seek. The Woodruffs held extravagant parties that Deanna and Cassie had spied on from the oriel window above the ballroom. But tonight was the first time she'd actually been invited to one.

Every window was ablaze with light. The Woodruffs had installed electricity throughout the house last year, and the lights were so much brighter than the gaslight they still used at Randolph House. Gaslight was softer but harder to see by; her father so far had refused to install the new lighting.

Deanna had to admit there was something garish about all that brightness. It took the mystery out of the façade: flattened out the scrollwork until it looked almost like a painting instead of intricately carved detail; and turned the turrets, belvederes, and gabled eaves into hard geometric shapes.

Her mother paused on the landing, looked down the sweeping steps, and cleared her throat. Deanna collected herself, lifted her skirt gracefully in one hand, and climbed the steps without mishap.

They stopped in the foyer, where backlit stained glass windows rained particles of color on the visitors as they entered. The majordomo showed them through to the ballroom as if none of them had been in the house before. Even Deanna had danced there, but only in the daylight, when Cassie and she would sneak in and twirl to the music in their heads until Cassie's governess found them and shooed them back to the schoolroom.

Tonight it had been transformed. The three giant chandeliers shone brilliantly overhead. Each crystal had been washed and dried and replaced by gloved hands, and they sparkled like diamonds. Wall sconces shot cones of electric light against the new "japonesque" wallpaper that Mrs. Woodruff had commissioned for the occasion. Chaises and chairs were placed for convenience around the dance floor.

The ballroom was already filling with people, the women's colorful dresses standing out among the gentlemen's dark evening wear as if bits of light from the foyer had followed them inside. Music floated down from the hidden orchestra alcove above their heads and filled the room with the latest tune.

The Randolphs made their way to their hosts, who were standing near the entrance to the ballroom. Mrs. Woodruff was wearing a gold-and-orange brocade evening gown with a ruffled scooped neck that showed off her ample bosom. A tiara of diamonds and amethysts was nearly buried in the curls of her coiffure. A diamond choker circled her rather plump neck and a corsage of pale lavender orchids embellished her left shoulder.

She was dressed lavishly but none too tastefully, and Deanna knew her mother would not approve. Mostly, her mother disapproved of Eleanor Woodruff because her wealthy silver-mining family, though rich in money, was poor in pedigree. Deanna thought that what Mrs. Woodruff lacked in taste and refinement, she more than made up for in generosity and good humor.

Fortunately, her mother had to put up with Mrs. Woodruff, because Francis Woodruff not only was a partner in R and W Sugar, but came from a family with both a staggering fortune and an impeccable pedigree. And why she'd allowed Adelaide to become engaged to Charles.

"Don't you look lovely tonight," Mrs. Woodruff said when it was Deanna's turn to be presented. "Cassie is somewhere around here. She's been looking for you all evening." She practically winked at Deanna. "Won't it be nice to be down here among the grown folks rather than peeking through the oriel?"

Deanna unconsciously glanced up at the peep window where she and Cassie had sat, heads together as they'd watched the dancers waltzing below. Mrs. Woodruff smiled and turned her attention to her next guest.

"And who is this beauty?" Mr. Woodruff took Deanna's

hands in his. Always a slight, lean man, tonight he looked positively frail. There were dark circles under his eyes. But his eyes were bright and his smile was genuine, and Deanna forced a smile to her lips.

"How do you do?"

"Just fine, my dear, just fine."

"There you are." Cassie Woodruff, swathed in layers of light rose taffeta, appeared out of the crowd. She was glowing with excitement, her cheeks flushed to the same lovely color as her dress. "I've been waiting ages. I want to introduce you to Lord David and his sister, Lady Madeline. She's gorgeous and so much fun. You're going to love them."

She took Deanna's hand and began leading her across the room, so close to the swirling dancers that Deanna felt dizzy. She quickly looked around to make sure her mother wasn't watching.

"Cassie, slow down."

"Oh." Cassie dropped her hand. "Sorry. I forgot this was your impression night."

"Yes. And don't pretend you're so old and jaded just because your parents brought you out a year ahead of me."

"Yes, and still an old maid," Cassie said. "Though Lord David is definitely delectable."

"Cassie . . ." Deanna began, but she couldn't chastise her friend for not taking Deanna's first Newport appearance seriously. Cassie loved parties, and she was naturally vivacious and high-spirited, sometimes embarrassingly so.

"There they are, over by the fireplace."

Deanna looked toward the far end of the ballroom, where a giant spray of peacock feathers screened the fireplace, lending an Egyptian feel to the gabled and gilded overmantel. The dance ended, and the crowd separated to the sides of the room, leaving them a full view of the sugar baron and his sister. But Deanna hardly noticed him. Standing at his right side was Joseph Ballard. He caught her eye, quickly excused himself, and walked swiftly into the crowd and out of sight.

Mortified, Deanna stood frozen for a full ten seconds, while heat flooded her face. What was wrong with her that Joe would be so anxious to avoid her? And why was he even here? So much for what Orrin said. She would make Elspeth promise to never use the words "Orrin says" ever again.

Deanna dragged her gaze from the empty spot next to Lord David and turned to Cassie.

"Why didn't you tell me he was going to be here?"

"Lord David? It's a party in his honor."

"I meant Joe."

"Joe? Is he here?"

"He was standing right next to your guest of honor. Didn't you see him?"

Cassie giggled. "No. I didn't even know he was invited. Shall we snub him all evening?"

Deanna shook her head. "I don't think that will be necessary." From the way he'd reacted to seeing her, she didn't think she had to worry about running into him again. How had she gone from friend to pariah so quickly? She wished their families had never cooked up that marriage scheme. It had ruined everything.

"Well, forget him and come meet our guests."

Deanna made a concerted effort not to glance around for Joe as Cassie guided her across the floor to Lord David and Lady Madeline. She forgot Joe the instant Lord David saw them and turned his smile on her. He was tall and thin with dark blond hair "kissed by the sun," probably from overseeing his plantation.

A full mustache and a sparkle in his eye made him look slightly roguish, like the hero of one of her dime novels.

And more handsome than Joe, who was dark and clean-shaven, though maybe just a tad taller than Lord David. And a tiny bit more muscular. And he *had* looked very distinguished in a crisp white shirt and black formal attire.

Not that she cared how Joe looked.

"Lord David, Lady Madeline," Cassie began a little breathlessly, "may I make my friend known to you?"

Deanna curtseyed to Lord David, then turned to his sister. "Lady Madeline."

"Do call me Maddie. I can tell we're going to be great friends." Madeline Manchester was as beautiful as her brother was handsome, with even lighter hair and the same sparkling blue eyes fringed in dark lashes. Her gown was a rich azure, trimmed in pointed lace that accentuated her tiny waist, and had a décolleté that hinted at, but didn't quite show, high, firm breasts.

Madeline was so bubbly yet so decorously assured that Deanna knew she would be an instant success in Newport, even with the more exacting ladies.

As well as the envy of every girl in the room.

Cassie was enchanted with both guests, though Deanna found the sister the more captivating of the two. So much so, that she was startled when Lord David asked her to dance. Recollecting herself, she curtseyed and let him guide her onto the dance floor.

Chapter
2

Joe Ballard stood in a shadowed alcove and watched Lord David lead Deanna Randolph onto the dance floor.

Of all the rotten luck. He'd been so intent on getting entrée to the Manchesters, he'd forgotten that Deanna had made her coming-out over the winter and would most likely be here, too.

"That was very unmanly of you. Not to mention rude."

"Grandmère." Joe turned quickly to encounter his grandmother.

Gwendolyn Henriette Laguerre Manon was a much smaller woman than her name implied. Joe had heard one of his father's friends say she was like Queen Victoria, but with twinkle. "My mother-in-law may look like that old prune," his father remarked, "but she has the spirit of a French—" He'd broken off immediately, remembering Joe was in the room, but Joe knew just what he'd meant.

Grandmère had a fire for living and had exercised that fire

in more than one *affaire de coeur*. Even now, she held sway over men who should know better. She had a distaste of the boring, anger at injustice, and wasn't afraid to speak her mind. Which evidently she was planning to do at the moment.

Joe bowed over her proffered hand.

"Joseph, was that really necessary?"

He looked up over their linked fingers. His grandmother's deceptively mild gray eyes flashed for an instant before she smiled. He didn't trust that smile; he hadn't missed her brief look of censure.

"I suppose you're talking about Deanna."

"Who else?"

"I didn't expect to see her," he said. "If that's what you mean."

"And what else would I mean?" She tapped his hand with her fan.

Joe was sure it looked like a playful act from a distance. But his skin felt the sting of her displeasure.

"Did you mean to give her the cut direct?"

"I did not."

"Well, that's what it looked like to me, if I didn't know you better. But other people might not be so astute. You could easily wreck her season by treating her like she has the plague."

"I would never do that."

"Then ask her to dance; stop all those malicious tongues before they start wagging—and stop skulking around the fringes of the ballroom like one of Allan Pinkerton's spies."

Joe flinched. "They're detectives, not spies. And I'm not skulking, Grandmère."

"And you can stop mooning over that girl from Barbados."

"I was not mooning. I was being polite."

His grandmother sniffed. "In my day we called it something else."

Joe gritted his teeth. Oh, he was making up to Madeline Manchester all right—and to the brother, too—but not for the reasons his grandmother imagined.

The telegram folded into the inner pocket of his jacket was his sole reason for being here. A request from his father that Joe go to the ball in his stead and make sure none of the guests trundled Lord David away to undercut his deal with R and W.

Joe knew it was a volatile time in the sugar trade. And that R and W, in which his father was a silent partner, needed the deal with the Manchester sugar plantation in order to stay in business. Joe knew his father was worried and wondering why the sugar baron and his sister had been in town for almost a week but had yet to venture into Manhattan to finalize the deal. Every minute's delay was a chance for someone to usurp R and W's claim on Lord David's raw sugar.

But it was clear Lord David intended to enjoy himself tonight. He'd been unimpressed when Joe introduced himself as envoy from R and W. He hardly had a word all evening for anything except his own pleasure.

"Stop avoiding Deanna Randolph," his grandmother repeated. "You don't have to marry the girl, but at least be civil."

"I—"

Fortunately, Bernie Ainsworth approached them and bowed formally over Gwendolyn's hand. "You promised me a dance."

Years were shed in a second as his grandmother took Ainsworth's proffered arm. "I'll probably bust a gusset."

"Nonsense," he answered. "You'll put them all to shame."

She'll cause tongues to wag as usual, thought Joe, but at least it stopped hers from wagging at him.

———•◦◦}◊{◦◦•———

D eanna was still dizzy from twirling and excitement when Lord David led her off the ballroom floor. He was an excellent partner, and she'd acquitted herself well.

She barely had time to catch her breath before Mr. Woodruff came over to introduce her to another young man, who accompanied her back to the floor and an extended quadrille.

Next came a schottische with Herbert Stanhope, a nice young man with a shock of red hair and a ready laugh. His father was one of the Boston Stanhopes; his mother was related to Henry Havemeyer, whose Sugar Trust was R and W's arch competitor.

Luckily, Herbert didn't seem to be interested in sugar at all. He was entertaining and funny and didn't take anything quite seriously. He was an enthusiastic dancer and kept her laughing through the entire song. When they finished, he offered to bring her some lemonade.

She met Cassie near the fireplace.

"Whew, it's hot," Cassie said, and fanned herself with the back of her hand.

"Maybe we should go up and be tidied," Deanna suggested.

"And chance missing the fun? Not me. I wonder where Maddie is. Do you see her?"

Deanna looked around the ballroom, but there must be two hundred people milling about. It was impossible to find anyone.

Herbert returned with her lemonade and entertained them with nonsense until the orchestra struck up again.

"Excuse me, ladies. I believe I have this dance with Lady Madeline." He hurried away.

He made a beeline across the floor, and soon they saw him swirling around the floor with Lady Madeline in his arms. Deanna also saw Charles and his father standing side by side, both watching the couple. Charles was smiling. His father said something to him, and Charles stopped smiling, bowed slightly to his father, and walked away.

Now, what was that about? Deanna wondered.

——◦◦◦◦——

J oe spent the next half hour cooling his heels, waiting for a chance to dance with Deanna in order to please his grandmother and Newport society. But the one time he attempted to approach Deanna, she latched onto Herbert Stanhope like he was the crown prince. Nor was Lady Madeline ever without a partner, including Mr. Woodruff, who should have left her for younger men. Lord David was constantly dancing or holding court with the other young blades about town. The one time Joe had approached Charles, his father had trundled him off to dance with a neglected young woman.

It was obvious he would learn nothing tonight. This had been a waste of time. The ballroom was stifling hot, and he could get nowhere near the Manchesters. He would just quietly take his leave. He skirted the dancing couples, bowing and smiling but never stopping long enough for anyone to introduce him to some poor girl who needed a partner.

Once in the foyer, he nodded to the butler and strode out the front door before remembering that he'd arrived in a borrowed carriage. He'd be walking back to his rooms in the warehouse tonight.

He walked down the drive, past carriages and dozing coachmen. As soon as he passed the front gates, he loosened his tie and pulled it from his neck. Not only had the evening been wasted, he'd irritated his grandmother and hurt Deanna's feelings. He'd seen it in her face before he'd turned his back on her.

For a moment he hesitated, deliberating whether to turn back and undo his bad manners, then looked at the tie in his hand. No. He'd go apologize tomorrow.

Besides, what he had to say could not be said in the middle of a crowded dance floor. He would explain that what had happened at the end of last season had had nothing to do with her. He'd just have to be on his guard not to say too much. None of this was her fault.

Joe set off down the street. He'd promised Bob that he'd watch over both the girls, though he hadn't really believed that the flu would carry him away. Adelaide didn't need much watching over; she was the most beautiful, most lethargic creature he'd ever known. But Deanna . . .

It was hard to believe the sisters were from the same family. Deanna was curious, vivacious, intrepid, smart. He'd been enchanted with her from the first time Bob had brought him home on holiday from Exeter, when they were both fourteen. She had just turned seven and was such a brat.

At ten, Adelaide already took her entry into society seriously, garnering the most attention from her mother, like any promising student would do. Deanna was left to the nursery and the care of her governess, who spent more time looking for the adventurous little sprite than actually teaching her anything. Deanna and Bob had a special rapport. Being an only child, Joe envied them.

Now Bob was dead.

Joe yanked the top button away from his throat and halted

momentarily, as ahead of him a gate in the wall that surrounded Seacrest opened and a dark figure slipped through to the street.

One of the maids sneaking out during an event this size? She was sure to be sacked if she was caught. The girl hesitated, looked furtively around, first left, then right in his direction. And in that brief moment, he recognized her. It was Daisy, one of the Woodruff maids, his apprentice Orrin's sweetheart.

"Daisy?"

Daisy let out a squeak and cowered back into the shadows.

"It's Joe Ballard, Daisy. What are you doing out here? And at this time of night?"

"Oh, Mr. Ballard, you about scared me witless." She took a couple of quick breaths and stood still, wringing her hands while Joe closed the distance between them.

"What's the matter, Daisy? Surely, Mrs. Woodruff didn't send you out on an errand this late?"

She shook her head. "No, Mr. Ballard. I need to talk to Orrin."

"At this hour?"

"It's—it's important. Awful important."

Oh Lord. Joe hoped to hell Orrin hadn't gotten her in the family way. "Is it something that can wait until the morning, Daisy? It really isn't safe to be out on your own." Especially if she were planning to walk to the Fifth Ward, the denizen of working class families and angry Irish men who after too many beers spoiled for a fight and would think nothing of having their way with an unprotected young girl.

"I know Mr. Ballard, but there's something I—something that—" She choked back a sob.

Joe touched her arm. "There now, Daisy. It can't be so bad. Can't you tell me?"

"It's—I don't know. You won't—please let me—"

She was cut off by raucous laughter coming toward them. Two young bucks leaving the party early, as Joe had done. Probably seeking more exciting entertainment.

Daisy shrank back into the shadows. Joe stepped in front of her.

The men slowed down. "Is that Joe Ballard?"

Joe recognized them as Cokey Featheringham, a dissolute younger son of a steel-mill baron, and his equally dissolute cousin Nathaniel.

Cokey stuck his neck out of his evening wear like a turtle out of its shell. "I do believe it is. What'cha doing lurking in the shadows, Joe, my boy?" He attempted to peer around Joe's shoulder and nearly fell over. "Ah. I see. Not 'nuff ladies in the ballroom for you?" He laughed. "Oh, that's right, heard you were taking up with the common folk down in the Fifth Ward."

Nathaniel grabbed Cokey's shoulder and pulled him away. "Sorry, Ballard. Didn't mean to interrupt."

"S'what happens when men start fraternizing with the 'footies,' meeting the help on dark street corners. Think he'll take her up against the wall?"

"Shut up, Cokey," Nathaniel said.

"No, no. If Joe here doesn't treat you right, just tell Cokey. I'll show you a good time."

They staggered off.

Joe turned back to Daisy. "Sorry about them. A couple of drunks with no manners and half a brain between them. And you stay away from both of them."

Daisy stepped away from the wall. "I know the likes of them. But they should'na talked to you like that, Mr. Ballard."

"They shouldn't have talked about either of us that way,

Daisy. Pay them no mind. Now go back inside. And don't walk out by yourself again. I'll send Orrin down in the morning."

"Mr. Ballard . . . ?" She bit her lip. "No. I'd best be getting back, I have to lay the fire for Mr. Woodruff's room. He's not well, Mr. Ballard. Nothing's going right in that house."

Joe studied the girl's worried countenance. "I noticed he was looking pale tonight, but what else is wrong?"

"Yes, sir, he—he . . ." Daisy shook her head. "I can't." She dropped an abrupt curtsey. "G'night, sir."

"Daisy."

"I can't," she said, and slipped back into the grounds and closed the gate.

Joe stood for a moment to make sure she didn't try to sneak out again. Had he missed an opportunity to find out what was going on with Francis Woodruff? Servants saw and heard a lot more than their employers realized. . . . Joe dismissed the thought. It was more likely that Daisy had problems of her own. He just hoped it wasn't the usual problem. First thing in the morning, he would have a little talk with Orrin—assuming it wasn't already too late.

—◦◦◦◦◦—

Deanna's evening sped by. She was claimed for every dance, which made her feet ache but her mother happy. In between she'd slip away to gossip with Cassie while they cooled their flushed countenances with lemonade in the lady's parlor, while Elspeth and Cassie's maid neatened their hair and straightened out their skirts. Then it would all begin again.

Twice Deanna shared scintillating waltzes with Lord David. He quite literally took her breath away. During the rest of the evening, she hardly saw the Manchesters except to watch

Madeline float by first with Mr. Woodruff, then with Charles, and after that on the arm of one gentleman after another.

She didn't see Joe at all, and by midnight, when supper was served, she'd forgotten all about him. She was escorted into supper by Herbert Stanhope.

The Woodruff dining room had been transformed into a sea of small round tables set for intimate conversations. A buffet table, so crowded that the silver chafing dishes sat almost edge to edge, lined the entirety of one wall. On another table, fresh fruit and sweets were arranged artistically around an ice sculpture that surely would melt before supper was over.

Herbert seated Deanna at a table with Cassie and Vlady Howe, scion of the Boston Howes and the object of Cassie's latest flirtation, before going off to the buffet to fill their plates.

Deanna was surprised to see Charles Woodruff seating Madeline Manchester at one table while Adelaide was seated at another with Colonel Morrell, an older British gentleman staying with his son's family in town. Adelaide looked paler than ever and bored, though Deanna couldn't fault her for that. The colonel did tend to ramble.

Shouldn't Adelaide be seated next to Charles? Of course, husbands and wives usually sat with some other acquaintance at dinner— not with each other. Her father was seated at a larger table with Mrs. Woodruff and Mrs. Van Alen; her mother with Tessie Oehlrich and two gentlemen who Deanna couldn't see.

But Charles and Adelaide weren't married yet. And it seemed like they'd had no time at all together this evening, what with Charles's duties as host. Deanna felt a little sorry for her sister. It seemed to her that Charles had been paying too much attention to Madeline during the evening and not enough to his fiancée.

The supper was delicious, with crab cakes and lobster rou-
lade, cresses, asparagus, and boeuf anglais. Deanna let Herbert
fill her champagne glass twice, though she kept in mind her
mother's admonitions not to drink or eat to excess. Dessert was
a glacé of mint and tiny cakes that melted in her mouth.

After supper, the ladies adjourned upstairs to freshen up
while the men took the opportunity to have a port and a cigar
or cigarette out on the terrace.

Deanna found Cassie and Madeline already in the withdrawing room.

"Look. I've torn my hem and no one can find my maid,"
Madeline said.

"I told you to watch out for Dr. Morrison," Cassie said. "He's
notorious for stepping on his dance partner's feet."

"Better my feet than my hem," Madeline said. "What am
I going to do?" She sank onto a nearby chaise.

"I'll send for Elspeth," Deanna said. "She's a dream with a
needle."

Elspeth appeared a short time later, carrying her sewing
basket.

"Oh, you are a dear," Madeline told Deanna, and stood
for Elspeth to examine the damage.

"Just hold still for a moment," Elspeth said, and knelt to
repair the fabric. It was only a few minutes before she stood
and fluffed Lady Madeline's skirts. "There, almost as good
as new."

"Oh, thank you, Deanna."

Deanna smiled perfunctorily. "It's Elspeth you should be
thanking."

"Oh, yes, she was wonderful," Madeline agreed.

"Will there be anything else, miss?" Elspeth asked.

"Not at the moment," Deanna said. "I seem to still be put together."

Elspeth curtseyed and left the room.

The three girls returned downstairs, where the orchestra had resumed playing and the floor was soon filled with dancing couples. The room became unbearably hot, just as Deanna's mother had predicted.

Between dances, Deanna stood near the French doors to catch a whiff of breeze. She was standing there when Cassie grabbed her hand. Her face was red against her pink dress.

"It's sweltering. Everyone's going out to the terrace. Come with me."

Deanna didn't need any persuasion. The thought of the mild ocean air had her moving through the French doors with alacrity. But once outside, she hesitated. "My mother . . ."

"Is an old fogey. Everyone under thirty is outside. And some of the old folks are, too." She nudged Deanna farther onto the terrace. "Whew! That's so much better," Cassie said, fanning her face vigorously and looking around. "I was afraid I was going to wilt. Oh, there's Vlady Howe." She lifted her eyebrows. "He's even richer than Lord David."

She started off and Deanna followed, past a knot of gossiping young ladies, several middle-aged men smoking cigars, and toward a quartet of younger men who'd managed to snag a bottle of champagne and were quietly and deliberately getting drunk.

"Ah, Cassie, you wonderful creature. Just in time." Vlady was a muscular young man, tall enough and certainly good-looking. A little too much of the playboy flair for Deanna's taste, but he suited Cassie just fine, and she'd been on the catch for him since last season.

"I'm parched." Cassie reached for the champagne bottle, but Vlady snatched it back.

"Not so quickly. Close your eyes."

Cassie closed her eyes.

"Open your mouth."

Cassie opened her mouth and tilted her chin up, which lifted her décolleté with it. Vlady openly admired it before he poured a stream of champagne into her mouth.

Cassie swallowed, choking and laughing as she batted at his arm, which had stolen around her waist and was pulling her closer.

No one offered to pour champagne down Deanna's throat. She was as disappointed as she was relieved. She turned to look out across the lawn, where couples were strolling down to the sea or looking for a dark niche in which to carry on an affair.

Deanna knew about these things, mainly from Cassie. And from Joe's grandmother—whom Deanna called "Gran Gwen"—who had explained the way of the world to her. "Since I know your mother won't, and God forbid you find yourself in a situation that can't be rectified by good manners."

Deanna smiled, remembering that first talk. She'd blushed then, but she'd been grateful. At least she had some knowledge of the world, if only vicariously.

Vlady pulled Cassie closer, and they started across the lawn.

"Oh, do come on, Deanna," Cassie said. "Herbert, bring Deanna along. There's a good boy."

Herbert Stanhope clicked his heels together in a way that made them all laugh and took Deanna's arm. She considered demurring, but everyone else was granted more freedom than her mother allowed, and it didn't seem fair that she had to miss all the fun.

They followed the brick walk to the cliff, passing between topiary beasts that sprouted from giant marble urns. The rising moon appeared and disappeared through the scudding clouds, and shadows of dolphins, peacocks, and rabbits dove before them as they laughed their way to the cliffs.

And Deanna began to enjoy herself immensely.

Two of Vlady's friends began an impromptu dance among the animals and then ran headlong toward the cliff. Deanna was about to cry out to warn them when they stopped abruptly, turned, and bowed comically to their audience of four and waited for them to catch up.

The air was so much cooler here, and the breeze from the water ruffled Deanna's hair. She lifted her face to sky, felt the salt air on her skin, and reveled in the unexpected freedom.

Until Cassie exclaimed, "Lord, what is that? Down on the rocks? Vlady, look. What is it?"

Her voice had become suddenly shrill. They all peered over to the rocks below. Something lay tangled in the shadows. At first it looked like spots of light against the dark of the rocks, but as Deanna looked more closely, she could make out the shape of—

"Good lord, someone is down there," Vlady said. "Hello there! I say! Are you all right?" He turned to the others. "I don't want to interrupt a tryst, but this looks— Cassie, stay here." He thrust Cassie aside, and she grabbed hold of Deanna as the men began to scramble down the steps to the cliff walk and then climb down the rocks below.

"What are they doing?" Cassie asked.

"I think someone is hurt."

"Who could it be?" Cassie moved to the edge of the walk. Deanna didn't want to get closer; she had a bad feeling about what they would discover. But truth be told, she couldn't stay away. She stood beside Cassie, both of them staring down at the rocks, perched at the edge of the walk like a couple of birds of prey.

Vlady and the others closed in around the figure.

"Vlady! Who is it?" Cassie called out. She lifted her skirts and would have started to climb down, but Vlady stood.

"No! Go back. Don't look." He stretched his arms out to stop them just as the moon slipped out of the dark clouds. It illuminated Vlady's pale, horror-stricken face. And revealed what he was trying to conceal from them.

Deanna froze. Beside her, Cassie let out a feeble cry.

A young girl, dressed in a maid's uniform, lay crumpled on the rocks, arms flung to the side, skirts twisted around her ankles, revealing only two small feet, clad in button-up shoes. Her head had fallen back, and a strand of loosened hair fell across her face.

Deanna leaned over as far as she dared, praying that it wasn't Elspeth. She could see the pale face in the glow of the moonlight. And she recognized her. "It's Daisy."

"Our Daisy?" Cassie asked, and fainted dead away.

Chapter
3

Deanna made an ineffectual grab for Cassie as she fell. Fortunately, their yells had attracted a crowd, and someone scooped up Cassie and carried her over to one of the marble benches that overlooked the cliff. Herbert's mother, Mrs. Stanhope, and another lady began chafing Cassie's hands and running a vial of smelling salts under her nose.

Seeing that Cassie was well taken care of, Deanna turned back to the gruesome scene below her.

Lord David stepped beside her. "What's going on?"

"It's Daisy. One of the Woodruff maids. I'm afraid she's fallen, or something."

"Something indeed. I hope *you* know better than to meet a lover on a cliff in the dark of night."

Deanna looked at him, confused. What was he suggesting? That Daisy had been out meeting her sweetheart on the night of a huge ball, or that Deanna was in the habit of meeting men alone at night?

"Maybe it's not too late. We must try to help her." She slipped past Lord David, picked up her skirts, and started over the rocks. It was child's play. She had climbed these rocks for years. Her skirts and delicate slippers made it a bit more precarious than usual and her slippers would most likely be ruined, but that couldn't be helped.

"Wait! Where are you going?" Lord David's voice.

Deanna hesitated. "Someone has to do something," she said. "Vlady and the others are just standing there gawking."

Lord David pulled her back and kept a firm grasp on her elbow. "Admirable, but I'm afraid no one can help that poor girl now. Look at her neck."

Deanna looked. And she saw what she hadn't seen before. Daisy's head was turned far too extremely to be normal, rather like a chicken that . . . Deanna brought her hand to her mouth.

Do not be sick. Do not be sick. Lady detective Kate Goelet wouldn't be so squeamish. But Kate Goelet wasn't real. Suddenly, the sea air was no longer refreshing, but clammy and evil. And Deanna would trade any manner of excitement to bring Daisy back from the dead.

Vlady looked up at them, spread his hands in a helpless gesture. Then he knelt by Daisy's body. When he stood again, he was holding something that looked like paper. "Found this in her hand," he called.

Deanna couldn't seem to speak the question in her mind.

Lord David did it for her. "What is it?"

"An envelope of some sort, too dark down here to tell, really."

The group gathered at the edge of the cliff grew to include some of the older male guests. The news must have reached the servants' hall, because at the edge of the growing crowd, several servants huddled together, risking their positions to see the news for themselves.

One of those stark staring faces belonged to Deanna's own maid, Elspeth. She looked from the cliff to Deanna, then with a sob she broke away from the group and rushed to the walk. Deanna barely managed to wrench away from Lord David and stop Elspeth from careering over the edge herself.

"Is it Daisy, miss? It can't be Daisy. Oh, please say it isn't."

Deanna put her arm around Elspeth. "I'm afraid so. I'm so sorry."

Elspeth began to cry.

Suddenly Deanna's father was there by her side.

"Don't be angry, Papa."

"I'm not. What has happened here?"

"There was an accident. It's Daisy. You know Daisy."

Her father nodded, looked over the edge of the cliff. "Vlad?"

Vlady shook his head.

"Then come away. There's nothing more you can do down there." Her father turned from the cliff and pointed to one of the footmen. "You there. Please take Elspeth here to the house and call for our second carriage to take her home."

"I should go with her, Papa."

"No, my dear. You'll see her when we return home."

Two of the male servants came to take Elspeth back to the house, but she held on, her eyes pleading. There was nothing Deanna could say. Daisy was dead, and there was an end to it.

The Woodruffs' butler, Neville, stepped toward her father. "I took the liberty of calling for the police, sir. I didn't think we should move the girl's body into the house before they . . . can make arrangements for her to be returned to her family. They should be here shortly."

The police.

Deanna's father turned to her. "You'd best get back to the ballroom and make yourself presentable before your mother sees you."

"But Papa—"

"Go now, Deanna. There's nothing you can do." He looked around the group. "In fact, none of you young ladies should be witnessing this. Go on, now."

"Yes, let us go." Lady Madeline was supporting Cassie, whose cheeks were completely drained of color. "Can you help me with Cassie? I'm afraid it's been a terrible shock to her."

To us all, Deanna thought.

"No, wait," whimpered Cassie. "Vlady's coming back. I want to wait for Vlady."

Vlady and Herbert were scrambling back up the rocks, and the crowd began pelting them with questions.

Vlady came straight over to them, and Cassie threw herself at him. "Now, now. Be a brave girl." He looked at Cassie with concern, then said to Deanna, "I think we should stay behind in case we're needed. You ladies can go up to the house. I don't think the police will want to speak to you."

"I should hope not," Lady Madeline said, taking hold of Cassie. Deanna nodded and took Cassie's other side. They were halfway up the walk when Deanna realized she hadn't asked Vlady about the envelope.

She turned back in time to see several policemen coming around the side of the house. Four of them continued straight to the cliff. One strode toward the butler and her father.

Deanna recognized Will Hennessey, a sergeant in the Newport police. A local boy, from an old Newport family, who'd been with Bob and Joe at Yale. He had an air of authority with enough polish to work among the inhabitants of Bellevue Avenue.

Will touched his hat to Deanna's father, and the two men walked away from the group.

Deanna strained to hear what was being said, but it was hopeless.

"Come, let us go," Madeline said, and Deanna reluctantly returned to the house.

Getting back inside without causing a stir was impossible. Most of the guests had heard of the discovery and were clustered, talking and speculating, on the terrace or in the French doors.

Deanna didn't see her mother among the onlookers, but she had no doubt her mother saw her and that she'd hear about it as soon as they got home. Madeline kept her wits and neatly herded Cassie and Deanna past the waiting crowds, through the nearly empty ballroom, and upstairs to the lady's withdrawing room to put themselves back together.

Cassie sank onto one of the wheat-colored satin stools. "Why did she have to fall off the cliff tonight of all nights?"

"Cassie!" Deanna snapped. "How can you say such a thing? The poor girl's dead. She was seeing Joe's apprentice. Imagine how he will feel. And her family."

"I know. It's just—" She burst into tears again. It took a few more minutes to calm her down.

"Oh, dear," Madeline said. "There's a man in the picture? That would explain it."

"What do you mean?" Deanna asked.

"Really, Deanna, you can't be that naïve. Why would a girl throw herself off a cliff?"

"Throw herself?" Deanna asked. "It was an accident, surely."

"Possibly. But consider. A young woman. With a lover? Perhaps she was jilted."

Deanna blushed. "She wouldn't throw herself to her death over a broken engagement."

"Perhaps not, unless maybe she was *enceinte.*"

"In the family way?" Cassie asked.

Deanna shook her head. "No. Orrin would never take advantage."

"Oh, my dear. Men will always take advantage. And leave us to take care of the situation."

"Why wouldn't she tell Orrin?" Deanna said.

"Ah," Madeline said. "Maybe she did."

Deanna frowned.

"Oh, come now, Deanna."

"Oh," Deanna said, making the connection. "You think that Daisy told Orrin and he spurned her, then she jumped off that cliff in despair? I don't believe it."

Madeline smiled sadly. "Jumped of her own accord . . . or worse."

Deanna stared at her.

"What do you mean?" Cassie asked.

"Perhaps she told this Orrin fellow he'd gotten her in a family way, and he pushed her off the cliff."

Cassie and Deanna stared at her.

"Don't you believe a man would do that? I assure you, most men would do that and worse if their lover became an inconvenience."

Madeline, who until an hour ago had been so cheerful and vivacious, now seemed a little cold, wise and jaded beyond her years.

Deanna shook her head. "Perhaps people in Barbados are like that, but not here."

"Of course they are, you silly girl."

Deanna wanted to snap that she wasn't silly, but maybe she *was* just a naïve, silly girl. She and Elspeth had read so many stories about betrayal and murder. Tales of scorned lovers; vengeful, spurned suitors; women overpowered by dastardly villains. They'd thought them exciting and fun. But this wasn't fun. Real life, unlike the stories, didn't always end with the heroine overcoming adversity.

"I think," Deanna said, standing and brushing out her skirts, mainly to recapture some semblance of a rational world, "I'd better go find my mother. She'll want to go home to see to Elspeth."

It was a lie. Deanna was the one who was worried about Elspeth. She didn't know what her mother would think . . . if she thought anything about it at all.

"We'll have to get Maddie a new maid," Cassie said.

They all stopped and looked at one another.

"That was the girl taking care of me?" Madeline asked.

Cassie bit her lip and nodded.

"Oh, dear. I didn't recognize her at that distance."

"Don't worry," Cassie said. "Let's find Mama. She'll know what to do."

The three of them went downstairs and found Mrs. Woodruff attempting to pull together the remnants of her gala evening. The orchestra was tuning their instruments. Footmen with trays of champagne began to circulate through the room. But it seemed a hopeless endeavor.

Cassie ran to her.

"Oh, my dear, your father and Charles have gone down to

the cliff to talk with the police. What a disaster. And it's not like Daisy has ever given us a moment of trouble. I just don't know what she could have been thinking."

Deanna didn't either; she just couldn't believe that Daisy had thrown herself over the cliff in despair, or worse, that Orrin had helped her do it. She excused herself and went to find her mother. She passed knots of guests talking in hushed whispers. No one was dancing, but no one was headed for the door.

It seemed to Deanna that everyone was taking a prurient interest in the maid's death. She was, herself. And that made her uneasy. She hadn't been able to take her eyes off that poor girl, her broken body draped over the rocks, her feet in her dark button-up shoes as small as a child's. *The Death of Innocence.*

Adelaide was sitting in an alcove looking sick. Their mother was standing over her, a watchful eye on the other guests as if one of them might suddenly go berserk and kill them all.

"There you are," her mother said as soon as Deanna approached them. "Where have you been?"

"Upstairs, refreshing myself." Deanna was careful to hide the soiled toes of her shoes beneath her hem.

"Ah, so you missed the, um, business on the lawn."

Deanna said nothing.

"Good. I've told your father we are taking the carriage home. The whole evening has been a strain on Adelaide. I knew how it would be. Stifling rooms . . ."

Deanna followed her mother's voice out of the ballroom. They stood in the foyer while their carriage was called for. Deanna listened for the sounds of anything coming from the cliffs—police whistles, voices, anything—but the night was eerily quiet.

And now that they were leaving, she was anxious to get home

to Elspeth. She decided right then and there that she wouldn't breathe a word of Madeline's surmises. Surely, she had been wrong. It had to have been a terrible accident.

As soon as they were home, her mother whisked Adelaide upstairs. Deanna was tempted to wait for her father's return to hear what the police had done, but first she needed to see Elspeth, who she knew would be waiting for her, ready to do her duty in spite of her grief. Deanna didn't think that she herself would be so loyal.

As soon as Deanna opened the door to her room, she heard muffled sobs coming from the dressing room. They cut off abruptly as Deanna entered the room. Elspeth appeared in the doorway, face blotched but composed.

"Oh, Elspeth, I'm so sorry." Deanna rushed to the young maid and put her arms around her. One sob escaped Elspeth, followed by a spasm of her shoulders, then she pushed away.

"Let's get you out of that dress, miss." Elspeth began fumbling with the buttons on Deanna's gloves.

Deanna stood docilely. She felt selfish and useless making her maid worry about her clothing when Elspeth was grieving for her friend, who would likely have become her sister-in-law.

But maybe doing the familiar would help her to cope with her feelings. It took a few torturous minutes to divest Deanna of her evening gloves, and by the time Elspeth rolled them down her arms, Deanna was ready to yank them off in frustration and be done.

But she held still. She often forgot to "keep her distance" with Elspeth; she was "too familiar" with the help, her mother said. But other than Cassie, Elspeth was the closest friend Deanna had. It seemed like most of the girls she knew were more interested in competing than enjoying one another's company. Deanna knew that was expected of her, too. But she was a miserable failure at it.

She turned for Elspeth to undo her gown.

No wonder Joe didn't want to marry her. No one would. Which was fine by her. She didn't want to be like her mother, content to visit people whom she didn't care for just because it was expected. To dine with people because of who they were and not because they were interesting.

She didn't want to spend half her life being fitted for dresses that would only be worn once and that cost more than most people made in a year. She didn't want to change clothes seven or eight times a day. For what? To give Elspeth more work to do? It was stupid.

Deanna stepped out of the dress and sat down at the dressing table while Elspeth carried it to the dressing room. Her dress had escaped the worst of the walk to the cliff, but when she stretched out her feet to look at her shoes, she felt a flutter of anxiety. They had been very expensive, and after only one wearing, the yellow satin was marked with grass and dew.

She immediately felt contrite.

How could she be worried about shoes at a time like this? A young woman was dead. No older than Deanna or Elspeth. Maybe younger. What had she been doing by the cliff? She wouldn't have been given time off on a night such as this.

Deanna kicked off her shoes. The stains appeared dark in the gaslight.

Elspeth returned and knelt down to pick up the shoes.

"Don't worry about any of this tonight. Come talk to me."

Elspeth looked toward the door to the hallway.

"We'll talk while you brush my hair." They wouldn't be reading any stories tonight. Especially not the one they had just started this past week, with Kate Goelet being chased by a madman—no, they wouldn't be reading that one for a long time.

Deanna turned around to face the filigreed mirror. Elspeth began to pull out the pins that held the pearls in place, then released the elaborate coiffure until Deanna's hair fell past her shoulders and she slumped with relief.

She watched in the mirror as Elspeth began to brush her hair in long, slow, regular strokes, concentrating on her work as if she didn't do this every morning and every night of her life and sometimes during the day, too. Occasionally, Elspeth's face would crumple, then, with a gasp of breath, the rhythm of the brush began again.

She always took good care of Deanna, and Deanna took it for granted, she realized.

"Do you want me to ask Papa if you can go to your parents' tonight? One of the men can send for a cab to take you."

"No, but might I go after the morning work? Just to see how Orrin is doing. Mr. Joseph will have told him."

Did Joe even know about Daisy? Deanna hadn't seen him since before supper. She certainly hadn't seen him out on the cliff.

"Oh, miss, why did she go out there?"

"I don't know, Elspeth. I would've thought she'd be working."

"She was. I saw her earlier. She seemed fine. She didn't say anything about going out." Elspeth sniffed. "I teased her into taking me up to that window, the round one that overlooks the ballroom. I just wanted to catch a glimpse of you in your beautiful dress."

"The oriel," Deanna said. "Cassie and I always looked down at the dancing from there."

"We saw you dancing with that Lord David. You were so

beautiful and he was so handsome, and I said to Daisy, 'There's a gentleman worthy of my mistress.'"

Deanna blushed.

"And Daisy leaned closer to the window to see. So close I was afraid someone might see her, and I started to pull her back, but she pushed away and said she had something she had to do. She ran off, and I really was afraid Mrs. Woodruff had seen her and would scold her, so I followed after her."

The brush had stopped, and Elspeth caught Deanna's eye in the mirror.

"When I came down the back stairs, I couldn't find her. I never saw her again."

"But why was she out by the cliff, Elspeth? What reason could she possibly have to go there?"

Elspeth shrugged. "Someone must have sent her."

"For what purpose?"

"I don't know. They say she done it to herself, but she would never. Poor Orrin. He had his heart set on marrying Daisy. Now what will he do?"

Deanna didn't want to think about what Madeline had suggested, that Daisy had found herself *enceinte* and had jumped to her death. She certainly didn't want to suggest such a notion to Elspeth. And as for Orrin—well, it was preposterous.

"Joe will help him through this." He'd always been a compassionate and caring friend, though lately Deanna had begun to feel she didn't know him at all.

Impulsively, she turned in her seat and put her arms around Elspeth's waist. "The police will find whoever did it and punish him."

The door opened.

"Deanna, just what is going on here?"

The two girls broke apart.

Mrs. Randolph stepped into the room and flicked a dismissive look at Elspeth. "You may go."

Elspeth made a quick curtsey and fled to the dressing room. Deanna stood to face her mother.

"Well?" Mrs. Randolph asked.

"Elspeth was upset. Daisy, the girl who died, was engaged to her brother."

"I've warned you about this before. Once you let servants become too familiar, you've ruined them. I'll have to let her go."

Deanna stared at her mother. She was strict, especially when it came to advancing her daughters in society, always talking about missteps and the importance of propriety. But she wasn't heartless.

"Mama, she's grieving."

"We all grieve at one time or another. We carry on."

Like when Bob died. Her mother had been stoical, and Deanna had been too bereft herself to wonder what her mother was feeling beneath her calm façade.

"Well, she's carrying on the best she can." Deanna noticed her ruined dancing pumps still sitting on the floor; she moved in front of them. "I'm going to ask Father to give her tomorrow afternoon off for family reasons."

"Are you indeed? I hardly see why that is necessary. That girl had no business being out at night by herself. I'm sorry for her, but really, if she hadn't been where she shouldn't, she wouldn't be dead, now, would she?"

"Mama!" Why was everyone so ready to accuse Daisy of wrongdoing?

"Learn proper behavior, or the girl goes."

"She's the only maid I'll have." Deanna heard the words

as they came out of her mouth, appalled that she couldn't stop them.

Instead of anger, her mother laughed. "Oh, really, Deanna, you should show as much gumption toward your inferiors."

Deanna managed not to snap, "Elspeth is not my inferior"— she could imagine how her mother would react to that statement. So she just stood silently while her mother gave her a final stern look and left the room. Now Deanna was in disgrace. Her mother would complain to her father, and he would tell Deanna that her mother was disappointed in her, and then she would feel terrible because it would sound like he was disappointed in her, too.

Elspeth's head appeared around the doorframe.

Deanna motioned her into the room. "Don't worry, Elspeth. If you go, I'll go, too."

"Don't say such things. If I lose my job, I'll go back to the Fifth and you'll forget me."

"Never."

"Get into bed, miss. You must be tired."

Deanna nodded. "I think no story tonight."

Elspeth shook her head. "Stupid stories. Good doesn't win over evil. If it did, Daisy wouldn't be dead."

Deanna wanted to tell her she was wrong. But tonight, Deanna was afraid that evil *was* among them. And she wasn't sure if good would have a chance.

Chapter
4

Joe was up before daybreak the next morning. He hadn't slept well. Seeing Deanna had been one thing, but Grandmère was right. The way he'd treated her had been infamous. And his conscience was bothering him.

Nor was he looking forward to the talk he would have to have with his apprentice later that morning. Hopefully, whatever had upset Daisy was merely a lover's quarrel and not an unexpected addition to the family.

He carried a steaming mug of coffee to his drafting room and office in the front part of the warehouse he was calling home. He'd converted the space from former offices and closed it off from the larger workspace, where he and Orrin spent hours a day perfecting and troubleshooting the various machines Joe had designed. He'd nearly finished a prototype for a bagging machine that would fill paper bags with granules of sugar, then fold and seal the tops, but there were still a few kinks to work out.

He'd rolled up his sleeves, sat down at the table, and reached for a pencil and protractor when there was a knock at the door. Too early for Orrin. Too early for anyone.

He went to the door, looked out the dirty window. *A uniform?* He opened the door.

Will Hennessey stood in the cobbled street. A large man, Will was stooped this morning as if he'd been working most of the night. Joe hoped it wasn't bad news.

Will, Joe, and Bob Randolph had become fast friends at Yale. When Bob continued in business and Joe went on to study engineering, Will became interested in the science of forensics. He'd joined the Newport police force, where he could use his new interest to advantage. In a few short years, he had been promoted to sergeant.

Joe opened the door wider and stepped back. "Will. What brings you here?"

"Nothing good, I'm afraid." He held up a preemptory hand. "Nothing to do with the Ballard family."

"Then who?"

"Your apprenticen Orrin O'Laren."

"You'd better come in. I just brewed coffee. I'll get you a cup."

"Thanks."

Will followed him into the "kitchen" Joe had constructed. It had water laid on, and he'd adapted an old Acme range to gas—much faster than waiting for the wood stove to create enough heat to boil water.

Will took his cup and followed Joe back to the office. Joe sat and Will pulled up a chair facing him.

"So, what's this about Orrin? Is he in some kind of trouble?"

"I hope not."

"That sounds ominous. What's happened?"

Will leaned back in the chair. "We were called to the Francis Woodruff ball last night."

Joe had started to drink, but he put his mug down. "Why?" *What could this possibly have to do with his apprentice?*

"The body of a young woman was found on the rocks below the walk there."

Cold fear ran through Joe's veins. "Who?" *Not Deanna.*

"It was a maid of the house. One Daisy Payne."

"Daisy? Good God." Joe ran his hand down his face. "She's Orrin's sweetheart."

"I'd like to speak to him."

"He hasn't come in yet. I told him we'd have a late start because I was at the Woodruff ball myself last night."

"I didn't see you there."

"I left early." He started to tell Will that he'd seen Daisy as he was leaving but held back. He wanted to know more about what had happened first. If it was an accident, there was no reason to suggest anything, other than to tell Orrin that his intended was dead. "Did you inform her family?"

"Yes. I just came from there. Very cut up about it. Of course, who wouldn't be? They loved their daughter—and depended on her salary. To add insult to injury, I can't return the body to them until the coroner finishes with her."

"The coroner? Is there some doubt about how she died?"

"Yes," Will said. "It isn't a steep drop at Seacrest, just tiers of scattered boulders. It's unlikely she would have slipped and fallen to her death. Maybe broken an arm or leg, but . . ."

"You suspect foul play?"

"Very possibly. The girl was a devout Catholic, and the family swore she'd never kill herself. Suicide is a mortal sin."

Joe nodded. He didn't like where this was going. But there was nothing he could do to stop it.

Will sipped his coffee, then held it in both hands and stared into the cup as if he could find the answers to his questions there. "Joe, between you and me, it looks like murder. Her neck was broken, but not necessarily by the fall. There were bruises." He sighed. "I'll have to wait for the autopsy results, but I think they could have been inflicted before she fell."

"There were over a hundred people at the ball—who would kill a girl where anyone might see? While people were probably out on the terrace or strolling through the grounds?"

"The same thought occurred to me, but you never know what people will do. Bad business, this. I'll need to talk to Orrin."

"You think Orrin killed her? He loved her. Wanted to marry her."

"Maybe they jumped the gun. And it scared him off."

Here it was. The obvious conclusion, that Orrin had gotten her pregnant. Joe had wondered that himself. It could easily be true. Loose morals weren't the sole propriety of the upper classes. But he didn't believe it. You couldn't work side by side with a man every day without learning his mettle.

"I thought more of you, Will."

"As well you should. Just because it is the most obvious scenario doesn't mean it's the correct one."

"Most wouldn't look further than the obvious."

Will gave him a penetrating look. "I'm not most. But I still need to question him." He stood, carried his cup over to the sink. "There's more."

Joe waited, expecting the worst.

"We think there was a letter."

"She left a note? I thought you were ruling out suicide."

"Actually, a witness found an envelope in her hand."

"Who?" He hoped Deanna hadn't seen any of this, though he had no doubt she would have come out to see what the commotion was about.

"A man named Vladimir Howe."

"Ah, Vlady. An envelope. And the letter?"

"The envelope was empty. We searched the area and her room." Will held out one hand. "Nothing."

"So what are you getting at? Someone sent her a letter to entice her outside?"

"We're not sure it was addressed to Daisy. There's writing, but as yet it's unreadable because of the ocean spray. I'll study it under the magnifier after it's dried and cleaned, but the first letter looks like it might be an 'O.'"

"That doesn't make any sense."

"Not yet. I interviewed several of the servants. No one had seen her since earlier that evening. She was an upstairs maid; it's possible that she was kept busy in the withdrawing rooms. Or that she'd already sneaked out of the house. Do you know where Orrin was last night?"

"No." Joe swallowed. "But I know he didn't meet Daisy. I saw her last night."

Will's jaw went slack.

"Not in the way you're imagining. Really, Will."

"Sorry. Not much surprises me these days. But that would."

"As I was leaving, Daisy was coming out of the servants' gate."

"What time was this?"

"Fairly early, before midnight for certain. People began arriving for the ball a little before ten. I only stayed at the ball for about an hour after that."

"Why so early?"

"I only went to stand in for my father, who couldn't get away from business in Manhattan."

"Hmm. So you were leaving the ball and what happened?"

"I saw Daisy and stopped her. She seemed very agitated and said that she needed to talk to Orrin. I, of course, jumped to the natural conclusion. I told her it was too dangerous to go out alone, asked if it could wait until the morning, that I would send Orrin down to her then. I wanted to give myself time to have a little talk with Orrin about doing his duty just in case she was in the family way."

"You think it was a possibility?" Will said.

"I don't know. I suppose. I sent her back to the house. I should have just taken her to see him. If I had, this wouldn't have happened."

"Or it would have happened at some other time." Will traced the rim of his cap between two fingers. "Joe, if you had any other relationship with this maid, tell me now."

"I did not. I was concerned because she was the sweetheart of my apprentice. That's all."

Will drank off his coffee and stood. "Fine. I have to go, but keep Orrin here until I return. It might be late. I also have to question those present on the lawn last night. Something I'm not looking forward to. I don't expect much cooperation. Just so you know, Deanna Randolph will be one of them."

"Deanna? Why on earth?"

"She was one of the party who discovered the body."

Joe groaned. "She would be."

Will smiled. "She was out on the lawn when I arrived. She looked amazing in a gold ball gown. I hardly recognized her. Seems like she changed from wearing pigtails and badgering us to death into being a very beautiful woman overnight. You're a fool, man, not to marry her before someone steals her away."

Joe laughed drily. "And have her live here with me? I'm sure her mother would have something to say to that."

"And you wouldn't give this up for her?"

Joe looked around. "This particular workshop?" He shrugged. "But my work? No."

"Not even for Deanna? I thought you and she—"

"She wouldn't respect me if I did."

Will shrugged. "Most men would jump at the chance."

"You?"

"If you think her mother doesn't approve of you, just imagine me showing up at the door."

"Well, it's academic. The families decided our marriage would be a good business move in the fight against the sugar monopoly. Neither one of us was ready."

"You might have missed your chance."

"Maybe. I don't think we're destined for each other."

"Oh, brother." Will adjusted his cap. "You'll have to break the news to Orrin about Daisy, I guess. Tell him I'll be back to speak with him. Make sure he doesn't run away. And Joe . . ."

"Yes?"

"The same goes for you."

—∞◦❀◦∞—

Breakfast in the Randolph household the next morning was a somber affair. Her father sat at one end of the breakfast room table reading his morning newspaper, the plate of eggs and ham growing cold before him. Her mother, dressed in a dark rose silk morning dress with alternating green and indigo ribbon-weave satin stripes, sat at the other end.

The chair opposite Deanna was empty. Adelaide was still down with her headache.

"Well," Deanna's mother said, "talk about a disastrous night. Poor Eleanor. The Woodruffs will be lucky if they're not social outcasts for the season. Maybe longer. Not that I'm at all surprised."

Mr. Randolph's paper lowered two inches, and he looked over the top of it at his wife. "Nonsense. The invitations will pour in; they'll dine all season on that poor girl's death."

Deanna looked at her plate. It was a cold thing to say, but it was true. People loved to wallow in scandal, even when it had a tragic outcome. They dwelled on the gory details, commiserated, accused, and gloated that it wasn't one of their own.

Jeannette Randolph lifted her finger and Dickerson, the Randolphs' butler, appeared at her shoulder with a fresh cup of coffee. He removed the old one and carried it away. "Perhaps we should distance ourselves a bit from the family."

Deanna glanced quickly at her mother, then away.

"And how to you propose to do that, dear?" Mr. Randolph neatly folded his paper and placed it on the table. "After all, Francis and I are business partners. And our daughter is engaged to be married to their son."

"Well, of course I don't expect you men to follow any sense of decorum. But you're gone all week and we aren't, although . . ." She trailed off, a quirk of conversation that never failed to get everyone's notice. As it did this morning with her husband and daughter.

"I'm considering taking Adelaide to Boston," Mrs. Randolph continued when she had their attention.

"Boston?"

"I was talking to Tessie Oehlrich last night, and she swears

that this doctor in Boston, Dr. Meerschaum, has worked won-
ders for her niece's migraines. These latest powders that Dr.
Lester prescribed are not helping with Adelaide's headaches,
so I see no point in taking her all the way to Manhattan for
more of the same. This is no time for her to be indisposed."

"By all means, take her and get to the bottom of these headaches." Mr. Randolph said. "This is as good a time as any, I
suppose. After all, it's just the beginning of the summer season,
and she's already engaged to Charles."

"One can never be sanguine about these things. She can't
take to her bed after every ball or soiree. She's in bed now,
with the drapes drawn. Something must be done."

Her father frowned, but Deanna understood. Her mother
needed Adelaide to be alert and vivacious. She hadn't missed
the attention Charles had paid to Lady Madeline. Deanna
doubted if any other woman in the room had, either.

"So, you will have Elspeth pack your clothes for a few days,
Deanna."

"Me? Must I go?" That would mean Elspeth would also
have to accompany them, and she needed to be with Orrin now.

"Really, Deanna, use your head. You can't stay alone in the
house."

Deanna shot a look at her father.

"Really, my dear?" Mr. Randolph said. "You don't want the
girl to miss all the festivities. You know Newport. They don't
even mourn their own for longer than it takes to leave a black-
edged visiting card. And the death of a servant? I'm sorry to
say, it won't slow them down at all. That poor girl—Daisy was
her name?—will be replaced and forgotten by sunset. And so
will Deanna, if she leaves now."

He picked up his paper and snapped it back into shape.

"I'm sure Gwen Ballard would love to have Deanna stay for a few days."

"Gwen Ballard? I blame her for this nonsense with her grandson. The woman is downright embarrassing. She was dancing with Bernie Ainsworth like some music-hall hoyden."

His father raised his paper. This time it completely covered his face.

Deanna wondered if it was to hide a smile or a frown. Gwen Ballard was one of his favorites. George Randolph had a modern streak in him; Deanna didn't know how he put up with her mother's anxieties and concerns about society.

"Whatever you wish," he said from behind the newspaper.

Deanna fought her rising exasperation. This was no time for him to retreat into the morning news. She cleared her throat. *Mention Lord David. She won't be able to resist.*

As if he'd received Deanna's silent message, her father lowered his paper several inches. "But unfortunate timing, my dear. I'm sure some young lady will snatch up Lord David while she's gone."

Deanna smiled inwardly. It was enough to make her believe in telepathy.

Mrs. Randolph templed her fingers and scrutinized Deanna for a long time. Before she could pronounce sentence, the door opened and the butler announced the arrival of Cassie Woodruff, who hardly waited for him to finish before she flounced into the breakfast room.

Except for the slight puffiness under her eyes, no one would ever guess she'd danced to all hours and seen a dead person the night before, let alone one closely attached to her household.

"Good morning. I'm sorry to interrupt." She curtseyed to Mr. Randolph and then to his wife. "But I couldn't wait.

Mama thought it would be ghoulish to organize badminton and luncheon on the lawn in view of the . . . tragedy. So we're all going to the Casino for tennis, and tomorrow there's to be dinner al fresco at Bailey's Beach.

"I came to invite Deanna in person. Lord David asked particularly if you would be there."

Deanna sighed and looked sad. "I'm afraid I have to go to Boston with Mama and Adelaide." She sighed again for good measure.

"Boston?" asked Cassie.

"Lord David?" Mrs. Randolph said.

"Oh, please, Mrs. Randolph? Deanna can't miss all the fun. She can stay with us until you get back. Couldn't you, Dee? Mama would love to have her."

Deanna looked expectantly at her mother. She could see the turmoil in her mind. It *was* like telepathy. She could practically read her mother's thoughts. *Deanna lost out on Joseph Ballard; this might be her chance to snag an even better prospect.*

"I suppose a few days won't hurt. George?"

"Whatever you think, dear," he said from behind his paper.

"I'll have to ask your mama."

"Oh, it will be fine."

Deanna gave Cassie a warning look.

"She's at home this morning if you'd like to telephone her. Deanna and I will wait upstairs in her room."

Deanna saw her mother stiffen ever so slightly. She was one of the sticklers who thought the telephone was to be used only for summoning servants, not conversing with others in one's society.

"Would that be all right, Mama?" Deanna said quickly.

"You could write Mrs. Woodruff a note, and we could take it over or have one of the footmen deliver it."

Jeannette Randolph gave a minute nod. "I'll discuss it with your father. You may be excused."

"Yes, Mama." Deanna stood, paused to kiss her father's cheek, and walked sedately out of the room. As soon as they were in the foyer, Deanna pulled Cassie to the back of the stairs. "What happened after I left last night?"

"The police were there for the longest time. They sent everyone back to the house, but we watched from the terrace while an ambulance came and took Daisy away."

"They didn't lay her out in your house?"

"Ew, no. Maybe they took her to where her family lives. Only, Vlady and Herbert overheard two of the policeman say they were going to perform an au—au—"

"Autopsy?" Deanna asked.

"Yes. Isn't that where they cut you up and see what's inside? I'd never let them do that to me."

"You wouldn't be alive to stop them," Deanna quipped, but she was thinking about the reasons for doing that operation. Because they weren't sure how she died. "How awful for her family to have her body desecrated on top of it all."

"They asked Vlady and Herbert all sorts of questions. I've never been that close to a policeman before, and it would have been great fun, except that Daisy was dead."

"The sergeant, Will Hennessey, went to Yale with Bob and Joe."

"He did? Why on earth would he become a policeman, then?"

"He was interested in forensics," Deanna said.

"What's that?"

"Using science to capture criminals. And putting clues together—things ordinary people wouldn't notice—that will lead them to the arrest. I'm not exactly sure how it works. The boys would always clam up every time I asked any questions." Deanna rolled her eyes. "When I'm mistress of a house, I'll let people talk about anything they want."

Cassie nodded energetically. "Oh, famous. We'll do anything we please. It will be such a lark. I'll come and visit you every day."

Deanna smiled. She sometimes wished she could be like Cassie, looking forward to being a society lady, but the very idea was so tedious. But that was in the future. There were other things that needed attention now. "Cassie, what did they ask Vlady?"

"How would I know? They took him away to the library, and I was suddenly so frightened that they would arrest him."

"Why on earth?"

"Because he found the body."

Deanna sighed. "We all found the body."

"Oh, right. Anyway, they were in there for ever so long, and when Vlady finally came out and Herbert went in, Vlady was all pale and everything. And he said he didn't want to talk about it."

"Did he tell you what he did with the envelope?"

"What envelope?"

"Don't be dense. The one he found in Daisy's hand."

"Oh." Cassie drew out the word. "He didn't say. Is it important?"

"Quite possibly. I wonder if he gave it to Will."

Cassie's eye widened until they looked like they might pop. "Do you think it was a clue?"

Deanna thought it might be. And if it was, she was afraid it would lead the police straight to the Fifth Ward and Orrin Payne.

"Can we go upstairs now, or do you want your mama to catch us hiding behind the stairs?"

They scurried out of their hiding place and were going sedately up the stairs when the front door bell rang. Deanna looked at Cassie and knew she was thinking the same thing. It was too early for a social call.

They hesitated, heard Dickerson say, "Good morning, sir."

"It's Will Hennessey," Deanna whispered, recognizing the visitor's voice. "Do you think he's here to talk to me?"

Cassie nodded and, without another word, bolted up the stairs.

Chapter
5

D eanna turned and descended the stairs to face Will across the foyer.

"Did you come to talk with me?"

Will nodded. "But not without your father present. Dickerson has gone to tell him I'm here."

He didn't move any closer and neither did Deanna. She didn't know whether to smile or be serious. Will was a large-boned man, handsome in a rugged way, like one of the frontiersmen portrayed in dime novels. Today he was dressed in a regular morning suit, not a uniform. Normally, she would be glad to see him, but she wasn't sure how to greet him this morning. There wasn't a rule in the etiquette books, as far as she knew, on how to deal with a man of the law.

She could hear her mother's voice as her parents moved from the breakfast room to the library, where they would receive Will.

Deanna swallowed. She'd really hoped her mother wouldn't have to be present. She wouldn't approve of anything that Deanna would have to say. She'd be rude to Will, outraged that the authorities would dare to besiege her home, and let everyone know about it.

Will looked just as uncomfortable as Deanna, only today, as policeman and witness, they couldn't laugh together and break the tension. She'd never been a witness before—not that she had actually witnessed anything last night—and she didn't know how to act.

Dickerson returned and showed Will into the library, then stood just outside the door.

As Deanna watched him, he held a finger to his lips. When he at last moved away from the door, he said, "I took the liberty of not saying that you were waiting here."

"Thank you, Dickerson."

"Chin up, Miss Deanna. They're ready for you now."

She steeled herself and followed him to the library door. Dickerson gave her a second to compose herself, then opened the door. She stepped inside. "You sent for me, Papa?"

"Yes, dear."

He and Will were both standing. Her mother was seated. The message clear: Mrs. Randolph wasn't leaving.

Her father turned his attention to Deanna. "You remember Sergeant Hennessey?"

"Of course. How do you do?" She risked a glance at Will. His eyes were kind, sympathetic, and a little amused.

"Have a seat, Deanna."

"Yes, Papa." *Chin up*, she told herself. She crossed the room to sit down; her skirt caught the leg of a chair and she almost stumbled. Her cheeks flushed red. Two signs of guilt. When confronted, the villains in the novels always gave themselves away by their nerves.

She managed to get to the chair near Will—Sergeant Hennessey—and sat down.

The gentlemen sat.

"The sergeant has a few questions to ask you about last night."

Deanna glanced at her mother. She hadn't told her that she had been outside on the lawn or even on the terrace. Deanna looked at her father.

"The sergeant has already informed us that you were among those who discovered the body of that poor girl," he said.

Deanna cringed. Now her mother would never let her stay with Cassie. At least her papa hadn't been the one who'd told on her.

Will Hennessey took a black notebook and a pencil stub from his pocket and looked at Deanna attentively. His mouth twitched, his apology for letting the cat out of the bag. Well, it couldn't be helped. She straightened in her seat.

"That's correct. Several of us were strolling on the path since the ballroom was unbearably close." She risked a small smile at Will, but her eyes were trying to telegraph to him that she didn't want to talk in front of her parents. Which was useless; it was too late to go back now. Besides, they would never let her talk to him alone.

The door opened. Dickerson stepped in, and Cassie swept past him. Now they'd really be in trouble.

"Sorry to interrupt. But, Mrs. Randolph, Adelaide seems awfully sick and I couldn't find her maid."

Jeannette Randolph's mouth tightened, clearly torn between

her duties. "I'll see to her." She rose and the gentlemen rose with her. After casting a glance first at her husband, then at the sergeant, she left the room. Cassie lingered long enough to wink at Deanna before she followed Deanna's mother out.

And Deanna almost laughed out loud.

The room seemed to exhale as the door closed.

Deanna turned to Will, who glanced at the door. "Can you tell me who you were with and what happened when you got to the walk?"

"Yes. Cassie—Cassandra Woodruff—Vladimir Howe, Herbert Stanhope, and several others who were behind us. But there were people all over. I don't see how—"

"Yes, thank you. Please continue with your movements."

"We reached the cliff walk and stopped to admire the sea. Like a lot of people were doing." She left out the part about the champagne. But from the way Will was looking at her, she thought he might have an idea of what they'd really been doing, and she blushed hotly.

"Then Vlady looked down and said someone was out on the rocks. At first we thought we had"—she looked at her father; he gave her an encouraging nod, then looked down at his ink blotter—"perhaps discovered a pair of lovers, or—but then we looked more closely and— Well, then Vlady—Mr. Howe—said someone was hurt, and he started to climb down the rocks. Then Herbert followed him. Cassie and I waited on the walk."

Will's eyebrows rose.

She looked away; she wasn't about to admit that she had tried to follow them and would have, had Lord David not stopped her.

"But even from there we could see who it was."

"From that far above her?"

"Well, it isn't that far, is it? Not like some places on the cliffs. She was just a few feet below us. Sort of at the edge of the rocks before there's a drop-off into the ocean."

"So you saw her clearly?"

"Yes. I told you—"

"Deanna," her father warned.

"Sorry. It was overcast, but the clouds were moving quite rapidly. While we were looking, the moon broke through and we saw that it was Daisy. We could see her face quite plainly in the moonlight. Her body was parallel to the walk, but her head—her head wasn't." Deanna took a breath, blew it out. "Her head had fallen sideways over the edge of the rock. She was staring straight up to the sky." Suddenly the image was very clear in her mind. She swallowed.

"You don't have to continue," her father said softly.

She shook her head. "It's all right, Papa. I want to help."

"Please, go ahead." Will's voice was calm, reassuring.

"She was lying almost straight, as if she were sleeping. I remember thinking her feet were so small." Embarrassingly, she teared up. She broke from Will's gaze. "Papa, is it all right if I give Elspeth the afternoon off?"

"Of course, my dear."

Realizing she might be implicating Orrin in the investigation, Deanna added, "My maid Elspeth and Daisy were friends. She's been upset."

Will nodded, turned the page of his notebook. "Did you see anything else?"

Deanna thought about it. Re-created the scene in her mind as she did when working on a still life after the fruit had been taken away. Her art teacher always said she had a good eye. Now she wished she didn't.

"Daisy was lying on her back. If she had jumped, wouldn't she have landed face-first?" Deanna wondered if that made any difference. Could Will's forensics determine something about the fall from the way she landed?

Deanna was dying to ask, but didn't. "She must have slipped and fallen, except—"

Will cleared his throat, and Deanna blinked furiously. She knew not to cry in public, and she really wasn't much given to crying. Until today, at least.

"Except what?"

"Except it wasn't the kind of place you fall from, and if she had somehow missed her way in the dark, she would have slid down and not landed that far from the path. Even if someone had pushed her . . ." She stopped.

"Deanna? Miss Randolph?"

She started. "Yes?"

"Did you think of something?"

"I . . . no." She darted a look toward her father. She didn't want to have to say more.

"Sergeant," her father warned.

"Just a few more questions, sir." Will continued without waiting for his okay. "What happened next?"

"Cassie fainted."

Her father made a noise halfway between a cough and a laugh.

"Mrs. Stanhope and Lady Madeline took her over to a bench to recover."

"And who is Lady Madeline?"

"Lord David's sister."

"If I may," her father interjected. "Lord David Manchester owns a Barbadian sugar plantation that R and W is contracting with. My partner, Francis Woodruff, visited him in Barbados and invited him to inspect our facilities and meet with us to assure R and W that he could supply us with enough raw product to run our processing plants."

"I see," Will wrote quickly. "And are these facilities here in Newport?"

Everyone knew they weren't.

"No, in Pennsylvania and Brooklyn. Lord David was to accompany Francis Woodruff to our New York offices today, once their introduction to Newport society was made, and then continue on to visit the refineries. Unfortunately, in light of what happened last night, and the fact that Francis is not well, their tour has been pushed back. I believe Charles Woodruff is planning to bring Manchester to the city in a couple of days."

"While they're in Newport, the Manchesters are staying with the Woodruffs?"

"As far as I know. I plan to ask Joseph Ballard to give them a tour of his workshop and explain his plans for modernization." He shot Deanna an arch look. "Wouldn't do to leave the man cooling his heels in Newport for too long."

Really, he was sometimes as bad as her mother.

Sergeant Hennessey returned to Deanna. Waited.

Deanna pulled her mind back to the discovery. "Oh. Vlady found an envelope grasped in Daisy's hand. He showed it to us. Though I suppose he should have left it as he found it."

Will nodded.

"I'm not sure what happened to it."

"The police have it in their possession."

"It was too dark to see any writing on it."

She waited for him to tell her what it said.

He didn't.

"Or if there was a letter or message inside."

Still, he didn't respond.

"Well, was there?"

He looked up. "I'm not a liberty to say, Miss Deanna."

Miss Deanna? She liked it much better when the boys called her Dee or Dee Dee or even Deedle-dum. She felt the doors of the future slamming on her past and on her fun. Her staunchest ally, Bob, was dead. Joe had still called her Dee the last time they'd met. But that was before he'd jilted her and ignored her at her first Newport ball. And now, here was Will, acting like a stranger.

"Then Elspeth came down with the other servants, and she was upset, and father sent her back to the house and told a servant to send her home in our carriage. Then I went back to the house, and that's all." Deanna crossed her arms.

Will's mouth tightened. But whether from annoyance or trying to hide a smile, she couldn't tell. And, quite frankly, she didn't care.

She suddenly felt suffocated. She wanted to be outside, away from society, away from restriction, running free on the beach like when they were children and she'd spy on the boys and learn all their secrets.

Why didn't women get more freedom the older they got, like men did? The older she became, the more confined her life was, the stronger the rules of behavior. It was so boring and demeaning.

Her father frowned. "Considering what has happened, perhaps it would be wiser if you traveled to Boston with your mother and Adelaide."

Deanna wanted to scream with frustration, but she merely shook her head. "No, Papa. It's like you said. It will all be forgotten by tomorrow. Isn't that correct, Sergeant Hennessey?"

"Unfortunately, that is usually the case."

"Is there anything else you wish to know?" she asked, glaring at Will, mainly because she didn't dare glare at her father.

"Not at this time. You have been most clear-sighted and informative. Thank you for your time."

She wanted to shake him and tell him to stop acting like such a stuck-up twit. But she merely stood, nodded in her most arrogant manner, realized she was acting like her mother, and finished off with her mother's dismissive smile. "Then I'll say good day." She nodded to her father. "I'll have Elspeth pack my things to remove to Cassie's. Good day."

And carefully avoiding chair legs and footstools, she swept from the room. As soon as the door closed behind her, she whirled around and stuck out her tongue at the men on the other side.

Cassie and Elspeth were both waiting for her when Deanna came upstairs.

"What did he say? What kind of questions did he ask? Is he coming to my house next?" Cassie's questions tumbled out.

Elspeth just looked wary.

Deanna collapsed onto her bed. "He just wanted me to tell him what I saw. I did. And there's an end to it."

"An end to it?" Cassie exclaimed. "Lord David said he wouldn't be surprised if there was a full-blown investigation."

Deanna frowned at her friend. Had she been up here frightening Elspeth the whole time Deanna had been gone?

"Is Adelaide really ailing?" she asked Cassie.

"I think so. Elspeth and I heard her maid coming in and out of her room." Cassie pursed her lips and widened her eyes innocently. "I was certain your mother would want to attend to her. Am I the cleverest?"

Deanna laughed. "Yes. Thank you. I was afraid she wouldn't leave and then we'd all be in for it. I'm sure she'll have plenty to say as it is."

"Adelaide *is* very sickly this morning," Elspeth confirmed. "Matilda says she's worse than usual—can't bear the light and can't hold a thing in her stomach, not even water."

"Poor dear," Deanna said. "I wish they would figure out what's wrong with her. I hope I never get those headaches. A selfish thought, I know. Maybe this new doctor will find something to prevent them."

"I can't believe your mama is willing to take Adelaide away even for a few days."

"Cassie, Adelaide obviously can't go through the season like this. I just hope I don't have to go with them."

"Go with them?" Elspeth blurted out, and immediately apologized.

"Oh, I'm sorry Elspeth. She wants to take both of us with them to Boston for Adelaide to see the doctor. We've asked her to let me stay with Cassie's family instead of going. That way you can stay here in town to be with Orrin."

"Oh, thank you, miss. I do appreciate it."

"We're not out of the woods yet. Now father is saying that it might be better if I went with them."

"Oh no," Cassie whined.

"I refused to go."

Elspeth and Cassie stared at her.

"Well, I *sort of* refused. We'll just have to trust in my father to persuade my mother. Now, I'm afraid you must dress me for tennis. Elspeth?"

"Yes, miss. The blue jaconet?"

"Yes, but Elspeth, please don't think I want to show disrespect to the dead."

"No, miss, I know you don't. It's what life is."

She went away to find Deanna's blue serge tennis frock.

Deanna sank into a chair. "I feel bad."

"It's not our fault Daisy died. Now get dressed and come to the Casino. Elspeth understands. She said so."

Deanna gave Cassie a half smile. Elspeth was right. It *was the way things were*. Not that it was right.

Elspeth returned with her blue tennis dress and helped her into it.

"You know, Dee, that dress just isn't . . . modern."

"Mama says it's appropriate to the game."

"Your mama would."

Deanna sucked in her breath as Elspeth cinched the belt at her waist. "Ugh. You've made it too tight. It's bad enough having to drag around heavy skirts and long sleeves in the heat just to get a little exercise." She wiggled until Elspeth sighed and released the belt by two notches. "Actually, I saw a tennis dress in *Harper's* over at Gran Gwen's house that looked ever so much better. This one was designed for annoyance."

"I saw it, too, but you'll never manage to get that dress past your mother. Besides, we're not really going to play tennis. We're going to be admired." Cassie pursed her lips until her dimples appeared. "Oh, I do hope your mama lets you stay. Lord David and Maddie are going to be here all week, until Papa's feeling better. Then he'll have to take Lord David to see the business. Such a bore. I don't want Papa to feel poorly, but I don't see why we can't just have fun instead of having to do business. It's the beginning of the season."

"Men never leave business behind," Deanna said.

"I know. Isn't it dull? At least Vlady's independently wealthy, and Herbert, too. So there will be some fellows around during the week to have fun. And Mama's planning all sorts of activities to keep us entertained. And there's there's to be a picnic al fresco at Bailey's Beach. Lord David has promised that he'll have Swan perform his magic tricks at the bonfire afterward."

"Swan?"

"He's Lord David's manservant. From Barbados. Huge and black as the night." Her eyes widened.

Deanna rolled her eyes toward Elspeth. "Oh, yes. Elspeth told me about him."

"He knows all sorts of magic." Cassie lowered her voice. "They say he can speak to the dead. He knows voodoo."

A brush clattered to the floor.

"Elspeth?"

Elspeth bent quickly to retrieve it, but when she stood, Deanna saw that her face had drained of color.

Oblivious, Cassie continued. "Madeline says her brother found him in an aboriginal village and was so impressed, he brought him back to the plantation and had him trained as a valet. He's frightfully exotic."

"He sounds ridiculous." Deanna gave Cassie the evil eye, hoping she would get the hint and stop talking about death and magic. "He's just a magician like you see on the stage. He doesn't really know voodoo."

"Well . . . something like voodoo. Honest. Madeline called it something else I can't remember, but it's like voodoo."

"Sounds like a bunch of nonsense," Deanna said. Honestly, sometimes Cassie could be so dense.

"Anyway, we'll be sitting out on blankets on the sand . . . with champagne. The chaperones will be all the way up on the veranda. It will be so romantic."

Relieved that the subject had changed to the beach, Deanna let Cassie prattle on. Still, she kept an eye on Elspeth. She was worried about her. She just hoped they weren't already gossiping in the servants' hall.

"Well, I'd better run home before Mama accuses me of neglecting our guests. Do try to get your mama to let you stay. We'll have such fun."

When she was gone, Deanna turned to Elspeth, who was standing stock-still.

"Elspeth, what's wrong? You're not frightened by all Cassie's talk about voodoo, are you?"

Elspeth slowly shook her head.

"What is it, then?"

"Nothing, miss."

"Elspeth?"

"Well, do you remember that book we read last month about the witch doctor? Do you think that could really happen?"

"You mean can somebody put a curse on you and you die?"

Elspeth nodded. "There was talk last night."

"Of what?"

"That Lord David's servant put a spell on Daisy and made her jump off the cliff."

Deanna suddenly felt cold. "Nonsense." She lifted her chin for Elspeth to straighten her collar. "That only happens in books. It was a terrible accident."

Deanna fervently hoped that she was right.

Chapter
6

Orrin O'Laren came into the workshop at noon. One look at the boy, and Joe knew that someone had already told him about Daisy's death. No one who saw his face could possibly think that he'd had anything to do with the tragedy.

No. Some other reason, accident or otherwise, had led to Daisy's death.

"Best get to work," Orrin mumbled, head bowed, his cap in his hand, his denim work clothes clean from a recent washing.

As he walked past, Joe said, "I'm so sorry, Orrin." Inadequate, but the best he could do. And he meant it. "If you want to take some time off . . ."

Orrin shook his head, took a step. Suddenly he spun around. "Why, sir? Why did she do it?"

Joe stood there like a lump. He didn't dare raise the specter of foul play. "Just a terrible accident."

"Weren't no accident. The police came. Officer Crum said they found her on the cliffs. Wanted to know where I was last night, he did. I didn't even know she was dead. How could I? I was home helping Ma all last night. I just don't understand." His face crumpled, and he turned and walked back to the workshop.

Joe just stood there. He couldn't begin to imagine what Orrin was feeling. It was hard enough losing a family member or a friend, but losing the girl you'd meant to spend your life with? Joe remembered his moment of cold dread when Will had told him they'd found the body of a woman at the Wood-ruffs' ball. And was ashamed of the relief he'd felt when he learned it was Daisy and not Deanna.

But for Orrin, the pain would only grow deeper.

Joe heard the centrifuge start up. He didn't think Orrin should be working around equipment in the state he was in, but it was probably better for him to keep busy and not have to think or feel.

He should warn Orrin that Will would be back to question him, explain to him that it was just a formality, that no one blamed him. But they would both know that was a lie. If it did prove to be murder, the police would look for a killer in the Fifth Ward first. No one, including the new mayor, wanted to accuse one of the powerful families on Bellevue Avenue.

Joe lifted his leather work apron off the hook by the door and went to the back, where Orrin was tinkering away on the heating gauge. The noise and the steam and the concentration needed for calibrating the right amount of pressure wasn't conducive to a heart-to-heart talk.

Relieved, Joe reached for a wrench and settled down to work.

⟞•∘○•▸◼◂•∘○•⟝

The Woodruffs' carriage let Deanna, Cassie, and Madeline off at the paneled entrance to the Casino. They were accompanied by Mrs. Woodruff's sister, Tillie. Unlike her sister, Tillie had not married well. Rumor had it she'd run off with a prospector who'd turned out to be a gambler, and her father had disinherited her. When her husband died, she'd come to stay with the Woodruffs. They'd set her up in a nice-size house in town, and as far as anyone knew, they had been supporting her ever since.

Deanna always wondered if Tillie had started out life as a bubbling, happy person like her sister. The sisters were nothing alike. Tillie was stern but also nearsighted and slightly deaf, which made her a perfect chaperone as far as Cassie and Deanna were concerned.

They moved like snails down the arcade to the piazza, where Mrs. Woodruff had already arrived in order to arrange luncheon. Some people thought the Casino allowed too many of the common people into the dances and concerts arranged each week, but Deanna loved coming here. She was always diverted by the many things to do, all under one roof. There was a theater, a ballroom, stores, restaurants. You could wander along its cool loggias, or sit in one of the numerous piazzas and niches that were perfect for chatting or just being quiet.

And, of course, there was tennis.

They finally reached the loggia that looked over the lawn tennis courts. Charles, Lord David, Vlady, and Herbert, dressed for sport, were standing at the ready by the nearest court, though Herbert and Vlady did seem subdued as they waved a greeting.

Lord David strode over to where the young women were standing. "Miss Deanna." He bowed slightly after showering her with a dazzling smile. If her mother could see that smile, she would be begging Mrs. Woodruff to keep Deanna in Newport. "Do you play?"

"Tennis?"

That smile again. "That is what we're here for, isn't it?"

Flustered, Deanna sputtered out the truth. "You, perhaps, but the women mainly sit in the shade of the promenade and watch, or if we're lucky, we are allowed to stand on the court doing nothing but holding our rackets until someone decides the sun is wrecking our complexion and calls an end to the game." Her hand flew to her mouth. "I shouldn't have said that. Yes, I do play on occasion."

He cocked his head at her. He had a charming dimple in one cheek. "I think you must be more intrepid than most ladies," he said. "I'll challenge you to a match, then."

"With pleasure," Deanna said, excited that she might actually get to play a worthy opponent before she recollected herself.

"Don't do it, Deanna," Maddie said, and laughed. "He loves to win."

"Doubles, perhaps," Deanna added, reproving herself for being unladylike. She had disappointed him. She could see it, though he recovered quickly.

"Doubles today. Who knows tomorrow?"

Vlady called to him.

"Our court is available. I shall return." And he bowed himself away.

Deanna watched him go.

"What would your mama say?" whispered Cassie so unexpectedly that it made Deanna jump. "Such flirtation." She trilled a laugh.

"Is your mama very strict?" Maddie asked.

"Rather," Deanna said. "Yours isn't?"

Madeline shook her head. "My mother died when I was a little girl. That's why I live in Barbados with David. Papa doesn't have much time to see to a daughter. Sometimes I wish . . . but never mind. Where do we sit?"

"Over here," called Olivia Merrick, one of the girls who had come out last year with Cassie. Olivia wasn't very pretty, but her mother was indefatigable about seeing her marry well.

They joined Olivia and some other young women who sat underneath the roof of the loggia, away from the sun and stray tennis balls, where they could sip lemonade and occasionally applaud the sportsmen when they weren't too busy gossiping to notice the game.

The four men took their places on the court. Vlady and Lord David against Herbert and Charles.

It didn't look to be much of a match. While the ladies' fans stirred the air beneath the roof, out on the courts the sun beat down mercilessly on the men in their white flannels. Soon they were all looking a little limp, except for Vlady and Lord David, who were completely taken up in the outcome of the game.

Deanna itched to be down there playing, too. She would do so much better than poor Herbert. But it quickly became obvious that today wasn't about the game, it was about court-ing: the men making flamboyant plays more intent on trying to impress than actually enjoying the game. It made her miss games with Bob and Joe more than ever.

The ladies soon lost interest in the sport, and conversation

turned to fashion and what they were going to wear to the
Vanderbilts' first ball at their new cottage, The Breakers.

"It has seventy rooms," Cassie exclaimed.

Olivia leaned forward and lowered her voice. "I heard there
were twenty bathrooms. And doesn't *that* just outshine Marble
House."

Cassie laughed. "I bet Mrs. Alva is mad as hops. Outdone
by the other Mrs. Vanderbilt." She turned to Madeline. "The
two wives of the Vanderbilt men. They're always trying to
trump each other."

"How droll," Madeline said.

Deanna wouldn't call the fight between the two most powerful women in society droll. They could be vicious—more like
tigresses, or Amazons.

"And this 'cottage' as you call it, The Breakers? It sounds
magnificent."

"Oh, everyone here has big houses. It's what we do," Cassie
said. "Don't you have big houses in Barbados?"

"We do, but nothing as splendorous as yours and these
others. I'd love to see inside of the others."

"You will. The season has just started. We'll be dancing,
dining, and having all sorts of fun until September."

Deanna's mind began to wander. How could they be talking
about bathrooms and dances when a girl had been murdered
only the night before? Her father was right. They'd already
forgotten about Daisy.

But Deanna hadn't.

She wondered what Will was doing, if he was still questioning guests. Had he questioned Orrin? Madeline had been so
quick to assume it had been about Daisy and Orrin's intimate
affairs. Deanna didn't know what to think or even hope for.

But if not Orrin, then who? A stranger? Had a madman lured her to the cliffs?

She looked out to the courts, where Vlady had just aced a serve.

One of her own set? When would any of them have had time during the ball? Of course, the men had been coming and going all night—ballroom, billiard room, terrace, gentleman's cloakroom. Sometimes it seemed like men spent more time outside of the ballroom than they did in.

And Joe had left early. She supposed anyone could have slipped out, but why?

The match ended with Vlady and Lord David trouncing the other two. They all shook hands and strolled off the court while four others took their places.

Deanna knew the men would stop to freshen up and perhaps have a drink or two or three at the bar before joining the ladies for tea.

The afternoon dragged on. Deanna hadn't gotten to play even one game. And now she had to listen to Ivy Bennett retell the anecdote of how her cousin had been responsible for building the Casino after being kicked out of the "stuffy old Reading Room" when he'd dared a friend to ride his horse onto the porch.

Madeline seemed to be enjoying the story, but the rest of them had heard it a million times. Mr. Bennett had behaved badly, but Deanna couldn't help being a little in awe of someone who could thumb his nose at propriety and go his own way.

When the gentlemen returned, they were accompanied by Cokey Featheringham and his cousin, Nathaniel. Ivy Bennett had managed to corral the Manchesters a few tables away, so Cokey and Herbert Stanhope joined Deanna and Olivia.

"You didn't ask me to dance last evening, Cokey. You bad boy."

"Oh, Olivia, I would've, but me and Nathaniel didn't stay long." He lowered his voice. "It was stifling, and we decided to meet up with some fellows I know at the country club."

"Well, you owe me a waltz," Olivia said coyly.

"Sure thing."

Their banter became tedious, and Deanna found herself doodling with her finger on the tablecloth. And was a little embarrassed to realize she'd been sketching the lines of a certain tennis player who was better than the rest. She looked up to see if he was still seated with Ivy.

He looked up at the same time and winked at her.

Deanna quickly looked around to see if anyone noticed, but they were all intent on their own conversations; Lord David broke into a charming grin, and her skin tingled in reaction.

As soon as luncheon was over, the ladies retired to the lounge to freshen up while the gentlemen sat over their port.

It was when Deanna was returning to the piazza that she passed Cokey, Nathaniel, and Herbert coming out of the library. Their conversation cut off abruptly and didn't continue until they'd rounded the corner.

They picked up again as soon as she was out of sight. "I kid you not. We left early. A dead bore if you ask me."

Deanna's steps slowed. They were talking about the ball last night.

"I'm sure it was the same girl they found out on the rocks. He had her up against the wall."

Deanna stopped.

"You don't think he killed her?" Herbert asked.

"Not sayin' he did. Just that he shouldn't be fraternizing with the lower classes out on the street and in a state of undress."

"I don't believe it. Not Joe Ballard."

Deanna turned cold and her stomach threated to expel her tea. They suspected Joe of . . . She shook her head and listened.

"Cokey's exaggerating about the undress. His tie was off and his collar was undone."

"That only means he was just finishing up or just getting started."

"Shut up, Cokey," his cousin said.

"Well," Cokey continued. "That's what you get when you throw off society and go to live down with the footies. Guess Joe's gotten a taste for low-class women. The Ballards have never been quite the thing, if you ask me."

"Well, I still don't believe it," Herbert said. "Joe's a gentleman. The Ballards are old money, a good family."

"Ha. He even stopped and talked to us. Brazen bastard."

"Actually," Nathaniel said, "he did try to step in front of her so we wouldn't see."

Cokey laughed. "Like we would care. It's not exactly unheard of to take a turn with the help."

"You would know, Cokey."

"Maybe I like a little skirt on occasion, but not out on the street like a commoner."

"It was dark," Nate reminded him.

Deanna moved closer and ducked behind a column so she could hear better.

"Heard he's friends with that police sergeant in charge of the case. Lucky devil. That kind of scandal would finish the family off."

"Wasn't he engaged to Deanna Randolph?" Nate asked.

"Yeah, but it went off for some reason." Cokey laughed. "Bet she'll be thanking her lucky stars. She could have been married to a murderer."

"Really, Cokey," Herbert said. "That's a terrible thing to say. You don't know that he murdered the poor girl."

"No? Then who did?"

Deanna reeled back. She wouldn't believe it. She'd heard that some men took advantage of their housemaids. But not Joe. And not with Orrin's intended.

And he certainly wouldn't have killed Daisy—or anyone. She wanted to run after them and tell Cokey he was wrong and to stop telling such vicious lies.

"Well, just keep it to yourself," Herbert said. "If it is true, he'll never be allowed back into society for doing something so . . . overt."

"Dare say. But things like this have a way of making themselves known. Not to worry. They'll never send him to prison."

"Maybe not," Herbert said. "But society will make his life a living hell."

"True. I sure don't envy him when it does get out," Nathaniel said. "Poor devil. He'll probably wish he were in prison rather than being a social outcast."

They passed out of hearing distance.

Deanna looked frantically around. At least it appeared that no one else had overheard their conversation. She had to do something. But what? She couldn't very well run after the men and make them stop telling such vicious lies. And she couldn't go looking for Joe down among the warehouses. She wouldn't be able to face him after having heard what she'd just heard.

She would go to Gran Gwen. It was the only thing she could do. Gran Gwen would know how to stop the malicious gossip. It might be devastating for her to hear such accusations about her grandson, but Gwen was a free thinker: She wouldn't believe it about Joe, and she wouldn't be ashamed to face society if it came to that.

Deanna would go right away.

No, she couldn't. She didn't have her carriage. She couldn't hire a cab, because she hadn't brought any money with her. Besides, she couldn't take the chance of her mother finding out and insisting Deanna accompany her to Boston. Deanna couldn't leave Newport when things were in such a state.

But the Casino had a telephone and so did Bonheur, the Ballard's residence. She hurried down the corridor to ask the concierge to put through the call.

Will Hennessy returned around four that afternoon. Joe had called a halt to work when it was clear that Orrin was too upset to concentrate. They were drinking coffee when the police sergeant came inside, looking as if he'd not slept in days.

Joe poured him a cup. Orrin had stood when Will entered the room, but at a nod from Will, he sat again.

"I'm sorry about Daisy, Orrin," Will said once he'd taken a cautious sip of the hot liquid. "I wish that you'd been told in a different way. Unfortunately, patrolmen are not always considerate when they're doing their jobs."

Joe knew what he meant. There were as many power struggles and snobberies among the men on the force as there were on Bellevue Avenue.

"Yes, sir. Thank you, sir." Orrin mumbled the words and didn't look up.

"I have a few questions if you're feeling up to it."

Orrin nodded. And Joe prayed that Will wouldn't attack him with accusations.

"Do you know why Daisy was down on the walk last night during the ball?"

"No, sir. She was needed upstairs to see that the ladies' room was kept aired and tidied."

"Did you have plans to see her later that night?"

Orrin shook his head. "We were going down to Easton's Beach on Daisy's half-day Sunday."

"Did you have any misunderstanding with her lately?"

Orrin looked up. "No, sir. What did you ask that for, sir?"

"Just trying to understand what happened. If maybe Daisy was upset about something."

"Not that she told me. And she woulda told me. She was my—my . . ."

"Yes, I know, Orrin. You were planning to marry her."

"Yes, sir."

"*Would* Daisy tell you if she were upset about something?"

There was a flicker of a smile that was heart-wrenching. "My Daisy can tell it like it is, she can. She—" His voice broke, and he hung his head, his shoulders racked with silent sobs. "But if you think—that she would get so she'd throw herself off the cliff? You're wrong. Killing yourself is a mortal sin. And my Daisy was pure . . . was pure."

Will and Joe exchanged looks.

Orrin sniffed, pulled out a much-used and grubby handkerchief, blew his nose.

"They found an envelope in her hand, but no note. Was Daisy in the habit of sending notes around to you?"

Orrin's head snapped up. He frowned at Will. "No, sir.

Daisy don't read or write. She's learning, but not enough to write a letter or anything."

"Just one final question. Was Daisy in the family way?"

"Course not. Her ma and mine woulda skinned us. We were waiting. Now we never will."

Will closed his notebook and returned it to his pocket. "That's all for now, Orrin."

"Yes, sir." Orrin pushed to his feet like an old man, Joe thought, not like a young man barely eighteen and looking forward to the future. It made him sick to think of what had happened to that poor girl. Orrin slumped out of the office and back to work.

Will passed his hand over his face. "Sometimes I hate this job."

Joe nodded. "Where do you go from here?"

"Keep asking questions. Wait for the results of the"—he lowered his voice—"autopsy. The family is pretty upset about it. The mother wailed like a banshee, and the only reason the father didn't kill me outright is that he's laid up with a broken leg."

"You haven't found anything that points to it being an accident?"

"No. And my superiors want it solved. 'A murder during the first week of the season, that's another month and a half to skewer the police force and incite every crazy out there to assault the citizens of Newport.' I quote."

"And they'd rather you arrest someone from the Fifth Ward than Bellevue Avenue."

"I've been told to stay away from the elite."

Joe smiled sympathetically. "The more things change . . ."

"The more they stay the same," Will finished. He picked his cap off the desk, where he'd tossed it, pushed back his hair, and shoved the cap on his head.

"Did you speak with Deanna?" Joe asked.

"Oh, yeah. The father is protective enough. The mother—what a gorgon."

"And?"

"Mrs. Randolph parked herself on a chair, and I was worried about how to pose questions to Deanna without getting myself thrown out."

"Did you manage to learn anything?" Not that Joe thought Deanna would know anything about what had happened except for discovering the body. At least he hoped she wouldn't.

"I'm just getting started, and the door suddenly opens and in walks Cassandra Woodruff. She must have been visiting. Told Mrs. Randolph that Adelaide was sick and she was needed upstairs. Mrs. Randolph had to excuse herself. Reluctantly."

"Was Adelaide really ill?"

Will shrugged. "Possibly, but I'll be damned if Cassandra didn't cut Deanna a wink as she left the room."

Joe laughed. "Those two."

"Yes, Cassandra is a minx. Deanna is another story."

Joe, who'd begun to relax, grew alert.

"That girl—young woman—I just can't get used to Deanna all grown up—is something out of the ordinary. I began my questioning being very careful to keep within propriety. Then *she* starts asking *me* questions. And the details she remembered, when everyone else was in a state of stupid shock. The girl has a mind like a trap. If she were a man and not upper crust, I would have enlisted her on the spot."

Will breathed out a laugh. "I tell you, Joe. I was on tiptoes trying not to be indecorous, and Dee comes out and says, 'We saw her face, she was lying parallel to the walk. If she jumped, she would have landed facedown.' I about swallowed my tongue, and I was afraid her father was going to faint."

"Oh Lord." Joe scrubbed his face with his hand. "You have to keep her out of trouble, Will. You told her to stay out of it, didn't you?"

"Of course. Not that it ever did any good before."

"Yeah, but that was child's play. Not a murder investigation."

"Well, I don't think we have to worry. Her mother is trying to take her to Boston while Adelaide sees a new doctor. Never knew a girl so middlin' as Adelaide. A shame, for she sure is a beauty."

"Above your touch."

"Don't I know it. Well, I'd best get back on it if I want to sleep tonight."

A thunderous knocking sounded at the door, making both men jump.

"What the hell?" Joe said, and went to open the door.

"Wait." Will crossed to the window to peer out. "I knew it was too good to be true. Reinforcements have arrived."

"Open up in the name of the Newport police!"

Joe looked at Will, shrugged. There was no use in prolonging the inevitable. The constables who patrolled the Fifth Ward had no more compunction about knocking down doors than they had about knocking heads together.

Joe opened the door and was pushed back with the force of several constables rushing in, followed by Sergeant Crum, a rubicund man with a barrel chest and receding hairline. He was the scourge of the Fifth Ward, more intent on punishment than protection—unless you were willing to pay, which not many people in the ward could afford to do.

"We're looking for Orrin O'Laren in connection with the death of one Daisy Payne."

Will stepped forward. "Thank you, Sergeant, but I am in charge of this investigation. And I will take a prisoner when there is evidence against him."

"You may eat out of the hands of the elite up on the Avenue, but this here is my turf. And I'll do the arresting on it."

"Can you show just cause?" Will asked calmly.

"I'll show you my fist. The swells been calling the chief demanding action. And since they won't hear of it being one of theirs, it's gotta be one of ours. I'm taking in O'Laren." Crum nodded brusquely to his constables. Two rushed into the workspace. A third hesitated, then with a small shake of his head, followed them.

Joe started to go after them.

Sergeant Crum stepped in front of him. He was much larger and taller than Joe, and he was used to intimidating his constituency.

Joe attempted to sidestep him, but Will stopped him with a gesture.

"That's right," Crum said. "You think you can come down here with all your money and try living like these people, throw your weight around, stir them up to trouble, but it doesn't work that way. You're just another Mick down here."

"Welsh and French," Joe said.

"All foreigners, if you ask me. You might can pass for American up there with those folks, but I know your kind."

He probably would have carried on some more, but the constables returned, dragging Orrin between them. He already had a swelling eye.

Joe's fists clenched.

"What's the meaning of this?" Will asked, stepping forward and cutting off Crum's view.

"Caught him trying to escape out the back winder."

"I was not." Orrin pulled against his constraints.

The cop jabbed him in the ribs.

"That's enough," Will said. "Go with them, son. Don't rile them. I'll talk to the chief, and if there's no evidence against you"—he paused long enough to give Crum a fulminating look—"or trumped up against you, you'll be set free by evening or someone can post your bail."

"We'll see about that," Sergeant Crum said.

"Yeah, we will." Joe stepped toward Orrin. "Stay calm. I'll come as soon as I can. Don't worry. I'll see that you get out on bail."

The sergeant leaned in until Joe had to force himself not to move away. The sergeant had been eating fish and onions for his lunch.

"You think you can have your way, but you can't protect him, and you'd better stay out of it or you'll be wishing you'd stayed up there in your fancy house on the cliff."

"Don't threaten me."

Will pointed at the constables. "If I find any marks on the boy, I'll report you to the captain."

The three men looked nervously toward Crum.

"Chief wants this solved. He's getting guff from the swells. So I expect he'll be happy to find the culprit living down here."

"Did he send you to do that?" Will asked.

"Something like."

"I don't believe it."

Crum laughed. "Maybe he don't like cops that look the other way."

Will smiled slowly, an expression so filled with intimidation that Joe was taken aback.

"Is that right? That may be. But I *know* he don't like cops who use brute force when it isn't necessary and are on the take."

"One day, Hennessey."

"Name it."

The sergeant lifted his chin to the men, who pushed a docile Orrin through the door. They were met with jeers and angry shouts from the crowd that had formed outside.

The sergeant turned on his heel and strode into the street. The crowd quieted until he passed, then became even more vocal.

"Can't you stop him?" Joe asked.

"Not here," Will said. "Jurisdiction is a sticky wicket. Some officers are more territorial than others."

"And no one wants Bellevue Avenue."

"Not even me," Will said ruefully. "I got it by default."

"They tie your hands?"

"Not totally. We have to turn a blind eye now and again. But it's the same in every city in the world. The rich get away with murder."

"And this time?"

"Joe, you know I'll do whatever it takes to find the real culprit."

"Even if it costs your job?"

"Even if it costs my job."

Joe nodded, clasped his friend on the arm. "Thanks."

"I'm not doing it for you. Now, let me get down to headquarters and make sure nothing bad happens to that boy."

Joe walked Will to the street, watched him stride off down the brick pavement until he rounded the corner, then shut the door. He had a lot of things to do.

The first order of business was to talk to his grandmother.

Then he would draw a draft on his bank and get Orrin out of jail if he could.

He quickly changed clothes, making himself presentable . . . enough. Then he closed down the machines and locked the warehouse. He pulled his bicycle away from the wall, clipped his trouser leg so that it wouldn't pick up grease, and maneuvered the machine through the door.

The crowd had begun to disperse. But a few stragglers remained, and one called out, "You gonna get that boy out of jail, Ballard?"

"I'm going to try."

"Just make sure you do."

It sounded like a threat, but that's what happened with desperate people. They turned on whoever was nearest.

Joe threw his leg across the bicycle and pushed off from the cobblestones. Lifting his hand to the crowd, he peddled away.

Chapter
7

It wasn't easy to convince Cassie to drop Deanna off at Bonheur, the Ballard family's seaside cottage. She and Madeline had a hundred questions. When Deanna said she'd remembered she was supposed to visit Gran Gwen that afternoon, Cassie frowned at her. "You didn't say anything about it this morning."

"I forgot until just a few minutes ago."

"But you're dressed in your tennis frock," Madeline noted.

"Oh, Gran Gwen won't mind," Deanna said with a lightheartedness she didn't feel, and hoped that the drive to the southern point of land where Bonheur sat alone would pass quickly.

"She's a great character, Maddie," Cassie said. "You met her last night briefly. She's Joe Ballard's grandmother."

"That handsome man who disappeared before I could claim him for a waltz?"

Cassie glanced at Deanna. "Yes. But we don't like him anymore."

"No? Why on earth not? I'm surprised one of you hasn't snatched him up yet. Or is he undesirable?"

He wasn't, though he might well be soon if Deanna didn't squelch the gossip.

"He, um . . ." Cassie hesitated.

"It's quite okay to tell her," Deanna said, a little more sharply than she'd intended. "Our families were in the process of arranging a marriage between us. A merger of businesses. Like a couple of barrels of sugar. Neither of us was ready for marriage or willing to be pawns of the sugar industry."

Madeline raised both eyebrows.

"Sorry if I shock you."

"On the contrary." Madeline smiled. "I think you were very courageous to cry off. But aren't you afraid that it will sour your chances of making a good match?" She placed her finger on her dimpled cheek, the one that corresponded to her brother's dimple. "Or do you already have someone else in mind?"

"No, of course I haven't."

Beside her, Cassie giggled.

Madeline leaned forward across the space between them. "Oh, do tell."

Fortunately, they turned into the drive of Bonheur, and Deanna busied herself with straightening her skirts and patting her hair. As if anybody at Bonheur cared a whit about hairs out of place.

"Oh my. Look at that. It's so . . . mysterious," Madeline said, looking up at the three-storied, stick-and-shingle "cottage" that dominated the point of land. The first floor was constructed of stone, like a castle fortress; the upper stories were covered with various patterns of weathered gray shingles that undulated in the sun like the waves on the sea behind it. "And spectacular." Madeline stared at the façade. "It looks like it's sitting at the end of the world."

"That's because of the cliffs," Deanna told her. "They drop straight down into the sea."

"Does anyone ever fall off?"

"No," Deanna said, knowing they were all thinking of poor Daisy. "Though the boys used to jump off them into the water. There are stairs down to a private beach. And also a marina, so Mr. Ballard can sail his yacht straight home instead of having to dock it in the town marina."

"Wealthy," Madeline said.

"Very," agreed Cassie. "Old money. Bonheur is *really* old. It's been in their family for several generations."

"Old money," Madeline echoed.

"But not all prim and proper," Cassie assured her. "Oh mercy. Gwen Ballard has a scandalous past. She still keeps tongues wagging, and she must be in her seventies if she's a day."

"But she's still invited to the best houses?"

Deanna started to say that Bonheur *was* the best house. But she held her tongue.

"Oh, good Lord, yes," Cassie said.

"The Ballards must be a powerful family."

"I guess so," Cassie said.

"Are they, Deanna?"

"They're a well-respected family."

Madeline smiled at Deanna. "They sound fascinating. You must introduce me one day. To the grandmother and to her handsome grandson. I love adventurous people."

The carriage came to a stop. The coachman let down the steps just as the front door opened and Gran Gwen came out to greet them. A small woman, she managed to exude magnificence in a maroon tea gown and a sleeveless gold caftan that floated around her in the sea breeze.

"And eccentric, I see. No butler?"

"Of course she has a butler," Deanna said, gathering her skirts to exit quickly. She didn't want to take the chance of having Cassie and Madeline join them for tea. "Thank you, Cassie. Fingers crossed that I'll see you tomorrow."

"Maddie and I are counting on it."

"Yes, do come," Maddie added. "I'm so looking forward to it."

Deanna smiled and hurried up the porch steps to Gran Gwen. As soon as they were inside, she let her smile slide.

"My goodness. Come out to the conservatory and tell me what has brought you here in such a hurry. You're probably swimming in tea already, but I'm not."

"Did you call my mama?"

"Yes, and all is well." Gran Gwen chuckled. "I told Dickerson I ran into you at the Casino and begged you to come to tea. A little white lie, but your mother was pleased. She may have set her sights on Lord David for you, but she hasn't totally given up on my grandson yet."

"Thank you. I didn't know what to tell her, and it's so very important that I talk to you."

They walked down the long wainscoted corridor toward the back of the house. Bonheur was decorated in dark wood and richly colored fabrics and always made Deanna feel safe. Just walking down the hall did much to assuage her agitation.

"Unfortunately, Laurette is away at a rally and won't be back for another week or so. Or did you mean to speak to me alone?"

Deanna nodded, relieved beyond words. "You." It would be hard enough to tell Gran Gwen. Having to tell Laurette Ballard what was being said about her son . . . she didn't think she could do it.

"I'm glad you came, regardless of this important thing you must tell me. I wanted to make sure you were recovered from last night—the ball and the death of that poor child. And . . . I've been meaning to talk to you about Joseph."

"That's why I've come." Though now that she was here, Deanna couldn't imagine what she was going to say. Gran Gwen had to be warned about what was being said about Joe. He might not care, but Deanna refused to let his mother and Gran Gwen be ostracized for his indiscretion—if it were even true.

They continued past the back parlor, through the morning room, and out to the conservatory, where they were enveloped by sunshine and the sea. In the distance, waves sparkled like so many diamonds. Tropical flowers flowed from hanging baskets and odd-looking palm trees spouted into the air from rattan tubs.

No matter how many times Deanna came here, stepping into the conservatory was always a surprise, and her smile returned, if only fleetingly.

Gran Gwen led her toward two cushioned wicker chairs that sat behind a small glass table. Almost immediately, a maid entered and placed a tea tray on the table.

Gran Gwen poured out tea, added milk and two lumps of sugar, and handed Deanna the cup. "Now tell me."

Deanna's mouth twisted. *Do not cry. Do not cry.* She was embarrassed and heartsick. And suddenly, she didn't know where to start.

"Are you in trouble, my dear?"

"Not me."

"Oh." Gwen sat back a little in her chair. Sipped her tea. "Maybe you should just start at the beginning and tell me everything."

So Deanna did. How Will had come that morning to ask her questions. How her mother wanted to take Adelaide to consult the doctor and bring Deanna along. How Elspeth was afraid that Lord David's servant had put a curse on Daisy, and how they were all afraid the police might blame Orrin for her death. About going to the Casino, about the tennis match and tea.

All too soon, Deanna reached the part she dreaded most.

"I was coming down the corridor and these men—they—"

"Were they rude to you?" Gwen prompted.

Deanna shook her head.

"To one of the other girls?"

Deanna shook her head again.

"Tell me just like it happened. Don't be embarrassed. We don't allow humiliation or hurt in this household."

"I—don't want to say it."

Gwen peered at her, then took Deanna's icy hands in her sinewy ones. "Then just spit it out like a bad taste. I won't judge you, if that's what you're worried about."

"Not me. I heard them laughing about something—someone—who had left the ball early." Deanna saw a spark of understanding in Gran Gwen's eye and faltered.

"Go on."

"They saw him with Daisy. Outside. They said he—he'd taken off his tie and unbuttoned his shirt and—Cokey said that he was taking her up against the wall." Deanna pulled her hands away from Gwen's and, hot with shame and embarrassment and feeling sick, covered her face.

"Go on." Gran Gwen's voice was calm, sympathetic, and Deanna felt worse.

"They thought he must have gotten a taste for the lower classes living where he did and that he must have murdered Daisy. They said even if he wasn't arrested, he would be ostracized by society and his family would be ruined."

"They were talking about Joseph?"

Deanna took her hands from her face and looked directly at Gran Gwen. "Yes."

"And you believed them?"

"No. I don't think so. I mean, I know men do such things but . . . but he wouldn't kill her. I don't believe it. You don't believe it?"

Gwen took a long time to answer. "I think I know my grandson well enough to say he wouldn't kill over a thing like that."

"But do you think . . . ?" Deanna couldn't ask; she was afraid of the answer.

"Wasn't Daisy his apprentice's intended?"

Deanna nodded, praying that Gwen would say it couldn't be true.

At last she said, "It isn't like Joe to betray a friend. I'm sorry you had to witness that bit of poor taste. Men like to revel in the more sordid side of life. Make it larger than it really is."

"Is that what happened? They were making it up?"

"I think they must have been. I certainly hope so."

"I didn't want to tell, but I thought—well, I wanted to warn you. Maybe you could do something to stop the rumors. I knew if I didn't tell, I would be abetting them. I'm sorry. I'm really sorry."

"Nonsense. Though, Deanna, I wouldn't share this with others."

"I'd never."

"Not with your father or Cassie or anyone."

"I won't."

"I'll talk to Joe, and then I'll see what I can do."

"I wish I had never gone to the Casino or heard those stupid men!"

"I'm very thankful you did, though I'm chagrined at your ears being sullied with such vulgar talk. Now finish your tea and I'll send you home. You are a very brave woman. You're also very smart, and I hope that you and Joe will one day see your way through all of this."

Skeptical, Deanna looked up at her.

"You don't believe this talk, do you?" Gwen asked.

"No." Deanna really didn't *want* to believe the talk. "But Joe doesn't want to marry me."

"Joe doesn't know his own mind. Do you?"

"I don't want to get married and take my place in society. I want a grand passion." She clasped her hand over her mouth.

Gran Gwen smiled and took her hand away. "My dear, you have plenty of time for grand passions. Have a sandwich, and let's get some color back in those cheeks."

Now that she was free from the burden of her message, Deanna was suddenly hungry. And with relief came speculation about who actually had killed Daisy. "Gran Gwen?"

"Yes, dear?"

"Elspeth is afraid that suspicion will fall on her brother Orrin, because the police always look for someone to arrest among the lower classes."

"Unfortunately, she is correct about that. But Will Hennessey is a good man. He'll find the real culprit if he can."

"It might not be up to him. He has superiors he must answer to."

Gwen nodded. "Who don't want to offend any of the Bellevue Avenue crowd."

"That isn't right."

"No, my dear. And someday it might change, though so far history has proven otherwise."

"Then what do we do?"

"The best we can."

"And give women the vote?"

"Absolutely." Gran Gwen lifted her teacup, and they finished their tea both feeling a lot better than they had when they'd began.

A few minutes later, Gwen walked Deanna out to the Ballard carriage, which was waiting at the front portico to drive Deanna home.

"Now, don't worry. I will get to the bottom of this."

"Thank you. And thank you for tea."

As the carriage door opened, Deanna saw Joe cycling up the drive.

He jolted to a stop. "Dee."

Her conversation with Gran Gwen and what she'd overheard came barreling back.

"Dee, I wanted—"

Deanna shook her head and scrambled into the carriage. The coachman closed the carriage door.

"Dee, wait. They've arrested Orrin for Daisy's murder."

For a second, the world went out of focus. Deanna's breath stopped, then came rushing back in again. She grasped the edge of the carriage window and leaned out. "He didn't do it, Joe. *You* know he didn't. You have to tell them."

"Well . . ."

"Don't say more." She turned away. "Drive on."

"Yes, miss." The coachman climbed to the box and they drove away.

———◦◦◦〉◀〈◦◦◦———

J oe turned to his grandmother. "What was that all about? Is she still so angry over last night? There are more important issues here. They've arrested my apprentice for Daisy Payne's murder. Why did she say that I knew he didn't do it?"

"Well," his grandmother said with a sigh, "I rather suspect she thinks *you* did it."

Joe stared at her. "Me?" It came out in a falsetto. "That's preposterous. Why on earth would she think that? She knows me better than that."

"She knew you better than that."

"What are you talking about?"

"You've changed in the last year, Joseph. You know you have."

Of course he had. "That doesn't make me a murderer."

"No, it doesn't. Come inside."

He followed his grandmother up the steps to the house and inside, where she went immediately into the parlor. He found her standing at the drinks cabinet.

"I can see I'm in disgrace. Did Dee come for a visit or just to accuse me of murder?"

"You fool!"

Joe took a step back. What had he done to deserve such raw disapproval from Grandmère? What had Dee been telling her?

His grandmother poured herself a sherry and carried it to the fireplace, now screened for the summer.

"I would have poured if you'd asked," said Joe cautiously.

"Fix yourself something. You may need it."

With mounting concern, Joe quickly poured himself a drink and sat down in the club chair but immediately regretted it. It put him at a disadvantage to the avenging inferno who stood at the mantel.

"Good God, what have I done that warrants this treatment? Is it because I was uncivil to Deanna last night or that you believe I actually murdered that poor girl?"

"Neither, but I want to know exactly what happened and how you're involved in it."

"Terrible business. Will Hennessey came down to the warehouse today. He has ordered an autopsy. While he was at the warehouse, Sergeant Crum arrived saying he had orders to arrest Orrin. Will's hands were tied. As soon as they left, I came here. I feel badly. Daisy was a housemaid at the Woodruffs'. I saw her last night as I was leaving the ball."

"I know. You were seen."

"Seen?"

"With the maid."

"What are you getting at?"

"Deanna, poor child, came to warn me. It seems she overheard Cokey Featheringham and some of his cohorts at the Casino today."

"Oh Lord. Daisy was sneaking out to see Orrin. They did pass by while I was trying to convince her to go back inside. Cokey made a few off-color jokes—you know how he is—then he staggered away. I can't believe they even remember seeing me, they were so drunk."

"Evidently, Cokey vividly remembers seeing you, the maid, the state of your undress, and I believe I quote, you were 'taking her up against the wall.'"

Joe's jaw dropped. "He actually said that?"

"According to Deanna."

"Deanna heard this? Is that what she came to tell you?"

"Yes, and that the scandal will ruin our family even if they don't hang you."

"Grandmère, you know it's pure bull. I never touched that girl. How could you even think that I might?"

Gwen didn't answer.

"Deanna believed them? How could *she* think such a thing about me?" Joe had started to stand, but he sank back into the chair. "How does she even know about things like that?"

"She's a woman, in case you haven't noticed."

"Of course I've noticed. You don't understand." He finished his drink. "Did *you* tell her such things existed?"

His grandmother slowly lifted one eyebrow. An expression that could make grown men cower.

Today it just made Joe angry. "Well, let me set your mind at rest. I saw Daisy sneaking out of the servants' entrance. I was not in a state of undress. I'd only removed my tie because of the heat. I sent her back inside. Now she's dead. I don't know how or why. I informed Will Hennessey of all of this when he came to the warehouse this morning.

"There's the whole truth, but please believe what you will." He stood, outraged and mortified that he could be so misunderstood. "And let Deanna believe what she wants."

"Oh, get off your high horse. It took a good deal of courage for her to come here and inform me of those things. She cares for our family very deeply."

"I know." Joe felt a laugh bubble up from deep beyond his anger.

"And just what's so funny?"

"The idea of Dee's righteous indignation. At least I hope

that's what it was. She really said that I took the maid up against the wall? Gad. How will I ever face her again?"

"If I were you, I'd be more concerned about convincing her that you didn't murder that poor girl."

"If she actually can believe that, I—"

"You should marry her."

"You think she needs a man to take care of her? That's not like you."

"Actually, I was thinking about you."

"I can't, Grandmère."

"Don't you love her?"

"I've always loved her. As a sister. I don't know about the other."

"Well, don't take too long to figure it out. She'll be snapped up quickly, I expect. She might be on her way to a Barbadian plantation before you know it."

Joe shook his head. "Not if I have anything to say about it. Grandmère, I can't explain now. But I need you to do two things for me."

"I'm listening."

"Use your influence with the mayor to have them release Orrin. His family is distraught and they need him. I'll guarantee that he won't flee. Though I may need to borrow some money for his, um, bail."

"And bribes. What's the other thing?"

"To convince Deanna to leave town with her mother tomorrow."

"Why? What aren't you telling me?"

"Nothing about Daisy Payne and her murder, I promise."

Chapter
8

Deanna meant to go straight to her room when she returned home. She was in a turmoil of disbelief, grief, and fear. She wanted to be alone, but she didn't want to have to think.

She was loath to face Elspeth and have to tell her that her brother had been taken to jail. And she couldn't tell Elspeth her fear that Joe, not Orrin, had been the cause of Daisy's death.

But it was not to be. As she walked up the front steps to Randolph House, Dickerson opened the door. "Good afternoon, miss. Your mother would like to see you in the morning room as soon as possible."

Which meant immediately. "Thank you, Dickerson. I'll go to her now." Walking more confidently than she felt, Deanna went to face her mother ready to plead, cajole, even prevaricate if necessary, in order to be allowed to remain in Newport. She couldn't leave now. Elspeth needed to be home. And how could she leave not knowing if Orrin—or Joe—would be charged with murder?

She reached the morning room all too soon, smoothed her skirts, pushed her shoulders back, and stepped inside.

Her mother was sitting at her escritoire, giving instructions to the housekeeper, Mrs. Beatty, but dismissed her when she saw Deanna.

"You wanted to see me, Mama?" Deanna said with as much aplomb as her racing heart would allow.

"I've spoken with your father. He assured me that this business with the maid is in no way dangerous for the rest of us. We agree that it would be best if you stayed here in Newport for the few days I must be away with Adelaide."

Deanna wanted to shout with triumph but she didn't dare. Any excited reaction would surely cause her mother to change her mind. "Yes, Mama."

"I hope to have Adelaide back here weekend next, but if it takes longer, it's preferable that you remain here and get to know Lord David better. Elspeth will stay with you. She's upstairs packing a few things for you. I expect you to carry yourself with dignity at all times. Cassie Woodruff is a sweet girl, but has had no proper guidance and doesn't know when enough is too much. Decorum, Deanna. Lord David may flirt, but he'll want a wife who knows what's expected of her."

"Yes, Mama."

"One other thing before you go."

Deanna stood still, trying to breathe evenly and not fidget when she really wanted to hike up her skirts and run up the stairs to Elspeth. She didn't understand how Adelaide could always be so demure.

"This is the worst of all possible times for Adelaide to be indisposed. I'm hoping Dr. Meerschaum can prescribe something to keep her on her feet. It's too bad for her to have to miss the festivities for Lord David and . . ." She gave Deanna intent look.

Deanna looked squarely back at her mother. "Lady Madeline?"

She saw the glint of surprise, then satisfaction in her mother's eye.

"So you noticed that." Jeannette Randolph didn't explain what "that" was. She knew she didn't have to. And Deanna thought that her mother's disgruntlement at having to confide in her younger daughter, even tacitly, was mixed with a smidgeon of pride that Deanna had been so observant.

"You'll have to keep an eye on that business. Men are a weak breed. They must be guided and kept from indiscretion."

Deanna didn't answer. She was much too overwhelmed by her mother's speech. It was the first time her mother had ever spoken to her as if she were another adult.

"I understand, Mama."

"Subtlety is key, Deanna. In all things."

"Yes, Mama."

"Now go and make certain Elspeth is packing all you need. Though I must say the girl knows her wardrobe." Mrs. Randolph turned back to the list she'd been discussing with the housekeeper.

Deanna walked demurely from the room. She even controlled herself up the stairs and into her own room.

There were two large trunks open on the floor. *You'd think we were going on a trip of weeks and miles away, rather than a few days and a few blocks' distance.*

Elspeth came into the room with a pile of linen underdresses draped across her arms. Her face was composed but her eyes snapped with fury.

She knows about Orrin, thought Deanna. And wondered who had broken the news to her.

"We'll be staying with the Woodruffs, Elspeth."

"Yes, miss." Elspeth gently laid the skirts in the first trunk, then went back into the dressing room.

Deanna stood where she was.

Elspeth came back with her orange-blossom silk evening gown, one of the new gowns commissioned from Jeanne Paquin, one of Deanna's favorite designers. The dress went into the second trunk.

"We'll find out who did that to Daisy," Deanna said while her brain cautioned, *Don't make promises that aren't in your power to keep.*

Elspeth's eyes flickered but she merely said, "Yes, miss," and continued to pack.

Deanna sucked up her courage and followed Elspeth into the other room. "Elspeth?"

Elspeth turned around, eyes blazing. "He didn't do it."

"So you've heard about Orrin."

"Ma sent one the of the little ones around to let me know." She lifted another dress from its hanger.

"I'm sure it's a mistake," Deanna said, following her and mentally crossing her fingers in hopes that the mistake didn't turn out to be Joe. "Joe will find a way to get him out of jail. In fact, he was at Bonheur just a few minutes ago talking to Gran Gwen. I'm sure that was why he was there."

Elspeth faltered. "Do you think he can?"

"Gran Gwen has much influence among the old Newporters. I'm sure she will pull strings if she can."

"I don't know how. They're always ripe to blame someone from our neighborhood. How do they know it wasn't someone from yours?"

Deanna swallowed. "Well, I'm not. And I'll help if I can. Even if it turns out to be someone from the cottages." She sighed, followed Elspeth into the bedroom, and watched as she deposited the new gown on top of the orange one. They would just have to have the creases steamed out again. "But at least we get to stay in Newport instead of accompanying Mama and Adelaide to Boston. We'll be on hand to help."

"Yes," Elspeth said, suddenly thoughtful. "And we'll be at Seacrest, the scene of the murder. Oh, miss, do you think we might discover a clue the police missed?"

Elspeth's words sent a chill up Deanna's spine. She sat at her dressing table and stared into her trunk. Deanna knew she should tell Elspeth to leave it to the experts, but she didn't feel that way. The police wouldn't be allowed to question the guests, and they would have limited access to the Seacrest servants. Deanna and Elspeth, on the other hand, would be staying at Seacrest for the next few days. And they did have experience—if reading about crime solving counted.

"Perhaps, but, Elspeth, don't get your hopes up. I know in our books the detectives always find the clue that leads them to the villain, but I don't think it's so easy in real life."

"I don't care if it isn't easy. And as soon as we get there tomorrow, I'm going to start looking. I'll tell them I'm to pick up Daisy's things so as to return them to her mother. And if they haven't been packed up, I can go to her room. Maybe she left a clue."

Deanna thought the police must have searched Daisy's things and taken away anything that might lead them to answers about her death.

But Elspeth didn't need to know that. Already she was get-ting some of her usual animation back. It would give her something to do while they waited to hear about Orrin's fate, and make her feel useful—make them both feel useful.

When the packing was finished (and Elspeth had slipped their two latest dime novels in with the linen), Deanna gave her the rest of the evening off to visit her mother, then went down the hall to say good-bye to Adelaide.

Her sister's bedchamber was dark. The drapes were pulled tightly over the windows, and Deanna started to back out of the room.

"Deanna?" Adelaide's voice was a mere whisper, as if the sound was unbearable.

"Yes?"

"What am I going to do? Mama is afraid I've lost Charles."

Deanna moved closer. "Now, what makes you say such a thing? Surely she didn't tell you that."

"No, but I'm sure it's what she thinks. She's not pleased with me, but, Deanna, I can't help it. My head hurts so."

Deanna took her sister's hand. They had never been close, had always had separate interests and different personalities. "You're not to worry about anything but getting well. I'm staying here and . . ." She leaned closer to her sister. "I'll make sure Charles behaves himself."

Adelaide's eyes filled with tears. "I saw him looking at her." She didn't elaborate. It seemed that everyone had noticed the attention Charles had paid to Lady Madeline.

"Don't cry. It will make your headache worse. Everything will be fine. I promise."

Empty words, but at least they seemed to soothe her sister. Deanna kissed her cheek and stood to go. "Be well, and hurry back."

Adelaide's eyes closed and Deanna tiptoed out of the room.

She didn't envy her sister having to take the long train ride up to Boston. But it would be better than returning to New York on the ferry. The waves would make Adelaide abominably ill. The rattle and lurch of the train would be torment enough.

—∞‐❊‐∞—

The following morning, Mr. Randolph saw his wife and elder daughter off at the station. Then he accompanied Deanna to Seacrest. Elspeth had preceded them with the trunks, and Deanna prayed that she wasn't off detecting without her. If someone saw them somewhere they shouldn't be, it would be hard enough to explain if Deanna was there. They would suspect the worst of Elspeth alone.

Deanna wished the horses weren't taking such a sedate pace or that her father wasn't so broody in the opposite seat. Surely, he wasn't having second thoughts about leaving her in Newport while he returned to New York.

"Does something worry you, Papa?"

"What? Oh, no. Nothing you should concern yourself with." And that ended the conversation.

Cassie ran out to meet the carriage as soon as it pulled up at her massive front door. She was wearing a light blue dress made of cotton lawn with a big dimity collar and sash. She lifted her skirts, skipped down the steps, and bobbed a quick curtsey to Mr. Randolph. "Lord, we've had visitors all morning. Mama has retired for a nap. But Papa's here, Mr. Randolph, if you'd like to see him."

"I think I will have a quick word with your father," Mr. Randolph said, alighting.

Cassie took Deanna by the arm and they followed him up the steps. "It's been so exciting around here with so many people leaving their cards. This is going to be so much fun. This afternoon we'll be completely lazy and sit out on the terrace. Mama insists."

They went inside, where the butler was waiting at the door. He pursed his lips in disapproval at Cassie, who gave him one of her saucy smiles, then he bowed to Mr. Randolph.

"Mr. Woodruff is in the library, sir."

"I think I will have a word before I leave for the city." He followed the buttler down the corridor to the library.

Cassie and Deanna followed more slowly while Cassie whispered a convoluted story about a game they had played the night before. "The Manchesters learned it in Barbados. And it's such great fun. . . ."

Deanna held Cassie back when they reached the stairs. She looked to make sure none of the servants were around. "Listen. There's something you must know before we reach my room. The police have arrested Elspeth's brother Orrin."

"For killing Daisy?" Cassie's eyes were huge.

"Shh. Yes, but of course he didn't. Just be careful what you say around Elspeth. She's very upset."

"I'm surprised your mother kept her on."

"I imagine she's distracted. Her thoughts are completely with Adelaide getting her treatment."

"And getting her back here before the season's over. I don't understand what's wrong with your sister."

"Migraines. She really suffers. I know everyone thinks she's insipid, and she is, but she doesn't pretend illness to be interesting. Though I don't know who would think being ill is interesting. Anyway, please don't tell anyone, especially the servants. They'll find out soon enough, but I don't want Elspeth ostracized for it. I'm sure he's innocent," Deanna repeated with as much conviction as she could muster. In her heart, if it had to be Orrin or Joe, she'd rather it be Orrin.

"I promise. Not a word. But I must say we'll all rest better knowing they've arrested someone."

Deanna didn't bother to point out that if Orrin was innocent, it meant the murderer *was* still at large.

"Now, just let me go say good-bye to Papa, and I'll change for luncheon."

They were almost at the library door when raised voices sounded from inside. Cassie and Deanna both stopped, looked at each other, and silently moved toward the door.

Mr. Randolph's voice rose above Mr. Woodruff's. "I don't understand this at all. Why hasn't this been completed?"

"Oh, it's just silly business," Cassie said, and started to pull Deanna away.

Deanna shook her off. Her father never really lost his temper, not at home anyway. *Is this why he's been so preoccupied lately? Something to do with business?*

Mr. Woodruff's answer was so quiet that she couldn't make out his words.

Cassie put her hands on her hips and waited none too patiently. "Let's go," she whispered.

Deanna put her fingers to her lips and moved closer to the door.

"What have you done?" her father demanded.

"Nothing, George. He just needs reassurances."

"A fifty-thousand-dollar retainer isn't enough good-faith money?" her father asked incredulously.

"He's had a better offer."

"What? Havemeyer, I presume. I thought we had a contract."

"We do, and he's willing to stick to our deal, but he wants to protect himself. To know that the money is there and we won't succumb to the Sugar Trust before he can sell to us. I'll take care of it."

"Just make sure you do. And, Francis, if this falls through, you'll answer to me."

They must be talking about the deal they had to buy Lord David's sugar. Deanna moved closer. Is that what had been worrying her father? Was their livelihood in danger?

"Perhaps I'd better talk to him before I go," Mr. Randolph said. "Havemeyer is a scoundrel and determined to control all the sugar refining in America. He's already taken over the refineries in Philadelphia. R and W is one of the last holdouts. If we fall, he'll own it all and you know what happens then. Prices will rise and he'll get richer on the backs of the consumers."

"What do you think we can do when the government couldn't stop him?" Mr. Woodruff answered weakly. Deanna thought he sounded tired.

"Is that it? You're throwing in the towel? By God, I'll run this company by myself if need be."

"George, relax. Things aren't so dire. I'm sure we can convince Lord David to honor our agreement."

"He'd better. Where is he? I'll invite him to New York and show him around myself."

"He and Charles have gone out. Let me handle it. You're needed in Manhattan to keep an eye on R and W business. Not play tour guide."

"I thought this was a done deal. If he's reneging, we'll have to look elsewhere and quickly."

"No, no, he isn't. I just—just—" Mr. Woodruff's voice broke off.

"If you're not up to taking him to see the factories, at least have Joseph show him through his warehouse. He'll be impressed by the efficiency of these new machines."

"I think—"

"Francis. We're depending on this deal. At your insistence, I might add. Just do what you promised to do."

Deanna stepped back. Her father sounded so angry. *What had Mr. Woodruff not done?*

The door flew open. Her father came out and stopped midstride. "Deanna?" He made a visible effort to calm himself.

"I just wanted to say good-bye."

"Well, yes, my dear. I was just going. Your mother or I will try to get back for next weekend. Have a pleasant stay." He kissed her forehead, nodded at Cassie, and strode off down the hall.

Deanna could see Mr. Woodruff sitting slumped over in a leather club chair, his face in his hands. She pulled Cassie away, afraid that she, too, had seen her father's despair.

"Deanna," her father called from the front door.

"Yes, Papa?" She walked to where he was waiting.

He pulled her aside, away from Neville who stood by the door. "Remember, if anything upsets you or if you decide you'd rather not stay here, go to Gwen Ballard. I know you and Joe have had some difficulties, but you can trust him to take care of you."

"I understand, Papa, but I'll be happy staying here." And she didn't need Joe to take care of her. She could take care of herself.

"Just remember what I say." He kissed her again and went out the door Neville held open.

Perplexed, Deanna climbed the stairs.

"What did he want?" Cassie asked.

"Oh, just . . . final instructions. What do you think they were arguing about?" she asked Cassie.

Cassie rolled her eyes. "How should I know? They sounded upset, but isn't that what they do all week, rant and rail about business and go to the club afterward?"

Deanna couldn't imagine her father ranting and railing, though she'd just heard him angry. But maybe Cassie was right, and it was just normal business.

Elspeth was in the lavender room, where Deanna had spent several nights during her younger years. It was frilly and soft and had a balcony that looked out to the sea.

Her trunks were open, and Elspeth was carefully hanging her gowns in the huge lacquer wardrobe.

Cassie openly admired the new orange Paquin. "You change into something cooler and meet everyone downstairs for luncheon on the terrace."

She bounced out of the room, the argument between their fathers and Orrin's arrest forgotten. Deanna went over to the windows and looked out. It was sunny, a perfect day for a lawn party. Someone had placed the croquet wickets in the grass ready for a game. It was hard to believe that, farther out on the rocks below, Daisy had met her death.

Deanna was still unsettled about what her father had said. Why should she feel uncomfortable here? Did he think she'd be afraid of living in a house where a servant had been killed?

Elspeth began undoing the buttons of Deanna's morning dress. "I wonder, miss . . ."

"Yes, Elspeth?"

"I told the housekeeper I was to fetch Daisy's things and bring them home. She said they were still in her room, since they hadn't had time to clean it out what with all the guests and things. She said I might collect them this afternoon if you don't need me."

"You may. But you'll have to wait for me."

"To do what, miss?"

"Well, didn't you say we might find a clue among her things?"

"We?"

"Yes, Elspeth. You must wait until later this afternoon when all the maids will be busy. I'll slip away from the others and meet you here."

"You, miss?"

"Absolutely. Do you think I would let you search alone? I'm going with you."

Chapter
9

Joe turned away from the Randolph home. He was too late; the family was gone, and Dickerson informed him that Deanna was staying with Cassie Woodruff. Joe had thought he could depend on Mrs. Randolph, that her extreme propriety would never allow Deanna to stay behind, especially not with the Woodruffs. He'd been wrong.

He decided to walk to Seacrest. He probably should have borrowed one of the Ballard family carriages and arrived in style. But he'd only planned to make the one stop to assure himself that the entire Randolph family was gone and out of harm's way. Just as he reached Bellevue Avenue, a carriage traveling in the opposite direction stopped in the street. Joe recognized the Randolph's brougham.

George Randolph hailed Joe over.

"Are you in a hurry, my boy? There's something I want to discuss with you."

"Certainly, sir."

"Hop in and accompany me home."

Joe climbed in the carriage and the coachman drove on. They didn't speak until they were back at Randolph House and safely ensconced in George Randolph's library with glasses of whiskey.

Mr. Randolph invited him to sit in one of the two wingback chairs that faced the unlit fireplace.

"Did you want to discuss business, sir? I know my father has been concerned about the finances."

"Business . . . among other things."

Joe nodded and waited for the older man to enlighten him.

"Have you had commerce with your father lately?"

"Some. Actually, I received a telegram two days ago asking me to be his envoy to the Woodruffs' dinner before their ball. He thought I might take the measure of Lord David."

"And did you?"

Joe shrugged. "Typical of other men I've met who were sent off to the colonies to make good. He seems to have parlayed the family's business into a good position. But the man himself . . ."

He hesitated, careful to keep his emotions out of his analysis. He had to admit that he hadn't watched Lord David waltz with Deanna without feeling a modicum of jealousy.

"The man?" Mr. Randolph prodded.

"Well, it was dinner and I was careful not to overtly bring up business, but I did get a chance to talk to him over port. He didn't seem very interested in discussing sugar."

Randolph chuckled. "One of these effete Englishmen who sit back and let their foreman keep the land productive?"

"I wouldn't be surprised. But I think something else worries you, sir."

"Yes, actually. Your father and I have been concerned for

a while about Francis's participation. Can I be assured that this will go no further than here?"

Joe nodded.

"The negotiations with Lord David seem to have stalled. The last telegram we received from him, he'd agreed to our terms. We sent Francis down to seal the deal. Now Francis is being cagey about exactly what he promised Lord David and how much Lord David has agreed to."

"So he hasn't signed the contract with R and W."

"It appears he's asking for more money up front."

"Appears, sir?"

"Since I haven't so far had access to him; whenever I tried, he wasn't at home. I don't know how well you are acquainted with Woodruff."

"Only through my father."

"Let's not tiptoe around this; I need to leave on the overnight ferry. And I probably won't be back for the weekend. There's work that cannot wait." He leaned forward, almost as if he were telling a secret. "Francis Woodruff is a spendthrift, a gambler, and a philanderer."

Joe nearly choked on his whiskey.

"Do I sound harsh? Well, so be it. He usually keeps himself in check, but recently I've been hearing about losses at the track. Extended parties on his yacht. Card games way beyond what he can afford. This is not the first time it has happened.

"Your father and I agreed that sending him down to Barbados might break the escalation and get him back on an even keel. We didn't want to do it, but we both needed to be here in order to keep one step ahead of the damn Sugar Trust.

"Now I'm afraid we may have made a mistake. As soon as

we get Lord David to our offices, we'll push for him to sign. But so far Woodruff has kept the man's social calendar filled to excess, and I can't stay any longer.

"I know that I can say for your father that we'd greatly appreciate it if you would keep an eye out for exactly what's happening here."

"I will," Joe said. "But what about Charles?"

"He's promised to bring Lord David to the city if his father doesn't rally in the next day or two. Though, if you ask me, Francis is just avoiding the situation. But you can't ask a son to spy on his own father."

"I see," Joe said. And he did. Mr. Randolph wanted *him* to spy.

"I knew you would, my boy. And there's one other thing. I wouldn't be surprised if Francis . . . makes use of the young female staff."

"You don't think he was involved with Daisy?"

"I don't want to. But Eleanor has had to dismiss servants before. I'm sure Deanna will be perfectly safe in that regard. He wouldn't dare stoop to molesting any young woman of his class. I don't like her staying there, but I also didn't want her at the mercy of her mother in Boston."

"Would you rather have Deanna stay with my grandmother?"

"Jeannette dislikes Eleanor Woodruff, but I think she's afraid that once your grandmother got entrée to Deanna, there would be no restraining her." He smiled ruefully.

"I believe you are right, sir. I'll try to keep an eye on that situation as well."

"I knew I could count on you. Can I drop you somewhere on my way to the terminal?"

"Actually, I was on my way to Seacrest when you stopped me. If you wouldn't mind dropping me at the gate."

—◦◦◦)◦(◦◦◦—

J oe took a moment to straighten his tie and adjust his hat, then he strode up the drive to Seacrest. It always felt to Joe as if he were walking into a marble wedding cake.

Of course even Seacrest had been eclipsed with the unveiling the week before of The Breakers, the Vanderbilts' massive new cottage. Grandmère had been invited to dinner, one of a select few who were granted the privilege of visiting before the ball that would officially open the mansion.

"Glorious excess," she'd said when asked about the interior. "It gave me the headache."

Well, Joe thought. If the The Breakers was glorious excess, Seacrest was merely excess, and not a very glorious one.

Neville opened the door and bowed with barely a trace of the condescension he saved for those who had fallen out of favor. And Joe had certainly fallen by moving to the lower-class Fifth Ward and by deciding to work for a living. He had to consciously not hide his fingernails from the supercilious butler. He could never remove the dredges of machine grease completely from his skin.

"How are you today, Neville?"

"Quite well, sir. Mr. Woodruff is not receiving visitors. He hasn't been well."

"I am sorry to hear that. Please give him my wishes for a speedy recovery. Actually, I came to see Lord David to extend an invitation to visit the warehouse this week."

"He and Mr. Charles are in the garden with the ladies."

Neville turned just as a voice from above them called out.

"Well, if that isn't Joseph Ballard!" Eleanor Woodruff stood on the landing above them waving her handkerchief like a passenger on an ocean liner.

Joe made a slight bow.

"The young people are out on the terrace. Neville, take Mr. Ballard back and get him something to drink. I'll leave you to it. Wouldn't do to be caught hovering like a nervous mama." She laughed and, with a final wave of her handkerchief, disappeared down the corridor.

"This way, sir."

Joe followed Neville through the house to the back terrace. He had to hand it to the Woodruffs. The house might be an architect's nightmare, but the view was spectacular—almost as spectacular as the view at Bonheur.

Charles, Lord David, Lady Madeline, and Herbert Stanhope were playing croquet on the lawn. Cassie was lounging in a chair with her feet on a footstool and glancing through the pages of a magazine while Vlady Howe serenaded her on an out-of-tune ukulele.

Deanna was sitting some yards away, in the shade of a tree, sketching in her drawing notebook. She was surrounded by bushes of blue hydrangeas and looked like a painting herself.

"Joe," Cassie said in a squeak. "We didn't expect you."

And probably wished him anywhere but here.

Deanna looked up at the sound of his name, scowled as only Deanna could scowl, and went back to her drawing.

A cry of victory went up from the croquet match, and the players came back to the terrace, where they immediately headed for the pitcher of lemonade that was set in a bowl of ice.

"Hello, Ballard," Lord David said. "Thought you would go back to New York City with the other men of industry."

"Actually I came to invite you and Charles to a tour of my

workshop. Since you've had to postpone the tour of our refinery, I thought you might be interested in viewing the modern
advancements of refinery machinery."

He glanced at Herbert, who was handing Lady Madeline
a glass of lemonade and seemed totally uninterested in what
Joe was saying. Herbert was a decent man as far as Joe knew,
but he was also a Havemeyer, if only by marrriage, and not
to be let in on any confidences.

Lord David smiled slowly. "But of course. Capital idea. I'm
beginning to feel quite the man of leisure."

"Shall we say tomorrow?"

"Tomorrow? What say you, Charles?"

"Sorry? I wasn't attending."

Too busy attending to Lady Madeline, Joe thought.

"Ballard has invited us to tour his factory."

"But of course."

Madeline Manchester, flushed with exercise and sheer good
looks, cried, "Oh, don't pull them away to work! We're having
a glorious time in your beautiful city."

Joe smiled, but he'd noticed Deanna close her sketchbook
and walk toward the water instead of coming to welcome him.
Well, what did he expect? She suspected him of murder. It
stood to reason that she would avoid him. He glanced around
the group; fortunately, it didn't appear that she'd shared her
suspicions with the others, at least not yet.

"Far be it for me to take away your pleasure," Joe said gal-
lantly. Deanna was almost to the cliff walk. *Damn. Where did
she think she was going?*

"I'm sure we'd all be pleased if you would join us for luncheon,"
Madeline cooed, dazzling him with a pair of glittering blue eyes.

Ordinarily, he would have been flattered, but today he had

only one thing in mind: talking to Deanna. And what he had to say certainly couldn't be said over luncheon meats with guests and servants listening. He turned to Cassie. "I went round to the Randolphs' earlier. Dickerson said the family had already left."

Cassie rolled her eyes. "Mrs. R. is taking Adelaide to Boston to see yet another doctor. But we convinced her to let Deanna stay with us. In fact"—Cassie looked around—"where is she?"

"Down by the water," Vlady said, and yawned. "Looking for clues," he said in a theatrically spooky voice.

"Oh, Vlady. She is not." Cassie pouted at him and shivered, which made Vlady put his arm around her.

"Well, do tell her hello for me," Joe said primly. He couldn't very well go running down the lawn in order to have a private conversation with her. He didn't want tongues to start wagging again. He'd have to bide his time. "And that I asked about her family. Until tomorrow, Lord David. Charles."

"Excellent. See you then." Lord David turned away from him and watched Deanna move behind the shrubs and out of view. "Do you think she should be out there by herself?" he said. "In view of the tragedy at the ball?"

Joe *knew* she shouldn't be out there alone.

"I'll just go get her before she wanders afar and misses luncheon." Lord David started across the lawn and down the path that led through the topiary hedges to the cliff walk.

Joe could only grit his teeth and take his leave.

⸺◦◦◦✦◦◦◦⸺

D eanna stopped to look out to the ocean. She wanted to turn back toward the house to see if Joe was gone but was afraid that he'd still be there and would know that she'd looked for him.

"You have a wicked turn of mind, my girl."

Deanna nearly jumped out of her skin at the sound of Lord David's voice.

"You startled me."

"I can see that I did. What are you doing, looking down on the scene of tragedy?"

"Was I?" Deanna said innocently. Of course she was. She'd wanted to see the place in the daylight, but she hadn't figured out how to leisurely make her way there until Joe had fortuitously appeared and distracted everyone. Besides, Cassie knew Deanna wanted to avoid him, and would explain as much to the others. So she was not a little annoyed that Lord David had interrupted her before she had memorized the scene.

But she had seen enough to be certain that, if Daisy had slipped, she wouldn't have fallen all the way to the boulder where she'd been discovered. She would have to have taken a flying leap or been pushed. An extremely strong push. It was just as she'd told Will. It looked like someone had thrown her over.

"If you've satisfied your curiosity, Cassie sent me to tell you that luncheon is being served." He smiled as if they had a secret. "Cassie has dismissed your—am I wrong to say?—your undesired swain."

Deanna laughed. "Really, Lord David. I don't know what you mean."

"Of course you do, my cunning young lady. I hope you're not flirting with me just to make him jealous."

"I don't flirt," Deanna said before she could stop herself. The idea that she was flirting with him brought the color to her cheeks.

"Of course not. Come, let us dine on cold lobster and

salad." He offered his arm and Deanna took it. She enjoyed their walk back to the house. She was just sorry that Joe wasn't there to see it.

They stopped by her chair to retrieve her drawing book. Lord David playfully tugged the book from her hands. She grabbed for it.

"Now, now. Let's see what you've been drawing while we were at play."

"Really, Lord David, you don't want—" No longer feeling playful, she made a grab for the notebook. He turned the page.

"Very nice." He cut her an expressive smile. "It seems I need a haircut." He turned the page for her to see. She'd captured several sketches of him, and Maddie, too.

"That's quite enough. Please give that back to me."

"Just a few more." He turned the page.

Deanna stilled.

"Well, what have we here? Is this what the poor girl looked like down on the rocks? You'll remember I wasn't on the scene until after our intrepid Vlad discovered the body."

"I—"

"You are a strange creature." He smiled his most charming smile. "And I mean that in the best possible way." He handed the notebook back to her. "Our little secret."

Deanna hugged her notebook under her arm. Why hadn't she gotten to it first? If she hadn't been so preoccupied with what Joe would think, she wouldn't have let that happen. What would Lord David think of her sketching pictures that belonged in the *Police Gazette*? Her mother would be furious.

They started back to the house. "You should give Maddie some pointers on drawing. I'm afraid she can't manage the difference between a horse and a dog. Proportion is the problem."

"Are you disparaging my artistic ability?" Maddie said from where she was "artistically" draped on a chaise lounge.

"Deplorable, sis dear."

Maddie sighed. "Alas, he's right. My needlepoint and embroidery are even worse. And please, please, for your own sake, never ask me to play the harp."

Deanna smiled. She wished she could be that carefree about the accomplishments young ladies were expected to have. Madeline Manchester might not be accomplished in the arts, but at least she got to travel and see the world. Someone like Lady Madeline wouldn't have to get her adventures out of books.

As soon as luncheon was over, Charles and Lord David left for the Reading Room, a place where, everyone knew, men drank, smoked cigars, and napped, but did very little reading. Vlad and Herbert took their leave soon afterward. Maddie and Cassie went upstairs to dress for their obligatory afternoon carriage ride. Deanna excused herself to write letters.

"Oh, come on, Dee," Cassie said. "Your mother isn't even here."

"I know, but with all the parties and events, I'm behind in my correspondence."

Cassie sighed loudly. "Her mother is a gorgon. Even when she isn't here."

For once Deanna was happy to use her mother as an excuse. "And she expressly told me not to neglect my duties." She smiled slyly, something she was proud of perfecting. "I'll get them all done while you're out and then I'll be free to play."

Cassie would have argued but Madeline pulled her away. "Let her get her duties out of the way. We have so many things planned for the week." The two young women went off arm in arm toward their rooms, and Deanna felt a momentary pang of conscience. She had no intention of spending the afternoon writing letters. She had another obligation to fulfill.

Well, maybe not an obligation. To be absolutely truthful, she *wanted* to search Daisy's room.

Elspeth turned from the window when Deanna entered her bedroom.

"Heavens, have you been standing there since I left?"

"I thought you'd never come, miss. I was about to go without you."

"Don't even think of acting without me. It might be dangerous."

Elspeth's eyes widened.

"Oh, I don't mean something physically harmful, just that you might get caught."

"I have permission to gather Daisy's possessions."

"But not to snoop around looking for evidence. Which I know you'll do."

"I have to do something."

"And we will. But carefully."

"And what happens if *you* get caught in the servants' quarters?"

"I'll say I had to come looking for my awful, disobedient maid who will answer none of my calls."

Elspeth grinned and started across the room, where she opened the door a crack and peered out into the hallway.

"It's empty. Hurry." Elspeth brushed through the opening of the door; Deanna pulled her skirts together and followed her.

Elspeth was already speeding silently down the corridor toward the back of the house and the servants' staircase. Without looking back to make sure Deanna was following, she opened the door and disappeared. Deanna followed right behind.

The staircase was narrow and poorly lit. If they met anyone, they would have to pass practically nose to nose. And how *would* Deanna explain being here? She crossed her fingers and followed close on Elspeth's heels.

Two flights later, when Deanna was beginning to feel out of breath, Elspeth stopped, again put her finger to her lips, and cracked the door to look out. She motioned for Deanna to follow.

They stepped out into another hallway, perpendicular to the main hallway below. The floors were wooden and there were doors leading off to each side. There was a single window at the end, and Elspeth hurried toward it. When she was two doors from the end, she stopped, turned the knob on one, and stuck her head inside, then followed it in. Deanna crowded in behind her.

They were in a tiny gabled space, smaller than Deanna's dressing room. Two painted iron beds stood against opposite walls. A washstand flanked by two small chests of drawers stood between. One side of the room was completely unoccupied, but on the other a summer coat hung on a hook and a photograph of a family was tacked above the bed.

"Is this where you're staying?" Deanna asked.

"No, miss. I'm a floor below in the nicer rooms, since I'm a lady's maid." Elspeth sniffed. "Daisy got extra duties and they didn't even give her a better room. It wasn't fair."

Deanna placed her hand on Elspeth's shoulder. "Courage," she said quietly. They would both need it.

Elspeth nodded. "The girl who shared the room with her was afraid to stay here by herself and moved in with two of the other maids, so we won't be interrupted."

She opened the first drawer. They both leaned over and peered at the contents.

It became obvious right away that they should have brought

a valise in which to carry things away, but when Deanna mentioned this to Elspeth, the maid merely lifted the coat from the hook, spread it across the bed, and piled Daisy's few belongings on top.

It was a sad testament to a life spent in hard work and a future cut off by some villainous creature.

Elspeth cleaned out the top two drawers and piled them on the coat. Chemises, cotton stockings, a faded skirt with tiny blue flowers. A change of undergarments made of coarse muslin that made Deanna's skin itch at the thought of wearing them.

And she felt a surge of guilt for being so spoiled.

Elspeth knelt down to open the bottom drawer. It was harder to open and scraped as she pulled it out. A pair of shoes and a small painted box were the only things it contained. Elspeth carried the box to the bed and sat down, then looked up at Deanna.

"Open it," Deanna said. Inside was a corsage dried between a folded piece of waxed paper, a seashell broken on one side, a roll of paper, a nub of a pencil, and two envelopes.

Deanna sat down beside Elspeth and waited while Elspeth unrolled the paper. The first page contained two rows of letters, one in a decent print, the second less perfected.

Elspeth bit back a sob. "She was practicing her alphabet. Orrin told her it was important to read and write." She shoved the rest at Deanna and groped for her handkerchief.

Deanna looked through the rest of the paper but it was all blank. She looked inside the envelopes. Empty. Had the envelope Vlady had found in Daisy's hand come from here? What had been in it if she could hardly read or write?

Elspeth closed the drawer, and Deanna returned the few treasures to the box. "Maybe Orrin would like to have this."

Elspeth took the box and added it to the pile of clothes on the bed. Her tears dropped silently on the dead girl's paltry possessions.

Deanna sighed and looked around at the bare room. "Should we pack up the blanket and pillow?"

"No, miss. They belong to the house. But where are the books you said I could loan her so one of the other girls could help her read them? She liked the poor-working-girl stories best. Like Cinderella, she said."

Those stories were Deanna's least favorite; the ones where the hardworking girl overcame a villainous master to find true love and riches. But maybe they had meant the world to Daisy. Elspeth, too.

"She always returned them. Kept them real neat, she did."

"Maybe she loaned them to one of the other maids."

"She would never." Elspeth looked around the empty room. She and Deanna both looked at the pillow at the same time. Deanna often stuck things under her pillow at home when her mother or Adelaide knocked at the door. She lifted it off the bed. "Nothing." She replaced it on the mattress.

Elspeth dropped to her knees and looked under the bed. Sat back on her heels and shook her head.

"The mattress," Deanna said.

She knelt next to Elspeth and together they lifted the thin pallet mattress. Sitting on the frame was a flat paper parcel. Deanna lifted it out while Elspeth held the mattress up. Then they both sat back down on the bed.

Deanna slid the cheap paper books out of the paper. On top was *The Pointing Finger*. Deanna remembered it from several months ago. The second novel's cover was missing.

"Oh, dear," Elspeth said.

"No matter. The books are so cheap, it probably fell off."

"No, miss. She was ever so careful. She told me she'd pretend like she was one of the girls in those stories. It was like having a magic door to somewhere special. Feels that way to me, too."

And to me, thought Deanna.

"She took good care of them. Not even a tear or a dog-eared page when she returned them."

"Well, it makes no matter now." Deanna returned them to the bag and placed the bag on the top of the other belongings.

Elspeth handed them back to Deanna. "No, miss. She wouldn't want to keep something that weren't hers."

Deanna reluctantly took the package and watched while Elspeth neatly tied up the bundle. "What are we going to do with it until we can return it to Daisy's mother?"

"We can leave it in my room. It's right downstairs."

"Will it be safe there?"

Elspeth gave her a sad smile. "Who would want it, miss?"

"I don't know, but I think we should keep it in my dressing room."

Elspeth nodded but insisted on carrying the bundle herself, and Deanna, grasping the package of books, followed uselessly behind. They stopped at the door and Elspeth peered down the stairs. "All clear."

They had just passed the entrance to the second floor when Elspeth sucked in a startled cry.

Deanna froze. Before them stood the largest, blackest man Deanna had ever seen. He was standing on the steps beneath them and yet he towered above them. A giant with massive muscles, a gold hoop hanging from one ear, and totally bald.

Deanna's mouth went dry. He was dressed in black livery, but in the dim light his stance, his eyes, and his demeanor all cried "savage."

Elspeth stepped back into Deanna, and Deanna fell against the wall.

He tilted his head slowly, then bowed slightly. "Ladies." His voice, deep and hollow, rumbled as if drawn from a cavernous pit and sent chills up Deanna's arms.

Elspeth let out a whimper and ran.

Chapter
10

Deanna wanted to run, was tempted to scramble screaming after Elspeth. But she wouldn't let her dignity slip. This must be the manservant Swan she had heard about. And he was everything she'd been told and more.

Praying that he wouldn't crush her with one blow, or put a curse on her, she took her skirt in hand and gracefully—as gracefully as one could manage with knocking knees—went down the stairs, followed by reverberating quiet laughter.

Elspeth had waited for her, but as soon as Deanna reached the second floor, she yanked Deanna into the hallway and slammed the door. The hall was empty and quiet, but Deanna was sure she could still hear that abominable laughing. Both girls grabbed their skirts and ran until they were safely inside Deanna's room.

"Do you think he'll tell?" Elspeth asked.

Deanna shrugged. "I don't think so. You have every right

to be in the servants' area. And he hasn't seen me before. Maybe he'll think I was just another servant girl."

Elspeth wrinkled her brow.

"Well, it's possible."

"Do you think he'll put a curse on us?"

"Of course not. Though he does look just like the witch doctor from *Lord Winston and the Black Death of Voodoo*."

Elspeth moaned. "I told you."

"Not to worry. Lord David wouldn't keep him as a servant if he put curses on everybody."

This rationale seemed to assuage Elspeth's worst fears. But not Deanna's. She didn't think Swan could put curses on anybody, but he had a look about him that frightened her. She wasn't sure what it was. Maybe it was just because he was so different. Deanna shook herself.

He's just a servant, and I probably won't see him again.

Elspeth carried Daisy's bundle into the dressing room; when she didn't come right back, Deanna put the novels down and went to see what was keeping her.

Elspeth was sitting on a bench, the bundle in her lap. "This is all that's left of her. It's just like nothing happened," she cried. "Your life goes on with your parties and dinners and fine houses and carriages. Them out playing games on the lawn when Daisy died just a few steps away. They didn't even think about her, did they?"

"I don't know about the others," Deanna said. "But I did."

Elspeth sniffed and fumbled in her apron pocket for a handkerchief. "I didn't mean you."

But she did. Deanna knew that in most ways she was no different than the others out there, taking their entitled lives for granted, everything around them extravagant and expensive. No wonder Mark Twain had called this the Gilded Age . . . but only for a select few.

Elspeth's and Daisy's families and others like theirs struggled every day to make ends meet. Although she was sure Joe was as generous with Orrin as possible, Deanna had no idea what Elspeth was paid.

Deanna sighed. "If Will Hennessey doesn't get to the bottom of this soon, you and I will. Now put Daisy's belongings away and come out so we can think."

Deanna sat at the Sheraton writing desk and opened her sketchpad. It wouldn't hurt to write some things down. But she stopped at the picture of Daisy lying on the rocks. She had died only two days ago, and already Deanna was forgetting details. Was the drawing missing something? The envelope. Vlady had found it in Daisy's hand. He hadn't said which hand or if it were crumpled or sealed. Did it matter? She'd have to ask Vlad when she saw him next.

She heard Elspeth come back into the room, and she quickly turned to a blank page.

"Come sit by me," Deanna said. "Let's get our thoughts organized."

Elspeth sat and stared at the paper while Deanna wrote *Woodruff Ball*. She left out her speculation about the discovery of Daisy's body. She'd go back and put that in when Elspeth wasn't around.

"Do you know if Will questioned everyone in the servants' hall?"

Elspeth shrugged. "He just asked everyone's whereabouts and when was the last time anyone saw Daisy."

"Who was the last to see her?"

"It was me, I guess," Elspeth said. "But I didn't tell him

that. I didn't want to get Daisy in trouble for showing me the oriel window."

"But Daisy is past worrying about," Deanna told her gently.

"Still, I didn't want to put a mark against her."

Deanna wondered how many of the other servants were holding out on the police for similar reasons. And if no one spoke, how was Will to ever find the murderer?

"I think it's important to tell Will. If you were the last person to see her alive and if we can figure out that time—and what time Vlady found her—we'll have a better idea of when she died." Deanna tapped her pencil to her cheek. "And if you weren't the last to see her, we need to know who was."

"And what if the murderer turns out to be one of the rich folks? They'll never arrest him, and they'll keep Orrin in jail forever."

"No, they won't. Father says the new mayor is an Irishman, and I'm sure he won't put up with favoritism." She said this with more assurance than she actually felt. She wasn't sure the new mayor would even care.

"So you and Daisy were watching the dance . . ." she coaxed.

"Yes. And you looked so beautiful. And Daisy said it ought be Mr. Joseph down there dancing with you, but we didn't see him anywhere."

Was Joe gone by then?

"And then what happened?"

"Like I told you. Daisy looked over the edge and then suddenly got up and said she had to go."

"Why?"

"She didn't say, but she'd seemed fine, then all of a sudden she got upset. She sounded real urgent—but not like she was going to kill herself. At first I was afraid she'd been seen, she was leaning out so far."

Deanna nodded. *Or she had seen something.* "Can you remember what time it was when you went to watch?"

"Well, it was soon after we arrived, because Daisy said that would be our best chance. You know, before we'd be needed to redo hair and adjust dresses and things."

Deanna closed her eyes. They'd arrived at the ball around ten. They hadn't gone outside until after supper and more dancing, which would put the time at two o'clock or later.

She counted on her fingers. "Four hours. Approximately."

"What is?"

"The time between when you last saw Daisy and when we . . . found her. Except . . ."

"What, miss?"

"It doesn't help much, but Lady Madeline tore her hem and was looking for Daisy right after supper."

"So?"

"She couldn't find her. You fixed her hem, remember?"

"Of course I remember," Elspeth said indignantly. "You think Daisy was already dead then?"

Deanna sighed. "I have no idea. But it gives us another piece to the conundrum. We need to find out if anyone else saw her during those times. Then we'll have a better idea of when she—when it happened."

"Oh."

"That way, if we can find out where everyone was during that time, we'll narrow down the possible killers."

"But what if it was a stranger who killed her, then ran away? It'll be hopeless."

Deanna shut her sketchbook. "Then we can just sit here and wring our hands and do nothing."

"No, no, I didn't mean that." Elspeth reached over and opened the sketchbook. "Ask me something else."

Deanna picked up her pencil. She wasn't quite sure what to ask, but she thought it would help lift Elspeth's spirits to think they were doing something to help. "Would Daisy have been enlisted to work in the kitchen for such a large affair?"

"No, miss. The Woodruffs hired out for extra waiters. She would've been upstairs straightening up the withdrawing rooms while everyone was at dinner, then readying the bedchambers for the night. I know Miss Cassie's maid was to go fetch her if Lady Madeline needed her. But I never saw her come down after the one time. Never saw her again at all." Elspeth sighed.

"Hmm." If Daisy had been needed for Lady Madeline in addition to following her usual routine, she should have been upstairs for most of the time in question. Except that she wasn't; she'd been on the cliff walk, about to die. Deanna shuddered. Why had Daisy gone there? Who had she been meeting?

Will Hennessey would never have access to the information he needed to make an informed inquiry. The cottagers put up with him, but they wouldn't help him. He was polished and educated, but he wasn't—and would never be—one of them. Not even their servants would cooperate.

Deanna and Elspeth could learn things he couldn't.

"Elspeth, do you think you could ask around—innocently, just conversationally—and find out who else saw Daisy? They might not want to talk to the police, but I bet with a little persuading they wouldn't mind gossiping with you."

"I suppose. You don't think it would dishonor Daisy's memory?"

"No, I think Daisy would want whoever killed her to be caught. And punished."

"Then I'll do it."

"I'll dress for dinner now, and then write some letters so I won't be found to be a total liar. And you can take a half day tomorrow to go visit Orrin and see if he needs anything. Find out if he has any ideas about why Daisy was out on the cliff walk."

Daisy went to prepare Deanna's evening clothes, and Deanna sat down to write her letter.

Dear Mama—

I hope that you and Adelaide arrived safely in Boston and that Adelaide was not too ill from the trip.

    Everything here is fine . . .

———∞>◎<∞———

Joe pulled the tie from his neck and tossed it over the back of a chair. He'd spent a trying day. Orrin was still in jail despite Joe's efforts to convince the chief of police to let him out on bail; they were both unwilling to rock the boat. They weren't even willing to let Joe see Orrin. He could only hope that his grandmother came through on her promise to talk with the mayor.

He'd had a nasty run-in with Officer Crum, who seemed to have appointed himself Joe's personal nemesis. The only reason it hadn't come to blows was that Crum had been restrained by several men on the force. Joe had no doubt he'd be back to settle the altercation.

And he hadn't managed to get Deanna out of town or even to speak to her.

He needed to keep a clear head, not to let his emotions cloud his judgment. There were underhanded dealings going on in R and W Sugar Refineries. He'd visited the plants three times over the winter. Production was steady, but there was an increase in minor breakdowns, accidents, and shipping problems that couldn't be explained away. Nothing big enough for outright accusations of sabotage, but definitely too significant to be coincidence. There were spies and saboteurs working at both plants.

There had been several attempted break-ins at his workshop as well. He'd had to hire some local men to keep an eye on it.

He knew who was behind it: H. O. Havemeyer.

The Sugar Trust had been ruthless with its other competitors. If they couldn't buy you out, they cheated you or burned your factory down. Though none of it had been proven so far; nothing had been done about it at all.

Havemeyer had powerful friends in Washington. His chief supporter was Nelson Aldrich, the senator from right here in Rhode Island, even though not a single sugar refinery existed here. That alone was enough to raise red flags. But no one had. At least not yet. Joe was determined to stop Havemeyer from overtaking R and W, but first he needed to find out who in R and W was selling them out. And how high up the conspiracy went.

Elspeth was sitting at Deanna's dressing table when Deanna returned to her room later that night. She jumped up and hid something behind her back.

"Oh, it's you, miss." She brought out the book she'd been reading.

"Are you reading ahead in the new Kate Goelet story?"

"No, this is the one Daisy borrowed. The one without the cover." She held it up. "It's about that man who killed his wife. You know, the Scottish doctor."

"The one who poisoned his wife's medicine, then played the grieving husband? That's an old one. I'd rather read about detectives."

Elspeth sighed and put the magazine away.

"So, did you find out anything?" Deanna asked.

"Some, but it's a little hard to gossip when the butler, the housekeeper, and the cook are all sitting there. After tea I managed to speak to two parlor maids Flora and Greta." She leaned forward and spoke more softly. "Flora said Mr. Woodruff likes the ladies, and the footmen told her that he takes actresses out on his yacht and parties for days sometimes."

"That's an awful thing to say."

"Even if it's true?"

Deanna didn't know what to answer.

"But the strangest thing . . . after Flora left, Greta told me that, the night of the ball, she'd looked out the window and seen Daisy sneaking out the delivery entrance."

Deanna sat up. "Did she say when?"

"It was before supper, but she wasn't sure exactly when. But the odd thing is, she said Daisy came back a few minutes later."

Was that when she'd seen Joe? Deanna wondered. She hadn't mentioned what she'd heard to anyone except Gran Gwen, and especially not to Elspeth. "Which means she must have gone out again later. But why?"

Elspeth shrugged. "Maybe she changed her mind, then changed it again?"

"Why?" Deanna began pacing. "Why do you come back to the house after you've left?"

"She decided not to go? Or she forgot something and came back for it?"

"What would she have forgotten? Where was she going?"

"Not to meet Orrin," Elspeth said.

"No, of course not. But we have to look at all possibilities to be thorough."

"Not Orrin."

Deanna sighed. "Okay, not Orrin." *And not Joe*, Deanna said to herself. But Daisy had gone out, then come back in and gone out again. What was so important that she'd tried to leave the house twice? Had she met Joe the first or the second time she left? Was that when Cokey had seen them? And did that mean Joe had no alibi for the time Daisy was killed?

"What, miss?"

"We have to find out why she went out that night and when." And unfortunately, Deanna knew just who to ask.

Chapter
11

By Friday it was apparent that Madeline and Lord David had passed muster with the Newport set.

Morning callers descended on the household, and the invitations poured in one after another until they filled the card tray. They may have forgotten Daisy, Deanna thought, but they were more than ready to gossip about the murder, and she was relieved when the door shut on the final visitor and the family was finally left alone.

They had just gone in to luncheon when Cassie came running into the breakfast room. "Just look what *Town Topics* wrote about our ball." Cassie thrust Colonel Mann's gossip newspaper at her mother.

Everyone turned their attention to Mrs. Woodruff.

"Friday night saw the introduction of Lord David Manchester and his sister, the lovely Lady Madeline . . ." She paused to smile at her guests and continued to read.

The ball had been a success. Colonel Mann praised the

newcomers, though he was less flattering to Mrs. Woodruff's décor and fashion, and cast all sorts of innuendos about the running of the Woodruff household and her inability to protect her staff.

Mrs. Woodruff was indignant. "That horrid old geezer," she exclaimed. "And he can put that in his paper." She cast the paper aside and appeared to forget all about Colonel Mann and his "dirty rag."

"But, Mama, what if everyone reads it?"

"Oh, pooh. Everyone will. I don't give a fig for what everybody thinks."

"What if Mrs. Vanderbilt, Mrs. Oehlrich, and Mrs. Fish get together and decide to snub us?"

"Let them. Mamie Fish is even less tasteful than I am, and as for Tessie Oehlrich, her papa made his money in the same silver mines as mine." She reached for a piece of toast. "Mr. Woodruff and I are very well placed, right in the middle of Mrs. Astor's precious four hundred. I'd like to see them try."

"Who are the four hundred?" Lord David asked. "It sounds like a cavalry regiment: 'On rode the four hundred.'"

Mrs. Woodruff flicked the air as if she were swatting at a gnat. "It's absurd. Her social secretary—odious man, may he rest in peace—he just died this year. The idea that only four hundred upper crust families are worthy of entering Mrs. Astor's Fifth Avenue house ballroom. Absurd. And I'm sure more than that will fit into Mrs. Alice Vanderbilt's new ballroom at The Breakers."

Lord David laughed. "Stop, stop. You confuse me. Astors and Vanderbilts and Fishes? You must remember, I spend my days in Barbados. And trust me, my dear lady, we don't come close to having four hundred society families, even if we had a ballroom that would fit them."

Mrs. Woodruff laughed heartily, then patted his hand. "We'll have to do something about that, now, won't we? Charles, what *are* your plans for Lord David's entertainment?"

Charles looked up from where he'd been practically forehead to forehead with Madeline. "Pardon me, Mama?"

"I said, do you and Lord David have plans for today?"

"We are supposed to take a tour of Joe Ballard's workshop, though there's a polo match that I don't want to miss." He turned to Lord David. "He's a brilliant man, his inventions are supposedly the wave of the future. But he starts talking and it's like Greek," Charles laughed. "But while I'm thinking about it, we'll have to go down to Manhattan, Mama. Sunday night for a couple of days . . . look over the business, that kind of thing."

Mr. Woodruff, who had hardly spoken at all, motioned for the wine decanter. "I'll come with you to New York."

"That isn't necessary, sir. I'm sure Mr. Randolph can deal with things to your satisfaction."

"Nonetheless, I'll accompany you."

"Now, dear, you must protect your health and not go traipsing around worrying about things that Charles and George Randolph can manage without you."

Madeline, who was sitting on his left, chimed in. "Oh, you can't be so cruel and leave us alone to while away the long days without you." She smiled at him, practically fluttered her eyelashes.

Deanna thought Mr. Woodruff would argue. But he merely smiled back at her, and said, "We wouldn't want to disappoint our guests," picked up the glass Neville had just filled, and took a long draught.

It seemed Lady Madeline had snared both Woodruff men

with her charms. Burning with indignation for Adelaide, Deanna stared at her plate. When she looked up, Lord David was watching her.

He smiled. "My sister is an incorrigible flirt."

"I am not," Madeline said, and smiled. "I just enjoy the company of handsome men." She looked from Charles to his father.

"So do I," Cassie said. "Am I a flirt, Lord David?"

"Absolutely, but none of you can hold a candle to the incomparable La Dame Woodruff." He lifted his glass to Mrs. Woodruff, who laughed heartily. Though to Deanna, it sounded just a little false.

When lunch was finished, Deanna asked to borrow a carriage, as she had forgotten some things in her hasty packing and needed to return home for them.

"Why don't you just send your maid?" Maddie asked.

Deanna sighed expressively. "She never remembers everything, poor creature," she explained with an air of hauteur for which she hoped Elspeth would forgive her.

She went upstairs and caught Elspeth just as she was leaving to visit Orrin.

"I've gotten the carriage. I told them I had to fetch some things from home."

"I could have stopped and gotten what you need on my way back from seeing Orrin," Elspeth said.

"I know, but this way is better. It gives us both an excuse to get out of the house."

"What are you up to, Miss Deanna?"

"I've decided that I'm coming with you."

Elspeth's jaw went slack. "You can't do that. The Fifth Ward is not a safe place for a lady."

Deanna was a little taken aback by that notion, but she stood firm. "We'll be in the carriage, and while you're visiting Orrin, I'll go around and visit Joe."

"You'd never."

"Yes, I would. There are a few things that I need to discuss with him. And I can't think of a better time."

———◦◦◦◦)◊(◦◦◦———

Joe was just returning from lunch at the tavern when a carriage pulled up in front of the warehouse. He was expecting Charles and Lord David; he was shocked to see Deanna Randolph instead.

"What are you doing here?" Joe quickly looked around. This would not do.

"I came to see you. Where have you been?" she asked, sounding annoyed as she took his hand and stepped down to the street. She was wearing a green morning dress with a braided jacket nipped-in at her waist. The color brought out the glow of her skin and the sheen of her dark hair. She looked so out of place on the dingy street, like a rare bird, slightly exotic—something he'd never noticed before—and something he had to admit he found compelling.

But this was no time for thoughts like that. "You'd better come in."

He stepped ahead of her and unlocked the door.

She brushed past him like an assured doyenne, but he didn't miss the flush of her cheeks. And he flushed also, remembering the conversation she had overheard at the Casino. Surely she wasn't here about that.

She'd stopped in the middle of the room, and Joe realized that his dirty dishes were stacked in the wash pan and his shaving kit was left on the counter with a crumpled towel next to it. The door to his bedroom had been left open and the bed was unmade. He crossed the room quickly and slammed it shut. He'd been in a hurry that morning. He hadn't expected company.

"This is where you live?" she asked.

Joe looked around at his living quarters, kitchen area, and the small bedroom off to the side. It had electricity, some running water, even a tub, if you didn't mind cold water. It was comfortable enough for him, but for the first time he saw it through someone else's eyes and realized how squalid it must look to Deanna.

"It used to be the manager's office. It's modest, but it's home." He'd shocked her. He could tell by her face. He took the defensive. "To what do I owe the pleasure? I'd ask you to sit down, but as you can see, there's not a comfortable seat in the place." Just two stools and one rickety straight-backed chair.

"Where are the machines you're working on?"

"In the back."

She gave him a look that he remembered well, and that reminded him of happier days, then she immediately walked off in the direction he'd indicated. He ran after her.

"You came to see the new condenser?" *Why the hell had she come?*

"Not really, but now that I'm here, I'd like to see what you're doing."

"I'm afraid it's rather dirty—and greasy—it's no place—"

"For a lady?" she finished for him. "Well, I hate being a lady." She grabbed her skirt in both hands and stomped through the door to the warehouse.

Joe followed. He didn't know whether to laugh or quake in his boots. He saw Grandmère's work here. If his grandmother wasn't careful, she'd derail Deanna's chances for a good marriage.

"Really, Deanna."

She spun around. "Did you kill that poor girl? Daisy?"

Joe staggered back.

"Did you?"

"No, of course I didn't."

She frowned at him, the scowl that had melted his heart the first time he'd seen her; it hadn't changed in all the years he'd known her.

She bit her lip, nodded slightly, then shook her head. "Cokey Featheringham . . ."

"I know. Grandmère told me. And if you're wondering, I didn't do that, either."

She blushed more hotly, shook her head.

"Is that why you came? To ask if I was a murderer? Don't you know me better than that?"

"I used to. Now you're not the same."

No, he wasn't. And neither was she, as much as she might not want to admit it.

"If you're satisfied that I'm not a murderer, can I put you back in the carriage?"

"I'm waiting for Elspeth. She went to visit Orrin."

"Look, I'm working on getting him out. Leave it to me. Go back home and wait. I'll send her word."

"Was it something I did?"

"What?" he asked, fumbling to switch gears to her train of thought. Deanna's lightning change of subject—a habit of hers that had always kept him on his toes—surprised him now.

"Why aren't we friends anymore? Was it that stupid marriage thing?"

"God, Dee. Do you want to marry me?"

"Well, no. I just want things to be like they were before."

"They—can't be." Because the same business that was supposed to bring them together until death them did part, was now just as likely to drive a wedge between them. Joe was afraid it was too late for them ever to be friends again.

She started to say something but changed her mind and stepped away from him. He watched her pick her way across the dirty floor, avoiding grease patches and metal shavings with a grace and assurance that belonged to a woman, not a girl. And yet she stopped in front of his latest work with the same curiosity she'd always had.

"What's this?"

"It packs refined sugar into bags."

"How?"

He walked over to it. "When I work the kinks out, the conveyor belt will drop a bag here, where the worker pulls on this lever and the sugar pours into the bag. Then the moving belt takes it to the next station, which I haven't yet constructed, where the bags will be folded and glued, then packed in larger containers for shipping."

"To stores?"

"Yes, you'll be able to buy it right off the shelves and pour it into a storage container at home."

"Hmm."

"It will be much more efficient and easier to use and store."

She turned, frowned at him. "Someone murdered Daisy. I want to help."

Again that unexpected change of subject. Joe realized it

was an efficient way of startling someone into saying more than he intended. But not Joe. "I'm working on Orrin's release. Be patient."

"I'm glad, but it doesn't solve the problem of who actually killed her. If the police don't find the killer, they'll go after Orrin again. It's what they always do."

"How do you know what they always do?"

"Don't be dense. The police are afraid to go after the cottagers, so they always come after people who live in the Fifth Ward because they are poor. Elspeth told me," she added in an afterthought.

"Well, there's nothing you nor I nor anyone else can do about that. We'll have to leave it to Will to find the real culprit."

"But how can he, if it turns out to be one of the Bellevue Avenue people?"

"He'll do the best he can."

"They won't cooperate."

Joe shrugged and tried to nudge her back into the front rooms. "Will Hennessy will do what he has to do."

She turned on him. "I'm staying at the Woodruffs'. I could ask questions. We've already found out more about Daisy's movements that night."

Joe skittered to a stop. "We?"

"Elspeth and I. We searched Daisy's room, and Elspeth asked the staff who had seen her. I can look for clues. Maybe it was someone at the party."

"You searched Daisy's room? Why?"

"Well, Elspeth let the housekeeper think she was supposed to clean out Daisy's possessions, so I went, too. Everyone said she died because she was meeting someone, and Elspeth swears Orrin would never have asked her to leave her duties to meet him on a cliff. I thought there might be clues in her room that the police missed."

"And did you find any?"

She shook her head.

"Dee, listen to me. Stop this now."

"Why?"

"Because it might be dangerous. You don't know whom you can trust. Please stay out of it."

"You and Bob always said that when you thought I couldn't keep up. But I always could."

That was true. And he *could* use a pair of eyes in the Woodruff household. . . . But it was too dangerous. He took her by the shoulders. "Dee, listen to me. There are things you don't understand."

"Then tell me." She fisted her hands on her skirt. Fierce, so like the young girl who used to follow them, got into scrapes just to be a part of the fun, attempted antics way beyond her size or ability. She knew no fear.

He smiled. "I see that coming out has done nothing to tame you."

"Tame me? Tame me? Is that what you want?"

"An unfortunate choice of words."

"Ugh. You're as bad as Mama. I don't want to be tamed or proper or any of those things. I want to be like Gran Gwen and travel, meet interesting people, and have affairs—" She stopped; heat suffused her face as Joe watched, tongue-tied. "Well, maybe not affairs, but you know what I mean. Let me help. I'll be careful. Just tell me what I can do."

"No."

"If you don't include me, I'll do it myself."

"Not if I telegraph your father and tell him to come get you."

"I won't go."

"Dee—" How could he tell her that what he was looking into might ruin the family of her best friend or, worse still, ruin her own? Maybe Daisy's death and his line of inquiry were unrelated, but that didn't make one less dangerous than the other.

On the other hand, Dee was fully capable of taking matters into her own hands.

It might be better to enlist her help rather than let her blunder around stirring up trouble that she wouldn't be prepared for.

His thoughts were stopped by a frantic knocking at the outer door. He went to open it.

Elspeth ran in and stopped in the middle of the room. "They wouldn't let me see him." She burst into tears.

Joe pulled out a straight-backed chair from under the scrubbed-wood table. Deanna sat Elspeth down, knelt down, and held her hands. "Tell us what happened."

"I went to the station and asked to see him. That nasty old Sergeant Crum said to go away and that Orrin wasn't allowed any visitors. I told them I was his sister and they didn't care. Nobody cares about us."

"Of course they do," Deanna soothed. "Joe and I do." She cast Joe a look.

"Of course we do," he said. "I've already been to the judge this morning to arrange bail, but he was out of town. I went to the chief of police, but he said I had to wait until the judge returned."

Elspeth looked up at him over her hands. "You'd do that for Orrin?"

"Of course. Grandmère is calling on the mayor today; hopefully, that will move things along. But, evidently, this envelope they found makes them think they have enough evidence against Orrin to hold him for trial."

"Why? What was in the envelope?" Deanna asked. "Will wouldn't tell me. Did he tell *you* what was in it?"

"In confidence."

Deanna waited. "We're not leaving until you tell us." She crossed her arms. Elspeth crossed hers.

Joe sighed. "Will said the envelope was empty, but Orrin's name was written on the outside."

Deanna frowned, pulled one of the stools close to Elspeth, and perched on it. After a few seconds, she said, "How could that implicate him? If she was sending him a letter, it meant she wasn't planning on seeing him. And if there was no letter in the envelope—"

"The police think the killer took it."

"But left the envelope clutched in her hand? Why not take the envelope, too?"

Joe pulled up the other stool for himself. "I asked the same thing. And they don't have much of an answer. They are saying that they may have struggled and she fell or was pushed over the cliff before he could get it."

"So why not climb down after it? It's an easy enough climb."

"Orrin didn't do it," Elspeth said.

Deanna was glad to see her maid's grief changing to anger.

"Besides, Elspeth says Daisy didn't read and write that well."

"She didn't write at all?" Joe asked.

Elspeth sniffed and pulled a handkerchief from her sleeve to wipe her nose. "Some, but she only came over from Ireland a few months ago, and she hadn't learnt to read or write much

over there. She couldn't have written a whole letter. Miss
Deanna saw her letters."

Deanna nodded and rested her elbow on the table. "She
would have had to ask someone else to write it for her. We just
have to find out who, and then we'll know why it was so
important for the killer to take it." She rested her chin on her
fist. "And why he conveniently left the envelope addressed to
Orrin behind."

Joe stood, took a couple of steps away.

"What?" Deanna asked. "Don't keep us in ignorance,
please."

He turned back to them. "I saw Daisy the night of the party."

"We already know that thanks to Cokey."

Joe gritted his teeth. "She was sneaking out to see Orrin as
I was leaving. She said she needed to talk to him about something. I made her go back inside. That's all I know or did."
He cast a look at Deanna, who met his eyes briefly but looked
away. He couldn't tell whether she believed him or not.

He turned his attention to Elspeth. "When did you last
see her?"

"It was when we were watching the dancing from the oriel
window. Miss Deanna was waltzing with Lord David. And it
was so beautiful. Then Daisy just up and rushed off."

Joe saw Elspeth's lip quiver, and he hurried on. "That must
have been right before I saw her. It was fairly early. I left right
after . . ." He hesitated.

"Right after you saw me," Deanna supplied.

Ignoring that minefield, Joe said, "A little later. And I sent
her back inside. You didn't see her again?"

Elspeth shook her head.

"Did she tell you what she had to do?"

"No," Elspeth said. "Just that she had something she had to do. She would have told me if she was planning on sneaking out of the house to meet Orrin."

"She may have just lost track of time," Joe said.

Elspeth gave him a look. "That's not the kind of thing that would have slipped her mind while she was watching the dancing. It was like she had forgotten to do something, like one of her chores. Like making up the fire in Mr. Woodruff's room or turning down Lady Madeline's bed. But when I went after her, I couldn't find her. It was like she'd just disappeared. Just like—"

"What?" Deanna and Joe asked together.

"Nothing really, only that while we were watching the dancing, I felt like someone was watching us. I turned around and a shadow moved away."

"Probably one of the musicians," Joe said. "Isn't that where they play?"

Elspeth nodded. "She must have left the house. That's why I couldn't find her."

"Okay, so we know that she left after she was watching the dancing, then went back inside. Then what?" Joe knew he shouldn't encourage them, but he had problems to solve, and frankly he could use some input.

"Then she went out again," Deanna said. "But if you saw her on the street the first time, why did she end up on the cliff walk the second time?"

"Maybe she was afraid someone would see her on the street, like I did. Maybe when I sent her back inside, she went straight through the yard to the walk and planned to take the long way around, but someone stopped her."

"No. She came right back inside the house."

"How do you know?"

Elspeth looked exasperated. "I asked."

"So she went out again later?"

"Must have. But I don't know when."

The three of them grew silent.

"We'll have to find out," Deanna said.

"Listen to me, Dee. Speculation is one thing; putting yourself in a possibly dangerous situation is not acceptable. Let Will figure it out," Joe said. "He's trained and he knows his job."

"And he'll do absolutely nothing," Deanna said.

"You're not being fair. He's doing his best."

"Perhaps," Deanna said, sounding haughty. "But neither master nor servant will tell him the whole truth. But they will tell us." She stood. "Come, Elspeth. We must be going."

She headed for the door. Joe barely reached it in time to open it for her.

"Remember, what I told you about the envelope was told in confidence," he said. "The less people know about the investigation, the more likely they'll be able to find the real culprit."

Deanna gave him an impish look. "Our lips are sealed."

She swept past him, Elspeth following in her wake.

Joe opened the carriage door and helped them inside. Then he leaned in after them. "I mean it, Dee. Keep your eyes and ears open if you must, but do not get into any trouble."

"We won't."

"And talk to no one about this but me or Will." He shut the door and the carriage moved away. He watched them go—two women, one intelligent and energetic, one fiercely loyal to her brother and her mistress, and both staying at Seacrest.

It was infamous of him to even think of asking for their help. But it was obvious that he couldn't stop them. He would just have to figure out a way to keep them from getting hurt.

Chapter
12

"All right," Dee said as the carriage rattled along Thames Street. "A quick stop at Randolph House, and we'll be back at Cassie's in time for tea." It was then that Deanna realized the coachman might be inclined to tell his mistress where he had driven them earlier. Unfortunately, she wasn't carrying enough money for an adequate bribe. Perhaps she could ask Cook for a loan from the larder money.

The coach drew up at the door of Randolph House; Elspeth climbed down, then waited for Deanna.

"We'll just be a minute."

The coachman touched his hat brim. "Yes, miss."

They went up the front stairs and rang the bell.

The butler answered. "Miss Deanna," he said, opening the door for her to come in.

"I just need to pick up a few things I forgot, Dickerson. We won't be but a moment."

"Very good, miss."

Deanna and Elspeth went upstairs. While Elspeth packed up a beach dress for the trip to Bailey's, Deanna emptied a lacquer box Bob had once given her for her pin money. It only took a second to pour the few coins and bills into her reticule, and she spent the rest of the time waiting for Elspeth, looking out the window, and thinking.

There must be someone who knew more about Daisy's movements the night of the ball. The house had been crammed full of people, not only guests but servants and visiting maids and valets.

She just had to figure out a way to get them to talk.

Dickerson stopped them as they were leaving. "Miss Deanna, a telegram came for your father yesterday evening after he'd left for Manhattan. Shall I keep it until his return?"

Deanna looked at the yellow rectangle of paper. "I'll take it, Dickerson. Mr. Woodruff will know what's best to do."

Deanna and Elspeth returned to Seacrest. Elspeth immediately took her things upstiars; Deanna stayed behind and had just emptied most of her purse into the coachman's palm to pay for his silence when Cassie opened the front door.

"Where have you been? You missed lunch and Mama was beginning to worry."

"I'm sorry. I'll go apologize to your mama."

"Fine, but later. The carriage is already here. We're going to take the air, and today you're coming with us."

"I'm not dressed."

"You look fine. Neville, please tell mama that Miss Deanna has returned and we're all going out." Cassie took her arm and propelled her across the drive to where Lady Madeline sat in the open carriage looking a little like Cinderella in a white-and-peach voile frock.

Deanna felt dusty and rumpled in comparison, and she was

sure her hem was loaded with dirt and machine oil. She patted at her hair and climbed into the carriage.

For the next hour they drove up and down Bellevue Avenue nodding and smiling at all the other coaches whose passengers were also enjoying their afternoon promenade and gossiping about the passengers.

"Was Elspeth able to see her brother today?" Cassie asked. "Elspeth is Deanna's lady's maid," she explained to Maddie. "Her family has worked for the Randolphs forever and she has, too. So we're all kind of like friends." Cassie puckered her lips. "I know you're supposed to keep your distance from servants, but I don't see why, do you?"

Deanna didn't think so, either, but it was too seditious an idea to agree with out loud.

"But if you don't," Maddie said, with an air of worldliness, "they get confused about their status and their duties. It's best to be the master and let them be the servants."

"I suppose." Cassie's attention flicked to a passing carriage. The three of them automatically nodded as the liveried carriage rolled by in the opposite direction. "There's Mrs. Goelet."

Deanna smiled.

"What's so funny?" Cassie asked.

"Just that one of the stories I read is about a lady detective whose last name is also Goelet. But she's nothing like the one who just passed by."

"Oh, one of your dime novels," Cassie said. "*Our* Goelets own Ochre Court. He's loaded, and she's one of the marrying Wilsons."

"The marrying Wilsons? Who are they?" Maddie asked.

"Three sisters whose mama was 'dead on the money,' as my papa said. Made fabulous matches for all her daughters, each husband richer than the one before."

"You certainly have colorful neighbors," Maddie said. "And they're all millionaires?"

"Multimillionaires."

"How about you, Deanna? Is your papa a millionaire?"

"I suppose so. I'm sure the business is worth several million."

"The R and W that David is in partnership with?"

Deanna nodded. She didn't know much about the business. Papa had taught Bob the fundamentals before he died, but Papa hadn't passed any knowledge to his daughters. Which was usually the case with fathers, Deanna thought.

She became restless about halfway down the avenue. She tried pretending she was Adelaide, who could sit perfectly still even though she didn't enjoy even the slowest carriage ride, since her head would begin pounding before they had gone half a mile. Perhaps that's *why* she was always so still, because moving hurt her head. Deanna felt a pang of conscience. She'd always made fun of Adelaide, but maybe her sister had adopted that air of languor as a way to stave off illness. Deanna suddenly felt ashamed and vowed never to make fun of Adelaide again.

"You're awfully quiet today, Dee. You're not homesick?" Cassie said.

"Heavens no. I was just thinking."

Cassie rolled her eyes. "Dee's always thinking. I never knew anybody to think so much."

Maddie laughed. "Don't you think women should think, Cassie?"

"Oh, I suppose so. When there's nothing else to do. Though, gee, there's always something to do. I hope tea's ready; I'm starving."

And Deanna just hoped the ride would soon be over. But

as luck would have it, they were stuck driving behind Mrs. Leggit, who stopped often to converse with the passengers of other carriages.

"I need my tea," Cassie complained when they finally stopped at Seacrest. "I hope no one has come to visit. I'm too hungry to change."

Fortunately, Mrs. Woodruff was alone, and she bustled them all into the lady's parlor, where a tea tray had been laid with a variety of delicacies.

"How is Mr. Woodruff feeling today?" Deanna asked Mrs. Woodruff as her hostess handed her a cup of tea.

"Oh, much better. He and Charles and Lord David said that they were going down to Joseph Ballard's to see his inventions."

Deanna nearly bobbled her teacup. She thought they had decided on the polo match. Thank goodness she and Elspeth hadn't run into the men at the warehouse. How could she ever have explained what she was doing there?

"But they went to see the match instead. I thought they might be back for tea, but you know how men get over sports."

Deanna relaxed a bit, but she'd have to be more careful in the future. The future? What was she thinking? She couldn't keep traipsing about like a . . . free person.

It had been exhilarating to be out on her own, to simply decide to drive down to the Fifth Ward and then do it without asking anyone's permission, knowing that she would never have been allowed to go if her mama or even her papa were here. And what Mrs. Woodruff didn't know . . .

She knew it wouldn't last, but until her mother's return, Deanna planned to take advantage of her absence.

After tea, the ladies went to their rooms to rest before dinner. Deanna was curled up in the bay window, reading the further adventures of Kate Goelet when she heard Elspeth go into the dressing room. A minute later she came to the door of the bedroom and cleared her throat.

"Can you come here for a minute, miss?"

Deanna frowned, but she closed her book and went to see what Elspeth wanted.

As soon as she stepped into the small square room, she understood why Elspeth had called her. A young maid with red hair and freckles so thick across her nose that each one ran into another, stood timidly by the door.

"This is Claire. Tell Miss Deanna what you told me."

The girl ducked her head and kneaded her apron.

"Go on," Elspeth prodded. "You won't get in trouble, I promise."

Claire flicked an anxious look at Deanna, then lowered her eyes.

Elspeth gave her a little nudge.

"When Daisy came back . . ."

Deanna leaned forward to hear her better.

"The other night—the night she died? She come to me and asked me to write something for her. She just come over from Ireland and can't read or write much. I can. I was born here and I study in my spare time. I was helping her."

Deanna couldn't imagine that she had very much spare time.

Claire seemed to have stalled.

"And did you write something for her?" Deanna coaxed as gently as her excitement would allow.

Claire straightened her apron, shook her head. "We didn't have paper. Then that awful valet to Lord David appeared in the doorway, just like the devil himself, and Daisy ran off. I thought she was getting paper, but she never came back." Claire gulped. "I didn't ever see her again."

"Did she say what she wanted you to write for her?"

"No, miss. Can I go now?"

"In a minute, if you please." Deanna cast a quick apologetic look at Elspeth. "Did Daisy ever talk about Orrin?"

Claire nodded. "They were going to be married. She wanted to get out of service, try to get a place at a milliner's in town. Now she—she won't never make any hats." Claire broke down into silent sobs just as a faint knock sounded at the door.

Deanna put her finger to her lips and hurried back into the bedroom, closing the dressing room door behind her. "Enter."

The door opened and Cassie came in. "You haven't even changed yet. What have you been doing all this time?"

Deanna sighed. "I don't know. Thinking, I guess."

"I hope what you mean is daydreaming about Lord David. Maddie says he thinks you're charming."

"I think he's lovely, too."

"Too bad they're not going to be here for dinner tonight. They've been invited to the Stanhopes," Cassie said in exasperated tones. "But Mama is having a few people over for drinks before they go, so wear something ravishing."

"The Stanhopes? With your mother and father?"

"Heavens, no. Mama and Mrs. Stanhope don't get along." Another knock.

"That must be Maddie. I told her to meet us here, since you're always running behind time."

"Am I?"

"Yes, what are you wearing tonight?" Cassie asked as she went to open the door.

Maddie came in wearing the most wonderful gown Deanna thought she'd ever seen. It had to be from Paris: gold *peau de soie* with diagonal brocade stripes and an overblouse of darker spangled chiffon. The pattern was repeated on the puffed sleeves that floated about Madeline's head like clouds of spun sugar.

It made Cassie's ruching and ruffles appear young and frivolous, though Deanna supposed they suited her.

"Oh, you're not ready yet," Maddie said.

"No. I—my maid—"

"I just saw her hurrying down the hallway with another maid," Madeline said. "I hope she's not up to things she shouldn't be. Surely, we've had enough of that kind of thing."

Deanna's mind went blank. Elspeth must have spirited Claire away as soon as Cassie came in. Neither of them had expected Maddie to follow. "I'm sure she isn't. She was probably on her way down to get my dress. I"—Deanna searched desperately for a believable lie—"spilled some cologne on it. It's probably ruined, but Mrs. Oates—"

"The housekeeper," Cassie interjected for Maddie's benefit.

"—said she thought she had a remedy that might work. Elspeth is probably getting it now." Fingers crossed that no one mentioned the nonexistent spill to Mrs. Oates.

Deanna heard Elspeth return to the dressing room and willed her to stay there. Elspeth stepped into the room.

"Ah," Deanna said. "Was Mrs. Oates able to get the stain out of my frock, Elspeth?" She sent Elspeth mind bending thoughts.

Elspeth didn't say anything for the longest moment, and Deanna's heart threatened to thump out of her chest.

"Not yet, miss," Elspeth said, eyeing Madeline's toilette. "I think the rose tulle for this evening instead?"

Deanna had to concentrate not to slump in relief. "Very well," she said with an air of languor she didn't feel.

Madeline pulled Cassie up from the chair. "I think we should go and let Deanna dress in peace."

"Oh, all right. But hurry, Dee." Cassie stopped at the mirror to adjust her waist and pull her neckline down, then shimmied her shoulders and flounced out of the room. Maddie looked at the ceiling and, laughing, followed after her.

"Someone oughta take that girl in hand," Elspeth said. "Now, sit and let me dress your hair."

Deanna sat and Elspeth began pulling pins from her hair. "Why did you lie to Cassie about why Claire was here?"

"Well," Deanna said, "firstly, I didn't want to get Claire in trouble, and secondly—"

Elspeth tugged a knot out of Deanna's hair. Deanna grabbed her wrist and pulled her down so she could whisper in her ear. "I think we should take Joe's warning seriously and not tell anyone about anything we find out. Not Cassie, not anyone."

"Because we might get into trouble?" Elspeth asked, her eyes wide.

Deanna nodded. "Or worse."

Elspeth sat down hard on the bench beside Deanna. "You think the murderer is someone we know?"

Deanna raised her eyebrows. "Don't you?"

⚬⚬❯◼❮⚬⚬

Dinner was a bit melancholy without the Manchesters, though Mr. Woodruff seemed to have rallied. Tonight there was more color in his cheeks and a twinkle to his eyes, and he seemed to be glad to be home with the family. He ate sparingly but teased the girls about their conquests at the ball.

Asked Charles about his revised plans for taking Lord David down to visit Joe's machine shop the next day. Told Dee to send his best wishes for Adelaide's speedy recovery.

Charles, on the other hand, seemed subdued, preoccupied. And Deanna wondered if he was missing Adelaide—or the presence of Madeline Manchester. This did not bode well for Adelaide's future, and her mother would have a fit if a second fiancé cried off.

But Deanna didn't see that there was much she could do about that. It would be up to Adelaide on her return. Which she selfishly hoped wouldn't be too soon.

Deanna was enjoying her new-found freedom, such as it was. She was beginning to get an inkling of what life would be like without a mother's constant supervision, though she supposed that when she left home, someone else—her husband or society in general—would take her mama's place. Still, she'd decided that she would never go back to being stifled and perfectly behaved. Though, at the moment, she didn't see how that could be achieved.

Exhaustion hit Deanna halfway through the first course, and she had to smother several yawns. Going to the Fifth Ward had been an adventure but it had taken its toll. And the conversation with Claire, and almost getting caught by Cassie and Madeline, had pushed her just over the brink. She was glad the Manchesters had gone out without the others.

Tonight she would soak in a hot bath, then read about someone else's adventures from the comfort of her own bed.

But it wasn't to be. As the ladies got up to leave, Mr. Woodruff announced that he would go out to the Reading Room.

"But, my dear, do you think you should go out? You're just rallying from the trip."

"Oh, don't fuss, Nell. I'll be fine."

Mrs. Woodruff looked as if she'd like to say more, but she didn't.

"Before you go, father," Charles said, "might I have a word? In the library?"

"Sure, my boy, but is it something that can wait? It's getting late."

"It will only take a minute. And I'd like to take care of it tonight."

Mr. Woodruff frowned. He had suddenly become . . . agitated, Deanna thought. As if he were in a hurry to leave the house. "Very well. Ladies, I'll say good night."

Deanna was thinking fast. Could Charles be about to tell his father that he wanted to break off his engagement with Adelaide? It did seem to Deanna that he had been wrestling with his thoughts all evening, and perhaps he had now come to a decision.

Mrs. Woodruff tried once more to convince her husband not to go out. Deanna took the opportunity to whisper to Cassie, "Excuse me," and quickly went down the hall.

There was a powder room nearby, and she hoped that Cassie assumed that was where she was going. Instead she turned into the servants' hall and slipped through the small servants' door at the back of the library.

If Charles was consulting his father about crying off, Deanna wanted to know about it now. She'd figure out what to do about the information—if there was anything she could do—later.

The library was decorated in dark wood and heavy furniture. Books lined one wall and a spiral staircase led to another level of books.

One lone reading lamp illuminated the darkness. Just enough

light for Deanna to make her way across the room without bumping into the two large club chairs and several reading tables and globe that stood between them.

She hurried across the lush Oriental carpet without making a sound, grabbed her skirts, and hurried up the stairs. She'd just reached the top when she heard the door from the hall open. She ducked into a reading alcove, a cozy niche with a window that looked onto the lawn and a cushioned seat just big enough for two young girls. Deanna and Cassie had found a picture book of Greek art there one summer and spent many wide-eyed hours giggling over the naked statues.

The downstairs lights came on, and Deanna blinked out of her dark corner. She could see the tops of the two men's heads below her, Mr. Woodruff's hair going bald in a circle at the crown of his head, but Charles's was still full and wavy.

"Well, what is it?"

Mr. Woodruff's voice was impatient. Deanna wondered what was so important at the Reading Room, where everyone knew men retreated not just to read their papers, smoke cigars, and talk about business, but to get away from their wives and daughters. It didn't sound all that interesting to Deanna.

She leaned forward.

"I'm concerned, Father."

"Oh, don't you start harping on my health."

"Not on your health, but on the health of R and W Sugar."

Deanna slumped in relief. Charles wasn't going to ask to break his engagement to Adelaide after all. He just wanted to talk business. And now she was stuck here until they left. Her bath was looking very far away.

"There's nothing wrong with the business."

"Isn't there, sir? American Sugar is buying up refineries all around us. This Lord David fellow was supposed to ensure us a supply of raw material in order to keep us competitive. In the meantime, our smaller suppliers are either signing on with Havemeyer or selling to the refineries out west."

"Don't you worry, Charles. Everything will be fine, fine."

"Then why isn't he out doing whatever you brought him here to do, rather than dancing and dining and spending our money and asking for more?"

"An investment. He could deliver twice the product if he were to plant all of his acreage. He just needs the capital."

"Let him use his own money."

"Don't show your ignorance, Charles. His capital is tied up in the plantation."

"Don't expect me to try to convince Randolph and Ballard to go along with this scheme. It's jeopardizing the whole future of R and W."

"Nonsense. Our future is dependent on it."

"With all due respect, sir, I don't even think Lord David's interested in the company. I offered to take him to see the refineries, and he couldn't have been less enthusiastic."

"I told you that I would take him when I was feeling better. Which I am. So stop worrying."

"I'll stop worrying when I know that all the money you gave him in good faith is actually being used to bring the raw sugar to our refineries." Charles took a step away, turned back to his father. "And now he's dining with the Stanhopes, who are thick as thieves with our competitors."

"Oh, enough. Yes, Stanhope's wife is a Havemeyer, but I'm sure she thinks no more about sugar than how much to put in her tea. And as far as Stanhope goes—the man hasn't dabbled in business in years. I assure you, he's only interested in his horses and mistresses. Our families go back generations, and I can tell you"—Deanna leaned forward—"more than one of the Stanhopes isn't playing with a full deck."

"Perhaps," Charles conceded. "But his son is."

"Herbert? Fun and games, that one. And air for brains. You just leave well enough alone, boy. I'll take care of everything. Now, I'm off to the Reading Room. I'll be back late. Tell the servants not to wait up for me."

Mr. Woodruff left Charles standing in the middle of the room.

Deanna eased back, willing Charles to follow his father out of the room. Tonight, telepathy didn't work. It seemed Charles had no intention of going anywhere soon. When he finally did move, he only went as far as the massive kneehole desk. He sat down, unlocked a drawer, and pulled out a blue ledger.

Several minutes passed with Charles bent over the ledger.

Then with an exclamation that made Deanna jump, he slammed it shut, tossed it back into the drawer, and locked it. "He'll ruin us," he said, as if he couldn't believe his own words. He slumped back in his chair as if he meant to stay there all night. "Damn and damn and damn."

Damn and damn and damn, agreed Deanna, and hoped to heaven no one would sound the alarm when she didn't return to the drawing room.

Chapter
13

Deanna awoke with a start. She thought she must still be dreaming, because she was hunched up in a tiny space, her head resting against a hard surface. She was in the hold of a ship like a slave or in a box like a magician's assistant.

Then she remembered.

Good heavens, she'd fallen asleep in the library alcove. The library was now completely dark. Charles must have left, and she hadn't even heard him. Was the family out looking for her? How would she explain?

She stood up; her foot must have fallen asleep as well, because it prickled painfully. But she had no idea of the time. She looked out the little window, but there was no moon, no stars. It was a cloudy night.

Gradually, her eyes became accustomed to the dark, and she made out the shapes of things below her. She groped for the rail that ran around the edge of the balcony and followed it to the steps.

Carefully, she placed her foot on the first tread and then the next. It took more time than she wanted, but she had no intention of breaking her neck. Not after what she'd heard tonight. Charles was worried about the business. Something he'd seen in the ledger had upset him. That terrible "He'll ruin us." And her father angry at something that Mr. Woodruff hadn't done about the contract with Lord David. And that it was serious.

It just didn't seem fair that Mr. Woodruff should be jeopardizing all their lives. But she did know that fairness had no place in business, at least not at the level that her father and the other men practiced it.

It was then she remembered the telegram sent to her father and that she had forgotten to pass on to Mr. Woodruff.

Perhaps she shouldn't pass it along after all. She wasn't sure what she should do. Bob would have known what to do. Joe would know. But what did she really know? Maybe she could ask Gran Gwen, who knew about a lot of things. But it would all have to wait. Right now, the most important thing for Deanna to do was go out and make up some excuse for being gone so long.

She felt her way across the room until she came to the desk. She wished she knew how to pick locks, but even if she got into the desk drawer, she doubted she could understand the numbers in the ledger. A few steps later she came to the door, groped for the doorknob, then opened the door to darkness.

Was this a dream? Why was everything so dark? She began to be afraid. Her pulse throbbed in her neck like something that didn't belong to her. All was quiet. Could it be so late that everyone had gone to bed? Why wouldn't they be out looking for her? She might be lying at the bottom of the cliff like Daisy.

How long had she slept?

At least Elspeth ought to be looking for her. Wouldn't she have sounded the alarm?

Cold, clammy fingers crawled up Deanna's spine. She turned and saw a soft glow of light ahead. Thank goodness. It was in the foyer. She hurried toward it. The foyer was empty. She crossed the floor and looked into the drawing room. All dark.

She climbed the stairs and had just reached the landing when she heard someone enter the front door and silently cross the foyer below her.

Her first thought was that someone had left the door unlocked and that a burglar was entering, then she scoffed at herself. A burglar wouldn't use the front door. It must be Mr. Woodruff returning from his club.

Deanna started toward her room. It wouldn't do to be found wandering the halls in the middle of the night. Then she heard soft laughter and a hurried "shh." It wasn't Mr. Woodruff, but Lord David and his sister, coming back from a late night at the Stanhopes.

Deanna blushed. This was even worse. Their rooms were in the opposite wing, but she'd never make it to her room without them seeing her. What would they think of her skulking in the shadows?

She'd hesitated too long. There was no hope for it. A few feet down the hall, a slatted chest held a vase of peonies. She ducked behind the far side, shrank down and pulled her skirts close to her feet, just as they came into view.

She could see them through the slats, and it made them

look like one of those new moving pictures that Mr. Edison had demonstrated. All flickery.

They paused. And Deanna held her breath.

"A successful night, brother," Madeline said, and smiled up at him.

"Indeed." Lord David wrapped an arm around her, pulled her close, and kissed her. Full on the mouth, like a lover.

Deanna swallowed a gasp. She knew she shouldn't be watching and yet she couldn't look away.

The kiss went on and on. His hand slid up her bodice, his fingers spread over her breast, but Madeline pushed him away, frowning. "We must be careful." Then she walked away, pausing long enough to smile back at him, and they both disappeared down the opposite hallway.

Deanna sat on the floor for the longest time. Maybe that hadn't been what it looked like. Maybe it was a Barbadian custom to kiss your sister on the mouth.

But it hadn't looked like a brotherly kiss at all. It was passionate in a way that made Deanna's stomach flutter.

Using the chest to steady herself, Deanna pushed to her feet and walked back to her room on shaky legs. Maybe it wasn't such a good idea to spy on people. Now she had knowledge she wished she didn't have, and she didn't know what to do about it, either. How could she possibly face them tomorrow like nothing had changed?

The light in her room was on. Elspeth was curled up in the chair asleep, but she woke up when Deanna closed the door and leaned against it.

Elspeth shook herself and jumped up. "Where have you been? I've been worried sick! I was afraid whoever killed Daisy got you, too." She looked around, picked up the brush from the dressing table, and threw it at Deanna.

"Ouch." Deanna stooped to pick up the brush, which had fallen to the floor after hitting her in the arm. "I'm sorry. I've had such a night. Did no one else wonder where I was?"

"Yes. Cassie came up and I told her you'd fallen asleep in the dressing room. That you were worn out and not to bother you. I don't know if I should have done that, but I was afraid to tell on you. I looked for you everywhere, even went back to Daisy's room—and that was not fun by myself, I can tell you. I didn't know what to do."

She sat down again and burst into tears.

Deanna hurried toward her. "I'm sorry, Elspeth. It wasn't my fault. Truly. Well, not exactly."

"What happened to you?" Elspeth asked from behind her hands.

Deanna sat on the floor at her feet. "Charles asked to speak with his father after dinner, and I was afraid he was going to end his engagement to Adelaide, what with all the moony looks he's been giving Madeline."

"They went to talk in the library, so I sneaked in the servants' entrance and hid up on the balcony."

"You didn't."

"I did."

"What if they had caught you?"

"I don't know. I was just afraid for Adelaide and— Oh, I don't know."

Elspeth lowered her hands and reached in her apron pocket for a handkerchief. She blew her nose. "Did he want to end the engagement?"

"No." Deanna told her what she'd overheard.

"You think Mr. Woodruff's doing something he shouldn't with the business?"

"Or not doing enough of what he should be doing. He went off to the Reading Room right after he talked to Charles."

"That still doesn't explain why you were gone so long."

"When Mr. Woodruff left, Charles got out a ledger and started going over figures. I couldn't leave without him seeing me, and I guess I fell asleep."

Elspeth rolled her eyes. "That's it?"

"Well, actually there's something worse."

Elspeth slipped off the chair to sit on the floor next to Deanna.

"As I was coming upstairs just now, Lady Madeline and Lord David came home from their dinner." Deanna stopped. Just thinking of what she'd seen made her feel queasy. She didn't know how she could tell it without sounding crazy.

"Everyone was in bed, and I didn't want them to think I was waiting up for them or spying on them, so I ducked behind that table in the hallway."

"You *have* been the spy this evening. Did they catch you?"

"No. But—I saw him kiss her. On the mouth. Like lovers do."

"But she's his sister."

"I know, but I saw them. I really did. And he put his hand where he shouldn't."

"Heathens! I told you."

"And Charles is worried about his father giving Lord David a lot of money."

"Why would he give Lord David money? He's a rich land-owner."

"I know. But evidently he wants even more to complete the deal. I don't understand any of it. It's probably nothing, or I misunderstood, but I think I should tell Joe, don't you?"

Elspeth nodded slowly. "I think you should . . . about the money. They were really kissing?"

—◦◦>─)◉(─<◦◦—

The sound of broken glass awoke Joe from a deep sleep. He lifted his head off the pillow.

Damned drunk, he thought, and lowered himself back into bed.

The second sound of smashing glass brought him out of bed and to his feet. That sounded more like a window than a whiskey bottle. He pulled on his trousers and reached under his bed for the pistol he kept loaded in case of a burglar or a saboteur, and made his way out of his bedroom. Everything looked fine from where he stood. The doors were bolted and all windows in the warehouse were grilled; no one could break in.

Still . . .

He moved stealthily toward the back work area and opened the door a slit. Saw the first explosion of fire. They were fire bombing his workshop. He stuck the pistol in his waistband and grabbed a burlap bag from the pile he kept for just such an occasion and a pail of sand. And ran recklessly across the floor to put out the fire that had begun to spread across whatever incendiary substance that had been in the bottle.

It was moving toward the rolls of brown paper that would go into making the bags for the bagging machine. He looked above him to the broken window. He poured the sand in a wide line between the flames and the paper, then began to beat at the flames.

More glass splintered farther down the room.

Damn them.

But no bomb followed. Just the sound of an angry mob. But Joe couldn't stop to see if the interlopers had been caught; he had his hands full putting the fire out.

Shots rang out, but Joe kept beating at the flames.

When the fire was finally doused and an extra pail of sand had been poured over the smoking ruins, Joe returned to his room long enough to pull on a work shirt and a pair of boots. Then he went outside.

"They got away," said Hiram Harkevy, an ex-boxer and one of the men Joe paid to keep an eye on the warehouse. "They had a wagon waiting for them and armed guards. But we'll get 'em next time."

There were verbal agreements throughout the knot of men who had come out of the tavern to help bust some heads. "And then they won't be doing any mischief ever again," someone yelled from the crowd.

"Thank you." Joe slapped Hiram on the shoulder. "No one was hurt?"

"Nah. A pack of cowards coming sneaking in the night."

"Still, thank you much." To the knot of men Joe said, "Drinks on me." He locked his front door, and with the promise of bringing them a pint, Hiram dispatched two men to stand watch at the warehouse.

The rest of men followed him into the tavern.

The attacks were escalating. Until tonight, they had been mere annoyances, but fire was a real threat. If Hiram hadn't stopped them, Joe could have lost months of work. He supposed it was time he hired full-time security.

He'd talk to Hiram tomorrow. And tomorrow he'd do something about securing the interior with more than glass windows.

———◦◦∘}◙{∘◦◦———

"Get up, sleepy head." Cassie bounced into Deanna's bedroom the next morning followed by a maid carrying
Deanna's breakfast tray.

Deanna groaned. "Go away." She pulled the satin com-
forter over her head.

"You've been sleeping forever. Are you sick?" Cassie pulled
the covers down and frowned at Deanna. "You look fine, so
come on. We're going shopping and to the Casino for lunch."

Deanna opened her eyes. Cassie's face was about a foot
from hers. She blinked. "I haven't had breakfast yet." Deanna
tried to turn over, but Cassie jumped onto the bed and poked
her. Deanna gave up.

"Okay, I'm awake."

"Oh, good. Just put the tray down over there, Bridget,"
Cassie told the maid. "And be a dear and bring me a cup."

The maid curtseyed and left the room.

"You'll never guess," Cassie said as soon as the door closed.

"What?" Deanna cleared her throat, gave up trying to go
back to sleep, and sat up.

"Joe's Gran Gwen telephoned to invite us to tea at Bonheur
on Monday. Maddie's dying to meet her." Clouds descended
on her face. "I thought it would be okay to accept, since we
can be sure Joe won't be there—it will be great fun."

"Oh, good," Deanna said, sitting a little straighter. Maybe
she would have a chance to speak with Gran Gwen alone.

"It will be just the three of us. Mama has to stay home.
Papa's under the weather again. Mama said he'd have to stop
traveling if this is what happens." Cassie frowned.

"Is he awfully bad? He said he was fine last night."

"I know, but this morning he didn't even get out of bed. I guess Mama was right about him not going out."

"Are you worried about him?" Deanna asked.

"Not really. Mama says he'll be fine, but she sent for the doctor, and we'll have to take Aunt Tillie with us shopping this morning, since Mama wants to be here when the doctor comes." Cassie made a face.

"What?"

Cassie laughed. "Aunt Tillie's such an old biddy and always says a dress is too daring just because it has an interesting décolleté. Well, I certainly don't care." Cassie was wearing an apricot visiting dress with a more than "interesting" décolleté, which she must have picked knowing that her aunt would be chaperoning.

"I don't think I—"

"Oh, no thinking today. We're just going to have fun."

Easy for Cassie to say; she hardly ever worried about things. But Deanna did. There was so much to worry about. Maybe "worry" was the wrong term—it was more like "wonder"—about things she didn't understand. Like how scientists could estimate how many stars there were in the sky, or how Thomas Edison figured out how to make a telephone. Or why Joe had given up everything to go invent machines. Or why Madeline let her brother kiss her like that. She was always thinking about something. Except now, she was just thinking about a cup of coffee.

". . . so we won't have a lot of time to shop."

"Wait, wait," Deanna said, realizing that Cassie was still chattering on about their plans for the day. "Start over."

The maid came in with another tray. Cassie poured a cup for Deanna and another for herself.

Deanna breathed in the steaming aroma and took a sip. "Bridget, please send Elspeth to me."

"Yes, miss."

"Invitations are pouring in," Cassie said. "Lord David and Madeline are the talk of the town."

Along with the murder at the Woodruff ball, Deanna thought wryly. Newport loved a good scandal. And even though the death of a maid wasn't at all titillating, the fact that her body had lain in full view of the Woodruffs' guests would be fodder for malicious tongues.

"So, do hurry up and dress. There's so much to do before the beach tonight. I must have a new frock to wow Vlady."

Deanna didn't mention that in the dark on the sand was hardly the ideal circumstance for a display of fashion. Not that those conditions would stop any of the ladies from dressing extravagantly.

"Now, what are you going to wear today?" Cassie headed for the dressing room. Deanna thought of Daisy's bundle, which Elspeth had left there. She didn't want Cassie seeing it and asking questions.

"Cassie, come back here."

Cassie stuck her head out of the door.

"Go sit in that chair over by the window. Elspeth will give you such a scold if you've messed anything up."

Cassie threw up her hands in mock fear but came back into the room. "Fine, but please do get up."

Deanna pointed to the princess chair by the far window.

Cassie sighed, flounced over to it, and plopped down. "You're worse than Maddie."

"Where is Madeline today?"

Cassie groaned. "Still sleeping."

"Which is what I'd like to be doing."

"Dee-ee."

Deanna gave it up and rolled out of bed. When Elspeth came in a few minutes later, Deanna's face was washed, her teeth were brushed, and she was sitting at her dressing table pulling out her braid, while Cassie finished off Deanna's breakfast.

Elspeth took one look at the breakfast tray and moved the plate away from Cassie. She poured Deanna another cup of coffee, then finished unbraiding her hair.

"So, anyway," Cassie said through a mouthful of toast and marmalade, "have you heard from your mama about when she's returning?"

Deanna shook her head. "No, but she's only been gone for two days."

"Well, I hope Adelaide is better, but I hope they stay away for another week. Because the Fishes are having a dress ball next weekend. And we know how your mama feels about the Fishes."

Deanna knew. It was the same way her mama felt about a lot of families whom she considered "fast" or "ill bred."

"Though I must say, Adelaide should get back here and claim her territory."

"Charles?"

Cassie nodded and took another bite of Deanna's toast.

"He's paying particular attention to Maddie, isn't he?" It seemed to Deanna that all the gentlemen were paying undo attention to Lady Madeline. Deanna squelched the thought. She didn't want to become like her mother, passing judgment on every little thing.

Cassie shrugged. "Well, you have to admit, she's very beautiful and charming, and with Adelaide always having the headache, it can't be much fun for him."

Or for Adelaide, Deanna thought.

"I wouldn't mind having Maddie for a sister-in-law but I'd rather have you. Besides Charles isn't a jilt." Her hand flew to her mouth. "Oh, Dee, I'm sorry."

Elspeth had been twisting Deanna's hair into a chignon, but she stopped.

"It's all right, Cassie," Deanna said. "Joe didn't actually jilt me, since he never got around to asking me."

"But the expectations. It must be so mortifying."

"Not really," Deanna lied. Though it did seem less important since Daisy's death. A lot of things seemed less important, and some things meant more.

"Miss Cassie, will you please be quiet so Miss Deanna will hold still?"

"Sorry, you grumpy old thing."

"Hmmph," Elspeth said. "She'd be ready sooner if you'd stop distracting her."

"Okay. I'll go pester Maddie. But hurry up or we won't have enough time to shop before luncheon."

"I'll be there in a minute."

Elspeth held on to Deanna's hair. "You're not going anywhere until you've had a proper breakfast, since yours seems to have disappeared. And some people have had two."

Cassie grinned. "Do you think I'm too plump?" She jumped up and twirled around. "Vlady Howe said he likes a handful."

"Miss Cassie!" Elspeth said.

"Well, he does."

"Shoo."

"He does," Cassie backed toward the door.

Elspeth raised her brush.

Cassie trilled a laugh and was gone.

"That girl will get herself in trouble if she's not careful."
Elspeth sniffed.

They were both silent as she finished Deanna's hair, both
thinking of Daisy and wondering if that kind of trouble was
why she had plunged off the cliff.

Chapter
14

It was an hour before Maddie appeared. She tripped down the stairs like she'd been awake for hours, so carefree that Deanna had a hard time believing she'd seen what she knew she'd seen.

Cassie and Maddie chatted away while Deanna tried to block the image of Madeline and Lord David locked in a passionate embrace. That kiss. The way his hand had roved down her back then around to her—she blushed even thinking about it. Or about how watching it or even thinking about it now made her feel.

"Come along, Miss Thinker," Madeline said.

"What? Oh." Deanna said and followed them into the parlor.

A few minutes later, Aunt Tillie's carriage stopped at the front door. Mrs. Woodruff waved at her sister from the doorway and told the girls to have a good time. The three young women descended the steps to where Tillie's coachman, a somber older servant dressed in dark blue livery, opened the carriage door.

"Chip chop," Tillie called from inside the closed carriage.

Cassie rolled her eyes and climbed first into the carriage. She took the seat next to her aunt, and Deanna and Madeline sat across. Deanna tried not to stare at the older woman, but since she was directly across from Deanna, it was nearly impossible not to notice her sunken cheeks and how the face powder caked into the lines around her nose and mouth.

It was hard to believe that Mrs. Woodruff and Tillie were sisters. Deanna wondered if people said the same thing about her and Adelaide.

It was stuffy in the carriage, which, like Aunt Tillie, was not in its first youth. There was the faint odor of mold and camphor, and Deanna imagined the carriage stored away with the rest of Tillie's off-season possessions, brought out only a handful of times, then forgotten.

Outside, the sun was shining, but it was not too warm or windy. It would be a perfect evening for their bonfire.

The carriage let them off outside the Casino, where a row of exclusive shops lined the first floor and opened onto the sidewalk.

Bellevue Avenue was reserved for the elite cottagers. It was delightful to stroll from shop to shop without being afraid a wagon would splash dirty water on your hem or some urchin would try to snatch your purse. Shopping in Newport was a relaxed affair, unlike in Manhattan, where dust carts and merchant wagons jostled fine carriages and fine ladies. Not that she was allowed to shop for herself. Most of her and Adelaide's clothes came from Paris.

Deanna didn't really need to buy anything. She'd had two

completely new wardrobes in the last year. One for the New York season and one for the Newport season.

Most of her winter frocks and gowns had already been sent out to the Sisters of Mercy charity, though what the sisters or their charges could do with them was a mystery. Hopefully, sell them to some down-on-their-luck society ladies—Deanna made an effort not to glance at Aunt Tillie when she thought that. The sisters could use the proceeds to support their work.

Madeline was especially gay and bought several bangle bracelets and a scarf of French silk.

They sat while Cassie tried on dress after dress until she finally chose a light yellow gauze confection that she thought would be perfect for the bonfire that night. Aunt Tillie thought it was scandalous, but Cassie merely pouted and told Madame to put it on her account.

"Yes, miss, do you wish it to be delivered?"

"Yes, please, but it must be there by three o'clock without fail."

"Very good." Madame saw them to the door.

They walked side by side down the sidewalk, Aunt Tillie content to follow a few feet behind, and stopped to luncheon at the Casino, where Vlady Howe, Herbert Stanhope, and Cokey Featheringham just happened to also be dining. They were nearly finished, but they pulled up their chairs to chat, much to the dismay of Aunt Tillie.

Vlady was outrageous in his compliments to her while he pressed Cassie's knee under the table. Deanna didn't know how Cassie's aunt didn't notice. Cassie had once told her that the chance of getting caught added to the thrill of her flirtations and misdemeanors, though to Deanna's knowledge Cassie hadn't yet gone beyond the line.

Though, what did Deanna know? It seemed she never got excited about the same things other ladies were interested in. Which brought her right back to the same quandary. She wanted to do something special with her life, if she only knew what and whether she had the means to do it.

"You're awfully quiet today," Herbert said.

"Just thinking. I can't help it."

"Oh, I don't know that it's a bad thing. People should think, shouldn't they?"

"Bert," Cokey burst out laughing. "Is that any way to talk to a lady?" He gave Madeline a meaningful smile, though Deanna was glad to see Madeline return only a demur one.

"I think Herbert has impeccable manners and is an interesting conversationalist," Deanna said.

Cokey rolled his eyes and Vlady joined in the merriment. Even Cassie giggled.

Aunt Tillie cleared her throat.

"Sorry, we beg your pardon," Vlady said. "Cokey, you must follow Herbert's lead in good manners."

Herbert had turned bright red, which clashed awfully with his carrot orange hair.

Cokey shrugged, yawned, and went back to flirting with Madeline.

Deanna didn't know how he could say things like he had about Joe and then sit here talking to her like nothing had happened. She'd like to pour her lemonade over his head.

She couldn't wait for lunch to be over. How could they all sit there acting so frivolous when someone had died practically in front of them, when Cokey had practically accused Joe of murdering Daisy, and when Vlady had actually found Daisy's body? How would they feel if they were suspected of murder?

That gave her pause. Vlady had found the body, practically led them to where Daisy lay. Could he have led them there already knowing what they'd find?

It sounded like something from *Beadle's Monthly*. Or even the *Police Gazette*, which her mother had forbidden her to read.

And Cokey. She'd never really liked him. She frowned, looked at him in a suddenly new light. Hadn't he bragged about liking a bit of skirt? Even Deanna knew what that meant. And he'd been close by when Daisy had tried to leave Seacrest.

Maybe Daisy had been going to meet him! And had run into Joe instead. But that would mean that Daisy . . .

She almost wished Cokey was the murderer. It would serve him right for being a cad.

Cokey laughed, breaking into her thoughts and bringing her back to the present. The annoying present. If she spent another second with Cokey, she might do something unladylike.

Fortunately, luncheon was soon over. But when the gentleman accompanied them out to the street, Deanna began to think of excuses to go home.

Cassie shooed them away. "Now, go away. Gentlemen are no good at shopping."

They left with much good-natured bowing and adieu-ing and created a bit of a spectacle on the sidewalk, which would have had Deanna's mother in a tizzy. Fortunately, she wasn't in Newport. Though, in her absence, Deanna was beginning to appreciate her attention to good behavior.

The young women stopped to try on hats, and Cassie and Madeline insisted Dee buy a new straw boater with a red band and gloves—of which Madeline and Cassie bought several pair. Deanna bought the hat but eschewed the gloves. They were on their way to a ribbon shop when they passed the bookshop.

Deanna would have stopped in, but Cassie and Maddie had already continued down the street. Deanna did manage to glance in the window as they passed by. The new issue of *The Old Sleuth* was in the very front.

"Go ahead, I'll catch up," she called. And before Aunt Tillie could object, she ducked into the bookshop and into the comforting smell of paper, ink, and old wood.

The proprietor came out from behind the counter to greet her. "Good morning, Miss Deanna. I expect you'll want the new issue of *The Old Sleuth.*"

"Yes, please." Deanna reached into her purse and realized she had given all her money to the Woodruffs' coachman.

"I'll be glad to put it on your father's account."

She hesitated. She liked to pay for her books herself, especially knowing that her mother disapproved, but today she'd make an exception. It had just occurred to her that he might also have a copy of the coverless dime novel that they'd found in Daisy's room. It probably meant nothing, but neither Kate Goelet nor Deanna's other favorite lady detective, Loveday Brooke, would leave a single stone unturned until she had followed the clues to a solution.

She asked him about it.

"I do have a copy of that issue left, but didn't you already buy that one?"

"Yes, but I misplaced it and hadn't finished the stories yet."

He flipped through a box of old dime novels, pulled out a copy, and wrapped both in brown paper.

There was a tap on the shop window. Outside, Cassie motioned Deanna to hurry.

The proprietor handed Deanna the parcel, then opened the door for her.

She hadn't managed to see the cover before he'd wrapped it up, and she was itching to peak inside. But it would have to wait.

"Aunt Tillie wouldn't let us go on without you," Cassie explained. "I hope you plan to come home with more than a hat and some old book."

At the next store, Deanna bought a pair of stockings and looked in the undergarment catalogue at the new knickers.

An hour later they were on their way to Seacrest for tea. Deanna hoped she'd also get a few hours alone in her room before the bonfire.

It seemed to take forever before she could get through tea and make her way upstairs. Cassie wanted her to come to her room while she tried on her new dress for her mother, but Deanna excused herself.

As soon as she was safely in her room with her package of books, she rang for Elspeth, then waited impatiently for her to make her way from the servants' hall to the north wing.

"Did you have a good time shopping?" Elspeth asked when she appeared from the dressing room.

"Yes. Come here." Deanna held up the parcel.

"New books?"

"And an old one." Deanna untied the string and pulled off the paper. The old issue lay on top. "This is the issue that Daisy had, the one with the missing cover."

"Oh," Elspeth breathed, and leaned closer to peruse the cover.

"Oh my," Deanna added.

They were staring at the red and black cover of *Pritchard the Poisoner*.

The infamous doctor had poisoned his wife decades before and had been the subject of lurid stories ever since. But this time it wasn't the story that caught Deanna and Elspeth's attention. The cover depicted the interior of an invalid's bed chamber. The doctor stood over the bed, pouring something into a vial—most likely the poison. Behind him, the door had been left ajar. A maid stood in the doorway, her face etched in horror.

"Oh, miss. Do you think Daisy saw something she shouldn't?"

"I think maybe she did."

"But why not tell someone? The doctor was here to see Mr. Woodruff—but he wouldn't have tried to poison him, would he?"

"I don't think so."

"But someone might have," Elspeth said.

"Yes, they might. He has been sickly since his return."

"I knew it. That voodoo man put a curse on him!"

"Really, Elspeth. If he put a curse on him, he wouldn't need to poison him, would he?"

Elspeth crossed her arms and rested her chin on her fist.

"But I bet Daisy was trying to send Orrin a message," Deanna said.

"With the cover?"

"Claire said Daisy had asked her to write a note to Orrin but was frightened away. If she thought she might not be able to get a note to him, she might have tried to send the cover to him, like a clue. To let him know she'd seen something suspicious."

"Oh, miss. Do you think that's what was in the envelope? If it fell out, maybe it's still down there on the rocks. I can go look for it while everyone is at the bonfire tonight."

"You will not. You will not go anywhere alone until this is cleared up."

Elspeth jutted out her chin.

"I mean it. Whoever killed Daisy won't think twice about killing you. Besides, the police searched the area. Will Hennessey is pretty smart. I don't think they found anything. It either washed away or someone took it—or we've been reading too many detective stories." She tapped the edition of *The Old Sleuth*.

"But I still don't understand," Elspeth said. "Why leave the envelope?"

"Because the envelope had Orrin's name on it, and the murderer wanted to implicate him. Daisy left a perfect setup."

"So, what are we going to do about it?"

"Well, I'm going to the bonfire. You're going to stay put and not go outside. And first thing tomorrow morning, we're going to figure out a way to go see Will Hennessey with what we've learned." Deanna slumped back against the chair. *And hope he doesn't laugh himself silly.*

———◦◦◦)◦(◦◦◦———

At seven that evening, Deanna went downstairs dressed in a blouson dress of white piqué draped by a light shawl of pashmina wool. Elspeth had dressed Deanna's hair in loose curls around her face and the rest twisted up to the top of her head, and she had insisted Deanna wear a short half corset, even though Deanna protested that they would be sitting on blankets on the sand and it would be dark and no one would see her anyway.

Deanna took her place in the carriage with Mrs. Woodruff and Cassie and Maddie. The men had gone ahead, and Deanna knew they would be at the bar when the ladies arrived.

The veranda of the Beach Club was lit with colorful paper lanterns. The mamas and some of the young ladies who pre-

ferred to stay away from the sand were sitting in chairs or
lounging on chaises. A carpet path was laid down across the
beach to protect shoes from the salt and sand. It was flanked
by two rows of torches to light the way.

To their right, the row of changing booths had been closed
for the evening. To their left, Reject's Beach was roped off, the
boulders behind it serving as perfect, if uncomfortable, tryst-
ing places.

Mrs. Woodruff took her place among the ladies sitting on
the veranda, and Deanna, Cassie, and Madeline followed the
carpet path down toward the water. The bonfire had not been
lit, but it rose behind the group like a small mountain against
the darkening sky. It looked almost ancient, like a pyramid—
or a funeral pyre.

Deanna shook herself. It must have been all that talk about
voodoo. Still, she couldn't help but look behind her, just to
make sure no one was following them.

It was just dusk, but little knots of people already sat on blankets brought for the occasion, while waiters carried trays of
punch and sandwiches to the guests, no easy feat due to the
shifting sand.

"Oh, there they are!" Cassie waved her bright yellow scarf
and began to pick her way across the sand to where Charles
and Lord David sat along with Vlady, Herbert, and Cokey.
Deanna had had enough of Cokey to last a lifetime, but she
couldn't very well snub him.

I'll just sit as far away from him as possible, she thought as she
followed Cassie and Madeline across the sand to the men.

There was a bottle of champagne in a standing silver cooler.
And another empty one neck down in the sand. They were
all in good spirits.

Charles, Herbert, and Lord David stood, brushing sand from their hands as the three girls approached. Vlady started to stand but lost his balance and fell back to the blanket, pulling Cassie with him and setting her off in a peal of laughter. Cokey was already too drunk to even attempt to stand. Maybe he would pass out and they wouldn't have to pay attention to him.

"Incomparable," Lord David said, and kissed Deanna's hand.

To her acute embarrassment, she felt the same tingle she'd felt when she'd seen him kissing Madeline the night before. His sister. He'd been kissing his sister.

Lord David smiled, no doubt thinking the shiver was caused by his gallantry. He offered his hand to help her sit, then sat beside her. He reached past her, and his arm brushed awfully close to her as he lifted the champagne bottle and poured her a glass.

The champagne was fizzy and tart, and went down quite easily.

The evening grew darker, the guests became livelier, Lord David filled Deanna's champagne glass a second time and ordered another bottle. Next to them, Cassie and Vlady were carrying on a lively flirtation.

Deanna's memory of the night before grew fuzzy in her mind, and soon she'd almost convinced herself that she'd misinterpreted the siblings' kiss. Lord David was being very attentive to her, the heat of his body compelling and seductive as he leaned close to speak softly in her ear.

Charles and Madeline sat on the other side of the blanket, their heads together, deep in conversation. Things were looking worse and worse for Adelaide. If she didn't hurry back, Deanna was afraid it would be too late to salvage her engagement.

Just as darkness descended in earnest, a murmured excitement swept through the guests. Deanna and the others turned to see a row of torches carried by the Beach Club's staff wind its way down the beach toward the water.

But instead of lighting the bonfire, they pushed the torches into the ground until a square of sand was lit up like a stage.

"My cue," Lord David whispered in Deanna's ear, setting off a delicious tightness in her stomach.

He got to his feet and strode toward the "stage." Everyone adjusted positions to see him better.

Lord David raised both arms. The light from the torches played along the planes of his body and face, making him seem to leap from the black of the night. He had certainly gotten everyone's attention. Some people stood and moved closer to see.

"Ladies and gentleman, my sister and I thank you for your warm hospitality. Tonight we have a special treat to share with you.

"Some of you may have heard that my servant Swan has some unusual powers far beyond the capabilities of a normal man. Now I would just like to set the record straight." He paused. Deanna shot Cassie an "I told you so" look. Lord David was going to dispel the voodoo rumors.

"Everything you've heard is . . . true." He lowered his voice, leaned toward his now rapt audience. "And more."

His voice sent a ripple of uneasiness down Deanna's spine.

"I discovered Swan in a village in . . ."

"What rubbish."

Deanna jumped at the new voice in her ear.

"Joe!" She turned and they nearly bumped noses, he was so close. She tried to move away but he grabbed her arm and held her in place.

"Shhh." He was crouched on one knee, leaning close to her. Too close.

"What are you doing here?" she whispered.

"Crashing the party, though I *am* a member, remember?" His face looked diabolical in the flickering torchlight. "I need to talk to you—but not here."

"Good, because I want to talk to you. Elspeth and I found something today."

"Dee. Stop it." His breath hissed in her ear and stopped the rest of her explanation.

In the following silence Deanna heard ". . . can conjure fire and wind, talk to the dead, read your palm, but tonight . . ."

"You're going to Grandmère's for tea Monday."

She leaned closer. "Yes, with Cassie and Madeline. Why?"

". . . so, without further ado, I present Swan the Obeah Man." Applause broke out.

"Joe, why do you—Joe?"

But Joe was gone. Vanished into the night like a magician.

Deanna looked around, hoping to catch a glimpse of him. Vlady and Cassie were clasped in an embrace. Cokey, cradling the champagne bottle, was sprawled out half on the blanket and half on the sand. Charles and Madeline were not where they'd been. Perhaps they had moved closer to get a better look. Deanna searched the crowd, but they seemed to have disappeared. And so had Joe.

Lord David returned and sat down beside her, a little closer than he'd been sitting before, Deanna thought.

"Where—" Deanna began.

"Watch," he told her.

Deanna looked at the place where the torchlight danced in the air, though there was no wind that Deanna could tell. Then, out of the darkness, appeared two white orbs that seemed to float above two yellow slashes. Coming closer and closer.

Lord David placed a supporting hand in the small of her back. "He's a gentle soul, just a magical one. Don't be afraid."

Slowly, the objects moved into the light of the torches and Deanna saw that the floating slashes of color were actually face paint and the orbs were merely two wide eyes.

She wasn't afraid—not really. She'd seen this apparition in the flesh on the back stairs of Seacrest. But tonight he looked even taller than she remembered.

Swan was dressed in a long red robe with a striped shawl tied diagonally across his chest. Two large feathers stuck up from a red turban. He began to chant, low and barely audible at first, then growing louder, sounds that Deanna had never heard before.

His chant became louder, the syllables quicker, until he stopped abruptly, words suspended. He began flicking his long fingers, sending sparks of red, green, blue, and yellow into the air until they surrounded him. They floated upward and spread into the night before they were gone in a poof of smoke.

There were gasps and nervous laughter and finally applause and a few bravos.

But Swan seemed oblivious. He began walking in a circle within the torches, his knees bent, body leaning forward, arms stretched outward, and his fingers playing the air like a harp.

He circled once, twice, drawing his audience into his spell. On the third time, he stopped in the center, and the ground lit up in a line around him, not with fire but with a phosphorescent glow.

"That's amazing," Deanna whispered to Lord David.

"And it just gets better."

Next, two large birds appeared from the folds of his sleeves and came to rest on each shoulder. Scarves appeared and disappeared only to be found in the audience. He glided up to a young woman; when he reached her, his hands shot from the folds of his robes and she screamed. Coins appeared between his fingers. He opened his hands and they dropped into the young woman's lap.

Everyone laughed as he backed away, grinning and leaving her dumfounded.

"Who has lost something?" His voice was mysterious, melodious.

One of a group of young men sitting nearby jumped to his feet and, laughing, called out, "I've lost something. Finally."

His companions laughed uproariously.

"Can you guess what it is?" the young man asked.

Swan pointed at him. "Do not mock the magic or it will come for you."

The man swayed and fell back into his companions. There were some concerned murmurs. One of his companions said, "No harm. Just a little tipsy."

"Look in your pocket, disbeliever."

The man rolled to his side and checked his trouser pockets. "Nothing."

"The left pocket of your vest."

The man reached in his vest, slowly pulled out his closed hand. Opened it and stared. "My ring. My signet ring. How did it get there? What did you do?"

"I never touched it with my hand but with my"—Swan's hand rose slowly and a long finger pointed to his temple—"mind."

"Huh," scoffed one of his companions. "He probably picked your pocket during the evening."

Swan slowly turned to stare at the man with the ring, who began to quake.

"He didn't. I lost this last week, before they ever arrived. How did you do that?"

Keeping his eyes locked on the man, Swan backed into the center of the circle. He broke his gaze and raised his hands to the side. Around him a ring of opalescent light pulsated on the sand. Sounds of amazement reverberated through his audience.

They were totally in his thrall.

Swan's hands stretched high above his head, moving in circles as if he were molding the air into a ball, holding something none of them could see. With a cry he flung the invisible object over their heads.

Everyone turned as the bonfire burst into flames. When they turned back, the torches had died. Swan was gone.

A bloodcurdling scream rent the air.

Chapter
15

For a moment there was dead silence, then several
ladies also screamed. There were titters of nervous
laughter, and then confusion.

Lord David jumped to his feet. "That scream wasn't part
of the act."

"It came from up there." Vlady Howe pointed toward the
tumble of rocks that rose along the far side of the little pocket
of sand that was Reject's Beach.

He and Herbert took off across the sand. Several other men
grabbed the lanterns that lit the canvas walkway and began
to run toward the rocks, while others began escorting the
ladies back toward the veranda.

"Lets go see," Cassie said.

Deanna didn't have to be persuaded. She had a bad feeling
about that scream.

Deanna and Cassie threaded their way through the crowd.
As soon as they were clear, Deanna began to run.

Deanna beat Cassie to the rope that separated the public Reject's Beach from Bailey's and slipped underneath, then held it for Cassie to wiggle through.

It took only a few minutes to get to the cliff base, another couple of seconds to hike their skirts into their waistbands—something they had done often in childhood—and start to climb.

They were both good climbers; you didn't forget a childhood of exploits just because you turned eighteen. And though the moon wasn't full, there was enough light to keep from falling.

Beyond them, men scrambled over the rocks, torchlight bouncing in and out of view.

"Here! Over here!" someone called.

"That was Vlady," Cassie said, and began to climb over the rough surface of the rocks toward the voice. They were upon him before they realized it, and Deanna sucked in her breath.

A girl lay crumpled in a little pocket of sand. Vlady stood over her, holding his torch like a centurion. Herbert had stepped back from the body and was a mere shadow. Across from Vlady, Charles Woodruff stood supporting a wilting Madeline. And kneeling beside the girl was Joe Ballard.

No one moved, trapped like the subjects of a painting.

Then Joe looked up and held Deanna's gaze.

Deanna brought a fist to her mouth, bit down on it as if to stop her own scream. This just couldn't be happening. She swallowed hard, inched forward. The black uniform, the white apron. She had to know who it was, but the maid's face was turned away.

"Good Lord. It's Joe Ballard. He's done it again." The words were slurred and came from behind Deanna, but she recognized the hateful voice.

"Shut up, Cokey," Herbert demanded. "You're drunk and witless."

"No I ain't." Cokey staggered past Deanna, and Dee was tempted to give him a push.

Joe stood and faced him. "I hear you've been making all sorts of accusations about me, Featheringham. This is neither the time nor the place. You may explain later. For now just be quiet."

Deanna didn't know how Joe could be so calm. He'd been leaning over the body when she and Cassie had arrived.

She pushed Cokey aside. He stumbled but she didn't care. She sidestepped around the scene until she was standing next to Vlady, where she could see the poor girl's face in his torchlight.

This time Deanna couldn't stop her choked cry of dismay. It was Claire. The maid who had come to them to tell them about Daisy. *Was* that why she was lying here dead? *Killed? Murdered?*

Because it must be murder, and that proved once and for all that Daisy's death hadn't been an accident or suicide, but murder. And that Orrin couldn't have done it, because Orrin was still safely in jail. Relief mingled with her sadness and anger—and guilt.

She was responsible for this. She had sent Elspeth to question the servants. She had encouraged Claire to tell all that she knew. She'd actually thought she could help find Daisy's killer. She couldn't. She should have left it to Will like Joe had told her to do.

But Claire would never have confided in the police. She'd been willing to speak to Deanna, though, had trusted her, and now Claire was dead, too.

What was she doing all the way out here? How did she get here and why? Two maids from the same household, both their bodies found on the rocks. Was a madman loose among them? Questions tumbled over themselves in Deanna's mind.

Joe stood over the body almost as if he were guarding it.

And the others . . . Slowly, Deanna became aware of the other two people who had been on the scene when she had arrived. Charles and Madeline. Charles had his arm around Madeline's waist, and she leaned into him as if she was about to faint. Charles didn't look uncomfortable or embarrassed. He didn't even seem to realize he was holding her; he just stared down at the dead girl.

Deanna wondered how they had gotten there so quickly, then realized that they must have already been close by when the scream cut through the night.

Which meant they'd been on the rocks together. And everyone knew what went on in the dark shelter of the rocks at Bailey's Beach.

A small crowd had gathered around them—mostly men and a few of the more adventurous young ladies—and murmurs of disbelief passed from person to person.

"Can you see who it is?"

"A maid."

"It's happened again. There's a madman attacking maids!"

"I'll keep mine close at home until they catch him."

"How can this happen?"

"Not in Newport."

Claire, thought Deanna. *Her name is Claire. And she's dead because of me.*

But why? As much as Deanna didn't want to think of a mad killer loose among them, even less did she want to think she might be responsible for Claire's murder.

A line of men stood on the walk above them. They'd probably come from the clubhouse, and they'd brought lanterns, which made it even easier to see those who crowded around the body.

One of them called down. "We've telephoned for the police."

Deanna saw Lord David standing with Mr. Woodruff among the men looking down on the scene. She hadn't even known Mr. Woodruff planned to come to the bonfire. Nor did he seem overly concerned with the fact that one of his own maids lay dead in the sand—assuming he even recognized her. He appeared to be trying to catch his son's eye.

Joe started toward Deanna.

"He's getting away!" Cokey yelled.

"Oh, stuff it, Cokey," Herbert said. "He's one of us."

"I saw him with the first one, too. I oughta know."

Joe stopped in front of him. "You don't know anything. And I'll thank you to stop making a spectacle of yourself and me." Then he continued around the group until he came to Deanna.

"I didn't do it," he said under his breath but not looking at her.

"I know." Deanna might question his culpability in seduction, and she could imagine him capable of killing if there were good reason, but she knew he would never attack defenseless young women.

They stood silent for what seemed like hours. Deanna didn't hear the clang of the police van, merely heard the pounding of the horses' hooves before it appeared. Of course they wouldn't use the bell. This was the cottagers' side of Newport. Discretion was everything.

A second wagon joined the first, possibly the Beach Patrol. Constables jumped out and came to stand in a line along the ground above the rocks. Deanna picked out Will Hennessey immediately. Tall, substantial, with an air of authority that stood out even in the dark.

Deanna had never been so glad to see him in her life.

Will stopped above them, surveying the scene. Deanna looked, too, trying to see what he was seeing. A small crowd huddled on the rock, lit by torchlight, carving the witnesses' faces into deep relief. Claire, lying dead on the sand before them. *Murder on a Rocky Beach.*

Will picked his way over the rocks to the knot of people standing around Claire's body. He paused when he came to Joe and Deanna.

"Did any of you touch the girl?"

No one had—except for Joe.

Deanna saw them exchange a quick look before Will knelt to examine the body. "Mr. Howe, bring your torch closer, if you will."

Vlady moved closer, handed him the torch.

"Thank you. Now, if you will all carefully step away from the victim. People on this side, you may return to the beach. Those of you on the left, I'm afraid you'll have to stay where you are unless you can find a safe but circuitous way to the road. Then you'll be escorted back to the club." Will motioned to his men. Two of them moved toward the retreating group.

Gradually, people moved out of the light and back to the beach, until only Deanna, Joe, Cassie, Vlady, and Charles and Madeline were left—and Cokey Featheringham, standing with his feet spread, his arms crossed, and glaring past the body at Joe.

It took only a few minutes for Will to examine the body. Deanna paid careful attention to what he was doing, trying to discern what he was looking for. Another envelope like the one Daisy had held?

But when he stood a few minutes later, he had nothing in his hand.

The first person he looked at was Joe.

It was everything Deanna could do not to blurt out, *He*

didn't do it, but she had no evidence that he hadn't. And in the meantime, poor Claire and Daisy were dead.

Please say it isn't my fault, Deanna prayed.

One of Will's officers came around and took all their names while a photographer who had come on the second wagon took pictures of the body. Deanna supposed they had done this for Daisy, too, but she'd been sent away before the actual investigation began.

Now she was mesmerized by what was happening. She thought about her sketch of Daisy lying on the rocks and how much more helpful it was for the police to have photography at their fingertips.

Deanna sighed, and she felt Joe put an encouraging hand on her back before he stepped away.

"It's him. He did it." Cokey pointed across Will's head to Joe.

Will's men stepped toward Joe, but Will waved them back. "That won't be necessary, will it, Joe?"

Deanna's head snapped around in time to see Joe frown at his friend and slowly shake his head.

"Tell him you didn't do it," Deanna hissed at him.

"All in good time."

Deanna grew cold as she watched the policemen climb over the nearby rocks, backs bent as they searched the crevices, their electric torches flickering in the darkness. The arrival of another van brought a doctor and two men who carried a stretcher. Too late for Claire.

The doctor examined the body more thoroughly, then said a few words to Will that Deanna couldn't hear. Once the doctor's examination was finished, the two men lifted Claire's body onto the stretcher and carried her away.

Will spent another few minutes inspecting the ground where her body had been. Finding nothing, or so it seemed to Deanna. He took a notebook out of his breast pocket, and while a constable held a lantern for him to see by, Will began to ask questions.

"Who discovered the body?"

At first no one answered.

"We heard the scream," Vlad volunteered.

"When?"

"Swan, Lord David's manservant, was just finishing his magic act."

Will looked over the crowd. "And where is Swan now?"

No one answered, so Vlad shrugged, and said, "Probably with the other servants, in one of the club staff rooms or back at Seacrest."

Will nodded.

"We found Joe Ballard kneeling over the body," Cokey said. "Didn't we?" Deanna noticed that he was no longer swaying or slurring his words. Shock. Finding a body must have shocked him sober. Now, if he would only shut up.

There were a few murmurs, but no one wanted to point the finger at a member of one of Newport's most respected families.

"I heard the scream, too," Joe said, glancing at Madeline. "I was just leaving and came to see if I could help. I was too late; when I finally found the place, the girl was dead."

"And was there anyone else about?"

"Not that I noticed."

Will jotted something down in his notebook. He must be making other notes, because it was taking him longer than it should have to write four words.

"But—"

Will stopped Joe with a look.

Deanna looked closely at both men. It seemed to her they were sending each other messages through that look. She mentally shook herself; she'd been reading too many stories about mind reading and summoning the dead.

Joe had said telepathy was all nonsense. And Deanna thought he must be right or the police would have no trouble apprehending villains; they'd just have to read their minds. And as far as summoning the dead . . . She shivered. Surely that wasn't possible.

"And who was the first to arrive after Joe?"

Everyone looked at someone else.

"I guess I was," Vlady said. His voice sounded a little shaky. "Me and Herbert." He looked around to get corroboration from Herbert, but Herbert was missing. "We—I saw something— someone lying in the sand and called to the others. When we— I—got closer, I saw—" He stopped to swallow. "I saw Joe kneeling over the body."

"I told you so," Cokey said triumphantly.

"And the rest of you?"

"Deanna and I got here next." Cassie smiled.

Will stifled a smile and turned toward Charles and Madeline, who were now standing even further apart.

"We . . ."

"I asked Mr. Woodruff to escort me back to the veranda." Madeline's voice was perfectly modulated, but Deanna thought she was prevaricating. "We heard a scream and, being close to where the sound came from, we naturally came to help if someone was in distress." She sighed. "Unfortunately, we were too late." Madeline flicked a glance at Joe, so quickly that

Deanna might have missed it if she hadn't been so intent on the fiction Madeline was telling.

The walk to the veranda from the beach came nowhere close to the rocks beyond Rejects Beach. Charles had definitely been with Madeline, but if they'd been innocently strolling back to the veranda, Deanna would eat her new straw boater. Surely Will could figure that out.

It was pretty obvious what they'd been out here doing, what most people did on the rocks in the dark. Charles looked disheveled and his waistcoat was misbuttoned.

Madeline, however, looked like she'd just walked away from her maid. She'd finally moved out of the circle of Charles's arm, and the two stood a respectable distance from each other.

But Deanna wasn't fooled, and she suspected it was too late for Adelaide to salvage her future with Charles.

Though that may be for the best after all, Deanna thought. She couldn't see Adelaide being happy with a man who'd started a flirtation before she'd even left for Boston. None of them had missed the attention Charles had paid to Madeline the night of the ball. And it had just gotten worse since then. It was better to find out now, before her sister was tied to him for life.

At that moment, Deanna swore that she wouldn't let her sister's happiness be sacrificed on the altar of business mergers. Surely Adelaide deserved more than that.

Deanna waited for Charles to say something, but when he spoke, he merely corroborated what Madeline had told Will. Protecting her honor? Deanna didn't think either of them was behaving very honorably. She wasn't mistaken about what the two of them had been doing. She just wasn't sure how far they had gone nor how much she should tell Will.

She looked up to find Madeline watching her. Deanna looked away. Between what she'd witnessed last night and tonight, she didn't like her new friend very much at the moment.

After another few minutes, Will released all of them with the request to contact him if they remembered anything else.

Vlady and Cassie started back with Vlady supporting her and helping her down the rocks she'd climbed up so nimbly and without thought just a short while before. Cassie was taking full opportunity to get closer to him, and once when he lifted her down from a boulder she'd been jumping from for years, she stayed in his arms. She was pressed so close to him that Deanna blushed for her. And then felt a little envious.

No one came to help Deanna over the rocks. She didn't need help, but it would have been nice if someone had thought about her. She squelched the thought. It was heartless to think of love when yet another poor girl had just been murdered.

Madeline and Charles followed them. Cokey stumbled along, due more to his lack of physical talent than to the amount of champagne he'd drunk that night. She glanced back over her shoulder. Joe was standing with Will right where she'd left them.

Her foot did falter then. Were they discussing the murder, or was Will going to arrest Joe on Cokey Featheringham's accusations?

Not if she could stop him. She turned back and clambered over the rocks and down into the crevice of sand.

"Deanna, you were supposed to go back with the others," Will said.

"You're not going to arrest Joe, are you?"

"No." He exchanged a look with Joe.

"No secrets. That's not fair."

"Dee—" Joe started, but Will interrupted him.

"Dee, this is not a game. You can't tag along. Two women have been murdered. This is a police investigation, not something you can be a part of."

She scowled at him, then at Joe, but neither of them succumbed to her expression this time. She sighed. "Fine. Then I won't bother to tell you what *I* know." Not that they would believe her now. They'd probably laugh at her for thinking Daisy had tried to leave Orrin a message by tearing off the cover of her book.

She started to pick up her skirts, realized they were still tucked into her waistband, and felt hot with humiliation. She looked ridiculous. How could she expect anyone to ever take her seriously?

She stomped off across the rocks, heedless of how she was going and managed to skid to the bottom without major mishap. That would have been the ultimate humiliation.

—oo)O(oo—

"Do you think she really knows something?" Joe asked.

"I wouldn't put it past her. And that could be very dangerous, very dangerous indeed."

"You mean whoever is killing these women may graduate from household maids to the female occupants?"

"Exactly what I mean," Will said.

"Christ. Well, at least we know for certain that Orrin wasn't the murderer. He's locked safely away in jail."

Will winced. "Unfortunately, that isn't the case. He was released just this afternoon."

"What? You released him? Why didn't someone tell me?" Joe passed his hand over his face. "Where the hell is he?"

Will smiled ruefully. "It was your grandmother's doing. At least, I assume it was. He was gone when I came in from my rounds this afternoon. Crum was not amused. He really doesn't like it when the rich call in favors."

"Nor do you," Joe reminded him.

"Nor do I, but in this case . . . well, until half an hour ago I was glad. I don't think that boy killed the first maid." He pulled his cap down. "I just hope he has an airtight alibi for tonight. Or heads will roll. Starting with mine."

"Do you think the fact that both maids worked for the Woodruffs and were killed within a week of each other makes this the work of one man?"

"Don't you?"

"It seems that way, but I bow to your expertise."

"I think it does. I plan to question every one of their servants strenuously. And then I'll question the household."

Joe choked back an involuntary laugh. "I don't envy you."

"I'm not looking forward to it. I might learn something from the servants, but I don't expect any cooperation from the family. Charles and I never liked each other by half."

Will started to climb back up the rocks to the road. Joe put a hand on his arm, stopping his progress. "You don't think Charles might have anything to do with these murders? My God, he was with the vixen sister from Barbados. They didn't admit it, but Charles Woodruff and Madeline Manchester were here first. I think it was she who screamed, not the maid."

"You saw them?"

Joe thought back. "Not at first. I was on my way home. I had just come out the front entrance and was walking toward the road when I heard a scream. It was coming from this direction, so I ran to see if I could help."

"And you saw them down on the rocks."

"I saw movement. I called out, and when I didn't get a response, I climbed down. That's when I saw the maid lying on the sand. I ran to her and felt for a pulse, but it was too late. There was nothing, and her skin was cool." Joe stopped, searched Will's face. "She wasn't killed just now."

Will shook his head. "No. Rigor mortis has set in. I'll have to consult the coroner, but I'd say she's been dead for several hours at least, possibly as long ago as last night or early this morning."

Joe stared at him. "How can you know that?"

"It's my job."

"I wondered what she would be doing out here in her uniform. It doesn't make sense. Is there a chance that this would clear Orrin? If he was still in jail when she was actually killed?"

"Possibly, but convincing the authorities of that a second time around might not be so easy."

The bonfire had lost its allure, and Swan's magic act had been forgotten. Most of the guests had retreated to the veranda, and those who hadn't hurriedly left the party were standing in clusters, except for several women who lay on chaises with their vinaigrettes.

Deanna found Cassie and Vlady.

"What took you so long?" Cassie asked, grabbing Deanna's hand and pulling her away from the others. One quick look around, and Vlady joined them.

"What was she doing out there? She's one of our maids." Cassie's voice trembled. "Why is he picking on us? Two girls from our household. Who will be next?"

"Stop it, Cassie," Deanna said urgently. "Don't you dare get hysterical. That's all we need."

Vlady had his arm around Cassie's waist again. This time it seemed to be more protective than seductive. "Dee's right, Cassie. You don't want all these people speculating about something that probably has nothing to do with us. Isn't that so, Dee?"

Deanna was pretty sure Vlady was seeking reassurance for Cassie's sake, but she didn't have much to give. The murders might have been committed because of some servant feud or some madman who preyed on young working women—she'd heard of that happening. And she and Elspeth had read many tales, though none quite this disturbing.

But Deanna seriously doubted that either of those possibilities was the correct one. She shuddered to think that Claire was killed because of Daisy, and Daisy was killed because of—what? Something the maid had seen? It sounded just like the title of one the stories they read. *What the Maid Saw.*

Deanna knew she had an active imagination. She'd been accused of that often enough by her mother and her governess. But she wasn't imagining this. Daisy had wanted Claire to write something for her. She'd been frightened away before she could tell Claire what it was. And then—

"Isn't that right, Dee?"

"What? Oh, I'm sure Will Hennessey will find the culprit. We just need to stay calm."

She hoped that answered whatever Vlady had asked her, because she'd become totally absorbed in her own musings. She smiled at him and went back to them.

Daisy had held an envelope with Orrin's name written on it but with nothing inside. Because she'd been taking it to Claire and had been stopped on her way? Or—

"Girls, girls, come along. We're all going home." Mrs. Woodruff waved to Deanna and Cassie. And Deanna became aware that people were leaving in droves. Didn't Will want to speak to any of the others? Ask if anyone had seen anything?

"I can't believe this is happening again. Mr. Woodruff has gone to summon our carriage. Charles and Lord David and Madeline have already gone in the first carriage. What did we ever do to deserve this?"

It was a good question, Deanna thought. Now, if they could just figure out the answer before it happened again.

"I'll see you out," Vlady said, and took Mrs. Woodruff's arm.

Deanna caught sight of Herbert standing off to the side, looking as far from the gregarious clown as he ever had.

Deanna was tempted to go over and see if he needed anything, but Vlady hustled them all off the veranda.

The one person she didn't see was Cokey, but the next time she did, she would give him a piece of advice not to make a fool of himself, and then she would give him a piece of her mind.

Vlady saw them into the carriage and shut the door. "I'll call on you tomorrow, if I may, to see how you're doing after this terrible tragedy."

Cassie reached for his hand as it was resting on the door, but at that moment the carriage pulled away.

"Well," Mrs. Woodruff said, pulling off her gloves, "I don't know what's happening to this town. Or to my staff. Why would someone pick on my girls?" She stopped, her hands arrested in the process of pulling off her second glove. "Unless they're not the only ones. Some madman might be killing housemaids all over Newport! No one will be safe."

Mr. Woodruff patted her knee. "I'm sure this is just an isolated villainy."

"Two, Francis. Two isolated villainies. And I take exception to being singled out. It's almost as if someone was doing it to spite us."

"Nonsense, dear. You're just upset. And you have every right to be."

Deanna was awed by how calm he was. His business was being questioned, members of his staff were being killed, his son was angry at him, and Deanna's father had argued with him, yet since his return from Barbados, Mr. Woodruff seemed to alternate between lethargy and agitation, joviality and depression. Tonight, he sounded dismissive of the two deaths, and that was very unlike him.

Something was going on that Deanna didn't understand. Whether it had anything to do with the murders of the two Woodruff maids was beyond her understanding. A mare's nest.

She looked around the carriage. The Woodruffs were the friendliest, most welcoming family she knew. They knew how to have fun, and if the higher social beings didn't always approve, their money kept them from being ostracized.

Monday they would go to tea at Gran Gwen's, and Deanna would tell her about her fears. She was sure that Gran Gwen would know what to do.

When they arrived back at Seacrest, Deanna went straight to her room and rang for Elspeth. It was close to midnight, and she had no intention of spending any more time with the people downstairs. She wouldn't be able to look Charles and Madeline in the eye. Or Lord David.

Elspeth came flying out of the dressing room. "Sorry, miss," she said between whoops of breath. "They've let Orrin out of jail. I ran down home to see Ma and the little ones and he was there." She sucked in a breath and let it go. "I didn't expect to see you back so soon. But when I was walking back, I saw the carriage coming up Ocean Avenue so I ran the whole way."

"Orrin is at home? They released him from jail?"

"Yes. Isn't that wonderful?"

"Oh no! Oh Lord, no. When did they let him go?"

Elspeth's mouth dropped open. "This afternoon." Her voice was quiet now. No longer excited, but wary. "What is it, Miss Deanna?"

Deanna pulled a chair close to the dressing table. "Sit down, Elspeth."

Elspeth stared at the chair like it was the pit of hell instead of a pink-slippered boudoir confection. But after a stern look from Deanna, she sat, hands clasped in her lap.

It tore at Deanna's heart. Elspeth looked like so many of the maids she'd watched her mother chastise. Of course, none of them had ever been asked to sit. But they'd all worn that same expression of bewilderment and unease that Elspeth showed now.

Deanna dropped down on her knees beside her.

"What is it, miss?"

"When did you go to see Orrin?"

"Orrin? Why, I didn't leave here until all of you left for the bonfire."

"And was he at home or at the workshop?"

"At home. Miss Deanna, you're scaring me. What's the matter?"

Deanna tried to swallow. Her mouth felt dry. She ran her tongue over her lips. Best just to say it and be done. "There's been another murder."

For several heartbeats, the two women just looked at each other. Then Elspeth's hand flew to her mouth and she started shaking her head.

"Elspeth, get ahold of yourself. I need to know when you saw Orrin."

"Who is it? Where?"

"The maid Claire. The one that came to us about Daisy wanting her to write a letter."

"Her? But no one said a thing downstairs."

"I doubt they know yet. We only just now found her body on the rocks near the Beach Club."

"What would she be doing there? The housekeeper here is very strict about girls stepping out any time of the day, but especially now after Daisy. . . . Besides, our folk don't go to Bailey's Beach. We're not allowed there. We go to Easton's. And Orrin wouldn't go either place. He can't swim. No. It weren't Orrin who did it. It can't be Orrin. I saw him. Why would he?"

Deanna let her run on until she had to take a breath. "I'm sure he didn't, but it's best to know what to expect. So, when did you see him?"

"I went as soon as you left. And I meant to come back earlier, but Orrin was there. Does that mean they won't arrest him?"

"I don't know. How long had he been home?"

"Ma said he came in while she was putting her take-in laundry through the wringer. Musta been about three or four."

"And he was there the whole time?"

Elspeth bit her lip. "I guess so. I mean, he wanted to go tell Mr. Joseph he was out, but Ma wouldn't let him out of her sight. They were squabbling about it when I got there. But he was going there now." Elspeth looked at the mantel for the clock. "I left him not twenty minutes ago."

Deanna let out her breath. "Well, we found her at least an hour and a half ago. So if he was home all afternoon . . ."

"Sergeant Hennessey won't let them take him again, will he? It'll kill my ma if they take him away again."

"I don't think so. I'm sure he's safe for now. Tomorrow we'll go make sure."

Elspeth nodded and slumped down in her seat. "Poor girl. Poor Daisy, poor Claire. What's happening in this house, Miss Deanna? Something's not right."

"No, it isn't."

"Did you see her? Claire?"

Deanna nodded. "Lord David's manservant had just finished his magic act—"

"The voodoo man," Elspeth whispered.

"He's just a big black man who knows magic tricks," Deanna said, trying to convince herself as well as Elspeth. But the timing of the scream just as the lights went out . . . It sent a shiver down her spine.

"We heard a scream, and Vlady said, 'Over there.' And we all ran to the rocks over past the common beach. And Vlady found her and we all went to see, and—" Deanna stopped. "Just like he found Daisy. Wait a minute. He found both girls. And Herbert. Herbert was with him both times."

"You think those two—"

"No . . . but doesn't it seem a little coincidental? Almost like they knew where to look. But no, they couldn't, because this time they found Joe kneeling over the body."

"Mr. Joseph? No, miss. He's not that kind of gentleman. Orrin says—"

"I think we can dispense with 'Orrin says' for a moment." Elspeth nodded.

"Then Will and some other men came, just like the other night. And a policeman took photographs."

"He never."

"He did. All around what Will called the 'crime scene.' But something strange happened."

Elspeth's eyes widened and she leaned forward.

"When we got there, Vlady had beaten us and he was holding a lantern overhead. There was Joe and behind them was Charles Woodruff and Madeline Manchester."

"They'd come to see, too?"

"They were standing beyond Vlady and Joe and the dead girl. I think they were already there, or somewhere nearby. And up to no good."

"Why, that— My ma would wash my mouth out if I said what she is. Making up to Adelaide's intended *and* doing those unnatural things with her brother. Mr. Charles should know better." Elspeth fell silent. "Maybe that voodoo man put a spell on him."

"I think if anyone's casting spells, it's Madeline and not Swan."

"Are you going to tell your mother?"

"I don't know. But until Will finds out who really killed those girls, I don't think you should go anywhere alone. In fact, I don't even want you sleeping in the servants' wing. Have one of the parlor maids make you up a bed in the dressing room."

"But, Miss Deanna, I might be able to learn something if I stay with the other maids."

"I don't care. From now on we stick together."

There was a *rat-tat* at the door and they both jumped. Deanna shooed Elspeth into the other room, then stood and fluffed her skirt. She glanced at the dressing-room door, where the door was left open an inch, just enough for an enterprising maid to keep an eye and ear on her mistress.

"Come in."

The door to her bedroom opened. Madeline slipped in and closed it behind her. "I think I should explain."

Chapter

17

It took Deanna a second to get over her surprise at seeing Madeline dressed in a white-and-gold night dress.

Her hair was unclasped but not yet put up for the night. It flowed around her shoulders like golden threads.

Madeline did owe them all an explanation, but Deanna wasn't sure she wanted to hear it. She considered playing dumb, and saying, "Whatever do you mean?" But Madeline was not slow. So Deanna motioned to the chair Elspeth had just vacated.

Madeline sat down. *Reluctantly*, thought Deanna. Well, she should be contrite. Then Deanna remembered what her old governess used to say about catching flies with honey. And even if Deanna couldn't quite accuse Madeline of being that disgusting insect, she still didn't like her very much right now.

Deanna sat on the dressing table bench. And waited.

There was a brief but awkward silence, then Madeline

blurted out, "I saw you looking at Charles and me on the beach, when we discovered Joe kneeling over the dead girl."

Deanna held her tongue.

"You're probably thinking that we shouldn't have been there—together."

Deanna tilted her head coldly. Having watched her mother all these years, Deanna knew how to make someone squirm. Unfortunately, it didn't have the usual affect on Madeline, who sat demurely looking into her hands, the picture of unhappiness.

Deanna started to thaw.

"We were just walking. I've seen Swan doing his magic show so many times, and Charles suggested that we look at the view from the top of the rocks. And it was so lovely, until—"

Deanna began to have doubts. Maybe Charles had loosened his waistcoat while he was sitting on the sand. Some of the fellows had taken off their jackets. In the dark he might not have noticed that he'd buttoned it wrong.

But they'd been standing so close. And they really shouldn't have been walking out alone, regardless, especially since Charles was an engaged man.

"We were standing there looking over the water, and I know it probably wasn't the correct thing to do, but you see, things are much different in Barbados, and I sometimes don't remember that manners are much stricter here."

Still Deanna waited. She wanted to believe Madeline, mainly for Adelaide's sake, but recalled the image of Charles with his arm around her, her head on his shoulder. . . .

"I was feeling faint, seeing that poor girl and Joseph Ballard leaning over her. It was such a shock." Her eyes brimmed with unshed tears. "It was terrible."

"Weren't you the first to find her?"

Madeline blinked quickly several times. "What? No. We were standing above, and Charles—well, I'll tell you, but please don't tell Cassie—Charles and I saw something, so we climbed down and there they were. And I screamed."

"That was you?"

Deanna didn't remember Madeline volunteering that information to Will. "Why didn't you say so when we were all there? We thought it must have been Claire."

"Who is Claire?"

"The girl who was killed. Her name was Claire."

"Oh." Madeline pulled a lace handkerchief from her sleeve and dabbed at her eyes. "I was afraid. I'm not one of you, and I thought people would get all the wrong ideas. That's selfish of me, I know. I suppose I am a selfish creature. But beyond that, how could I say anything when I would've had to tell them that your friend Joseph was the murderer?"

"He wasn't." The denial rolled out before Deanna could stop it.

"Oh, my dear, I know he's your friend, but he was there, kneeling over her. What else was he doing there, down among the rocks?"

This wasn't what Deanna had expected. Another damning accusation against Joe. She needed to talk to him and get him to tell her exactly what was going on. What he was doing on the cliff, when he'd just left her a few minutes before. Meeting the maid? It didn't make sense.

And what could she say to Madeline, looking lovely and repentant and innocent, and yet whom Deanna had seen kissing her own brother? Deanna could barely repulse a shudder.

"I don't usually get so hysterical. But with the murder of

the first maid and now this? Well, things like that just don't happen in Barbados . . . at least not that I've ever been privy to." Madeline lowered her head, the golden curls reflecting the light. "Can I tell you something?"

Deanna nodded slightly. "I guess." She wished she'd tell her something that made sense.

Madaeline looked up. "And you promise you won't tell anyone?"

Deanna wasn't sure about that, but she crossed her fingers and nodded again.

"You may hate me."

"Just say it." Deanna smiled quickly, hopefully looking sympathetic while she chastised herself. *More flies with honey, more flies with honey.* "You can tell me. Anything." She smiled again, but her heart was pounding. She didn't like misleading people, but in her few months in society, she'd learned that it was common practice and sometimes necessary. Besides, Kate Goelet had been known to prevaricate in the course of an investigation. And what was this if not an investigation?

"I do like Charles. Actually"—Madeline paused to dab at her eyes—"I love him. And he loves me. I know he's engaged to your sister, and I don't blame you if you never speak to me again, but I have to be honest. We didn't mean for it to happen. It just did. I think he was feeling depressed because Adelaide is so sickly and he's afraid that she will always be sickly."

Cassie's words burned in Deanna's mind. *With Adelaide always getting the headache, it can't be fun for him.*

"I know we're doomed not to be together."

Deanna had a hard time keeping her countenance. Charles Woodruff was no Romeo.

"But I'll be leaving soon. As soon as David finishes up this sugar business with your father and Mr. Woodruff, I'll go back to Barbados, and Charles will forget about me and marry your sister." Two large tears appeared from her swimming eyes. This time Madeline didn't try to stop them from rolling down her cheeks. "And I—well, I'll get over him, too—in time."

Deanna didn't know what to do with that confession. Her first reaction was to say, *Take him. Why would Adelaide want someone so fickle and disloyal?* But she didn't know what Adelaide would want, so she held her tongue.

"Please forgive me, and don't say anything. Nothing will come of it, and everything will go back to normal when we're gone."

Deanna doubted that. She'd never be able to look at Charles Woodruff again without thinking he was a two-timing cheat.

Madeline looked heartbroken sitting there with her head bowed, the light shining down on her penitent pose, but Deanna just wanted to tear that lovely blonde hair from her head. *Innocence Driving the Harlot from Her Home.*

But Deanna wasn't exactly innocent and Madeline wasn't exactly a harlot . . . was she? *Flies with honey*, she reminded herself.

Deanna stood. "Well, it's unfortunate, but it isn't too late to save your"—Deanna nearly choked on the next word—"reputation. And if Charles truly loves you, then what can I say to it?"

Madeline looked up, searched her face through her tears.

"You should probably get some sleep. Things will look better in the morning," Deanna said.

Madeline stood slowly. "Thank you." She took Deanna's hand and pressed it, then hurried from the room.

Deanna waited until the door closed before she wiped her hand on her skirt.

Elspeth stuck her head out the half-closed dressing-room door. "Is she gone?"

Deanna nodded.

Elspeth stepped into the room. "I don't like her."

"No. Nor do I trust her." Deanna sank back on the bench. "But what are we going to do about her and Charles?"

"I say good riddance. Maybe when the Manchesters go back to Barbados, they'll take Mr. Charles with them."

"But just think of the humiliation to Adelaide."

"Women get over humiliation, if they're smart. You don't get over a loveless marriage."

"Elspeth, I had no idea you were so philosophical."

"It isn't philosophy. All you have to do is look around. Hardly any woman in your class is happy."

Shocked, Deanna said, "My mother is."

"Because she always gets her way."

Deanna couldn't deny that. "What about Mrs. Woodruff?"

"Because what she don't know don't hurt her."

"What do mean?"

"Sometimes I wonder about you, Miss Deanna. Because Mr. Woodruff's quite a womanizer . . . among other things."

"No," Deanna replied, shocked. "I know some men are, but not Mr. Woodrfuff."

Elspeth sighed. "Most of your menfolk are. Mr. Woodruff is no exception. You know all those trips he goes on?"

"For business."

"Well, he's not against mixing some pleasure with it."

"Mr. Woodruff? I don't believe it."

"Well, the laundry maids know better than you or Mrs. Woodruff."

"The laundry maids? He wouldn't."

"Wouldn't he? Most of the men take advantage of the servants or keep a fancy lady in town. Then there's the gambling."

"All men gamble a bit. It's expected."

"And how many have blown their brains out because they lost their wives' money?"

Deanna blinked.

"Maybe it's best you don't know about these things. We're so busy reading about poor working girls and lady detectives . . . They oughta write books about poor rich women. They say Mr. Woodruff already spent his inheritance. All this house and stuff was paid for by Mrs. Woodruff's money. And half this side of town laughs at her behind her back."

"How do you know these things?"

Elspeth sighed. "Miss, if you want to know what really goes on in these fancy houses and these richer-than-anything families, just ask someone belowstairs. They hear and see it all, and they are not above talking about it. Heck, that Colonel Mann with his *Town Topics* will even pay for a good tidbit for his newspaper. The rich will pay him even more to keep it out of the paper."

"They do?"

Elspeth nodded. "Where do you think he hears all that nonsense he writes about?"

"Do you gossip?"

"You gonna let me go if I do?"

Deanna thought about it. She would have to tell her mother. "What do you say about us?"

Elspeth smiled slyly. "Don't you wish you knew?"

"Elspeth!"

"Oh, don't be such a priss. I only tell enough to get by. Mainly about your mother and how she rules you girls with an iron glove. I make fun of her, just a little bit, so's I'm one of them. Just enough so people will share what *they* know. You can't survive in service if you don't tell the others a little something. They won't take to you. And that makes life miserable. But don't you worry none. I don't tell anything too bad." She laughed. "Actually, they all think I have a dull time of it and feel sorry for me. I've never had anything that the newspaper would pay for."

Deanna just looked at Elspeth in bewilderment. She was Deanna's best friend besides Cassie. Had she been wrong to trust her?

"Oh, Miss Deanna, get rid of that puss. You know I'm true blue to you." She grinned. "And a poet."

Deanna tried to smile, but her world had just shifted. Had her mother been right about her letting Elspeth take too many liberties? But she didn't want some aloof companion who saved her from fashion faux pas, and even saw her naked, yet whom she couldn't trust.

Elspeth turned serious. "I shouldn't've told you all these things. But it's the way of the world. Servants talk. So does the butcher and the dressmaker, and sometimes you folks tell on each other. But don't you worry none, Miss Deanna. I would never betray you. You should know that by now."

Deanna sighed with relief. "I believe you."

"You should. We got each other's backs, and that's the way it oughta be."

"That's why I want you to sleep next door," Deanna said, harking back to the conversation they were having before Madeline interrupted them.

"And I told you—"

"I know. But two maids tried to tell someone something. And both are dead."

"Everyone's scared downstairs. But you should be careful, too."

"You think whoever it is will start murdering the cottagers?"

"I don't know about that. But I do know one thing."

"What's that?"

"You'd better watch out for that Lady Madeline. I don't trust her not to try to take Mr. Joseph, too. Some women just can't help themselves."

"And some men can't, either, as we've learned about Charles. Like father like son. And if Joe is one of those men, she can have him, too."

"Oh pshaw. Mr. Joseph ain't like that at all. Orrin sa—"

"Don't."

"Sorry, but Mr. Joseph is a good man and my brother says so." Elspeth grinned at Deanna and ducked as the hairbrush whizzed by her head. She picked it up. "You gotta aim better than that." She placed the brush back on the table.

Deanna fought a smile, lost the battle, and laughed. "You are so provoking."

Elspeth laughed, too. "I'll go get your nightdress. You pick out what we're going to read tonight."

Deanna knew what she wanted to read. She'd glanced through the coverless copy they'd found in Daisy's room. But now that she had a copy with a cover on it, she would start at the beginning.

She reached into the dresser drawer and lifted out the brown wrapper that held her two new magazines, slid them out on the bed, and saw the yellow paper sticking out of the top one.

The telegram. She still had the telegram for her father. She pulled it out turned it over. She'd meant to give it to Mr. Woodruff as her father's proxy, but after overhearing his conversation with Charles, and seeing the way Charles had been acting with Madeline, she was afraid to trust either of them with it.

If Mr. Woodruff took advantage of the house servants, would he kill the girls to keep them quiet?

Did her father expect as much? Surely he wouldn't have left her here if it wasn't safe. But it was becoming more obvious that her father didn't trust Mr. Woodruff with their business.

Maybe Deanna shouldn't trust either of the Woodruffs with this telegram. The only person who had knowledge of the company business and whom she could truly trust was Joe.

Or she could just open it herself.

⸺•◦○◦•⸺

Joe paced along the brick floor of the shop. The machines were all shut down, and his footsteps echoed in the cavernous room.

He hadn't bothered to turn on the lights, and he could barely discern their shapes in the darkness. But these machines were his future—he hoped. And the future of R and W. Just because he didn't enjoy the day-to-day running of the business didn't mean he didn't care about it. He cared a lot. And he had something concrete to offer.

He'd asked his father to give him a year to try to increase efficiency in the refining and the delivery processes. Improving efficiency and producing at a higher volume was the only way they could compete against the giant Sugar Trust.

And his machines would be safer for the workers.

They would still have to buy sugar from growers who had no concern for the men and women who worked their plantations under hideously hot and dangerous conditions.

Joe didn't think things had to be like this just to get a profit.

He was in the minority, of course. He'd been called an air dreamer, a nutcase, a communist, and a fool. Let them call him what they would. Soon they'd all be coming to him, or someone like him, to increase their profits, and Joe would make the life of the workers just a little better at the same time.

Meanwhile, he'd be damned if he'd let American Sugar take over R and W like it had so many other refineries. Bought them up or shut them down, paid them off, cheated them, sabotaged them, destroyed men's livelihoods. Havemeyer, who controlled the trust, didn't care. So far nothing had stopped him in his insatiable hunger to control all sugar refining in the country. Not strikes, not the courts, not his conscience.

Havemeyer wasn't alone; there were the Rockefellers and Vanderbilts, Carnegie, Gould, Fisk, Morgan. Lust for power and wealth was cutting out the middle class in every arena; it trounced the working class, took advantage of the poor.

Joe supposed it had always been like that. And maybe he was a communist to think that people should live in harmony with one another. An attitude his father attributed to Grand-mère and her freethinking ways.

But tonight he wasn't just thinking about sugar.

He was trying to figure out why two maids in the same household had been killed. Was it coincidence that Cokey had run into Joe and Daisy on the street? Why had Joe been the one to find that second maid? Were they the victims of some madman? Could it be someone from the Woodruffs' own household?

Joe really needed to get Deanna out of Seacrest—the sooner the better.

Deanna.

He rested his elbow on the mechanical arm of the bagging

machine. He loved machines, wanted to spend his entire life among them. But he would also like to go home to something—someone—warm and soft who would talk back to him, laugh with him, make love to him.

But that would have to come later. How much later, he couldn't pretend to know. It was imperative that they get this raw sugar deal and that he make machines that could help them compete in a shrinking market.

R and W wouldn't go down without a struggle. Not if he had anything to do with it.

Chapter
18

Deanna ripped open the telegram. "This is from Joe's father."

```
ANOTHER OFFER FR. H FOR MY SHARE OF R & W.
IMPORTANT THAT WE TALK PLEASE RETURN TO CITY
```

Deanna turned the telegram for Elspeth to see.

"Who is H?"

"It has to be Mr. Havemeyer. He's the head of the Sugar Trust, and he's been trying to buy R and W for years. Now he's trying to get Joe's papa to go against mine and Mr. Woodruff."

Elspeth shook her head. "I don't know why they can't leave each other's businesses alone. I guess men are just plain greedy. Like boys and their marbles."

Deanna frowned. "I suppose so, but with a lot more at stake than some colorful glass."

Elspeth rested her chin on her fist. "But your papa is already in the city."

"I know. And surely Mr. Ballard has contacted him by now. But what if he hasn't? What if he doesn't expect him in the city until Monday? We'll have to go to the telegraph office first thing Monday and send papa another telegram telling him to see Mr. Ballard first thing. I hope it isn't too late."

"Well, it's too late for you to still be awake. Now turn around or we won't have time for any reading tonight."

Deanna changed into her nightdress, then sat down to have Elspeth comb out her hair. While Elspeth began pulling out pins, Deanna reached into the drawer.

She didn't open the magazine but spent a long time looking at its cover. "I think we need to turn this over to Will." Deanna yawned. "But for tonight . . . I've had enough about poisoning and murder for this week. How about Loveday Brooke in *The Ghost of Fountain Lane*?"

<hr/>

The breakfast room was empty when Deanna came down Sunday morning. She was relieved not to have to make conversation.

She didn't feel much like eating, but she also didn't want to sit in her room like the others were doing if they weren't still sleeping. She hadn't slept well at all, and she knew her eyes were a little sunken and her cheeks were pale. The thought made her feel a little sad, because it made her think of her mother always telling Adelaide to pinch her cheeks.

Deanna looked around to make sure she was alone, then pinched her own cheeks. *Mama was right about some things*, she conceded. And wondered what her mother would do if two of their maids had been murdered.

Her lip trembled; she wasn't exactly laughing and not exactly crying. But uncomfortable. Her mama would never allow murder in Randolph House.

The baize door opened and Neville entered carrying a coffee tray.

"Good morning, miss. Coffee?"

"Yes, please." She felt embarrassed to be sitting here alone like the mistress of the house. It was a lonely feeling. Maybe it was because the Seacrest breakfast room was almost as large as Randolph House's dining room.

Neville poured coffee, moved the sugar and cream closer to her. "Do you care for toast? There are eggs and ham on the sideboard. As well as porridge. But if there is anything else you desire . . ."

Deanna shook her head. "No, that will be all."

Neville bowed and left the room.

Deanna quickly brushed a tear away. She was feeling a little homesick this morning. Which was silly. Still, she wished she were home. If she were at home, she would be going to church. She liked church, especially here in Newport. But of course she wouldn't go by herself, and this morning, when she'd been told that the Woodruff family would not be attending, Deanna had actually felt relieved.

She knew people would be paying more attention to the Woodruffs and whispering about their two murdered maids than attending the words of the sermon.

She finished her coffee and went upstairs to get her sketchbook, then walked out to the cliffs to sit by the sea. There were several boulders perfect for sitting, so she didn't bother to ask for a chair to be set out on the lawn.

She skirted the topiary hedge and cut through the garden. The hydrangeas were in bloom, fat and delicate as glass that had been filled with the color of the sky.

Deanna continued until she was at the walk. No one was about, so she sat down and opened her book. But she didn't start drawing, just looked out to sea.

Her world had shuddered this week. That two servants of a prominent family could be murdered here in Newport—or anywhere, for that matter—was just beyond comprehension.

She didn't believe the maids had done anything wrong, though both had worked for Mr. Woodruff, and if what Daisy said was true . . . But that just made no sense. If all gentleman carried on in such a way, there would be no reason to kill the objects of their . . . feelings.

It must be something else that bound both girls together. Was it that Daisy and Claire were friends? Or that Claire had been teaching Daisy to read? Could it have been one of the other servants?

That must be it. A jealous servant, or one who had interfered with both of them and killed them when they'd threatened to tell.

But surely Daisy would have told Orrin or Elspeth if that was happening. Unless she'd been too ashamed. It wasn't fair that the maids were preyed upon and then brushed aside. Leaving them without reputations or references was bad enough. But to kill for that?

Abominable.

Someone must know something. Even if it was one of the

guests, someone must have seen. Though she supposed that, from a distance, maid and killer would look like any other couple. No one would pay any attention. Might not have noticed if she suddenly disappeared.

Vlady had discovered both bodies. Was that significant or just coincidence? Vlady was always doing adventurous things. It was reasonable that he *would* find something like that.

She sighed. It was just as reasonable that he'd known where to find them. But why lead everyone there? To keep from being suspected? No one would think of accusing the person who'd pointed out the crime. But how many stories had she read where the villain appeared as a friendly, well-mannered gentleman who, after gaining the heroine's trust, turned out to be a horrible monster?

Herbert Stanhope was friendly and well-mannered, kept them all laughing. He'd also been at both discoveries. Now that she thought about it, he hadn't stayed to wait for the police at Bailey's. She'd looked for him and he'd been gone.

But that didn't make *him* the murderer.

And then there was Joe . . .

"Miss Deanna."

Deanna yelped and her sketchbook slid off her lap.

"I beg your pardon," Neville said as he stooped to collect her notebook and the pencil that had fallen with it.

"You startled me." She scrambled to her feet.

"My apologies, miss." He handed her book and pencil back. "Miss Cassie and Lady Madeline asked me to say they desired your presence in the morning room."

"Oh, is that all?" Deanna brushed off her skirt. "I'll come at once."

He bowed, and she preceded him up the lawn to the house.

Cassie and Madeline were sitting in the morning room, a carafe of coffee and tray of pastries between them.

"We're picnicking," Cassie said, with what Deanna thought was forced enthusiasm. "To soothe our wounded souls," she said, and sighed theatrically.

Deanna thought the idea of eating pastries as a display of mourning missed the mark.

"Mama sent our regrets to Mrs. Callum that we wouldn't be attending her 'hen' luncheon today. She said it would be unseemly in view of recent events."

"Is your mama feeling under the weather?" Deanna asked, glad of the cancellation. She hadn't relished lunching with a dozen women, all chattering about whatever came into their heads.

"Not ill, exactly. She just isn't quite the thing this morning."

Who could blame her? Though, eschewing society because of something as scandalous as murder might only cause more speculation. Sometimes it was better to just brazen it out and get it over with.

"Perhaps spending a few hours reflecting wouldn't hurt us," Deanna offered.

Cassie rolled her eyes. "Oh, Dee, sometimes . . ."

"She's right," Maddie said. "We've been so busy partying that we've barely thought about those poor girls. We're very self-absorbed creatures aren't we, Deanna?"

"Yes, we are," Deanna agreed. Though Lady Madeline's attitude won her back a smidgen of Deanna's esteem.

"I suppose you want to read sermons," Cassie said on a yawn.

"No. What a thoughtless thing to say."

Cassie huffed. "I know. I'm sorry. It's just so boring to sit around and do nothing. And then Papa and Charles insist on taking Lord David to New York on the ferry tonight. They might be gone all week."

"Well, at least there will still be plenty of men to dance with," Deanna consoled.

"Yes, but . . ." Cassie glanced at her. "But won't you miss Lord David?"

"I'm sure we all will, but I don't want to sit here and dwell on our misfortune." With that, Deanna left the room, primly she supposed Cassie would say. But she just had no patience for her friend's whining today.

But on one score she was right. It was going to be a long day.

The gentlemen left for the ferry around five o'clock, joining the other husbands, sons, and guests who took the ferry back and forth each week.

Some kept their yachts at the ready so they didn't have to wait for the ferry, but the ferry was almost as sumptuous as one's own parlor, and there was plenty of entertainment for the men.

Dinner, like most Sunday dinners without the men in the family, was a desultory affair. Newport seemed to sigh with relief once the ferry pulled away from the wharf. Though Deanna wasn't fooled. It was the matrons who ran Newport, and any seeming relaxation was only a momentary pause to reenergize themselves for the power struggles that would begin again on Monday.

———◦◦◦>◦◦◦———

Cassie and Madeline and Mrs. Woodruff were in the breakfast room when Deanna came down on Monday morning. Deanna helped herself to eggs, tomatoes, and sausage from the buffet.

"Well, I think it's a bore," Cassie was saying. "What are we supposed to do while they're gone?"

"I'm sure you'll think of something," Mrs. Woodruff said.

As far as Deanna was concerned, they could stay gone. Hopefully, Mr. Ballard and her father could finally cinch their deal, and Lord David and his sister would leave before Adelaide got back.

Cassie sighed dramatically. "Stuffy old business. I'm sure Lord David would have rather stayed here," she continued. "Who's going to escort us to the musicale tonight? And we were supposed to go on Vlady's yacht this week. And the Howes' soiree. Oh, and the theater. Oh, Mama, don't say we'll have to miss the new play."

"Perhaps Vlady and Herbert would escort you to the theater."

"Vlady hates the theater. Well, he likes the farces but not real plays." Cassie sighed again. "I can't say as I blame him. Plays are boring, long-winded things."

"Well, I have an idea." Mrs. Woodruff smiled and twinkled at the girls. "We have the Latham-Jones musicale tonight, but why don't we have an impromptu get-together tomorrow night with games and maybe a few dances? It won't be a yacht party but it will help all our moods. Nothing too big, just the regular boys and girls. I'm sure Vlady will give up one yacht party. They can all come here."

"Oh, Mama, that sounds wonderful. Don't you think so, Madeline?"

"What? Oh, yes. Wonderful."

"What about you, Deanna? I promise not to invite Joe."

"Oh, you may invite anyone you care to. I'm sure it makes no difference to me."

Cassie raised a disbelieving eyebrow at her. "Well, this is a change."

Mrs. Woodruff dropped her napkin on the table and rang the bell. "Well, I'm sure I don't care what people are saying about young Ballard. I say invite him. But I must say, I don't know if you girls should encourage him until this"—she waved her hand as if to drive away an unpleasant word—"affair is concluded."

"Oh, Mama, you're beginning to sound like Deanna's mama. No offense, Dee."

"None taken," Deanna said.

"And if anyone doesn't want to come here because two maids have died, let them stay home." Mrs. Woodruff sniffed and reached for the telephone that connected her to her servants. "Neville, please inform Cook that we're planning a little get-together tomorrow night, just the young folks, but we'll need some light refreshment."

She rattled off several dishes she would like served, then hung up the device and clasped her hands together. "This is just what the doctor ordered. Fun and games. And a little champagne punch."

"Charades," Cassie said. "Maddie, do you play charades in Barbados?"

"In London, when I visit, but not often in Barbados."

"Let's see. Oh, I know. Blindman's bluff. That's always great fun." Cassie threw a roguish look toward Deanna. Deanna had no trouble reading her meaning. Blindman's bluff afforded excellent opportunities for a hug or a misplaced hand.

"And forfeits."

Mrs. Woodruff laughed. "Well, you girls plan it all out, then telephone a few of your friends." She heaved herself out of her chair.

Deanna rose, also.

"Where are you going?" Cassie asked. "Mama says we have to return calls this morning, and then there are invitation calls to be made."

"I actually have a few errands I need to do."

"Again? Send Elspeth. Besides, you can't neglect your duty calls just because your mama is out of town."

"Fine, I'll give you my card to leave along with yours. If you actually go in to visit anyone, say I was feeling peaked."

Cassie crowed with laughter. "You've never felt peaked in your life. Leave that to Adelaide."

Deanna couldn't help glancing at Madeline. Really, if she were going to keep looking so cast down and guilty every time someone mentioned Adelaide, people would start asking what was wrong.

"I'll just explain to your mama." She resolutely went into the solarium only to find that Mrs. Woodruff wasn't there. The doors to the garden were open, so she stepped out onto the brick terrace. Mrs. Woodruff stood at the edge, looking past the rosebushes to the sea.

Something checked Deanna's step, and as she stood there, Mrs. Woodruff brought a handkerchief to her eyes.

What on earth?

She started to tiptoe back into the house as Mrs. Woodruff turned. She sniffed, then put on a smile. "These roses are so lovely, but they always make me sneeze."

And your eyes water, and your lip tremble, thought Deanna. Mrs. Woodruff was walking toward her, and Deanna impulsively hugged her. "Is there anything I can do?"

"Oh, my dear, you're so kind."

"Whatever it is, I'm sure it will be all right."

"Of course. You're right, my dear. It's my nerves, with Mr. Woodruff being so poorly, then running off to the city with the young men. I don't mind telling you, I'm worried about him. He just doesn't seem himself. I thought he was rallying, but yesterday he looked positively ghostlike. I begged him not to go, Charles tried to reason with him, but to no avail. He insisted on going with them. Oh, listen to me carrying on. Pay no attention, dear."

"I'm sure Charles"—*the scoundrel*—"will take good care of him. And my father, too." At least her father wouldn't join him in his philandering. Would he? Did all husbands have mistresses?

It was a daunting thought. Well, if she were ever married, she wouldn't put up with it, not for a second.

"Now, I know you didn't come looking for me to see me at my unprettiest. What can I do for you?"

"Nothing," Deanna said, forcing a smile. "It's just that—oh, nothing. I just was wondering if you wanted me to come calling with you this morning."

"Of course I do. You're like one of the family."

Deanna nodded. "I'll just get ready." She'd have to send Elspeth to the telegraph office to— She stopped with her hand on the banister. No. Elspeth couldn't go out alone, even in the daylight. They would have to send one of the male servants. But whom could they trust?

No one.

——∞⊙∞——

Joe stripped off his shirt and poured water into the basin. He splashed it under his arms, then on his face and neck and was groping for a towel when it appeared before him.

Joe took the towel from Orrin, dried his face, tossed the towel onto the back of a wooden chair, and looked in the wardrobe for a shirt that was clean enough to wear to Ocean Drive. He'd never been bothered by the inconveniences of living in a factory during the winter, except that it had been devilishly hard to heat, but trying to go between his life in the Fifth Ward to his old life on Bellevue Avenue during the summer season was a first-class pain. He'd have to stop by home and refortify his wardrobe if he was to continue this double life much longer.

It was bad enough that someone had been siphoning funds out of the business for a long while. And the fact that R and W's entire survival was held in the hand of this sugar baron who had taken their money but, as far as Joe knew, hadn't committed his syrup. Didn't even seem interested. Neither Charles nor his father had brought Lord David by to inspect the new machinery. Will seemed to be making no progress in solving the murders. And Joe didn't know how he was supposed to watch over Deanna if she wouldn't even have anything to do with him.

He buttoned his shirt, realized a button was missing. Shrugged out of it and threw it on his cot, then sat down after it.

He didn't like being away from the workshop long for fear of spies and saboteurs. And he liked even less having Orrin stay alone while he was still under the eye of the police. One false move—or a move perceived as false—would have him back in jail. Besides, one lone man against armed saboteurs would be no contest. Joe didn't have any illusions about them not striking again, but surely they wouldn't attack in broad daylight. The workshop should be safe until Hiram's men came on duty. He'd just have to send Orrin home.

"There's a clean shirt in the drawer underneath," Orrin said. "Your grandma's servant brought a whole bunch of things down yesterday. I put 'em away for you."

Joe looked up. His tall and gawky apprentice, still grieving for his love, was taking care of the man who should be taking care of him. "Thanks."

He pulled open the drawer and found clean socks, underwear, and shirts, all neatly folded. Bless Grandmère.

Five minutes later, dressed in a pinstripe suit and with his hair parted, he stuck a straw boater on his head and stepped into the street. Orrin locked up and started down the street in the direction of his home.

Joe took one look at his bicycle and he decided to take a cab.

A few minutes later, the hackney stopped in front of Bonheur. Joe paid the driver, then trotted up the steps to ring the bell.

An echo of gongs rang from inside, and a minute later, Carlisle, his grandmother's ancient butler, opened the door.

"She's expecting you."

"Is she?" Joe asked, handing the butler his hat.

His grandmother was writing letters in the back parlor. She was swathed in a turquoise morning wrapper embroidered with humming birds and hyacinths. Her gray-streaked hair was swirled to the back of her head and held in place with an ivory comb of monumental proportions. She didn't bother to turn around when he hurried in, merely stuck out her hand to be kissed.

"You're a witch, you know."

She laughed. "Ha."

He held her hand and kissed it. "A very fetching witch—bewitching."

"You should be that charming with someone closer to your own age."

"Grandmère—"

"Don't bother, I've heard it all before. They are coming to

tea this afternoon, the three of them. Cassie, Deanna, and their visitor, Lady Manchester."

"Are they?"

"Yes. I want to get a closer look at the Barbadian beauty."

"Good. I'd like your opinion of her."

His grandmother raised a disapproving eyebrow.

"Not for any personal reasons. I just value your insights. But that can wait. I came to borrow a carriage."

"Ah."

"I need to talk to Deanna alone. And don't comment. I'm afraid she's in danger in that house."

At this, his grandmother turned and gave him her full attention.

"Then she must come here to stay. Why her mother left her in the care of the Woodruffs is beyond me. She should be giving her attention to Deanna instead of Adelaide, but it's always been the same. Do you think she'll go along with your scheme to speak to her alone?"

"Yes, even if I have to throw her over my shoulder and carry her to the carriage."

"Oh, how I should like to see that. But don't you dare. She's already survived one of your misdeeds. You don't want to wreck her first season. Give her some time to develop her cachet."

"I suppose you're going to encourage her to become an iconoclast like you and mother."

"I have no doubt that, given the opportunity, she will surpass us both."

"I shudder to think. So may I have a carriage?"

"Yes, of course. But take an open one and drive her down Bellevue so tongues will stop carrying on about how you jilted her."

"I did not jilt her! And now tongues will wag that we were seen together."

"Can't control tongues—might as well have them wag in your favor. Which leads me to mention, there are some nasty things being said about you around town."

"It's that damn Cokey Featheringham. He's always full of gas, and I don't think anyone actually believes him."

"I suppose you're just waiting for Will to find the real culprit."

"Do you have a better suggestion?"

"I'm afraid not."

"Right now, I have a greater concern than what people are saying about me. I want to talk to Deanna, and then I may have to make a trip to New York."

"Ah, are things coming to a head there?"

"I'm not sure. There's something very underhanded going on."

"And you will find out what, no matter the cost."

"Would you have me do less?"

"Not I. Now go, before the ladies have left for their morning calls."

"One other thing."

"Yes?"

"I plan to bring her here before tea. Will Hennessey will be joining us."

She nodded. "Ah. The plot thickens."

Chapter
19

With Deanna promised to go out with Mrs. Wood-ruff, she and Elspeth were trying to figure out how to get Elspeth to town without going alone or causing suspicion, when there was a knock at the door.

"I don't care if it is daytime," Deanna said. "I'm not taking any chances with your safety. We'll have to think of something else. Come in."

The door opened, and Cassie rushed inside and closed the door. "You'll never guess who's downstairs."

"My mother?" Deanna asked, her stomach turning itself into a knot.

"No. Joe Ballard. And he's come to take you for a drive."

"Joe? Here?"

"Yes. It's a bit early for driving out, but maybe living down there in the Fifth Ward, he's forgotten the finer points of court-ing." Cassie stopped and frowned. "Do you want me to send him away?"

"No! Wait. I mean, no. I'll see him. I suppose I will have to talk to him sometime. Tell him to wait and give your mama my apologies."

But Cassie made no move to leave. "Are you two going to make it up?"

"No, we're just friends."

"Oh, you're no fun. I'll tell him you'll be with him shortly." She bobbed a curtsey and finished with "miss" before she flounced out the door.

"That's so strange," Elspeth said. "Why do you think Mr. Joseph's here?"

"I have no idea, unless . . . maybe he read my mind."

"Oh, miss, that's not funny."

"No, it isn't, but I'm glad he came. Now he can take care of these things." She picked up the novel and the telegram.

"They won't fit in your purse."

Deanna looked around. "Bring me the moiré paletot. It will go well enough with this dress."

Elspeth looked skeptical but went to fetch the jacket and helped Deanna into it.

"Now put these down my back." She handed the book and telegram to Elspeth, who wrestled them into her waistband.

"Don't move around too much. You don't want them falling out."

"No, I don't. I'll be careful," she said, and let Elspeth pin on her new bonnet. "Wish me luck."

"Good luck," Elspeth said begrudgingly. "I wish I was going with you."

"I'll tell you everything when I get back."

Elspeth opened the door for her, and Deanna walked out, careful not to disarrange the book and telegram.

Neville greeted her at the bottom of the stairs. "They're in the parlor, miss."

"Thank you, Neville."

He crossed to open the door for her, and she went inside.

Joe Ballard was sitting on the edge of a chair, listening attentively to whatever Mrs. Woodruff was saying.

"Ah, here she is," Mrs. Woodruff said. "Deanna, look who's come to take you for a drive."

Joe stood and faced her as she came toward him.

"Joseph, how nice of you to call," Deanna said at her most poised—and stuck up enough to put him out of countenance, she hoped. She needed him, but he deserved a little comeuppance.

She held out her hand and felt totally ridiculous, especially when she saw him trying to smother laughter. His eyes twinkled and she wanted to smack him. But, unfortunately, those days were gone.

He leaned over her hand, kissed the air above it, and let it go, but not before he winked as he lifted his head.

She felt the blush flood her cheeks. *Damn him.*

Mrs. Woodruff beamed at the two of them. "Joseph has asked to take you for a drive and then to his grandmother's. I don't think your mother would mind."

Deanna shook her head minutely. Her mother would not mind if it were Lord David asking her out to drive, but Joe had fallen in her mother's good opinion when he'd refused their engagement and moved down with the "riff and raff," as Mrs. Randolph called the families who lived in the Fifth Ward.

Her mother had never cared for Gran Gwen or Joe's mother, Laurette, considered them too bohemian, despised them for their ideas on women's suffrage, and suspected them of espousing free love. But even the latter had not been cause enough for her to turn her back completely on their society or their money.

"Shall we go?" Joe said politely, but there was mischief in his eyes.

Deanna gritted her teeth to keep from bursting out laughing at the stupidity of the situation.

Joe bowed to let her pass through the door to the foyer, where Neville waited to see them out. He handed Joe his hat, and they went down the steps to Joe's curricle, which was drawn by a pair of beautiful bay horses.

Joe helped Deanna into the seat, slipped the post boy a coin, and then climbed in the other side. They were soon through the gates.

Deanna immediately turned to him. "What the heck was that all about?"

He glanced at her, surprised. "Which part? The part where you said, 'How nice of you to call,' sounding like an elocution teacher, or the part where Mrs. Woodruff said your mother wouldn't mind?"

"I meant the part where you kissed my hand and acted like Herbert Stanhope. Which is okay on Herbert but ridiculous on you."

"Alas."

"And who's taking care of these horses while you're living down at the warehouse?"

"Ah, leave it to you to get to the important stuff."

"Well?"

"I keep the stable hands on. And I take them out when I can, which isn't often. I've been quite busy."

"So it would seem."

"Oh, Dee, cut it out. It's one thing to act like Miss Priss in front of other people; they expect it. But can you drop the attitude with me?"

Deanna frowned at him.

"That's more like it. I've missed that scowl."

"I'm trying to rid myself of it."

"Did your Mama tell you it wasn't ladylike?"

"For years." Deanna sighed and dropped all artifice. "It's been like a holiday, having her gone. I'm sorry Adelaide is unwell, but it's such a relief not having to try to please Mama constantly—and failing most of the time."

He reached over and tugged one of the carefully controlled curls that hung about her ear. "Well, you can scowl at me anytime. As long as you don't really mean it."

"How's Orrin?"

"Okay. But jumpy. He expects the police to come back and arrest him at any moment. I don't like to leave him by himself for too long."

"Then why have you?"

"Because you and I need to talk. Besides I sent him home."

"Oh." She adjusted her seat. The magazine was beginning to slip, but she couldn't very well take it out while they were on a public road.

"Is something wrong? Are you uncomfortable?"

"No, but—" Deanna templed her hands at her mouth. "Joe, maybe I did a bad thing."

"It wouldn't be the first time. What?"

"Well, when we left you the other day, I stopped by my house to pick up some things. And there was a telegram for my father. I took it, meaning to give it to Mr. Woodruff."

"Did you give it to him?"

"No. Something happened before I could that . . . well, it's complicated. But I decided that if it was important, I would somehow get to the telegraph office this morning and send Papa one telling him what it said."

"After you read it, of course."

Deanna shrugged. "Well, how else would I know if it were important or not?"

"Fair question. So, what did it say?"

"It was from your father, saying that Mr. Havemeyer had made him another offer for his shares in R and W, and for Papa to come to New York immediately. But he's already there."

"Yes, and they've met. I heard from my father."

"So I don't need to send it on after all?"

Joe shook his head. "My father sent it to urge your father to come back early, which he did on his own and went straight to my father. I think they will be able to handle this on their own."

They'd been traveling south on Ochre Point Avenue, but now Joe turned west.

"Your father isn't going to sell, is he?"

"Of course not. But there are . . . troubles with the company."

"Troubles? What kind of troubles?"

Joe looked straight ahead.

"You can tell me. I know a little bit about business."

Joe gave her a smile that said he was humoring her.

"I know if R and W goes under, we could lose everything."

Joe glanced over. "Not everything, Dee. You'll be okay."

"Is the business in trouble because of something Mr. Woodruff has done?"

Joe's hand tightened on the reins. The horses came to a nervous stop. "What do you know?"

"I overheard him and Charles talking."

The horses pranced in place, anxious to go.

"Where are we going?"

"To Grandmère's. I hope you don't mind. Will is meeting us there."

Deanna perked up. "A powwow."

Joe laughed out loud. "Something like. So you can tell us both what you overheard."

"I will if we can go down to the beach before the others come for tea."

Joe didn't answer.

"Joe, I haven't been to the beach since we arrived in Newport except to that horrid magic show. I want to get my feet wet." She heard herself and knew she sounded like the peevish brat she'd always been when she tried to get her way. Well, she didn't care. She was being stifled by corsets and good manners. And following the rules. She wanted to get her way for a change. Even if just for a walk on the beach.

Joe turned to look at her. It was a look that she didn't recognize. Not sad, not like the old fun-loving Joe, but something that made her feel unsettled, heated, and very close to bursting into tears.

"Please, Joe. Don't you ever miss the old days? Remember when we would go down and go wading in the surf? You and Bob would swing me out over the waves."

He sighed. "Good days gone forever."

He sounded so resigned that it made her sad. Bob had been his best friend, and she had been . . . his best friend's little sister. She shook herself.

"Why? Why are they gone forever?"

"Because Bob is dead and you will soon become a society lady."

"And what about you, Joe?"

"Me?" He smiled—wistfully, she thought. "I'm going to revolutionize the sugar refining business."

He turned away and settled back on the seat. Clucked the horses into a trot.

Deanna didn't try to talk anymore. It seemed they could never go back to the way things had been. *Good days gone forever.*

A few minutes later they turned onto Bellevue Avenue and drove south again toward Bonheur. Joe stopped the curricle at the front steps and helped her down while the groom led the horses away. Joe followed her up the steps, but before ringing the bell, he said, "If we have time before the ladies come, we'll go down to the beach. But don't you dare let it get back to your mother."

"I won't." Deanna smiled, feeling truly happy, she realized, for the first time since the end of last season.

Gran Gwen was sitting in the conservatory with Will Hennessey.

"Ah, there you are," she said, and motioned Deanna and Joe in. "I've told Carlisle that I'm not at home—to anyone. We'll have lunch on the terrace. It's a lovely day and no wind to speak of."

Was it a lovely day? Deanna had barely noticed it. Nor did she notice it now, because she was studying Will's face. He didn't look happy, and she was afraid he had more bad news to report.

Will stood, shook hands with Deanna, and nodded to Joe. They all sat down again, creating a circle with Gran Gwen as its focal point. And Deanna remembered younger days, when Bob had been alive, how the four of them would sit at Gran Gwen's feet listening to her spin tales of exotic places and people, never quite sure if she were telling actual happenings or making it up.

But today wasn't meant to be entertaining or spent reminiscing, and Deanna fidgeted in her seat thinking of what she knew she must tell them.

"My dears, let's get this nasty business taken care of so we may luncheon without black clouds hanging over our heads."

Joe and Will both turned to Dee.

"Well," Will said. "Tell us what you know and wouldn't tell us at the beach the other night."

She swallowed or at least tried to. Her mouth was dry, and her throat seemed paralyzed.

Gran Gwen gave her an encouraging look.

Deanna told them about Charles wanting to speak to his father. "I was sure he was going to break his engagement, the way he's been mooning over Madeline. And I thought, *Forewarned is forearmed*."

"Very right," Gran Gwen said.

"So I hid in the Seacrest library and listened."

"Oh my Lord." Joe shot his fingers through his hair.

Deanna ignored him.

"But instead, Charles confronted Mr. Woodruff about the money he'd given Lord David without getting a binding contract, and that now he wants to give him more."

Joe leaned forward. "Mr. Woodruff planned to give him more?"

"I think so. And Charles was upset about that and about the Manchesters dining with the Stanhopes since Mrs. Stanhope is a Havemeyer." Deanna frowned at them. "I think Charles suspects a . . . a . . . double cross."

Her announcement didn't have the effect she'd thought it would. Will put his hand over his mouth. Joe laughed outright.

Only Gran Gwen looked serious. "When you two boys get over the giggles, you should mark Deanna's words. That scoundrel Havemeyer will use anything at his disposal to get what he wants. Always has. Though he isn't alone. Seems there's not one honorable man in business these days."

"Excepting my father," Joe said, suddenly serious. "And Dee's father. And perhaps Woodruff, but that remains to be proven."

Grandmère raised a dismissive hand. "Francis has always been a fool. The only intelligent thing he ever did was to marry Nell Peabody and join forces with George Randolph and your father to create R and W, though I suspect she had a hand in that as well. It was her money to be sure.

"He's already gone through his own fortune, and he'll go through Nell's, too, if she doesn't watch out. If he hasn't already." Gran sighed, a weary sound. "But women invariably choose to look the other way. Even someone as savvy as Nell Woodruff."

She pointed a finger at Joe. "But that's her choice. As far as the business goes, Joe, if he's playing fast and loose with the company's money, he'll have to be stopped. Sooner rather than later."

"That's the other thing," Deanna said, feeling a bit more courageous. "After he left, Charles looked through a ledger and whatever he saw in it upset him terribly."

"You didn't get a look at it?" Joe asked, but Deanna knew he was just being facetious. She wished she could hand it over.

"No. He locked it in Mr. Woodruff's desk."

"Dee, you have to stop doing these mad escapades."

Deanna jumped up. "They're not escapades. Elspeth and I have found out more than you and Will both."

"She's got you there," Will said from where he was lounging in an overstuffed chair.

"Father and I will take care of it," Joe said.

"How? And what about my father? You don't think he's cheating the company do you? How could you?"

Joe stood. "I don't think that. But someone is monkeying with the company's funds. There are rumors of R and W stock floating round. If they get into Havemeyer's hands, we're in big trouble."

"Stop yelling at me!"

"I'm not yelling!"

They realized at the same moment that they'd both stood and had been arguing over Gran Gwen's head.

"Oh, I am sorry, Gran Gwen." Deanna sat down abruptly.

Joe sat more slowly.

Gran Gwen waved the air. "Don't mind me. I love a good squabble."

"I think this is more than a squabble. Joe practically accused Papa of being a thief."

"I did not."

"Children, enough. Joe has said he doesn't think that. But remember what that delightful character in Mr. Conan Doyle's novels says."

Everyone looked at her.

"Well, I forget exactly what he says, but it's something about looking at all the possibilities, even if they don't seem possible, until you come to the right one."

Deanna forgot for a minute what they were talking about. "You read Sherlock Holmes?"

Gran Gwen put on a prim expression. "I read a lot of things."

"Excuse me, ladies," Will said. "But could we get back to our own situation?"

"Sorry," Gran Gwen said.

"So what happened after Charles returned the ledger to the desk?" Will asked.

"Well, I don't quite know."

Will waited.

"I was tired, and emotionally . . . wrung. And he stayed so long. I was up in the balcony and I couldn't get out until he left. I—I . . . fell asleep."

"You what?"

"Shut up, Joe."

"Yes," said Gran Gwen. "Do shut up."

"Anything else?" Will's mouth was twitching, and Deanna thought if he laughed at her, she would just get up and leave. She didn't need to be laughed at when she was trying to help, and besides she really wasn't looking forward to telling them about the other thing she'd witnessed that night. But it might be important, though Deanna didn't know how or why. Still . . .

"Is that all?"

"Not exactly."

Across from her, Joe groaned and hid his face in his hand. Which was just as well. She didn't want to see his expression when . . . She cast an anxious look at Gran Gwen.

"It's all right, dear. You just tell them what you know."

Deanna took a breath. "When I woke up, it was late, and Charles was gone, so I climbed down and went to bed."

Will closed his notebook and started to put it back in his breast pocket.

Deanna rushed ahead. "I was almost up the stairs when the front door opened. The Manchesters had been out to dine at the Stanhopes—"

"The Stanhopes again," Joe mumbled.

"Shh," Gran Gwen said.

"So I hurried up the stairs hoping I could get to my room before they came up. I didn't want them to think I was spying on them."

"Oh no, not that," Joe said with a laugh.

"Joseph, if you can't mind your manners, you'll be sent from the room."

"I beg your pardon, Grandmère. And yours, Deanna."

Deanna didn't think he looked sorry.

"And did you make it to your room?" Will asked.

Deanna looked at him gratefully. He always was more serious than the other two. More sympathetic. More understanding.

"Deanna?" he prompted.

"No. They were coming up the stairs, but I knew I couldn't get down the hall before they reached the landing, and they might see me running away, so I slipped behind a cabinet in the hallway." She glanced at Gran Gwen, who nodded to her. The small gesture gave Deanna the courage to blurt out the rest.

"When they got to the landing, they stopped and she— he—they—kissed. But not like a sister and brother kiss. Like lovers kiss. Then his hand . . ."

"That's quite enough, Dee," said Gran Gwen. "And very succinctly told. I believe we all get the idea."

Will was staring at Deanna like she'd sprouted horns. Joe was staring at her, too. He wasn't laughing now. But she couldn't tell what he was thinking.

"Are you sure it was not brother-sister affection?" Will said cautiously.

"Bob never kissed me that way. And I don't think brothers and sisters kiss that way in Barbados, either."

"And then what happened?"

Deanna thought back. She'd been so shocked, she hadn't been paying attention. "She pushed him away and said they had to be careful, but that it would only be a little while longer."

Joe sprang to his feet. "Until what?" He faced Deanna.

"That's all she said. Then they went down the hall to their rooms, and I went back to mine."

Joe began to pace the room. Stopped and addressed Deanna. "Are you sure of what you saw?"

Deanna nodded.

"Not that their relationship has anything to do with the sugar industry," Gran Gwen said.

"Maybe not," Joe said. "Regardless, the man's not even interested in sugar. From the little he's said to me, I doubt if he knows the difference between a condenser and a centrifuge."

"Perhaps, my dear, he's one of those effete Britishers who'd rather ride to hounds or sit back with his sherry and let the overseer take care of the business. He does have an impeccable lineage."

Joe snorted. "Lineage doesn't run businesses."

Will cleared his throat. "I know you're all worried about the company, but I don't see how disappearing money from R and W, or even the antics of the Manchesters, can possibly have anything to do with the murder of two maids."

"The murders are my fault," Deanna said.

Chapter
20

"What?" Both men and Gran Gwen stared at Deanna. "Well, not Daisy, but I'm responsible for the second one, Claire."

"How do you figure that?" Joe asked.

"Just let her talk," Will said. He turned to a new page in his notebook.

There were so many things starting to add up in her mind, but how to present them so that they made sense and didn't have the boys—men—rolling on the floor laughing at her?

"Let her tell it in her own way with no interruptions." Gran Gwen gave Joe an intent look.

His mouth tightened as if he were holding his argument in.

"Go ahead, Dee."

Deanna nodded.

"To begin with, Elspeth was worried about Orrin, so when Mama had to take Adelaide to Boston, and we went to stay with the Woodruffs, we . . . Well, Elspeth asked if she could take Daisy's things back to her family, and Mrs. Oates, the housekeeper, said that she might. So we—"

"We?" asked Will.

"With a murderer loose, I didn't want Elspeth to go alone."

Will nodded. Joe just looked horrified. Deanna was afraid to look at Gran Gwen. She had no idea what that lady might be thinking of her.

"We gathered up Daisy's clothes and found her books under the mattress."

Will nodded. "I remember seeing them."

"We always loaned Daisy our dime novels when we finished them." Deanna cast an apologetic look at the other three, who looked slightly scandalized. "Well, they're more interesting than the young ladies' magazines."

This time it was Gran Gwen who laughed.

"But we found one with the cover stripped off. You didn't take it, did you Will?"

Will shook his head.

"Oh, come on," Joe said. "Those books are so cheap most of the covers do come off."

"I know that, but Daisy was always very careful to return them in good condition. We didn't know what to make of it, until . . ." Deanna stood.

Surprised, the two men hastily stood also.

They all watched as she pulled back her jacket and reached behind her waist.

"What on earth . . . ?" said Joe.

She pulled the magazine gingerly from her waistband and held it out. "There."

Will lifted the book from her hand and studied it. "Dr. Pritchard, the poisoner? I remember the case. Scottish doctor who poisoned his wife. It was a sensation in its time, but that was years ago," he pointed out.

"I know, but they're still writing stories about him. And, more importantly, look in the background." She pointed to the image. "Look at the maid in the door, witnessing the poisoner."

Deanna saw the change in his expression. "You think Daisy saw something she shouldn't."

Joe took the magazine from Will and perused the cover, then handed it to Gran Gwen.

"But why tear the cover off?" Gwen asked. "She didn't want anyone to see it?"

"We wondered, too. So Elspeth went down to the servants' hall to see what she could find out."

She had everyone's full attention now.

"Nobody much wanted to talk to her. But later, Elspeth brought Claire to my room, and Claire told us that Daisy had tried to sneak out the night of the party to tell Orrin something, but someone stopped her."

Joe sighed. "That was me. So if anyone's to blame for Daisy's murder, it's me."

"Oh, piffle," Gran Gwen said. "Neither of you is responsible for those murders. But someone else is, and they must be stopped before it happens again."

"Let's stick to one thing at a time," Will said. "What did Claire tell you?"

"That when Daisy couldn't see Orrin, she asked Claire if she would write a note to him. Daisy doesn't read or write very well. I mean she didn't." *And now she would never learn.* "It isn't fair."

Gran Gwen reached over and patted her hand. "No, it isn't, my dear. But we can depend on Will to catch the monster that did this."

"None of the maids came forward when we asked them for information," Will said.

Deanna gave him a disbelieving look. "Are you surprised? The police aren't exactly their friends."

Will looked chagrined. "No, we have a lot to answer for in that department. Did Claire tell you what she wrote?"

"She never got a chance to write anything. Daisy was frightened away before she could tell her."

"You think Daisy tore off the cover as a message?"

"Yes. She couldn't write and she didn't have time to go back to Claire, so she put the cover in the envelope. She had an envelope when you found her."

"Yes, but it was empty."

"Because whoever killed her took the image."

"Why leave the envelope behind?"

"Don't be dense. Because it had Orrin's name on it. And you arrested him."

"It wasn't just because of the envelope. He had no alibi for her time of death."

"A lot of people didn't," Deanna said. "But everybody's ready to accuse Orrin, just because they heard his name was written on an envelope."

Will leaned forward, every muscle tense. "What frightened her away?"

"Lord David's man. Swan. He came down the stairs and Daisy ran."

"I think maybe I'll go have another talk with the magician valet."

"But he was performing at the bonfire when Claire was killed."

Will looked at her long and hard. "Claire was killed at least twelve hours earlier and someplace else. Her body was dumped there after she was already dead."

"How do you know this?" Gran asked.

"Forensics is a science. It can tell us much more about a murder than hot-tempered policemen who are willing to arrest the most convenient person while the real perpetrator goes free."

Deanna sucked in her breath. That was the most passionate speech she'd ever heard from Will. "So *that* explains it."

"Explains what?"

"When we heard the scream, we thought it was someone in danger. But it wasn't Claire who screamed. It was Madeline."

Will scratched his head. "Dee, you amaze me. She certainly didn't volunteer that information to the police."

"She told me," Deanna said. "She was trying to give me an explanation for why she and Charles were together in the dark on the rocks." Deanna turned to Joe. "It's terrible. She said they were in love and I wanted to scratch her eyes out. What do I tell Adelaide? She can't marry Charles now."

Will cleared his throat. "And did she say that she saw Joe kneeling over the body when she screamed?"

"Yes, but I don't believe anything Lady Madeline says anymore. She probably just wanted to take the attention off herself. Just out walking, indeed. Charles's vest was buttoned wrong. His valet would never let him leave the house in such a state."

Will leaned back in his chair and raised his arms in victory. "If I had even one officer with your brain, the crime rate in Newport would be cut in half overnight."

"Don't encourage her," Joe said. "You're not staying another night in that house, Dee. You can come stay here with Grandmère, you and Elspeth."

"Dee knows she's always welcome," said Gran Gwen. "Shall I send one of the footmen to collect Elspeth and your things?"

"Thank you, but we're no closer to catching the killer," Dee said. "We can't stop now."

"You can and you will," Joe said. He was practically yelling.

Deanna stood. "May I remind you, you have no right to tell me what to do." The barb hit the mark. Joe's suddenly ruddy cheeks drained just as quickly.

"I'm aware of that," he said in a subdued voice.

Will slowly shook his head. "None of the staff remembers seeing or not seeing her during the day. Either she was very unmemorable or, more likely, they decided not to cooperate."

"They're frightened," Gran Gwen said.

"All the more reason to help the police find the killer before he strikes again."

"Again?" said Deanna.

"No," said Will. "That's just my frustration talking. I beg your pardon. Still, please be careful."

"I will."

"And don't question the servants anymore."

Deanna shook her head. She'd learned her lesson.

"Good. That's settled," Joe said. "I don't have to worry about you. Because right now I'm more concerned about Woodruff's subterfuge."

"Well," Deanna said, shooting him a sour look, "with Mr. Woodruff and Charles having taken Lord David to see the refineries, Mrs. Woodruff is giving a party for the young people tomorrow night. I'm sure she will invite you, Joe." She cast an apologetic look at Will. "Though probably not you, Will."

"I'm quite used to being left off the guest lists. But I must say,

Joe, with you *and* Deanna on the scene—and the other men out of the house—there's no telling what you might find out."

Joe frowned at him, then there was a sudden glint in his eye. He was making a plan, Deanna thought. But would he include her?

Gran Gwen clapped her hands. "Good. Deanna can finagle you an invitation while we're having tea today, to which neither of you gentlemen is invited. And I'll plan a little soiree myself for an evening later this week. See what we can ferret out." Gran Gwen shared a smile with Deanna, then reached over to ring the bell. "It's time for luncheon. All this sleuthing has given me an appetite."

———◦◦◦)◦(◦◦◦———

There was no talk of murder during lunch. Gran Gwen was forward-thinking, but as she pointed out, manners were manners. Will stayed for lunch, but once he left, Deanna reminded Joe of his promise to go down to the beach with her.

"Delightful idea," Gran said. "But, my dear, you cannot go down to the beach in that dress, not if you plan to wear it to tea." She tugged at the bell pull. Two minutes later, Carlisle appeared. "Ask Minerva to take Miss Deanna upstairs and find something of Laurette's to wear to the beach."

"Does she have one of those new bathing costumes?" Deanna asked.

Gran Gwen raised an eyebrow. "As a matter of fact, she does. But you won't be wearing it when you're on the beach with Joseph and unaccompanied by a chaperone."

Deanna's face fell.

"When this is all over, we'll order you one of your very

own." Her dark eyes twinkled. "But we'll keep it here, and you won't wear it to Bailey's. Your mother would have a stroke."

"Oh, thank you. I've wanted one forever. And a tennis dress, like the one I saw in the Harper's catalogue."

"Very well, but go upstairs now and change into a day dress if you want to get down the cliff and back before the others arrive."

Deanna practically ran out of the room.

"Joseph," Gran Gwen said as soon as Deanna was gone. "That girl needs some freedom before that mother of hers sucks the life out of her."

Joe, who had just picked up a copy of the *Newport Mercury*, put it down again. "If you ask me, she manages to find plenty of freedom. Always has," he added.

"Yes, she's clever, but to no useful purpose."

Joe groaned. "Oh, Grandmère, don't say you're going to make a free thinker and suffragette out of her."

"Do you want a biddable ninny for a wife?"

"No. But I'm not marrying Deanna."

His grandmother shrugged.

"It surprises me that you would want me to honor an arranged marriage."

"Oh, piffle. How your two fathers came to make such a mess of things is beyond me. They are usually smarter men."

"You would have tricked us more subtly?"

"Is that's what is upsetting you?"

Joe sighed. "No. It's just that I'm . . . selfish."

This statement got two raised eyebrows—his grandmother at her most disapproving. "And how so? You've never been selfish."

"Because I have my work."

"And you can't have a life also? Are the two mutually exclusive?"

"I can't go traipsing around to balls and yacht parties with grease under my nails. Or talk about the latest winner at Saratoga when I'd rather drive one of the new motorcars."

"Heaven forbid."

"And I wouldn't marry someone and leave her sitting alone in one of our cavernous houses, unlooked after and free to carry on all sorts of liaisons."

Gwen threw back her head and roared with laughter. "Oh, my dear boy, give her a wrench and put her to work on one of your inventions."

Joe stared at his grandmother, but before he could think of anything to say, the door opened and Dee walked in wearing a white frock with slimmer sleeves than the current fashion and with a short enough hem that he could see her feet and ankles. It took his breath away.

He heard his grandmother humming a tune under her breath.

"Shall we go?" Dee said formally, then exploded the mood by running to his grandmother and twirling in a circle. "It's so beautiful. Much too beautiful for the beach."

"My dear, it's exactly what to wear at the beach. And it looks just ravishing, doesn't it, Joseph?"

"Ravishing," he said. He gestured toward the French doors. "Shall we?"

"Yes, we shall." Dee cut him a saucy look, not flirtatious but triumphant.

As soon as she reached the lawn, Deanna took off, arms stretched in the air. For a moment all he could do was watch. He hadn't been around for her New York season, but seeing her now, free like the old days, made him realize how stifled she'd been and how much she deserved to be out from under her mother's thumb.

It was all well and good for Adelaide. She was made for society. But Deanna . . . Deanna should have been born a Ballard, that would be the atmosphere in which she could thrive. The thought brought him to his senses.

He had to run to catch up to her.

She was already sitting on a boulder, her skirt hiked up to her knees, her shoes sitting neatly to one side.

She glanced up at him. "Don't look."

Joe shook his head and turned away, but when he felt her lean over to pull off her stockings, he looked anyway.

"You weren't supposed to look."

Joe shrugged.

"Well, take off your shoes, too. Or have you grown too old and decrepit over the winter?"

"I'll show you decrepit." Joe shucked off his jacket and untied his tie and tossed it after his jacket. Then he took off his shoes and socks, and rolled up his pant legs. When he turned back, she had tucked her skirts up and was already clambering down the wooden steps that led to the secluded beach.

"Dee, slow down. It might be slippery." The warning only made her go faster. She didn't slow down when she reached the sand, but ran straight to the water and didn't stop until she was ankle-deep in the surf.

"Ah," she said as Joe picked his way painfully across the rocky sand.

She watched him approach, shaking her head the whole time. When he got close, she kicked water at him, spraying his ankles and wetting the folds of his trousers.

"Hey."

She kicked again.

"Stop it."

She laughed and leaned over to use her hands.

Joe gave up. If she wanted a water fight, she would get one, and his grandmother's maid could have the dubious pleasure of putting her together again before tea.

He, on the other hand, would take a hot, luxurious bath— one of the things he missed most about living as he did—then change into one of the many suits that still hung in his closet.

Water sprayed his face.

"Okay, that's it." Joe ran into the water, and a kicking war commenced and didn't stop until they were both drenched and out of breath from laughing.

Suddenly Deanna stopped. The joy fled and she became serious again.

He stepped toward her and saw there were tears in her eyes. "What is it?"

She shrugged.

He stepped closer, gave her a little shake. "Come on, Deedle-dee, you can tell me."

She looked up at him, tried to smile. "I miss my old life."

When she was younger and she'd skinned a knee or her governess had scolded her, he'd sit beside her or put an arm over her shoulders and cajole her out of her unhappiness. But he didn't think that would work now. And he knew that putting his arm around her now wouldn't have the same effect it once had. At least not for him.

He wasn't sure about her.

He did take her hand. "Let's climb over the rocks and look for tide pools, and you can forget for a while that you have to put your shoes back on and sit through another abominable tea."

"It won't be abominable, not here. And it might help things if Gran Gwen can observe Madeline Manchester."

"You don't like her."

"I did at first. She's very beautiful and fun-loving, but how could she be in love with Charles when she kissed her brother like that? And how could she let Charles fall in love with her, when he's affianced to Adelaide?"

"I'm afraid that happens more than we'd like."

"I know men continue to have affairs after they're married."

"Have you been talking to Grandmère again?" He tried to make light of things but she wasn't having any of it.

"Elspeth says Mr. Woodruff is a philanderer. She said she doesn't know whether or not Papa is, too. But if she knows about Mr. Woodruff—"

They'd been walking at the water's edge but now Joe stopped her.

"I don't think your father has affairs, and I think that's to his credit."

"Because Mama is so controlling?"

"Most men would look for relaxation elsewhere, but he loves your mother. My father said so." Joe grinned. "And if my father said it, it must be true."

"Does *your* father have affairs?"

"I don't know. My mother travels a lot, as you've probably noticed. But . . ." How did he explain that his father and mother behaved more like a man normally did with his mistress? "They have a somewhat unusual situation among their class. Let's just say they make each other happy."

She gave him a quizzical look.

"Really, Dee, let's talk about something else."

They started walking again.

"Okay, what are we going to do tomorrow during the party?"

Joe looked toward heaven. "I haven't worked it out, but I have to find out what is in that ledger. You're going to stay at the party and make sure no one follows me when I leave the room."

"That's no fun."

He dropped her hand, grabbed her shoulders with both hands, and turned her around. "This is not about fun. This is about finding out who killed two members of the Woodruff household. It's about saving R and W from imminent bankruptcy. It's about making sure no one else gets killed. It's not an adventure."

"You mean it's not an entertainment. I'm not so stupid as to think it is. But I want whoever did it caught, too."

"Then do what I ask."

She nodded. He could tell she didn't like her role, but he also knew Dee. She would do what was needed.

Chapter
21

Thanks to Gran Gwen's maid, Minerva, Deanna was safely changed back into her visiting dress, her hair dry and repaired, and she was sitting with Gran Gwen when the door chimes rang and Carlisle showed Cassie and Madeline into the front parlor.

Tea was served, the conversation was vivacious, and Deanna heard Gran Gwen laugh several times at things Madeline said. Deanna tried to join in, but she was torn between trying to hold on to the feeling of freedom she'd had with Joe at the beach and worrying about what he planned to do tomorrow and if it would be dangerous.

Though when Gran Gwen mentioned her plans for a soiree, she thought she did a good job of showing as much enthusiasm as Cassie and Madeline. They were back in the carriage before Deanna realized she should have been listening more closely.

"What's the matter, Dee?" Cassie said as the carriage made its way back to Seacrest. "Did you and Joe have another fight?"

Deanna shrugged and looked out at the passing vista. "We had some things to . . . talk about." She couldn't tell them what was really worrying her.

"Did you make up or did you give him his congé?" Madeline asked.

"I'm not sure, though I did take the liberty of inviting him to the party tomorrow night. I hope that's okay."

"Of course it is. Why do you even ask? Are you sure you're feeling well?"

"Yes, fine. I'm just—"

Cassie trilled a laugh. "Thinking. Deanna's always thinking, Maddie. She's so droll."

"I think women should think," Madeline said. "Don't you?"

"Yes," Deanna said.

"Oh, I don't know," Cassie said. "I suppose it's okay if you have nothing else to do. But there always seems to be something to do." She took in a deep breath. "I think about Vlady and what we almost did on the beach the other night."

"Cassie," Deanna said, "don't do something stupid."

"Not that. Just enough to keep him interested."

Madeline laughed. "Slowly reeling him in, Cassie?"

"Well, I sure as heck hope so. He's dreamy and rich, and doesn't have to go to an office or business everyday." She cast a saucy look at Deanna. "Not like Joe."

"Joe likes to work. He's creative." And he was probably richer than any of them, or would be when his father died.

"Well, he must be back in your good graces."

"Not really. Can we talk about something else?"

Conversation turned to talk about their own party the following night. Cassie and Madeline had spent the day telephoning or calling on their friends in person with invitations to the evening's fun and games.

"There'll be as many as thirty people coming, maybe even more. I told Vlady that he and the boys should bring their friends. It will be such a crush." Cassie sighed and looked at Dee. "Too bad Lord David will miss all the fun."

Deanna could tell by the look that what she was really saying was: "Too bad Lord David won't be there to outshine Joe."

"My brother will be sorry to miss it," Madeline said. "He loves games, and he's great at charades and twenty questions." She sighed. "But business comes first."

They were two blocks from Seacrest when the sky suddenly turned dark.

"Just an afternoon thunderstorm," Cassie assured Madeline. "I just hope it doesn't keep up all night. I thought it would be fun to play forfeits outside in the moonlight tomorrow."

"Cassie, really."

"Oh, Dee, you're getting a bad as your mother."

"I'm not." Was she? She wasn't shocked at Cassie's behavior. She didn't even think it was wrong necessarily. But the outcome of a passionate dalliance could have long-ranging repercussions, from gossip and innuendo to worse. It would be horrible for Cassie. Or any girl.

As soon as they arrived at Seacrest, Cassie and Madeline went to their rooms to rest and dress for dinner and the musicale they were invited to that evening. Deanna went to her room to do the same, but also to apprise Elspeth of what had transpired with Joe and of their plans for the next evening.

"What should I do?" Elspeth asked as she scooped Deanna's dress from the floor.

"I guess just make sure none of the servants come up to light a fire in the library or anything, or try to warn Joe before they get there."

"I doubt if they would. With Mr. Woodruff out of town, no one else will likely go in there." Elspeth picked up the stockings and shoes Dee had discarded.

"Did you go to the beach?" Elspeth held up the stockings. "Sand."

"Yes, at Bonheur. And Elspeth, it was so much fun. I miss having real fun. Fun without having to answer to Mama or any of the old biddies in town or my peers or to some man."

"Did Mr. Joseph go with you?"

"Yes. But today he was Joe. The Joe he's always been." Deanna threw herself backward onto the high poster bed. "And I liked him so much more than I remember."

When Elspeth didn't leave to carry her things away, Deanna turned her head to see what was keeping her. "What?"

"You could do worse than Mr. Joseph."

Deanna rolled to her side. "Not you, too."

"I'm just saying what's what."

"Well, don't. I think I'll wear the peach organza and taffeta tonight."

"Yes, miss." Elspeth gave what Deanna called her ironic curtsey.

Deanna turned to her other side. She'd felt something different for Joe today. And she was intrigued about what he'd said, about his parents making each other happy. She had a feeling he didn't mean over the breakfast table, but in more intimate situations, and she found herself curious as to what those things might be.

On that thought she closed her eyes and didn't open them until Elspeth awoke her to dress for dinner.

Deanna really wasn't in the mood for a musicale at the home of the Latham-Joneses. She normally loved music, but she had too many things on her mind to be able to concentrate on the performers, of whom Deanna was sure there would be many.

They were already going to the Howes' later in the week to hear a famous soprano who was appearing at the Metropolitan Opera House.

She distractedly let Elspeth dress her in her new gown, which had arrived only a week before from Paris. Her mother had insisted on it, though Deanna had complained that the sleeves were so puffed that she couldn't see around them.

Her mother's only comment was, "Don't be ridiculous, Deanna." And she'd ordered it delivered at their Newport address. It seemed like a lifetime ago. The dress was made of a light ecru paneled in a floral motif of blue, gold, and aubergine, cinched at the waist with a brocaded aubergine sash and bow with matching sleeves. Elspeth was already buttoning it before Deanna realized what she was wearing.

"Not this one," she complained.

"Your mother will ask if you wore it. And this is as good an evening as any. And then we can pack it away."

Deanna sighed and pulled at the neckline. Deanna's figure was slight; she didn't have a "handful," like Cassie had, anywhere. But there was nothing she could do about that.

Elspeth gave her a sour look.

"I know, it's hopeless. I'll never have an 'interesting' décolleté. I hardly have any décolleté at all."

"Nonsense. Don't you listen to Cassie. You have just what you need. Now, turn around and let me fix that bow."

All four of the ladies climbed into the carriage at eight o'clock. None of them looked very enthused about a musical evening. And Deanna knew it was going to be a long evening when she saw the harp being set up for Olivia Merrick.

At least they didn't have to sit and listen as if they were in an opera house. People wandered into and out of the rooms in which entertainment flowed. There were naturally more women than men, with many of the husbands away in the city, but Mrs. Latham-Jones had supplied a few well-looking young men from Fort Adams to make themselves useful, engaging in conversation and fetching lemonade and cakes for unescorted ladies.

Deanna noticed that while most everyone welcomed Mrs. Woodruff and Cassie with sympathy and concern, there were a few who kept a wide berth. The Woodruffs had fallen off some hostesses' necessary lists. Deanna just hoped it didn't ruin the family entirely.

At least her mother was not privy to the happenings. She'd have made Deanna leave for certain. Sullied reputation by association.

The evening finally dragged to a close, and they drove back to Seacrest.

"I think we'll have a quiet day tomorrow and rest before our party," said Mrs. Woodruff.

They all agreed and went off to bed.

It seemed to Deanna that she had just closed her eyes when Cassie and Madeline woke her up the next morning. They were all excitement about the upcoming party.

But they hadn't stayed up half the night with Elspeth as she had, discussing what had transpired at Gran Gwen's, wondering about Joe's plan, and figuring out something that Elspeth could do to help. Then they read a few pages of a detective story until Deanna's eyes became too heavy to stay awake.

The day was overcast and dreary. It looked like it would be too rainy a night for playing forfeits in the moonlight. They'd be lucky if it didn't storm.

Somehow the day passed, even with Cassie's numerous stops to look out the window, sigh, and predict awful rain to ruin the evening.

Madeline finally ordered her to sit down and help with the charade phrases.

Everything was ready early, but they decided against the afternoon airing. It had already started drizzling, and no one wanted to get wet while being seen by the same people who always saw them on the five o'clock drive.

Since Neville was setting up a buffet in the dining room, they had an enjoyable dinner in the breakfast room.

Deanna was just going up to change for the party when she heard the door gong. And before she reached the landing, Neville said, "A telegram from your mother, miss."

———⊶✦⊷———

"So what did you make of Madeline Manchester?" Joe asked his grandmother as they sat over a dinner of boeuf en croute and asparagus.

Gwen patted her mouth with the fine linen that she used even when she was the sole occupant of the house. His grandmother had class—inborn, and through and through. It balanced out her adventurous streak, which would have gotten many another woman ousted from society.

"Charming enough. Though I don't recall the family. I

mean, how does one keep up with the English peerage? When their chins start to recede, I lose interest."

Joe choked on the sip of wine he'd just taken. "Really, Grandmère, you shouldn't say those things when the wine is red. I'm lucky I don't have to change my clothes before I go out."

His grandmother looked him over, as much as she could see above the tabletop and dishes. "You do look rather elegant tonight, though do you think wearing a white summer suit while rummaging through someone's office is quite the thing?"

"I suppose you would rather I wear all black and climb up by a rope to gain access through the window?"

"No, but I imagine Deanna would be impressed."

"Do not teach her to be reckless, please."

Gwen, who had just cut a bite of beef, put her knife and fork on her plate. "My dear, the girl is eighteen. She knows her own mind—she lacks only the liberty to exercise it. I'm thinking about asking Jeannette to let her come to Paris with me in the fall."

"I doubt that she'll countenance that. You know you are not Mrs. Randolph's favorite person."

"I would be horrified if I were. But I do know more European aristocrats than half the people in Newport."

"No details, please."

She laughed. "Those were good days—alas, gone forever. But," she said, growing serious, "I think she may be convinced of it, considering this situation with Francis Woodruff and the circulating stocks, and the possible disaffection of Charles—though once the scandal breaks, I doubt Jeannette will want to align her family to the Woodruffs. Still, having two girls jilted in successive seasons will be a blow to her ego, if not her standing in society."

"I did not jilt Deanna."

His grandmother waved away his denial. "That's between you and Deanna. As for Lady Madeline—I suggest you watch yourself around that one. She may have a bluer-than-blue-blooded lineage, may have been schooled in England, may have impeccable manners, may have an engaging façade she shows to the world . . ."

"But?"

"I can't put my finger on it, but there's something off about her. She's one who knows what she wants and is used to getting it."

"Maybe it's the way she kisses her brother."

"My dear, that sort of thing I'm sorry to say is more prevalent than we acknowledge, though you don't want to hear my views on that ninny Anthony Comstock and how his puritanical laws have forced so many relationships behind closed doors. The man's a fool, not to mention his attitude is downright criminal."

Joe nodded—the only safe response when his grandmother got going on Comstock, the self-proclaimed upholder of Victorian morals.

"His actions have sent people to jail, kept women from safe relations, and—"

"Grandmère."

Gwen sat back in her chair. "Yes, well, in the meantime, be careful. I don't need you in jail for burglary."

Deanna didn't open the telegram right away. She dressed in an elegant but deceptively utile dress in case Joe needed her to do something that required freedom of movement.

"You'd better go on and open it," Elspeth said. "You don't

want your mother showing up at the door tonight while you and Mr. Joseph are committing a crime." She picked the telegram off the dressing table. "You want me to read it to you?"

"No." Deanna took it, sat down on the bench, and sliced it open. Read through it twice.

"Well?" Elspeth asked.

"The good news is she's taking Adelaide to Switzerland for treatments and I don't have to go."

"Then why are you all mopey?"

"The bad news is she's sending Aunt Harriet to chaperone me."

"Is that the old— I mean, is that your mother's sister from Boston?"

Deanna nodded. "And she's even more strict than Mama."

Elspeth sat down beside her, and they both stared at the open telegram as if they could change what it said.

"I might as well go to Switzerland for all the fun I'll have."

"Me, too," Elspeth said. "Your Aunt Harriet don't like me by half."

"If it's any consolation, Aunt Harriet doesn't like anyone." Especially not the Woodruffs, and even more especially not Gran Gwen.

Elspeth stood. "Well, we'll worry about it tomorrow. Right now you'd best get downstairs. There's work to be done."

"You're right." Deanna gave herself a quick final look in the mirror, pulled her bangs to the side, went over last-minute plans with Elspeth, then went downstairs.

She thought it must be a slow night in Newport, for the guests began arriving soon after nine o'clock. Or maybe everyone just wanted to beat the worst of the rain. The drizzle had already turned to a steady rain. Thunder had begun rumbling in the distance right after dinner and had moved progressively closer. There would be a downpour before long.

The footmen had opened the pocket doors between the two parlors to create twice the space. Deanna was glad to see that the chairs and sofas were facing away from the door to the hall. Joe would only have to wait until everyone was absorbed in the games before he sneaked away.

It was a festive atmosphere with no chaperones other than Mrs. Woodruff and her sister, Tillie, who mostly sat in a corner of the room, unnoticed and unheeded as she knit her way through the evening.

The windows were open and a breeze came in off the water, and though it was evening, most of the men had opted for summer suits and the ladies were dressed in summer frocks for the informal get-together.

Deanna's mother would be dismayed by such a slip in form, but she wasn't here—nor was her aunt, yet—and times were changing. Deanna could feel it. Soon women would have the vote, and they'd be able to play tennis without tripping over their skirts or fainting because their corsets were laced too tightly.

She'd already seen young women riding bicycles along the streets. Joe had a bicycle. Perhaps he would teach her how to ride.

Joe arrived with a group of young men, and she had to admit that he stood out from the others with his dark hair and eyes, and his muscular frame inside his finely tailored jacket and trousers. Girls had always been casting their lures for him . . . until he'd moved to his workshop. Then mothers couldn't remove their daughters from his vicinity fast enough.

Male and female guests were pressed together on the several

sofas that had been pushed together to form a small arena for
playing charades and other games. Cassie was holding court
from a cushioned chair. Vlady Howe sat on the arm, looking—
Deanna rolled her eyes—down Cassie's dress. Herbert Stanhope and Cokey Featheringham stood before her. Madeline
was talking to a group of girls over by the pianoforte.

Joe didn't come too close to her except to say hello. He moved
from group to group, and Deanna noticed that some of the
people snubbed him. Two girls actually walked away when he
approached.

Deanna burned with indignation on Joe's behalf.

Punch and cakes were served, then they all took their places
back on the sofas while Vlady fetched the bag with the charade
phrases that Cassie and Madeline had written out earlier that day.

"Wait, wait," Vlady said. "We need some atmosphere." He
went around the room, adjusting some lamps and turning off
others until the room was dark except for a large oval in the
center of the room.

Everyone applauded. Just as Vlady took a bow, thunder
cracked behind him and the rain began in earnest. Two footmen rushed to close the windows.

"Now, this is cozy," Vlady continued. "Who will go first?"

Joe caught Deanna's eye and a thrill, half anticipation and
half anxiety, shot through her. It was starting. She turned to
join the guessing, and Joe slipped from her view.

The games started calmly enough but quickly grew boister-
ous, and Deanna was aware that Joe had left the room. Everyone was enthusiastic and jumped from their seats or called out
silly answers to the pantomimes.

The room filled with laughter but Deanna kept alert, listening for the door to open or for Joe to reappear, but he didn't

come. They would soon be moving on to a different game. Possibly a quiet game, and someone might notice he was missing.

What could be taking him so long? It was everything she could do not to go out after him. But she had her orders, so she stayed put.

The game continued, becoming more raucous with each new participant. Deanna smiled and laughed and kept one ear always on the door.

Perhaps that was why she heard the carriage arrive.

Mrs. Woodruff was nowhere to be seen, but Madeline must have heard it, too, because she quickly slipped from the room. Deanna didn't hesitate to go after her. She could always plead a trip to the ladies' withdrawing room.

Madeline had stopped just outside the room, and Deanna nearly bumped into her. Madeline whirled around, surprise written on her face. Then the door opened and Mr. Woodruff hurried through. Rain dripped off his hat brim, and his clothes were limp and wet.

"Welcome home, sir." Neville's voice didn't betray the surprise that he must have felt. The men hadn't been expected to return to Newport until the weekend. The butler tried to take Mr. Woodruff's hat, but he brushed him aside.

"The young people are gathered in the parlor. I believe Mrs. Woodruff is there, too," Neville said.

"Don't tell her I'm here. I'm only here for a moment to get something and leave again."

He pushed the butler away. And Deanna froze. He had turned and was practically running down the hall. To the library. Where Joe was rifling through the books.

"Mr. Woodruff!" she called, and hurried after him.

But Madeline had the same idea, and she reached him first.

"My dear sir, you look unwell. Come, have some wine. Surely your business can wait a few minutes."

Mr. Woodruff reared back like he'd seen a monster.

Deanna saw that his eyes were dilated and he looked feverish.

"He's ill," Deanna said, forgetting for a moment about Joe.

"He is indeed," Madeline said calmly. "Now come, dear sir. Let me help you to bed. You don't want to alarm Mrs. Woodruff. Neville, please have Cook prepare Mr. Woodruff some hot milk."

Neville bowed and hurried away. Deanna thought how much Madeline sounded like she was already mistress of Seacrest.

Mr. Woodruff shook his head, but he allowed her to lead him upstairs.

Deanna didn't know whether to follow them or try to warn Joe that Mr. Woodruff was home.

Joe won out.

She took one quick look around, then ran down the hall.

Deanna knocked at the door. No answer. She knocked again. "Joe. Joe." She waited impatiently, sure that at any moment Neville would return and see her.

Finally she tried the doorknob. The door opened. The desk lamp was on but the rest of the room was dark.

"Joe?" she said into the darkness.

Fear lifted the hairs on her neck and arms. Where was he? There were papers spread out on the desk, but it looked like they had been thrown there.

Deanna crept toward the desk. Something was terribly wrong. When she drew closer, she saw that all the drawers were open and papers were strewn across the floor. Joe would never have left such a mess.

She climbed over the papers intending to turn on another lamp, but her foot caught on something and she fell forward, just managing to catch herself on her hands and not step on the recumbent figure.

She turned around, tucked her skirts under her. "Good heavens, Joe. Get up! What's wrong? Oh—"

A clap of thunder was followed by lightning, and she saw what she had feared: Joe lay crumpled on the carpet. She didn't see any blood. She leaned over him until she could feel his breath on her cheek. *Alive. Thank God.*

Another clap of thunder and the rain pelted the panes of the French door that led outside. Then the lights went out.

A few screams of surprise that must have come from the party, then the sound of running. They couldn't be found here. Joe's reputation was already questioned because of Cokey's accusations. If they found him here with the desk obviously broken into—well, she couldn't let that happen.

"Joe, you have to get up." Desperate, she shook him, but he didn't stir. She grabbed his arm and pulled as hard as she could. But she couldn't budge him.

She tried again and managed to drag him six inches. If she could just get him outside, she would think up some excuse later. She just knew they couldn't be caught in the ransacked office. If Joe hadn't been unconscious, she would have kicked him. He'd obviously been knocked out by some unknown assailant who had then ransacked the library.

There were too may odd things going on in this house to stop and question the hows and whys now. They had to get out of this room. As she pulled, he rolled to his back, and she saw that he'd stuck some papers in his vest.

"Joe, so help me." She grabbed him under both arms and

hauled. She'd just gotten him to the French doors leading outside when she heard voices.

"We're just getting a torch. Mrs. W. says there's one in the library."

Sheer terror gave Deanna the strength to drag Joe to the door. She unlocked it, opened it, and rolled him outside into the rain just as someone opened the other door.

She saw the library light come on. Someone's gasp of surprise. Shear panic had her dragging Joe into the shadows, hopefully out of sight.

"I say, there's been mischief here!"

"The French doors are open. He must have gone this way."

Deanna pulled Joe close to the wall and squatted in the rain, praying they wouldn't look for the thief outside.

Joe stirred. "Wha—"

She covered his mouth with her wet hand. "Shh. Not a sound."

"I don't see anyone out here." Deanna recognized Herbert Stanhope's voice. He stepped out to the terrace, looked one way, then the other—right at Deanna and Joe.

Deanna tightened her hold on Joe and held her breath.

Then Herbert turned away and went back inside. "Nothing out here. He must be long gone." He closed the doors.

Joe blinked a couple of times, but Deanna wasn't sure if it was in disbelief or to keep the rain out of his eyes.

Herbert must have seen them huddled in the rain. And yet he'd held his tongue. It made no sense. Perhaps he planned to confront them later. Perhaps he hoped they would give themselves away and he wouldn't have to.

Joe's eyes cut to hers. Hers rounded in reply. Understanding passed between them. She hauled Joe to his feet. He took only a second to recover. He wrapped his arm around her shoulder, and together they stumbled toward the back of the house, where they could stand under the eaves of the servants' entrance, though it was little enough shelter from the rain, which bore in on the house at a sharp angle.

There was no way of getting back inside now without everyone knowing they'd been caught out in the rain. They were both soaked. Hopefully, no one would put together the ransacked office with their disappearance.

Deanna's teeth began to chatter. Joe pulled her closer, but he wasn't in any condition to shelter her. She suspected that the wall was all that was holding him on his feet.

She was sure of it when she tried to step away and he sagged against her.

And then from the darkness came not a sound, but a feeling—a big hand clamped around her arm, and before she could scream, the mate to that hand covered her mouth and she was dragged into the dark.

Chapter
22

Deanna struggled, but it was no use. She tried to call Joe's name, but it was muffled by the massive palm that covered her mouth and nose, and made it almost impossible to breathe. She tried to think. There had been a wall behind her just seconds ago, and now there was just emptiness as she was pulled inexorably into even deeper darkness.

Suddenly, she was thrust away and she staggered, disoriented in the dark.

"Miss. Miss." An urgent whisper.

Deanna blinked and still couldn't see anything. She stretched her hand out, and it was grabbed but this time by a small, cold hand she knew well.

"Elspeth?"

"Yes, but shh."

"Where are we?"

"The coal-delivery door. This is the chute to the basement."

First rain, then coal dust? Her clothes would be ruined.

How would she ever to get back in the house without being found out? *And what a stupid thing to worry about now.*

Deanna twisted behind her to see Joe being half carried, half dragged into the narrow space, then thrust against the wall. The door closed. It was a small space for four people, especially when one of them was so large. She heard a scrape and then saw a bit of light. A lantern and the sound of a shutter being drawn back.

"Swan!" Deanna exclaimed. "What are *you* doing here?"

"Saving your bacon," Elspeth said.

"My head." Joe gingerly touched his scalp. "Someone hit me." He squinted at Swan. "Was it you?"

"No, sir." That deep voice, with its slight singsong quality, sent shivers through Deanna.

"How did you know where to find us?" she asked.

"Swan sees all."

Deanna stepped back involuntarily. *Nonsense*, she told herself. *He's a magician, not a witch doctor.*

"So does Elspeth," Elspeth said, mimicking Swan's tone. She didn't seem at all intimidated by the man, who only yesterday had sent her into the quakes. "Besides, you told me to stay out of sight but to keep my eye on the parlor door to make sure that no one came out and followed Mr. Joseph," Elspeth said. "So I did."

Deanna didn't think she'd been that specific but she wasn't going to quibble.

"I hid in the closet at the back of the hall there. I saw Lady Madeline, then you, come out. Then Mr. Woodruff come running in looking like he was being chased by one of them banshees. And suddenly this here gentleman's gentleman stepped right in front of my hidey-hole so I couldn't see nothing.

"Then Mr. Woodruff started rambling something about the library. I woulda run outside to the window to warn you, but this big oaf was blocking the way." She paused. "So I kicked him."

Deanna cast an approving look at her lady's maid.

Swan growled low in his throat.

"I knew I had to do something, so while he bent over to rub his leg, I banged the door into him, and when he turned around, I slipped out and ran the other way thinking I might be able to get you out before anyone found you." Elspeth looked at Swan. "I guess he followed me."

"Amazing," Deanna said. It was all she could manage.

"We thank you," Joe said, still nursing his head. "But we can't stay in the coal tunnel all night." He started toward the door they'd been dragged through.

Swan stepped in his way. "They will be looking for you."

Joe huffed out a sigh. Winced.

"Besides," Deanna said. "How are we going to explain all this when we do get out?"

Joe seemed to notice for the first time that they were both drenched. "Hmm. We'll just say we went out to get some air and got caught in the downpour." He grinned, looking maniacal in the lantern light. "You've had your swim, after all."

"Very funny."

"Can you think of something better?" Joe asked, feeling the bump on his head. "I can just leave and let everyone assume I have bad manners. But you? Even if you change, your hair will still be wet. You could send Elspeth down to say you have the headache and have gone to bed."

"I could not. Adelaide has the headaches, not me."

"No, you *are* the headache."

"Stop fighting," Elspeth said. "We can't stay here. And he's right, miss. You can't go out looking like that. Your reputation—"

"Will be made?" Deanna grinned, though she was feeling a little frightened. More of her Mama, though, than of being caught as a thief or having the whole of society think she was fast.

Swan moved toward the door, put his ear next to it, shook his head, and leaned against the door barring their escape.

Deanna could hear Neville shouting orders. He must be organizing a search for whoever broke into the library.

"What happened?" Joe asked Deanna.

"You'd been gone forever and I was getting worried. Then I heard a carriage come up the drive. Everyone else was intent on the game, but I went out to see who it was. It was Mr. Woodriuff. He'd returned early. I came to warn you, but when I got to the library, it had been ransacked and you were lying on the floor. I knew we couldn't be found like that, so I dragged you outside."

"That I remember."

"And then he, Swan, pulled us in here."

"That, too."

Swan had put his ear back to the door, listening.

"Did you see who it was who attacked you?" Deanna asked. "The room was torn to pieces. Like they were looking for something."

Joe cut a look at Swan, then looked back at Deanna. Touched his chest. He'd gotten what he wanted.

But who in the world had hit him and what had *they* been looking for?

Swan turned slightly toward them. "I hear no one. You go now."

Joe took Deanna by the wrist.

"But what do we say?" Deanna asked.

"We were out looking at the stars."

"Joe, it's raining. There are no stars."

"It's a euphemism, Dee."

"Oh."

"And it came on to rain and we took shelter under a tree."

"That would be a stupid thing to do, because—oh, is that another euphemism?"

Joe groaned but Deanna didn't think it was because of his head.

Swan's teeth flashed in the darkness. A smile, perhaps. "It's safe. You go now." He opened the door a crack.

Joe peeked around the doorjamb. "Shall we?" He stepped back out into the rain and pulled Deanna with him. She pulled back when she realized he was moving toward the library doors.

"We were out and about and saw the commotion," he said. "Act surprised and mystified." He pulled her forward—and closer.

The French doors were closed, but Deanna could see several men standing in the library and surveying the state of the room.

Joe knocked on the glass, and when Vlady opened it, Joe ushered Deanna into the room. "Good heavens, what happened here?"

Everyone turned.

"The question," Vlady Howe said, "is what happened to you?"

"Caught in the rain. Alas, we'd barely gotten outside before the sky broke over our heads."

Deanna nodded, hoping the admiration she was feeling for Joe's acting skills would appear as infatuation and not idiocy.

Herbert stepped forward. Deanna held her breath.

"There's been a break-in. Did you happen to see anyone out there?"

Joe shook his head, smiled. "But quite frankly, I wasn't really paying attention."

Deanna saw the knowing smiles from some of the men. Her reputation would be ruined after tonight.

The only one who appeared not to find it amusing was Herbert Stanhope, but he held his tongue.

What was he up to? Deanna wondered. He'd never shown any real interest in her, so it couldn't be that. Then she remembered that his mother was a Havemeyer—had *he* been the one to ransack the office and attack Joe? Surely it couldn't be that, either. She hadn't noticed one way or the other whether Herbert was participating in the charades. He could have slipped out, bashed Joe on the head, and come back into the foyer to join the ruckus.

Herbert was fun-loving, dependable, could keep his friends laughing for hours, and didn't seem to care a whit about business. On the other hand, wasn't that an excellent disguise for a spy?

"Did they steal anything?" Joe asked, addressing Neville, who was standing in the doorway.

"I don't know, sir. Mr. Woodruff has been put to bed. He isn't well and madam has called for the doctor."

"Mr. Woodruff is back? Where are Charles and Lord David?"

"They didn't return with the master. Perhaps they are following."

"Shouldn't you telephone the police?" Deanna asked.

"I believe Mr. Woodruff would prefer that we handle this ourselves."

Joe whispered in Deanna's ear. "Too late for that, I'm afraid."

What had he found out? The evidence of misdoings? He held the answer inside his vest.

"Under the circumstances, I think we should make it an early evening and leave the family in peace." Vlady began rounding up the guests, and soon everyone was heading for the front door and their carriages. He stopped by Neville. "Give our sincere wishes for Mr. Woodruff's speedy recovery."

Deanna tried to catch Joe's eye, but he, too, was following the others toward the door. How could he leave her without letting her know what he'd found? She had half a mind to go after him, then remembered her damp and wrinkled state. She'd caused enough scandal for one night.

⚬◦❯❮◦⚬

Outside, carriages had already begun to line up on the drive, and Joe was feeling uncomfortably damp. His head spun whenever he moved it too quickly. He'd sent the Ballard carriage back earlier, meaning to return to the warehouse after the party. He wasn't looking forward to walking back to the Fifth Ward now. In fact, he was fairly certain he wouldn't make it that far.

Herbert Stanhope caught up to him. "Can I give you a ride? I know you've probably come on your bicycle, but I'm sure they won't mind if you leave it overnight, considering the weather."

"Kind of you, Herbert. Thank you."

"I'm down there." They strode past various equipages until they came to a shiny black-and-red-trimmed tilbury. "I feel sorry for those folks who drove open carriages tonight. I could have told them it was going to rain."

"You were right about that," Joe said ruefully before he climbed onto the carriage seat.

Herbert snapped the reins, and they started off, Joe bracing himself against the throbbing in his head.

"Are you going to the factory or to Bonheur tonight?"

Joe eased out his breath. "Bonheur, I think. I could use a hot bath. Do you mind going out of your way? You can take me back to town and I can hire a hackney."

"No, actually I wanted to have time to talk to you alone."

"About tonight?"

"I'm sure you have your reasons for that. Something else. They might possibly be related."

Joe immediately grew wary. "You didn't hit me over the head and ransack Woodruff's office, did you?"

Herbert coughed out a laugh. "Is that what happened? Did you get what you were looking for?"

"Perhaps," Joe said warily.

"Fair enough. So here is something you might find interesting: I was reading the *Tribune* the other day at the Reading Room. My father and my brother, Thornton, were there discussing business as usual, and I happened to overhear my father mention that Uncle Henry said he'd bought shares in R and W to the sum of a third of their assets."

"What? That's nonsense."

"Well, the Havemeyer side of the family doesn't deal in nonsense. So if Uncle Henry says he bought it, you can believe he bought it. My father said he had arranged to transfer the stocks next week. I suspect that's why you were rifling Woodruff's office tonight."

"Actually it was an informational quest, but if Woodruff is involved with the sale of that stock, it could answer a lot of questions," Joe said. "But if the stocks haven't transferred, your uncle doesn't actually own them yet." The carriage wheels set up an accompanying pounding in Joe's head. It was making it hard for him to think clearly. "It's not too late to stop him."

Herbert laughed. "Good luck. Stopping my uncle is about as impossible as climbing the Matterhorn. You may reach him, but you won't survive the trip back down."

"Like the Douglas party of climbers."

Herbert nodded more slowly. "One goes down and drags the rest of them down with him."

"Did anyone else overhear?"

"Not that I know of. We were the only ones there at the time."

"Well, he didn't buy them from my father," Joe said. "He's tried to. Several times. My father has refused, and I don't think he would sell to him on principle. No offense, Herbert."

"None taken. Uncle Henry's a hard, driven, greedy man. And indefatigable until he gets what he wants."

"I'm fairly certain that Mr. Randolph wouldn't give in to his demands. He's been particularly supportive of my work to improve efficiency. And I know my father trusts him."

Herbert crowed out a laugh. "My dear Joseph, you can't trust anyone in business." He became serious. "Or in families, as far as that goes. But I think you already suspect who the weak link is. That's what you were looking for in Woodruff's study tonight. Evidence."

"Why are you telling me all this?"

"Because I like Deanna, and her father is an honest man—honest enough. But the climate isn't favorable for honest men."

"No, it isn't. Especially now that the Sugar Trust has the antitrust committee in its pocket."

"They'll put you out of business before it's all over. They've gobbled up most of the refineries on the East Coast and have started on the West Coast. He's determined to go after the holdouts. My uncle doesn't make idle boasts, and he won't quit until he gets what he wants."

"Are you warning me or threatening me?"

"I'm telling you to watch your back. I don't have a horse in this race."

"Are you sure? For someone who has always laughed through life, you seem to know a lot. Are you certain they're not grooming you for the family business?"

"Me? That is a laugh. I'm not interested."

"You can't keep playing for your entire life."

"My friend, I don't intend to. But not in sugar. Can you keep something under your hat?"

Joe nodded. "If doing so is not detrimental to my family or my business."

"Fair enough. I'm leaving Newport."

"Throwing us over for Saratoga or Tuxedo Park?"

"Germany. I'm only going back to the city long enough to pack my bags."

"It's a little early in the season for the Grand Tour isn't it?"

"I'm going to stay for a while. A long while maybe. There's a guy named Daimler there."

"The motor car engine designer?"

"Yes. That's going to be the future. Automobiles. They're having a bit of trouble over there." Herbert paused to laugh. "Daimler got caught up in licensing his engine to some Brits who then ousted him and his main designer and took over. But he's working back in Germany, and when he gets things running, he'll have my inheritance to help keep him going." Herbert smiled. "Unless I bring the whole outfit back to the States to run."

If Joe's head hadn't been aching like it was about to explode, he would have slapped Herbert on the back. "Good luck."

"And God knows I've learned enough about power—mechanical and human—just being around it. I don't plan to misuse it, but I do plan to be out there on the advance guard."

"Damn. I think I've underestimated you, Herbert."

"That's okay. Everyone does."

⋘◦✦◦⋙

It was nearly a half hour before all the carriages were summoned and the guests had been sent on their way. Deanna had changed into dry clothes, hidden her hair under a scarf, and come back downstairs.

With Mrs. Woodruff in attendance on her husband, the responsibility for the farewells had rested with Cassie, but she was so worried about her father—not to mention frightened by his appearance—that Madeline often had to say her good-byes for her.

Even Deanna helped out, though her mind was not on farewells, but on trying to figure out what was happening. And she was worried about Joe. He'd left without a word to her. God forbid he had decided to ride his bicycle back to the warehouse in the rain. He would have an accident for certain.

"I wonder how your papa is," Madeline said to Cassie when the last guest had departed.

"I don't know. Mama hasn't come down to see to any of the guests. It must be bad. You were a big help, so calm. All I could do was stand in the doorway and stare."

Madeline gave her a quick hug. "It's because it's your papa. If it had been mine, I would have been standing and staring, too."

Cassie gave her a watery smile.

"I just hope I didn't overstep."

"Of course you didn't. Did she, Dee? I'm sure Mama appreciates it."

Cassie and Madeline smiled at each other. Deanna felt like the odd man out, which of course she was. It seemed to her that Madeline had assumed the role of mistress of the house too easily. Did she and Charles already have an understanding? And where was Charles? Why had Mr. Woodruff come home without the other two? What had he needed in the library? The same thing that had upset Charles so much, and which, if Deanna guessed correctly, was currently residing in Joe's vest?

They had just turned to go upstairs when the front door opened and Charles ran in, drenched and looking almost as wild as his father.

Neville, who had just been going into the parlor, strode out to meet him.

"Did my father come home?"

"Yes, sir. He's upstairs now. With Mrs. Woodruff. He was not feeling well."

"And is Lord David with him?"

Neville blinked. "No, sir. We thought he must be with you."

"Oh, Charles," Cassie said. "Thank God you've come. Papa's not himself."

"No," her brother echoed. "And no one has seen Lord David?"

"No."

"But where is he?" Madeline asked. Her voice was strident with worry. "Why didn't he come in with your father or with you?"

"Perhaps he did, miss. I'll summon his valet to check his room."

Madeline nodded disjointedly. "I don't understand. Didn't you come with them, Charles?"

"No, I had some business in town, and when I returned to the hotel, the concierge said they had taken a hack to Grand Central Terminal. I thought they must be retuning here via Wickford," Charles said. "Fortunately I ran into Dickie Hermann and imposed upon him to run me back here on his yacht—we made excellent time. It's the only reason I got here when I did."

Swan appeared at the top of the stairs. He came no farther, just stood, tall and massive, and shook his head.

"Swan. He must be here," cried Lady Madeline, clasping her hands under her chin as if beseeching him or praying. "Did you look everywhere?"

Swan nodded.

"I'll go myself."

Charles stopped her. "If he were here, surely he would make himself known to us."

"We'll have to call the police."

"No, Maddie, I'll take care of it. We'll just have to ask my father where he is." Charles climbed the stairs.

Cassie sank down on the staircase as if she were still a little girl. "I don't understand what's happened. They weren't supposed to be back until the weekend."

Deanna sat down next to her. "I don't, either. We'll just have to wait for Charles to tell us."

"We have to find him. He may be lying hurt somewhere, or—or worse." Madeline cried and began to pace in front of the staircase. "What if your papa has left him somewhere to die?"

Cassie jumped up. Deanna pulled her back down. "She's distraught. She doesn't mean it."

It was the first time Deanna had seen Madeline lose her

aplomb, and Deanna felt a concern that surprised her. But she knew what it was to lose a brother, and she fervently hoped that Madeline would find hers alive and well.

"But Papa wouldn't hurt anyone."

"Of course not," Deanna said.

After a while Neville came out to say that a fire had been laid in the back parlor if they would like to wait there. But neither Cassie nor Madeline, who had finally sat down next to Deanna, moved.

"Thank you, Neville, but I believe we'll wait here for a while," Deanna said.

"Very well, miss."

"I'm sorry, Cassie," Madeline finally said. "I didn't mean it. I'm just so scared."

"That's okay," Cassie said, and sniffed.

They fell silent again.

Deanna had just about given up seeing Charles again that night when he descended the stairs.

All three of them jumped to their feet.

"Any news?" Cassie asked.

"Does he know where David is?" Madeline asked.

Charles looked frightfully white. "He's out of his head. I think I should go into town and see if someone saw them at the docks or if they got off the ferry together."

The doorbell gonged.

They all turned, then moved as one toward the door.

Neville somehow managed to get there before them. He opened the door and stepped back.

Lord David stepped in. His clothes were muddy, his trouser knees were torn, his cheek was bruised, and there were smears of dirt across his cheeks.

"David!" Lady Madeline rushed toward him and threw herself at him. He staggered back. "Easy, sister. I've had a bit of a time of it."

"There's a fire in the back parlor," Deanna said.

Charles nodded. "Neville, send for Lord David's man, and bring the whiskey."

"I'm fine, I assure you. Just an adventure. Did your father make it home?"

"Yes, he's upstairs in bed. Not well, I'm afraid."

Lord David shook his head. "Thank God he's safe. I tried to stop him." He swayed. "I think I will have that whiskey before I change into some decent clothes."

Neville bowed, Charles took Lord David's elbow, and they all followed the two men to the back parlor.

As soon as he was made comfortable in a wingback chair pulled close to the fire and was holding a glass of whiskey, Lord David filled them in on the adventure he'd been through.

"After you left the hotel this morning, Mr. Woodruff received a call. He told me to wait for him at the hotel, which I did. He didn't come back for maybe two hours, and when he did, he was very agitated. Said there was only one thing he could do. I had no idea what he was talking about, but of course I was alarmed and vowed to myself not to let him out of my sight. He went straight to the train station. I was close enough to hear where he was going. So I purchased a ticket and got on the train, too. I didn't want to confront him in such a public place.

"I waited until I thought he was calm enough and then presented myself to him. The train ride seemed to have soothed him. He seemed better, but when we arrived at this Wickford place, he once again became agitated. Asked me to get him a glass of whiskey. I did, and when I returned, he was gone.

"By then I'd missed the ferry to Newport and had to pay

someone to take me across. No sooner had I reached the New-port wharf than I was set upon by some of your rougher element. I must say I acquitted myself quite well, but they managed to relieve me of my money and watch. So I was forced to walk here. And arrived as you see me now."

"Oh, David," Madeline cried. "I wish we had never come to this place."

"Now, now, Maddie. I'm quite fine. Though I do relish a hot bath."

"By all means," Charles said. "Just one more thing." He looked around at the others. "Did father say anything as to why he was so distraught?"

"Alas, no. I'm afraid he wasn't making much sense."

"I see. Please have your bath and anything else we can provide. I appreciate this, more than you can know."

"Charles, Charles. It's nothing, I assure you. I'm just sorry that I wasn't faster on the uptake. And now I'll say good night."

Madeline tried to go up with him, but he kissed her fore-head and turned her away. "I believe that between Swan and me, I'll be able to accomplish a bath quite well without you. Charles. Ladies."

Charles waited until he was gone, then went into the library and shut the door.

Deanna wondered how long it would take him to find that the ledger pages were missing.

Deanna was shaken awake. She had no idea what time it was. Surely it couldn't be morning.

"Miss Deanna, get up. There's a commotion outside in the hallway. Mr. Woodruff has taken a turn."

Deanna sat up. Elspeth was already pulling off the bed-clothes. By the time Deanna slid out of bed, Elspeth was holding a robe for her to put on.

Elspeth was wearing a checked housedress, and her hair was braided down her back. "Hurry."

"What's happening?"

"I don't know, but they've fetched Mrs. Woodruff."

"Oh no. Do you think he's died?"

"I don't know. Hurry."

Elspeth held the bedroom door open. Several servants were running up and down the hall. Elspeth and Deanna padded barefoot toward Mr. Woodruff's rooms.

The door had been left ajar and Deanna slipped inside. Mr. Woodruff's valet was standing on the far side of the bed attempting to hold his master, who was thrashing violently. Two maids and Neville stood nearby waiting for orders. They were all in various states of dress. Neville had managed to put his trousers and jacket on over his nightshirt. The valet was wearing an elaborate smoking robe, and his usually impeccably oiled hair was sticking out, leaving patches of bald skin showing through the strands. A tragic tableau vivant. *In the Sickroom.*

There was nothing she could do, but she wanted to lend her support to Mrs. Woodruff if she could. When she saw Cassie huddled in a chair the corner, Deanna crossed the room to her.

"I heard them come for Mama," Cassie whimpered. "What's happening to him?"

"I don't know, but your mama will know what to do."

Deanna put her arm around Cassie and watched as the valet motioned for Neville to take Woodruff's other side.

While the two men tried to calm his thrashings, Mrs. Woodruff, her hands as calm as if she were reaching for her atomizer, opened a small bottle and measured several drops of liquid into a small medicine glass. Neville held Mr. Woodruff's head while his wife poured the liquid down his throat.

Deanna was mesmerized by the motion, by the utter calm of it. She looked for Elspeth and saw her still standing in the doorway, her mouth slightly open. Her face etched in lines of surprise and horror—like the maid on the cover of *Pritchard the Poisoner.*

Mr. Woodruff coughed and spluttered but sank back on the pillows.

"There," Mrs. Woodruff said, returning the glass to the bedside table. "He'll rest now that he's had some of his medicine." She seemed to notice the others for the first time. Cassie ran to her. "Now, now. Everything will be fine. You know your papa has these nervous attacks. Let's let him get some rest."

She herded them all toward the door. Deanna lagged behind trying to memorize the way Mr. Woodruff looked, the shape of the bottle, and what was written on it.

She didn't believe Mrs. Woodruff would poison her husband. But it was uncanny how close to the novel cover the scene had been.

Mrs. Woodruff stopped at the door. "Deanna, will you take Cassie back to her room? There's really no cause for alarm. He'll be better directly."

Deanna took Cassie and helped her down the hall.

She heard Mrs. Woodruff say, "I'll just stay a little while longer, Neville."

"Yes, madam." And the door closed.

Cassie's maid was waiting at her bedroom door. "Thank you, miss. I'll take care of her now." She practically shut the door in Deanna's face.

The hallway had slowly emptied of servants. Deanna hadn't seen Charles, whose bedroom was farther along the same hallway, nor had Lord David or Madeline made an appearance, though they probably were too far away to have heard the commotion.

"Did you see that?" Elspeth asked the moment the door had closed and they were alone in Deanna's room. "It was just like the bottle in the picture."

"Yes, but . . . you don't believe Daisy saw Mrs. Woodruff poisoning her husband and was killed for it? She would never. Besides, she had several hundred guests the night of the ball, spent every minute making sure everyone had what they needed, overseeing servants and making sure the champagne was chilled.

"Do you really think she could've lured Daisy out to the cliff, pushed her over, and then returned to the ballroom, smiling and not even breathing hard?" Deanna snorted. "Ludicrous."

Elspeth helped Deanna out of her robe. "You just don't want it to be true because of who she is. Now, get back into bed. I want to go down to the servants' hall before the excitement dies down and see what's what."

She hurried into the dressing room but was back almost immediately. Her face had drained of color. She was holding a folded piece of paper.

"What is it, Elspeth?"

Elspeth came forward and held out the paper with a shaking hand. "This—this was shoved under the door."

Deanna took the paper and opened it. Written in large scrawling letters was a short message:

Take your mistress away from this place. Bad bad juju. More bad is coming. You must leave this house.

"Oh, miss. It's from the voodoo man. I just know it. What does he want with us?"

"I think he wants to warn us," Deanna said with more calm than she felt. "He helped us once. I don't know. Maybe he is trying to help us now."

"But we can't leave in the middle of the night."

"We're not leaving. But we're going to be very, very careful. You're not going down to the servants' hall. You can sleep in here on the chaise tonight."

Elspeth nodded, ran into the dressing room, and pulled her linens into Deanna's room. She threw them on the chaise on the far wall and jumped under them.

Deanna waited until she was settled, then turned off the lamp. *What more bad things are coming?* she wondered as she finally drifted off to sleep.

Before dawn, Mr. Woodruff lapsed into a coma.

Chapter

23

Deanna knew something was wrong the moment she entered the breakfast room the next morning. And not just because of the warning from Swan.

The breakfast room was sunny but empty. The chafing dishes were set up, but either everyone else had already eaten or was still abed. Which was possible, since they'd had a trying night.

Deanna didn't have much appetite, but she knew that not eating never solved anything except maybe being a bit too fat. Usually hunger just made people irritable and too quick to lose their tempers. So she took a plate from the warmer and peeked into the first covered dish. As she spooned a dab of eggs on her plate, the butler entered with warm toast and hot coffee.

"Good morning, Neville. Has everyone been here and gone?" she asked.

Neville set the toast rack by her place and poured coffee. "Mr. Charles left early this morning."

"Oh? Did he return to the city?"

"I don't believe so. He said he would be back after luncheon. Mrs. Woodruff is taking breakfast in her room. None of the others have been down as yet."

"And Mr. Woodruff?"

The butler shook his head. "It doesn't look good, miss. The doctor was summoned earlier this morning."

"Did he say what is wrong with him?"

"I couldn't say, miss."

"Neville," Deanna wheedled, drawing out the butler's name as they'd used to do as children when they tried to make him unbend.

Neville leaned in and poured more coffee. "The doctor says he must have had a stroke. He's not responding."

"Oh, dear. Thank you, Neville."

The butler bowed. "Ring if you require something else, miss."

"I'll be fine."

He bowed again and left the room.

Her mind racing, Deanna ate her breakfast alone.

She was sitting over her coffee trying to decide on a course of action when the door opened and the footman entered and presented a silver salver. There was an envelope on it. *Please, not a letter from Mama.*

It was from Joe. He had to go to Manhattan. Today, of all days? She needed to tell him about Mr. Woodruff's collapse and ask his advice about what to do.

Deanna wished she knew what was really going on. Something serious must have happened for Joe to go off to the city. Was it because of the papers he'd appropriated from the library? His note said he was going to talk with his father. Something about the business, then. Was it because Mr. Woodruff,

Charles, and Lord David had returned from the city earlier than expected?

Deanna hated not knowing what was going on.

And she was worried about being an imposition at Seacrest with Mr. Woodruff in such a sorry state. But maybe she could be of use to Mrs. Woodruff and relieve her of some duties so that she could sit with her husband.

After breakfast, Deanna went upstairs and quietly knocked on Mrs. Woodruff's bedroom door.

"Come in."

Deanna slipped inside and shut the door.

"Oh, Deanna. Come here, child."

Deanna crossed to where Mrs. Woodruff was stretched out an a chaise of wine-and-gold brocade. She was wearing a light green taffeta dressing gown embroidered with lilac bunches and green ribbons. Delicate lace frothed about her shoulders and neck.

She looked like a confection, except for the pallor of her face and her sunken eyes, which even the artful machinations of her lady's maid hadn't been able to conceal.

A round table with a cup of untouched tea and a plate of uneaten toast sat at her elbow.

She held out her hand, and Deanna took it and dropped to her knees on the floor by the chaise.

"How are you? Is there anything I can do for you?" she asked Mrs. Woodruff.

"No, no, I'm afraid there's nothing we can do. Nothing."

"Oh, ma'am. It can't be as bad as that. Surely he'll recover."

"Recover?" Mrs. Woodruff laughed. Her voice sounded strange, not like her normal jovial trill, and Deanna began to be really concerned, not only for Mr. Woodruff, but for his wife.

"We had some good times, Francis and I, especially at the beginning. Oh, the laughs and the jollifications we had. Every day was an adventure. I met him when we were both visiting Chicago. And fell in love almost at first sight." She paused, frowned slightly. Her shoulders began to shake, and Deanna leaned forward to comfort her and realized that she wasn't crying, but laughing. And Deanna grew really afraid.

"Shall I call your maid?"

"No, no. There's nothing she can do." She sat up suddenly, grabbing Deanna's wrist. "Don't leave me. Serpents. That's what my papa said. Serpents, every last one of them."

She was raving. Deanna tried to ease away just long enough to reach the bell pull, but Mrs. Woodruff held on tight.

"Don't be afraid. I'm not crazy. Not anymore. The doctor says Francis is not likely to recover. He won't wake up, you know. I shall miss the old reprobate."

Reprobate? Surely she shouldn't be talking about her husband in such terms, especially not to Deanna.

"Why don't I send for more tea?" Deanna said. "You'll feel better if you have something warm."

"You're such a sweet girl. I hope you'll be a friend to Cassie."

"Friends with Cassie? Of course I will. Always."

Mrs. Woodruff sniffed and applied a lacy handkerchief to her eyes with her free hand. "Great times. He knew how to enjoy life. I loved that about him, But it seems he enjoyed it too much. Be careful when you marry, Dee dear."

"Yes, ma'am."

"Get a steady man. The dashers are charming but dash doesn't last—they grow old, lose their hair, gain a belly. And when the dash is gone, there isn't much left but the bills. So you just get yourself a steady man."

"I will. I will," Deanna said, her alarm growing. "Please let me get you some tea. Or a cordial."

"That woman. All those women. All of them," she continued. "Deanna, ring for my maid. I must get up. There are things to do."

"Of course, ma'am."

Her maid came in immediately, almost as if she'd been awaiting the summons. She gave Deanna a quick glance, dismissing her. Deanna leaned over and kissed Mrs. Woodruff's cheek. "I'll come back later."

"But you'll stay. Cassie needs you. And you're all invited to the theater tonight."

The theater? Surely that outing would be cancelled. But Deanna nodded and fled the room, then stood outside the bedroom door trying to piece together what had just happened. Mrs. Woodruff seemed to have lost her mind one minute and in the next seemed perfectly normal. But the reminiscing and talk of private matters was disconcerting.

Elspeth pounced the moment Deanna was inside her room.

"Where have you been?"

"At breakfast, and then I went to see Mrs. Woodruff, and oh, Elspeth, she seems funny in her mind."

"Forget her for a minute. When I went down for my tea, I heard that the Manchesters are leaving today."

"What? Who said?"

"One of the parlor maids. She said the voodoo man was upstairs right now, packing their trunks."

"Well, good riddance."

"Do you think it's because he warned them about the evil thing in this house?"

"I don't think so. I think that was just his own way of trying to understand all the events that have happened. I imagine they offered to leave because of Mr. Woodruff's illness. I was thinking that we should go, too, but Mrs. Woodruff asked me to stay."

"You mean we're not leaving?"

Deanna shook her head. She knew just how Elspeth felt. She wished they could both go to Gran Gwen's, where it was safe and comfortable. Joe's grandmother always had a way of helping her with things she didn't understand. But Mrs. Woodruff had requested she stay, though Deanna wasn't sure whether she'd meant to stay close by or just remain at Seacrest.

Deanna snatched an embroidered pillow out of the way and slumped into the upholstered boudoir chair.

"She's probably afraid to be in the house by herself," Elspeth said.

Deanna snorted out a laugh. "She has a house full of servants and Cassie and Charles. I don't think she's alone."

Elspeth stuck her nose in the air. "You know what I mean. And that kind of laughter is very vulgar."

Deanna tossed the pillow at her. "So, what do you think we should do?"

—∞•◦►◄◦•∞—

Joe's head was still pounding the next day as the steamer he'd taken from Newport docked in Manhattan. He'd spent what was left of yesterday night at Bonheur, picking up a change of clothes and enlightening his grandmother on what had transpired at Seacrest.

"I don't like having to leave, but I need to take these papers to my father. See if you can get Dee to move in here with you. There is something sinister going on over there. I can't be in two places at once. Why are you smiling? This is not a humorous situation."

"Don't worry about us. We'll be fine."

"I'll try to return late tonight, if I can catch the last steamer."

"We'll be fine. You're the one who should watch yourself."

He'd dashed off a note to Deanna to let her know where he'd gone, and his grandmother had sent him to the station in her carriage. At the last minute, she'd run out to the carriage carrying a parcel.

"Cook insisted." She'd thrust it at him.

When he'd looked inside, he'd found an apple, bread, and cheese, and a packet of headache powders, which he'd realized he needed as soon as the steamer's warning horn split the air— and his head.

He'd stopped by the telegraph office and sent word to his father that he would be in the city that day to see him. He hadn't had time to wait for an answer; he'd just hoped that his father was at home.

The city was teeming with activity. It was going to be a hot day. Already he could feel the perspiration pooling under his arms. He'd forgotten the traffic, the noise, the stench. Manhattan was not the place to be in the summer.

He was deliberating whether to take the omnibus across town to the Ballard residence on Gramercy Park, where his father would hopefully be waiting for him, or to stand in line for a hansom cab when he heard his name being called by Darby, their family's town coachman. His father had sent the carriage for him.

Dodging people, street offal, and urchins vying to carry baggage for a penny (or steal it as an alternative), Joe made his way to the dark maroon town carriage. Darby held the carriage door open as Joe climbed in, then they set off through the jumble of conveyances toward the East Side.

Gramercy Park was a haven of peace and shade in the crowded, sweltering city. Joe paused outside on the sidewalk just to look up at the townhouse. The Ballard home was Italianate, with balconies surrounded by heavy iron grillwork that somehow evoked security and ornament at the same time. The home had been in the family for several generations, and Joe hoped it would stay in the family. He could see himself and *his* family—if he ever had one—living here. He'd been busy during the winter and hadn't had too much time to miss home. But now he was so glad his father hadn't sold it and joined the exodus uptown to build yet another opulent marble mansion.

He shook himself from the unexpected reverie and climbed the steps to the front door, which was opened by their ancient butler, Harrison. He'd been in his prime during Joe's grandfather's time, had served the next generation well, and now was too old and loyal and tenacious to be "let out to pasture," as he himself had pointed out.

"Harrison," Joe said, handing him his fedora.

"Your father is in the library, sir."

"Thank you. How are you keeping?"

"Fine, sir. This way."

Joe followed the old man, concentrating so as not to tread on his heels. As if he'd forgotten the way to his own library. Or was he being treated like a stranger as punishment for choosing to live with the hoi polloi? Harrison was more of a social stickler than Joe's father or grandfather had ever been.

His father was sitting at his desk, though he was completely hidden behind an open copy of the *Tribune*; his identity confirmed by the cigar smoke that curled above the edges of the paper.

The paper came down. "You're here. Fine. I suppose you're hungry."

"Ravenous, sir."

He father reached back and rang the bell. "Marthe has made you a feast. I think she hopes to lure you back with her cooking."

Joe forced a smile. His father understood his need to invent, but he didn't like it. Of course, his father's father hadn't liked it when Joe's father had decided to "dabble" in business. They were all cut from the same cloth, the Ballard men. Joe could be looking across the desk at himself in another thirty years. And if he raised his eyes to where his grandfather's portrait would be looking down at them, he would see the stages of his own life.

He should turn out so well. His grandfather had lived to a spirited eighty-five years, and his father still had a full head of dark hair, intelligence in his even darker eyes, and was fit enough to keep up with much younger men on the polo field and in the boardroom.

"I told her to serve it in here if you don't mind. I've already eaten."

"What? Oh, luncheon. Thank you."

"So what tears you from your work to bring you to the city?"

"Murder, sir."

His father blinked, carefully folded his paper, and stubbed out his cigar. "Open that window, will you, son? Marthe will tell on me if she smells cigar smoke."

Joe did as he was bid. No hustle and bustle or street noise here. It was pleasant. Comfortable.

"Now, what's this about murder?"

"It started with the death of a maid. Daisy Payne, my apprentice's sweetheart."

His father didn't ask questions but waited until Joe finished telling him about the deaths of both Woodruff maids.

"And what does this have to do with R and W?"

"I'm not sure, but Will Hennessey is convinced that it's linked somehow, and so am I. Plus, there are other things that Dee discovered that just add to the speculation."

"Deanna Randolph? George said she was staying with the Woodruffs while Jeannette has gone to Boston to have Adelaide quacked. I say they should take off that girl's corsets and send her to the country. But what else did you find?"

"To begin with, the Manchesters have been here almost two weeks yet only just came two days ago to seal the deal? What businessman in his right mind would wait that long when the sugar market is so volatile? For all Lord David knows, R and W could fall to the Sugar Trust, and then he'd have a useless contract and no market for his cane. Charles was meant to bring him to the warehouse to view my new condenser and bagger. They never bothered to come, and the few times I spoke with the man, he seemed to have no idea what I was talking about. Oh, I realize he just grows the cane, but I can't believe that he doesn't have any clue at all about the refining process."

"The idle rich perhaps?"

"Perhaps."

"Plus, you don't like him."

"I don't."

"Prowling around Deanna, is he?"

"Yes."

His father laughed.

"It isn't funny. He could be a dangerous man."

"Indeed. He could. But this isn't what has brought you so hurriedly to town."

"No. Two things specifically. I confess I did something underhanded. Dee overheard an argument between Charles and his father in the Woodruffs' library. Charles was very upset about something related to the business, and when Mr. Woodruff left, Charles spent a long time going over ledgers"—Joe grinned; he couldn't help himself—"trapping Dee in her hidey-hole until she fell asleep."

"Now, there's a girl who will never succumb to the vapors." His father immediately grew serious. "And what did this lead to?"

They were interrupted by the door swinging open and two footmen carrying trays walking into the room, followed by a butterball of a woman with her sleeves rolled up, apron stretched across a vast expanse of bosom. "Monsieur Joe," she said in a warble of French. "*Mon petit chou.*"

Joe cracked a laugh. "Not so *petit* anymore."

"Skin and bones." She gestured in the air, and the footmen unloaded plates and cups and wineglasses, then slipped quietly from the room. "Now you eat. *Mon pauvre,* don't those nasty fishermen feed you?"

Marthe had never been to Newport, and somehow in her mind she imagined fishmongers and brothels on every corner.

"Thank you, Marthe," Lionel Ballard said.

"Ah, *mon pauvre.*"

Joe half expected her to pinch his cheeks, but she merely broke into a string of lilting French and hurried from the room.

"She's going a little batty, I'm afraid," his father said. "But she still cooks as well as any chef. Now, sit down at the table and finish your tale while you eat."

Joe changed seats and looked over the repast that Marthe had prepared. Cold beef, ham, and cracked partridge. Salad and petits pois and potatoes lyonnaise. He filled his plate, took a couple of bites, and savored the delicate seasoning.

His father poured him a glass of wine and took one for himself, then perched one hip on his desk and waited.

"So," Joe continued after a few more bites, "during a party last night at Seacrest, I slipped off to the library and took a look for myself. And . . ." He put down his fork, reached into his inside pocket, and took out the folded papers he'd kept safely hidden there; he handed them to his father. "These aren't the official financial records. They're personal expenditures. As you can see, Woodruff is broke, cleaned out."

His father perused the pages. "I suspected as much. And these certainly substantiate my fears."

Joe nodded. "I thought I might need these figures as proof."

"Something to hold over his head, if need be?" His father's eyes twinkled. "You're pretty mercenary for a creative soul. You tore these right out of his ledger?"

"Yes. I had just put them in my jacket when someone hit me over the head. Knocked me clean out."

"Good Lord, and you weren't caught?"

"No, and that's another story. But the upshot is, while I was unconscious, someone ransacked the library. I was very neat, I assure you. Whoever hit me must have been desperately looking for something."

His father relit his cigar, puffed on it until the ash glowed red. "But they didn't search you." It was said as a statement, not as a question.

"No."

"Perhaps if you tell me your second reason for coming, we can glean more of the situation."

Joe told his father how Herbert Stanhope had said his uncle, Henry Havemeyer, had bought a big bundle of stock in R and W.

"We've been hearing those rumors, too. At first we thought they were just more of Havemeyer's intimidation ploys."

"So did I," Joe said. "But considering the state of Mr. Woodruff's finances, he might be motivated to sell off his shares. Is that why he came to town finally?"

His father shook his head. "No. No, Francis came to town to ask for more money, ostensibly to give to Lord David. George and I were already suspicious. I'd already sent a wire to Lord David's bank in Barbados to see if the money had been received."

"And?"

His father's cigar had gone out and he dropped it into the ashtray.

"It hasn't been. Yet Francis went down to Barbados with a bag of cash and a cashier's check, at his own insistence."

"What happened to them?"

His father shrugged. "The bank down there is checking its transactions, but my guess is Francis took the money *and* sold his shares to Havemeyer, who would willingly buy them for a lot more than they're actually worth."

"I can't believe he would betray the two of you like that."

"I don't think he meant to. Francis has always had a bit of a volatile streak. He keeps up a good front. None of us had any idea just how bad his situation was until recently." His father refilled his glass. Lifted the decanter toward Joe, who shook his head.

"He never had a penny to fly with. Even at Yale, he'd outspend his allowance before it hit his pocket. Women, drink, gambling. Like his father before him. He would have fallen sooner if Eleanor Peabody hadn't come along."

"Did you confront him yesterday?"

"Yes. I'm sorry to say George and I laid a bit of a trap. We sent Charles and Lord David off to the refineries and presented papers to Francis to sign that ceded his stocks to the company for a little above face value." His father perused the contents of his glass.

"He agreed, only he couldn't produce the stocks. He made excuses about how they were in the safe at Newport. He refused to hand over the money, insisted Lord David had it. Accused us of trying to queer the deal. But he caved in the end, admitted that he couldn't have sold his shares to Havemeyer, because he'd already lost the stocks and the money in a card game on the way down to Barbados."

"How could he do that? A betrayal of his own partners."

"It's like a sickness," his father said.

"That's no excuse." Joe shook his head. "Then why is Lord David here, acting like he's committing his sugar crop to R and W? I don't trust the guy. He's playing deep."

"My guess is Francis has been putting him off the same way he's been using us. Never trust anyone in business, son."

"A sad commentary on the world," Joe said.

"Perhaps, but it's the way the world works. For myself, I try to stay on the moral side of the fence, though sometimes it's necessary to straddle that fence. And sometimes . . . Look, son, I could afford to lose R and W. It's a hefty amount, but I'd recover. But George Randolph and I go a long way back, and he's just stubborn enough to go down with the R and W ship.

It's only a matter of time until Havemeyer beats us. He's taken just about everything else in his path."

"You can't let that happen."

"We can't stop it. But we've taken precautions."

"And those would be . . . ?"

"Last week I convinced George to dissolve R and W. We've sold it lock, stock, and refineries to the Eastern Sugar Company."

"What? Why?" After the support his father had given him for his inventions? It didn't make sense. "I've never even heard of them."

"That's because they just came into being. In New Jersey. On Friday." His father smiled.

"You?"

"And George."

"So the R and W stock Woodruff sold is worthless."

His father nodded.

"Can you do that? Is it legal? Could you incorporate that quickly?"

"The answer to all three of your questions is yes, if one has the money and is willing to grease enough palms. You look shocked. Don't be. Keeping sugar out of the hands of that greedy monopolist will benefit your struggling workers, the shippers, the store owners, and ultimately the consumers of sugar.

"It's always the same; Fisk, Gould, Carnegie, Vanderbilt. For a while service is convenient, prices are low, but as soon as they control the market, prices go up, wages go down."

"And you think this new company of yours can change that?"

"I'm not so naïve. The Eastern Sugar Company will probably fall eventually. We're counting on you to revolutionize the industry with that machinery of yours. You'll hold the patents, and the Eastern Sugar Company will become the Eastern Refinery Machine Company."

Joe was floored. "That's quite a responsibility."

"I have utmost faith in you. Just one thing."

"Yes?"

"Don't tell your mother or grandmother about any of this business. They'd never let me hear the end of it."

Chapter
24

Deanna knew she couldn't stay in her room all day. But she didn't want to sit around the morning room trying to think of conversation, assuming either Cassie or Madeline had even left their rooms yet. There had been plans to go to the theater that evening, but Deanna thought they must have to cancel.

Elspeth had gone to the servants quarters even though Deanna protested that it might be dangerous. Deanna didn't really believe in voodoo or whatever Swan said was in the house, but she thought it was better to be safe than sorry.

Not Elspeth.

And Deanna knew if she insisted on going with Elspeth, the servants would clam up until she left again.

She could visit Gran Gwen and see if she knew why Joe had taken off for the city, but that seemed a little like abandoning a sinking ship.

Perhaps she would take her sketch pad out to the cliffs. That way, she wouldn't need to bother Elspeth for a change of clothes. Her muslin shirtwaist was fine for drawing. She went into the dressing room and chose a wide-brimmed straw hat, went back to the mirror, and studied her reflection intently as she tied the silk ribbon into a bow close to her ear.

It looked awful—one tie was longer than the other and one loop drooped. Her second attempt was better. It wouldn't pass her mother's or even Elspeth's inspection, but they weren't here and the cliff rocks wouldn't care.

She took her art bag into the hallway and practically ran into Cassie. So much for solitude.

"Oh, there you are. What are you doing?"

"I was just getting my—"

"Maddie and Lord David are planning to leave today because of Papa's illness. Mama has sent me up to convince them to stay. You know Mama, she's happier surrounded by people. Even with Papa so poorly."

"How is your papa today?"

"Still the same. The doctor says only time will tell." Cassie's eyes filled.

Deanna gave her an impulsive hug. "I'm sure he'll be fine. And we must keep up your mama's spirits."

Cassie sniffed. "That's why we have to convince Maddie not to leave."

She started down the hall, pulling Deanna with her, and Deanna was momentarily reminded of the night of the ball and Cassie pulling her across the ballroom floor to meet Lord David. So much had happened since then, and most of it hadn't been good.

Madeline was in her room overseeing the packing of her trunks. She was already dressed for going out in a brown-and-puce visiting dress with a bodice of accordion-pleated mousseline de soie. It was a perfect complement to her hair and complexion. Deanna felt downright clownish in her floppy straw hat.

Cassie took Madeline's hands. "Mama asks that you please not go. She has so many nice things planned."

Madeline smiled; her lips trembled a bit. Deanna wondered if she was sad at having to leave Charles. "I hate to go, but David says that we are an imposition with your papa so ill and that we should remove to a hotel to take the strain of entertaining us from your mama."

"Oh, pooh. Mama wants you to stay. She gets melancholy when left too long to her own thoughts."

"I don't think he'll change his mind."

"Oh, but he must. He will if we all insist. Deanna thinks so, too."

"Oh, yes," Deanna said, attempting to look concerned but suspecting that she was not nearly as convincing as her favorite fictional detective, Kate Goelet, would have been. Part of her wanted to see the back of the Manchesters, the sooner the better. But unlike Kate, Deanna had a real murder—two of them—on her hands, and she felt she should keep everyone here until Joe returned.

"Indeed," she added for good measure.

"Is he in his room?" Cassie asked. "Come on, we'll go on a strike, stand in front of his door, and not let him go until he relents." Cassie turned and marched down the hall.

For a moment Deanna and Madeline were left looking at each other, Deanna wary, Madeline with a flash of something that might be happiness, but might just as well be anger, in her eye. Then she shrugged.

"How can anyone say no to Cassie?" Madeline took Deanna's elbow and trundled her out of her room. The two of them walked arm in arm down the hall after Cassie.

Madeline seemed to have recovered her good spirits, and when they caught up to Cassie outside Lord David's door, she knocked. "Brother," she said in a coaxing singsong. "I have two lovely ladies here who want to talk with you." She smiled at the others and giggled. Cassie joined her. Deanna smiled but couldn't summon much mirth.

The door opened. Cassie gasped and stepped back into Deanna.

Swan looked down on them. He was dressed in a normal valet suit of black with a pristine white shirt and impeccably tied tie. It was the first time Deanna had seen him in full daylight. His head was completely shaved, but he otherwise looked like a very large, very black gentleman's gentleman, except for the gold ring in his left ear.

His eyes narrowed slightly when he saw Deanna, then he bowed solemnly and opened the door for them to enter.

Lord David was just shrugging into his suit jacket. "Ladies, a most charming vision," he said coming to greet them. "I'm afraid you find me in dishabille at the moment, and my chambers rather disorganized."

They looked perfectly fine to Deanna except for the trunks and the carefully folded clothes neatly stacked on the dresser. A decanter sat next to the clothes and a glass was half-filled with dark liquid.

As Deanna looked at it, Swan moved silently to re-stop the decanter and carry it and the glass away.

"David, Mrs. Woodruff would like us to stay and keep her company for a few days until her husband is better."

Lord David made a slight bow. "Thank your mama for us, but of course we are an intrusion at this difficult time. We've decided to remove to the Ocean House Hotel."

"Oh, you can't stay at that stodgy old place," Cassie protested. "No one who's anybody stays there these days. Please, Lord David. You can't desert Mama. Come with me and she'll tell you herself."

"She would be polite of course, your mama is such a giving person, but it would not be fair."

"Oh, yes, it will. Won't it, Dee?"

Deanna smiled. "But of course." She saw the sudden glint in Lord David's eye. It was mere flirtation, but Deanna didn't welcome it, not anymore.

Lord David turned to Swan. "The rooms have been confirmed at the hotel?"

Swan nodded slowly, keeping his eyes on Lord David.

Lord David turned to his sister.

Deanna wondered if Swan really could read people's thoughts, because he turned away and began taking things out of the half-packed trunk.

Lord David shrugged slightly, a charming acquiescence.

"Let's go tell Mama the good news," Cassie said.

Deanna walked behind Cassie and Madeline, wondering what exactly had just happened and which one of them had made the decision to stay.

She pondered the relationship between brother, sister, and servant while she sat at luncheon. Surmised while Elspeth retied her hat. Listened distractedly while Elspeth scolded her for wrinkling the ribbon.

At last she managed to slip away to sketch. She sat on a boulder at the edge of the rocks, but the wind was brisk, and after a few minutes of wrestling with her skirts and clamping down on her paper, she gave up and returned her sketching to her bag.

Deanna stood and looked around for a more protected space. She was several yards from where Daisy had fallen or been pushed to her death. She tried not to look. It seemed a macabre thing to do. Voyeuristic almost.

There had been few items about the deaths in the paper, and Deanna wondered if Charles or Mr. Woodruff had paid to have others withheld. Society thrived on intimate details of the rich. The cottagers were always being examined for any little slipup, any breath of scandal. And they were open to all forms of blackmail. Deanna wondered how much Mr. Woodruff had paid over the years to keep his peccadilloes secret. And she wondered if her own father had done the same.

She shied away from thinking about that possibility. It was enough to put her off getting married. Just look at what Adelaide would face. But Deanna wouldn't let that happen. She'd have to tell her sister about Madeline and Charles. And if Adelaide chose to ignore Deanna's warning, then she would have at least tried.

Her eyes drifted back to the rocks where Daisy had died.

There had to be an answer to why first Daisy and then Claire had been killed. Deanna put down her sketchbook, stood, brushed off her skirt, and climbed down until she was near the rocks where Daisy had lain. It looked so innocuous in the sun.

Suddenly, the back of her neck prickled. She brushed at it, thinking it must be a stray hair, but when she looked up, she saw Swan standing on the path above.

Deanna caught her breath. She couldn't have moved if she'd wanted to.

Slowly, he shook his head, then stepped back out of her view, leaving only sunshine. And Deanna wondered if her eyes saw true or whether he had been an apparition.

Either way, she'd lost the desire to study the rocks or even sketch. Throwing caution and decorum to the wind, she began to scramble up to the path.

"Oh, there you are. It's teatime." Cassie stood with Madeline and Lord David above her on the lawn. "Dee, it's absolutely morbid the way you keep coming back to look at this place."

"I was out sketching, and I . . ." She could not see Swan anywhere. Where had he disappeared to so quickly? "I thought I saw someone, so I came to see." She smiled up at them. "But I was mistaken." She finished the climb toward them. Lord David offered his hand for the last step.

They had tea on the veranda and were joined by Vlady Howe, Herbert Stanhope, and two young ladies from their set whom Deanna didn't know well. Charles joined them a few minutes later, looking harassed and like he hadn't slept in days. He must be worrying about his father and trying to prepare for the worst, Deanna thought. He took his tea to a chair and sat morosely contemplating his cup.

Mrs. Woodruff even made an appearance. She'd changed into an at-home robe of turquoise sateen, covered in red peonies, a chinoiserie theme she seemed partial to.

"Are you going to be with us long, Lord David?" Herbert asked when the conversation lagged for a moment.

"We will be here for a few more days, and then I have business in Manhattan, and Madeline will visit friends in Saratoga."

This was the first that Deanna had heard of it. Charles's head snapped up, and both Cassie and Mrs. Woodruff looked surprised at this news as well.

Lord David didn't elaborate. "And what about you, Stan-hope? Do you stay in Newport for the summer, lazing the warm weather away?" He said it in a joking way, but Herbert colored slightly.

"Until August, then I go abroad."

"Will your mama and sisters go with you?" Mrs. Woodruff asked.

"No, ma'am. I take myself. I plan to be there some time."

"You'll be back for the season of course."

Herbert smiled. "Perhaps."

Cassie laughed. "Oh, Herbert, you are so droll. You know you wouldn't miss the season. Europe has nothing to compare to New York when everyone is in town. Madeline, you and Lord David should stay for it. It's ever so much fun." She shot a flir-tatious look at Vlady, who lifted his eyebrows and smiled back.

"I'm afraid my sister and I must return to Barbados long before that. I do have a plantation to run."

"But surely Maddie could stay. She doesn't have to run the plantation. Charles, support me in this."

Charles merely shook his head.

Madeline laughed. "I don't have to run the plantation, but I must take care of my brother. When he's busy, he'll forget to sleep or eat if someone's not there to remind him."

"My dear sister exaggerates. Fortunately, I have an excellent foreman who keeps labor working smoothly and an estate manager to see to the business. Mainly, I just make sure that they are doing their jobs."

Deanna half listened to the conversation. She was begin-ning to feel uneasy. She didn't know why. It would be such a relief when the Manchesters were gone and the summer went back to normal.

"I suppose you're expecting us all to go to the theater as planned," Charles said to his mother.

"Of course. Your father wouldn't want everyone sitting around moping just because he's a little under the weather."

Charles's expression didn't change, but Deanna sensed that he knew his father wouldn't be recovering.

"Very well, mother. I wouldn't want to disappoint father." Charles stood and returned his cup to the tea tray. "I'll see you for dinner. I have business to attend to."

"Poor Charles," Mrs. Woodruff said. "He feels the weight of his responsibility."

They all murmured something. But what could they really say?

At least they would be going to the theater. There would be no need for conversation outside of the common banalities of discussing the play.

Maybe it would keep Deanna's mind off Joe and worrying about what he was doing and when he would return.

But now she had to go upstairs and tell Elspeth that she would be staying at the house while Deanna was out, and to insist that she spend the evening until their return downstairs in the company of the other servants.

—ooo-)O(-ooo—

The play was well written, the actors admirable, the plot engaging, and yet none of the Woodruff party seemed to be paying much attention.

Deanna kept thinking about the night before—Mr. Woodruff's wild entrance and his look of madness when Madeline stepped in to stop him. Charles's race back on his friend's yacht. Lord David being outwitted by the ailing man and having to walk from the wharf.

Now, *there* was a story for the stage. Except what would the ending be? Mr. Woodruff lying insensible. The Manchesters intending to leave. And who could blame them? Deanna would be inclined to leave, too, if she could. But Cassie and Mrs. Woodruff needed her support, if only as a sympathetic ear. And even though Mrs. Woodruff put on a brave front by sending them all to the theater, Deanna could see the strain on her face and in her voice. And Deanna knew that, when they returned, Mrs. Woodruff would be sitting by her husband's bedside.

Deanna was so lost in thought that she started when the final curtain came down and the audience broke into applause. Charles was already standing before the curtain calls were finished. And the others quickly collected wraps and purses and hats, and were hurrying through the crowded lobby, where people were chatting about the play or stopping for refreshment, making plans for supper or when to meet at the yacht races. People at their leisure.

But not the Woodruff party. Deanna was as anxious as Charles to get back. She was worried about Elspeth being left by herself. She'd said she would spend the time with the other members of the Woodruff staff, but Deanna wouldn't feel relieved until she saw her maid, safe and unhurt.

That was the state of her mind. And there was nothing she could do about it. They'd brought the family's closed carriage so that the five of them could travel together. No one talked or even fidgeted, including Deanna, so intent were they on their own thoughts.

Neville answered the door almost immediately, as if he had been waiting for them. His face was more pallid and expressionless than usual. Deanna prayed Mr. Woodruff hadn't taken a turn for the worse.

"I think I'll go up to see my father," Charles said as soon as he stepped into the house.

"I think the rest of us should all go to bed," Lord David said. "It's been a very eventful few days." And indeed, he looked exhausted.

Charles started for the stairs before the rest of them, but Neville called him back. "Sir, if I might have a word."

A sense of dread stilled Deanna steps.

Charles frowned. "Now, Neville?"

"If you please, sir."

"Yes, well, all right."

He went toward the library, and the butler followed. Lord David escorted Deanna, Cassie, and Madeline up the stairs.

Deanna said a quick good night, squeezed Cassie's hand, and went into her room.

"Elspeth? Are you here?"

She was about to call again when Elspeth stepped out of the dressing room. Deanna froze with her hand on the bell.

The maid's hair was pulled from its bun. Her apron was torn and her face was white and stricken.

"Elspeth? What happened? Are you hurt? Did someone hurt you?" Deanna rushed toward the girl but stopped several feet from her and reeled back. "Good Lord. What is that smell?"

"It's me, miss. Something awful's happened." And Elspeth burst into tears.

Trying to breathe shallowly, Deanna moved toward her. The smell was overpowering now and seemed to be coming from Elspeth's clothes.

"No, miss, stay back. It's rum . . . among other things."

Deanna sniffed, gulped. "You haven't been drinking?"

For the briefest moment, Elspeth looked outraged, which

is what Deanna had hoped for. It only lasted a second, then Elspeth sobbed uncontrollably.

"Did someone attack you?"

Elspeth shook her head.

"And you're not hurt?"

Another shake of her head.

"Then let's get you out of that dress and you can tell me all about it."

Deanna marched her back to the dressing room, turned her around, and untied her apron and slipped it over Elspeth's head. Looked at it, then gingerly bundled it up and threw it to the farthest corner.

But when she tried to unbutton Elspeth's collar, the maid rebelled. "I don't have anything to change into."

"We'll send for your things later, but for now, get out of that dress."

Elspeth shook her head.

"Now."

Reluctantly Elspeth undid the buttons of her dress while Deanna rummaged in the wardrobe. She found a simple cotton exercise dress and brought it out.

As Elspeth let her uniform fall, modestly covering her camisole with her hands, Deanna slipped it over her head.

"Oh, miss—"

"Don't argue," Deanna said in her strictest voice. It came nowhere near her mother's, but it worked. Elspeth turned around and let Deanna button up the dress.

The hem dragged along the floor, and Elspeth had to grab the skirt with both hands to keep from tripping over it, but it would have to do.

Deanna led her into the bedroom and shut the door behind

them. Then she sat Elspeth down in the slipper chair and pulled up the dressing bench.

"It was the voodoo man. He—I . . ."

"Go on."

"I was down with the others, but it was boring and I thought I'd go get my book from my room. The Cad Metti one."

Deanna nodded. Cad Metti was Elspeth's favorite detective. Streetwise and working class, she was a master of disguise, and she could even outsmart her boss. Elspeth's kind of heroine.

"So I did. And I was coming out of my room when I heard a moan coming from down the hall, where the men servants live. And that voodoo man, he comes staggering down the hall. I was too scared to move. I thought I was a goner.

"When he gets right up to me, he says, 'Poison,' and falls down dead at my feet."

"Swan's dead?" Deanna exclaimed.

"Dead drunk. Leastways, that's what I thought at first. So I'm sorry to say I gave him a little kick. Just to see if he was alive. Then I got to worrying if it really was poison, so I got him turned over and he didn't look like no drunk man I ever saw. Turning all gray like.

"I called for help. But I was afraid to wait, 'cause he was looking worse and worse, so I stuck my fingers down his throat and got him to get it all back up until he was just about empty. That's why my dress is so smelly."

Deanna shivered. "I see."

"By that time, Mr. Neville came, then went off to call the police like I told him to do . . ." Elspeth stopped to give Deanna a little smile. "The voodoo man was getting some color back, but he still didn't wake up. Now I'm thinking something don't seem right, so I leave him lying there and tell one of the fellas to look after him. They didn't want to, chicken-hearted so-and-so's. And I went into the men's hall—might get into trouble over that."

"Not to worry," Deanna assured her.

"There was a rum bottle on his table. But then I see that something's on the floor. It's a piece of paper. So I picked it up. It's a note."

"What did it say?"

Elspeth pulled up her skirt. "I thought I'd better keep it safe, so I put it in my knickers pocket." Holding it by the edge, she pulled out a rectangle of cheap paper. "Just hold it like this, miss, just in case the police have one of them fingerprinting machines."

Deanna doubted it, but she took the paper by the edge and read the crooked printing there.

I killed those girls. I am bad man. I must die.

Deanna looked up.

Elspeth nodded. "I'm thinking that something doesn't seem right. A man poisons himself and then stumbles down the hall for help?"

"Maybe he changed his mind."

"Hmmph. Somebody that big oughta not succumb to fear at a time like that."

"Did you show this to the police?"

"No. I wasn't taking any chances of some flat-footed police-man treading all over it. Or some maid thinking it was trash and throwing it out. I was going to show it to Sergeant Hennessey when he came."

"Good thinking," Deanna said. "Did you show it to Will?"

"By the time he came and they took the voodoo man away and Will had questioned everybody, you all had returned from the theater and I had to go. He told me to wait because he wanted to talk to me. And he told me not to say a word about anything that happened. So I figured I'd tell him later. But I did see the police taking the bottle away, so maybe the sergeant suspects something, too.

"What do you think, miss? Do you think that the voodoo man wrote that note and killed those girls? 'Cause I'm thinking something don't smell right, and it ain't just me."

Chapter
25

It was another hour before a maid tapped on Deanna's door to say the police had requested to talk to Elspeth.

"I told him you'd likely be in bed, but he insisted. Mr. Neville is down there with him, but he told me not to wake up the missus."

"That's exactly the way it should be. We'll be glad to come down." Deanna turned to Elspeth. "Now, aren't you glad I convinced you to change clothes?"

"Yes, miss. Though I can smell the liquor still."

"It's just in your mind."

"If you say so." Elspeth patted the pocket that now held the suicide note.

They went downstairs to the little study where Neville had placed the sergeant to wait.

"I thought you would be more comfortable here, miss," Neville said.

"Yes, thank you." Deanna nodded slightly, which was what

her mother did when she was dismissing someone. She hoped it would work on Neville.

Neville didn't move. "Wouldn't you rather I stayed, miss?"

"No thank you, Neville. You go on to bed. I'll let Mr. Hennessey out when we're finished."

"Thank you, miss, but I'll be waiting in the hall to accompany the sergeant to the door." He bowed and left the room.

"To the servants' door, I bet," Elspeth groused.

"Hush." Deanna turned to Will so quickly that he barely managed to wipe the grin off his face.

"You did that very well," he said.

"I've had the best training," she said ruefully.

Will smiled. "Yes. One look from your mama and even Satan would turn tail and run."

"So, what did you learn?"

"I believe that's my question."

"Is he dead yet?" Elspeth asked.

"Swan? He's at the hospital with a guard. He hasn't regained consciousness but he's still with us. At least when the guard checked in with me twenty minutes ago. But"—he held up a finger and turned to make sure the door was fully closed—"I think we can keep his condition to ourselves."

"Oh, yes," Deanna said. "Just what Elspeth and I were thinking. If the note was a fake—"

"What note?"

"The suicide note that Elspeth found."

"Elspeth." Will stuck out his hand.

She reached into her pocket and, holding it by the edge, put the note on the table before him.

"Why didn't you tell me about this earlier?"

"Well, I didn't want everyone to overhear, did I? 'Cause if we keep it secret, then the person who tried to kill him will be listening for that bit of detail. And when they don't hear it being talked about, they'll get nervous and slip up. Then we'll catch them."

"Where do you get these ideas?"

"Well, wouldn't they?"

"They might. But don't you go trying to press them into doing something desperate." Will leaned over the note. "I suppose you two handled it while you were studying it for clues."

"Yes, but we were careful not to disturb any fingerprints."

That startled Will into a crack of laughter. "Is that what they do in those adventure stories you're so fond of?"

"Yes, and Mr. Sherlock Holmes, too," Elspeth said. "*He* can tell all sorts—"

"Yes, thank you. I've read Mr. Conan Doyle's stories."

"Can you do all the things he does?"

"Me personally? Probably not. Theoretically, the department could, if we had the money and time—and the inclination—which, alas, we do not. Now, tell me again exactly what happened."

Elspeth told him. And finished with, "Did you take the bottle of liquor?"

"The rum? Yes, we did, and yes, initial tests show that it contains some kind of poison. The hospital is running more tests to see what kind. Hopefully your quick thinking saved his life."

"That's nothing; everybody knows to stick your finger down a little one's throat when he swallows something he shouldn't."

"I'd hardly call Swan little."

"No, but I used more than one finger."

Will grimaced. "Poor man."

"It wasn't too much fun for me, neither."

"No."

"Will he be okay?" Deanna asked.

Will shrugged. "Too early to tell. However, I haven't made anyone in the house aware of the incident. I'm sure the staff will gossip, and I'll come to give a report to Manchester in the morning. Until then, mum's the word."

"And what about Mr. Woodruff's tonic?" Elspeth asked.

Will looked startled. "What about it? Do you think he's being poisoned, too?"

Elspeth looked at Deanna and she took up the story.

"He hasn't been well since he returned home. At first everyone assumed it was seasickness, but it's lingered. And then, two nights ago, he rushed into the house like a crazy man, Will—I mean Sergeant—"

"Never mind. How was he acting crazy?"

"He ran in, saying he had to get to the library, and his face, it was all contorted. Fortunately, Madeline was there. She helped him upstairs, and he went with her, completely docile. It was odd," Deanna said. "Then Charles came in looking for him, and finally Lord David. It seems that Mr. Woodruff was running from both of them.

"Later in the night there was a commotion, and Elspeth and I followed one of the servants to Mr. Woodruff's bedroom. He was thrashing about and the bedcovers were on the floor. He was out of his head, fighting and ranting. They had to hold him down while Mrs. Woodruff mixed medicine into a glass. She forced him to drink it and he calmed down after that, but he hasn't awoken since."

"And you think Mrs. Woodruff might be poisoning her husband?"

"No. But—"

"We saw it in a magazine," Elspeth blurted out. "The one

that Daisy was reading when she was killed. You showed him that cover, didn't you, miss?"

Deanna nodded.

"Well, it was a man in the book, but the maid saw it; she was standing in the doorway and she saw the whole thing. And Daisy must have seen it, too, and that's why she got killed."

"Elspeth, that's just a story." Will looked over to Deanna.

"As crazy as it sounds, Will, it makes a certain kind of sense."

Will nodded. Deanna could tell he was tired and had no patience for their story. But she also knew he was listening and would think about it later.

"And Claire was killed," Deanna voice cracked, "because she talked to us."

"Okay, supposing just for the sake of argument that Daisy did see something and Claire knew about it. Why try to kill Swan?"

"To keep him from talking," Elspeth said, exasperation heavy in her voice.

"Maybe Swan also saw something he shouldn't have. Or maybe he knows who killed the maids. He warned us to leave." Deanna shuddered at her thought. "He said something evil was going on in this house. And I think he's right."

"So do I," Will said. "And I wish the two of you would remove to somewhere else."

"I can't until Mama comes home"—*or Aunt Harriet arrives*—"and besides, you need someone on the scene."

Will stood so fast that his hat, which had been balancing on the edge of the table, fell to the floor. "Dee! How can I get you to understand?"

"I do understand. This is not a game. I'm aware of that. Two young women have been murdered, and Swan may make the third victim. We're all scared. You think Elspeth and I are silly girls who read too many dime novels, but who else do you have in the house as your spies?"

Will didn't answer. A muscle jumped in his jaw. "Dee," he began more quietly, "Joe would kill me, and so would your mother and father, if anything happened to you. Bob would haunt me from the grave. He expected Joe and me to take care of you and Adelaide."

"Oh!"

"Dee? Why are you looking like that? Are you ill?"

"No. You said Bob would haunt you from the grave."

"Yes, and he'd find a way, too." Will looked abashed. "Sorry, Deanna, I didn't mean to upset you."

"I'm not upset. It's given me an idea."

"Deanna, what are you thinking?"

"'Haunt you from the grave.' Maybe we can use the voices of the dead to flush out their murderer."

"What are you concocting?"

"We'll hold a séance. Let the dead speak for themselves."

J oe took the overnight steamer back to Newport. His father had decided to return for the weekend and offered to take Joe on his yacht the next day, but now that Joe felt confident that the business end of the matter was being handled, he was impatient to return home. He didn't like Dee staying in that house with God knew what all. A partner who was an embezzler and a betrayer, and a shady plantation owner who might or might not hold a huge amount of R and W money but was making no move to sign any contracts.

There was something off about the man, Joe thought. Or was his father right, that the real reason he didn't like David Manchester was because he was getting much too familiar with Dee?

Joe didn't join in the card games or drinks in the first-class parlors; he just went straight to bed and slept like a log. He awoke in time to dress, shave, and be standing at the gangplank when the ferry docked.

He went straight to the warehouse, where he found Orrin and Will Hennessey drinking coffee and eating a hearty breakfast.

Orrin jumped up when Joe opened the door. "We thought you'd be coming in on the ferry."

"And you didn't come to meet me?"

Orrin grinned. "Wait until you hear this."

"Good news?" Joe looked the question at Will.

"Yes and no," Will said.

Orrin poured Joe a mug of coffee and set it on the table. Joe pulled up a stool.

"Good for Orrin, not so good for someone else."

"You'd better start with whatever happened while I was gone." Joe said, his mug cradled in both hands.

So Will started with how he'd been called to Seacrest the night before, how Elspeth had saved Swan's life and found the suicide note and the poison.

"Stood there as bold as brass and told me she thought the man was innocent and someone, possibly the real murderer, had poisoned him and tried to make it look like suicide. I tell you, Joe, those two women are formidable."

"I suppose the other woman you're talking about is Deanna."

"Who else? She'll never be happy as somebody's society wife."

Joe passed a hand over his eyes. "So is Swan dead?"

"Not yet. They pumped his stomach at the hospital, though I have to say, Elspeth did a pretty good job of emptying it before we got to him."

All three men grimaced.

"I'm not letting anyone see him. Lord David was already at the station this morning making inquiries. I had them fob him off—not hard to do, because nobody much likes a rich guy demanding things when two women of their class have been murdered. Everyone at the station is now betting that one of the cottagers did it."

"And what do you think?" Joe asked, though he was afraid he already knew the answer.

"I'm afraid they're right."

"Ha!" said Orrin, who'd been silent so far. "So which one of the cottagers did it?"

"That, my lad, is the question."

"So, what we need is to trap them."

"You considering becoming a policeman?"

Orrin's face suffused with red. "No, sir. I just thought—"

Will punched him lightly on the arm. "I'm just kidding you. You're absolutely right. Do either of you have any ideas?"

Orrin shook his head.

"No," Joe said slowly.

"Well, don't worry, my boys, because Deanna does. I'm meeting her at Bonheur later this morning. She told me to say you may come if you're back."

"Why Bonheur?"

"Deanna will be there consulting with your grandmother."

Joe closed his eyes. "Oh Lord."

SHELLEY FREYDONT

Deanna slept well into the morning. She and Elspeth had stayed up after Will left, proposing and discarding various plans for smoking out the killer. They had agreed to play dumb with the others about whether Swan was alive or dead, and promised to say nothing of the suicide note. Elspeth was still asleep in the dressing room with the door between them open. But as soon as Deanna pushed back the covers, Elspeth padded into the room, holding up one side of the nightgown she'd borrowed from Deanna.

"Just give me a few minutes, though I don't know how I'm going to get to my room without people talking and asking questions."

"You're not going anywhere. We'll ask one of the other maids to fetch all of your clothes and move them here."

"That's going to cause a stink belowstairs. They'll think I'm acting above my station."

"Well, too bad. We aren't going to be here much longer. And you're not going back to that room while we're here. You can tell them I'm afraid to be alone." Deanna rang for the chambermaid.

When she appeared a few minutes later with a coffee tray, Deanna gave her request. The girl looked a little reluctant.

"I will truly appreciate it."

A flicker of understanding glinted in the maid's eye. She would be amply rewarded. "Yes, ma'am." The maid bobbed a curtsey and started to leave.

"Be thorough. Don't leave anything behind."

"No'm."

"And what will you be wearing today?" Elspeth asked. "Is

the grenadine walking dress or the flowered muslin better for plotting and planning?"

"The yellow gauze; it's lighter and cooler, and don't bother with the half corset."

"The yellow it is." Elspeth fisted both hands at her hips. "*With* the half corset."

Deanna stuck out her tongue at Elspeth's retreating back.

By the time Deanna had finished dressing and Elspeth had twisted her hair into a soft knot at the top of her head, the maid returned with Elspeth's belongings.

Deanna dropped the rest of her pin money into the girl's hand. The maid's eyes lit up. "Anything else, miss?"

"No, that will be all."

"Thank you, miss." She curtseyed and backed out the door.

As soon as she was gone, Deanna turned to Elspeth. "I wonder if everyone is at breakfast?"

"It's late enough. Why?"

"See if you can find an empty bottle in the dressing room."

"How big?"

Deanna held her fingers three inches apart.

"What are you up to, miss? Mr. Hennessey said not to do anything until we saw him again."

"I'm just going to tell Mrs. Woodruff that I'll be out this morning, and on my way out I'm going to just pop in for a minute to check on Mr. Woodruff."

Elspeth's eye bulged. "Not without me, you're not."

"Of course not. Now you find a small bottle and meet me outside Mr. Woodruff's bedroom in five minutes." And she went out to visit her hostess.

Mrs. Woodruff was lying on the divan in her room, looking harried and tired. Deanna just meant to stay long enough to reassure her, but as she got up to leave, Mrs. Woodruff grasped her wrist.

"What is it, ma'am?"

"Nothing, nothing. You're a good girl. A friend to Cassie."

"True blue," Deanna said.

"Run along. Have fun."

Deanna smiled, but Mrs. Woodruff had closed her eyes. Deanna tiptoed away.

Elspeth must have been watching from the door, because as soon as Deanna left Mrs. Woodruff's room, she came hurrying down the hall to meet her.

"Did you find something?"

Elspeth nodded and looked down to where she was clutching her skirt. "In my hand," she whispered.

"Give it here."

"I'm coming, too."

"Yes, but you're going to guard the door while I pour."

They moved quietly down the hall, stopped outside the bedroom door, and looked both ways down the hall.

Deanna knocked softly. Waited to see if Mr. Woodruff's man would open the door. When nothing happened, she slowly turned the knob and opened the door just wide enough to look inside. The room was empty except for Mr. Woodruff, who lay motionless on the bed.

On the side table was a pitcher of water, two small glasses, and the bottle of medicine. She stepped inside, Elspeth pushed in after her.

"Give me the vial and stay here to make sure nobody's coming."

Elspeth handed over the tiny bottle, then she closed the door until it was barely open, and peered out.

Deanna quickly crossed to the bed. Still no movement or sound from Mr. Woodruff. She uncapped the vial and laid it on the table while she unstopped the medicine bottle.

Then she carefully poured a small amount of the medicine in the vial. When the bottle was returned to the table and the vial was in her skirt pocket, she took a minute to look at the recumbent man.

It was shocking. The normally robust, fun-loving man looked like he was already gone, his face almost as white as the bed-clothes. Deanna didn't hold out much hope of a good outcome.

She sighed and joined Elspeth at the door. Fortunately, the hallway was empty, and they hurried back to Deanna's room. Just as they reached the door, a maid came out of the opposite room.

"Good morning, miss. Let me get the door for you."

"Go-good morning," Deanna stuttered, and waited impatiently for the maid to put down her bundle and open the bedroom door.

As soon as they were inside, they both let out huge breaths.

"I can't believe we did it," Elspeth said.

"Nor I, or that my hands managed to pour the liquid without spilling a jot. They were shaking like anything."

"You know, if we had been a minute later, we might have run right into that maid as we came out of Mr. Woodruff's door."

"I know," Deanna said quietly. And she knew Elspeth was thinking the same thing. Is that what had happened to Daisy? Just a chance encounter that had led to murder?

"Now what?" Elspeth asked, breaking the spell.

"Now you're going down to the kitchen for something to eat, I'm going to join the others for breakfast, and then we're going to Gran Gwen's to confer with Will about catching a killer."

Chapter
26

"You slept late," Cassie said, waving a piece of toast at Deanna as she stepped into the breakfast room.

"Maddie and I are dying to hear what happened last night. Maddie's so worried about Swan. Lord David left earlier to visit the police station, but he hasn't returned. No one told them last night that Swan had taken sick."

Madeline looked like she hadn't slept well, and Deanna felt a momentary pang at their thoughtlessness. But only for a moment.

Deanna took a plate and studied the contents of the chafing dishes. She took her time; chose a piece of ham, some eggs, and braised tomatoes; passed on the kippers; and took her place at the table.

"Well?"

Neville entered and poured her a cup of coffee. "Thank you, Neville; you can leave the pot."

"Yes, miss."

As soon as he was gone, Cassie and Maddie both leaned forward.

"Well," Deanna said between bits of food, "Elspeth was so frightened last night that I made her sleep in my dressing room."

"We wondered," Cassie said. "We stayed up waiting to find out what was happening, but Will Hennessey must have left without talking to mother."

"Perhaps he didn't want to bother the family, considering your father's illness."

"Oh, that must be it," Cassie said, frowning slightly. "So, what did happen?"

"All I know is that Swan got really sick and they called for an ambulance. I guess Will was on duty and came along with the others."

"Did they say what's wrong with him?" Maddie asked. "We're so worried about him. We didn't even know that he'd been sent to the hospital until this morning."

"I suppose we'll have to wait for Lord David to tell us. Because I certainly don't know."

"Elspeth didn't say anything more?" Cassie stuck out her lip. "The maids were talking that she stuck her fingers down his throat and made him—" She shuddered. "You know."

"Was it a stomach complaint?" Maddie asked. "Something he ate? Is he going to be all right?"

"I have no idea. But Elspeth said he looked awfully bad and he was barely breathing." Deanna took a bite of ham. She was feeling distinctly queasy just thinking about Elspeth's heroics.

"Did they find anything?" Madeline asked.

Deanna stopped. "Like what?"

"Like something he'd drunk or eaten?" Cassie said. "None of the other servants are sick."

"I don't know. Elspeth didn't say. Though I suppose if they had found something, she would have told me."

Madeline's face grew even paler.

"Madeline, are you feeling all right?" Deanna asked.

Madeline nodded. "It's just all so terrible. Swan has been with us for a long time. Things like this don't happen in Barbados."

"Food poisoning?" Deanna asked innocently.

"Or murder."

"Really? How amazing. I thought every place had murders . . . and murderers."

"Not where we live. Well, maybe the natives do, but I never hear about it. As soon as Swan recovers, I'm going to make David take me back home."

"Oh no. Not so soon. The season is just beginning," Cassie said. Deanna added her halfhearted pleas to Cassie's. But when Cassie began to enumerate all the parties and events they were invited to, Deanna pushed her chair back.

"I have some errands to run this morning," she told them. "I won't need a carriage. I'll walk. I'll take Elspeth with me. I think she could use some fresh air, poor thing."

"Oh, yes, poor thing," Cassie said. "Perhaps she'd feel better in one of the open carriages. No one is using the gig this morning."

"Thank you, but I need the exercise, even if Elspeth doesn't."

"Well, don't be long. We were going to Bailey's this morning, but what with everything, Maddie decided she should stay here and wait for Lord David."

Deanna nodded sympathetically.

"Couldn't you stay here with us? Can't your errands wait?"

"No, I'm sorry, they can't." Deanna stood. "And now I must

rush if I'm to be back in time to dress for tea. Is tonight the night of Mrs. Howe's musical soiree?"

"Yes, and don't forget, tomorrow night is Gran Gwen's mysterious fete."

"Oh, I won't." Deanna turned to Maddie. "Gran Gwen always has the most amusing gatherings. It will be such fun. And don't worry, Madeline. I'm sure Swan will be better directly."

She didn't wait for a response, and as she left, she heard Cassie still cajoling Madeline to stay for the season.

Deanna and Elspeth set off down the cliff walk toward Bonheur.

"What if she isn't at home?" Elspeth asked, puffing to keep up with Deanna's long strides.

"Carlisle will let us in to use the telephone, then Cook will ply us both with tea and something she's just baked. And we'll get to eat in the kitchen because there'll be no one there to tell on us. And it will be just like the old days."

Elspeth frowned.

"Don't be a sourpuss."

It was a sunny day and there was a slight breeze, so the walk was pleasant. When they arrived at Bonheur, Deanna led Elspeth around to the kitchen door and knocked.

"Lord, Miss Deanna, what are you up to this time?" Cook asked. She was a dumpling of a woman. All the Ballard cooks were hefty women. Gran Gwen insisted that women cooked as well as any man, and without nearly the same amount of drama.

"Is Gran Gwen at home?"

"She is, which you would know if you went to the front door as is proper."

Deanna looked chastised. "We thought you would at least give us a cup of tea."

Cook picked up a wooden spoon and tapped a tattoo in the air. "Up to your old tricks are you? And you almost a grown woman."

"Ugh. Don't remind me."

"Well, you're in luck; the kettle is already on the boil and I baked these this morning." She opened the larder door and came out with a tray of fragile tea cakes. "You can each have two. The rest are for the guests tomorrow night."

Deanna took two for herself, and when Elspeth hesitated, she took two more and handed them to her. Elspeth glanced at Cook.

"Egalitarian is what you'll get in this house," Cook said, turning her spoon to Elspeth. "Just be sure not to overstep."

Elspeth glanced sideways at Deanna.

"She just means we all get tea cakes when we want them." Deanna wiggled the tea cakes at her.

Elspeth took them and bit into one, sighing with delight. Deanna followed her example, and both ate enthusiastically as they waited for the tea to brew.

Cook filled the teapot, then went over to a wall panel holding two rows of buttons. She pressed one, and after a few minutes, Carlisle appeared.

He barely registered surprise at finding Deanna in the kitchen, well trained as he was. "Good morning, Miss Deanna."

"Good morning, Carlisle. We need to see Gran Gwen." She looked toward Elspeth. "*Both* of us need to see her."

"You'll have your tea first," Cook said.

"I'll tell her you're here." Carlisle made a dignified exit, though Deanna did see him glance at the tea cakes as he passed.

Cook was just pouring the tea when Gran Gwen swept into the kitchen. "Is this a private party?"

Elspeth jumped up, nearly upsetting her cup.

Cook quickly wiped her hands on her apron. "Would you like a cup, madam?"

"Yes, please, and, Elspeth, please sit down and relax. I often take tea in the kitchen." Under Elspeth's startled gaze and Deanna's amused one, Gran Gwen sat down at the table. "Oh, dear," she said. "Have I scandalized you, Elspeth?"

"No, ma'am."

"You did, Gran Gwen. She's such a stickler," Deanna said, shooting Elspeth a smug look.

"And to what to I owe the pleasure of your visit?"

"We wanted to use your telephone."

Gran Gwen frowned at Deanna. "Is the one at Seacrest broken?"

Deanna shook her head. "Nor the one at home. But we wanted to come here."

"Ah, tea cakes."

"They're for the party tomorrow night," Cook said. "You can only have two."

Gran Gwen took a handful from the tray.

"I hope it's all right," Deanna said as they munched cookies, "but I asked Will Hennessey to meet us here. I told him I would telephone the station when we arrived. And . . . and I wondered if you had heard from Joe?"

"You're in luck. Joseph sent Orrin round this morning with a message." Gran Gwen shook her head. "Joseph's head is already living in the twentieth century, yet he doesn't own a telephone."

"We don't have a lot of telephones down in the Fifth," Elspeth said.

"I know, dear. But that will change in time. Anyway, he

said they are both coming for lunch. Until that time, why don't you fill me in on the goings-on at Seacrest."

By the time Joe and Will arrived, Gran Gwen had been brought up to date on all the "goings-on" at Seacrest, the tea cakes were gone, and Cook had started a new batch.

———◦◦◦❯❮◦◦◦———

It was several hours later when Gran Gwen sent Deanna and Elspeth back to Seacrest in the family carriage. Their planning meeting had gone so long that Deanna had to hurry to change clothes in time for tea.

Mrs. Woodruff even came down to pour. She looked resigned but rested.

Deanna hadn't expected Lord David to be back from his vigil at the hospital, so she was surprised but glad when he and Charles came down the steps together. She had plenty of questions she wanted to ask.

"How is your poor manservant?" Mrs. Woodruff asked.

Lord David shot the crease of his white linen trousers and sat down across from her. "Alas, not well. I wasn't even allowed to see him. They said he barely clings to life and cannot be disturbed."

"How awful!" Mrs. Woodruff said, sympathetically.

Lord David shrugged slightly. "We can but hope for the best. He was a good worker. Took very good care of me and my wardrobe."

She handed him a cup of tea. "Well, I'm sure Neville can find you a replacement. Until he's better of course. He might not be as unique as Swan, but he should suffice until you can make other arrangements, or . . ."

She trailed off and looked over to where Charles stood separated from the others, his hand resting on the fireplace mantel. "Charles, do you care for tea?"

"Hmm? No, Mama, I do not care for tea. Manchester, where is your sister?"

"I'm here," Madeline announced floating into the room, the skirts of her tea gown floating behind her. "Mrs. Woodruff, please forgive me for being so late to tea." She sniffed daintily. "It's all been just a bit much for me."

Deanna was tempted to roll her eyes. The few times she'd seen Madeline and Swan together, Madeline hadn't been very nice to him, and she'd called his magic tricks boring. Though Deanna supposed that it might get boring if Lord David was constantly pulling him out to perform for their friends. And it was true that some things and people aren't missed until they're gone.

"We're so sorry, dear, that this has happened while you were here. Nothing like it has ever happened before, I assure you. Come sit here on the settee by me."

Madeline did as she was bid and accepted a cup of tea but none of the sweets from the three-tiered tea tray.

Deanna tried to join in the conversation, but she could hardly look Mrs. Woodruff in the eye. She felt so guilty for filching some of her husband's medicine and for even momentarily wondering if this woman could be poisoning her husband.

Cassie kept looking at Deanna with a confused and worried countenance, and Deanna breathed a sigh of relief when she was finally back upstairs in her own room.

"I don't think I can stand it until tomorrow night," she told Elspeth as she changed out of her dress. She jumped up on the bed and lay down, arms stretched out to the side. "Oh." She sat straight up.

"What, miss? Did something pinch you?"

"No. But Elspeth, what if Mama hears that I've gone to a party at Gran Gwen's? Especially without her. She will not be happy. You know how she feels about the Ballards."

"Well, by the time she does, it will be too late to stop you."

"True. And even if she gives me one of her lectures, it will be worth it if we can catch a killer."

Dinner was a quiet affair. Madeline and Charles were both brooding; Lord David kept the conversation going, though Deanna could tell he was only half paying attention.

After dinner the ladies climbed into the Woodruffs' barouche while Charles and Lord David followed in the smaller spider phaeton.

Deanna had never visited the Howes before, though her mother and Adelaide often called on Mrs. Howe. They lived in one of the newer cottages at the south end of Bellevue Avenue.

Vlady must have been waiting for them just inside, for as they entered the music room, which gleamed with gold brocade walls and upholstery, he strode up to them to say hello. Charles and Lord David had stopped to speak with several of the gentlemen, and Mrs. Woodruff waved to someone across the room and left to say hello.

Soon the performance was announced and everyone found a seat. Deanna looked around for Cassie, from whom she'd been separated, and caught sight of her and Vlady slipping out of the room.

Deanna turned back to the singer just as Herbert and Cokey sidled into the room. They stopped one on each side of her. She nodded and smiled.

"Where's Joe?" Cokey asked. "Have they arrested him yet?"

"Enough, Cokey," Herbert hissed across Deanna. "You're no longer amusing."

"Deanna thinks I amusing, don't you?"

"No, I don't. Now please be quiet."

Old Mrs. Bigelow turned around and frowned at them.

The music began. The soprano, a coloratura from the Metropolitan Opera, sang an aria from *The Magic Flute*. Appreciative applause followed her song and her next song and the next.

When the singer left the stage for the intermission, Herbert and Cokey took their leave.

"That's enough screeching for me for one evening. I'm for the Casino. Herbert?"

Herbert agreed.

Cokey bowed slightly. "Well, if you'll excuse us, we'll see you tomorrow at the Ballard fete. At least we can depend on Joe's grandmother to keep things interesting."

You don't know the half of it, Deanna thought as she watched them both walk away.

By the end of the second half of the program, even Deanna was ready for some quiet.

But when they returned to Seacrest after the musicale, there was a policeman waiting for them. He was sorry to have to inform them that Swan had passed away.

They were all shocked, even Deanna—who wasn't sure if it were true or one of the lies Joe and Will had concocted as part of the act.

Madeline let out a little cry and Cassie put her arm around her. Lord David accepted the news stoically and asked when he could pick up Swan's body for burial.

"Well, now. The captain has ordered a postmortem examination."

"No," Madeline cried. "Oh no!"

Even Lord David looked like he might cry. "But we want to take him home."

"And you can, sir. When the coroner's finished with him."

"It's heathen," Madeline cried. "Godforsaken! Oh, why did we come here?"

"Now, now," Mrs. Woodruff said. She took over from Cassie and helped Madeline to the sofa in the front parlor. "Neville, send for my maid to bring some salts."

Lord David walked out with the policeman. Deanna could still hear him arguing with the man.

"It *is* heathen to cut the poor man up like that," Cassie said. "How awful."

"Yes, it is," Deanna said. "Just awful."

—⚬❍⚬—

Joe, Will, and Orrin arrived at Bonheur at daybreak. Cook had guessed as much, and the buffet groaned beneath her eggs, ham, steak, bread, and porridge. Orrin refused to eat in the breakfast room, so Joe and Will joined him in the kitchen.

"Don't you young people make a habit of this," Cook complained. "I need room to work."

They'd worked out most of the plan with Deanna and Elspeth the day before. But they had intentionally left the women in the dark about certain things so their reactions would be genuine.

"I just hope they don't faint dead away," Will said as he unrolled a drum of wire across Bonheur's music room floor. They'd decided on that room because the French doors opened off to two sides, one which led to the terrace and the other which led to the lawn and the cliffs. They would use the terrace door for their spirit visit, since the second parlor was where they would work the machinations of the evening.

"Those two?" Joe said. "Not likely. Though it might be better if Deanna did. Then we could just tell her afterward if it worked and not have to worry about her getting in the way."

Will straightened, holding the drum of wire in both hands. "You know, Deanna's changed, Joe. Just in the last few days, she's become sure of herself. More confident. Courageous. It's kind of amazing. I think her mama is going to be in for a big surprise when she returns to Newport. I don't think Deanna will go back to the way things were."

"Heaven protect us," Joe said, and spliced the wires onto a thin wooden board.

"Maybe. But lest you forget, it was Deanna who thought up this scheme."

"Don't remind me. Roll."

Will shook his head and went back to rolling a spool of wire along the floor.

When he was finished, they carefully relaid the carpeting to cover it and placed the games table right in the center.

Then Joe went into the next room, where the other end of the wire led to another board that had been secured to a second table. An alphabet was printed on the board, and under each letter was a red light. A row of switches ran along the table corresponding to each letter.

"Everything working, Orrin?"

"Yes, sir. So far, so good."

"Let's give it a test, then call Grandmère out to have a go."

Joe pulled a chair up to the table in the music room and opened a box. He took out a Ouija board, a fad that had swept the country and that, whether it actually communicated with the other world or not, would serve their purposes just fine.

He set the board on the table and a wooden planchette on top of the board.

Will sat down and they each lightly touched the planchette. It began to move across the two rows of letters, first to one letter, then another.

"Strange," Will said. "Are you moving it?"

"Not intentionally. Okay," Joe called to Orrin, who had stayed in the other room.

He looked at Will, who returned his gaze, and the planchette moved.

P. The planchette moved again. *O.* It moved again.

"You're not doing this?"

Joe shook his head. "Orrin is. Electricity and magnets. Let's call in Grandmère. Then we'll figure out the rest of the evening's entertainment."

Deanna thought the day would never end. She hated being left out of the preparations for the evening's experiment. She was the one who'd had the idea of calling the spirits of the dead maids. Elspeth had volunteered to act the part, but Joe and Will had nixed that idea. They would find someone on their own.

Now they were over there making plans, and they'd excluded Deanna and Elspeth from joining in.

Joe said she had to go back to Seacrest and act normal, that it would be more effective if she and Elspeth didn't know quite what to expect, but just to be sure to watch everyone's reactions very carefully.

Deanna was sure they would catch the culprit; Gran Gwen

had invited everyone in their immediate circle and they'd all agreed to come. Including Mrs. Woodruff, who declared that she'd been neglecting her visitors long enough, and since Mr. Woodruff was still abed but not getting worse, she would be pleased to attend.

The only problem was how to get Elspeth to the party. She refused to sit at Seacrest while all the excitement was at Bonheur. It was finally decided that Deanna would give her the evening off and Orrin would pick her up in the gig outside the gates of Seacrest.

By the time Deanna came upstairs to dress for the evening, she was a bundle of nerves and anticipation. Elspeth wasn't much better.

"Where have you been? I've worn a path in the carpet while you've been lollygagging about."

"Sorry, but Cassie was determined to convince Madeline to stay by dragging us from store to tea room to ice cream parlor. She chatted on about all the soirees and balls, the regatta races, the tennis matches, and the golf tournaments, until I was ready to scream."

"Did she convince her?"

"No, I don't think she did. I don't think this is what Lady Madeline expected from the social season in Newport."

"Well, nobody did, now, did they?"

"Well, once Will arrests the killer, I say good riddance. I'm heartily sick of both of the Manchesters."

Chapter
27

Gran Gwen had gone all out for her fete.

Authentic Japanese lanterns lined the drive and stood sentry along the front of the house. A silken canopy came to a point above the entrance and floated down to either side. There was a light layer of fog rolling in from the sea, and clouds scudded across the sky hiding and exposing the three-quarter moon like a mise en scène.

Deanna thought it was a perfect night for conjuring the dead.

When the Woodruff party arrived, only five people were drinking champagne in the conservatory, where a cool breeze wafted in through the open windows and a string trio played from the far corner. Deanna recognized Quentin Asher, a handsome widower whose name had been linked to Gran Gwen's in an earlier decade, or so Deanna's father had said.

"Oh dear," Mrs. Woodruff whispered to Charles. "Did we arrive too early?"

"I don't think so, Mama. Gwen Ballard is known for her intimate dinners. I think this one is to be extremely intimate."

"Well, that's no fun." Cassie looked around the room. "Where are Vlady and the others? They said they were coming."

Deanna began to wonder that herself. She didn't really want to suspect any of their friends of killing the maids or Swan, but Vlady Howe and Herbert Stanhope had been together both times they'd discovered the bodies. And Herbert had seen her and Joe after the break-in and had said nothing. Because he also had a secret?

Gran Gwen came to meet them. She was the embodiment of the exotic in a gown of damson purple encrusted with jet beads. Her hair was pulled back and stuck through with two golden ostrich plumes. Deanna thought she looked magnificent.

She took both of Mrs. Woodruff's hands. "Ah, Nell, my dear. I'm so glad you could come. How is Francis?"

Then she said hello to the others, saving an arch look for Deanna.

"My goodness," Lord David said, walking Deanna into the conservatory. "Madeline said she was quite unique, but I'd say she is nothing short of amazing."

"She is," Deanna said.

Lord David smiled, took her arm. Deanna tried to think about something else.

A few minutes later, Vlady and Herbert arrived, followed shortly by Cokey Featheringham, his cousin Nathaniel, and several young ladies, including Ivy Bennett and Olivia Merrick.

"Ugh, it's Cokey Featheringham." Cassie said. "What is he doing here? I'd have thought Gran Gwen wouldn't invite someone who'd been spreading such nasty rumors about Joe."

"I haven't the faintest," Deanna said. "Just ignore him."

Dinner was announced soon after that. Joe was conspicuously absent; Mr. Asher led Gran Gwen in to table.

Deanna found herself once again on Lord David's arm. "I'm not sure what to expect," he said. "Shall we have lamb and couscous and eat with our fingers, or rice and raw fish and eat with chopsticks a la japonaise?"

"I imagine it will be something closer to home. Her cook is excellent but American."

"Ah, I can't wait."

Sixteen people sat down to dinner, which at Gran Gwen's was never more than five courses. Though lately, people had been moving away from the usual four-hour dinner to much shorter ones, Gran Gwen's dinners had always been delicious, sparkling with conversation, and never more than two and a half hours anyway.

Tonight was no exception, though Deanna wished people would eat faster. She for one had no appetite and more than once thought to excuse herself and go search out Joe and Will to see what they were doing.

After dinner the ladies went back to the conservatory to wait for the gentlemen to finish their port and cigars.

Deanna was ready to jump out of her skin when at last the gentlemen returned and Gran Gwen stood and went to the door. "For your entertainment I have planned a little game, if you'll all join me in the music room."

They followed her across the hall and behind the curving staircase to the music room. The music room was really that, with a grand piano in one corner, a dais for chamber music, and usually a grouping of chairs for listening. Tonight the chairs had been replaced by a small table with two straight-backed chairs. A green cloth was laid over the surface, concealing some-thing beneath. There was a slight lump in the center.

"This way."

Gran Gwen stopped by one of the chairs. "Last month in the city I spent the most interesting evening playing a game that I'd heard of but had never played before." She paused, looking over her guests. "I say game, because that's what it's supposed to be. But that night, we were witnesses to something profound. Something inexplicable. Something my grandson, Joseph, would say is sheer fakery."

A ripple of quiet laughter.

"So I decided to put it to my friends. And the young people here are much more clever than I."

That was a whopper, Deanna thought. Still a thrill zinged through her. It was happening. Tonight they would catch a killer.

Unless the killer really was one of the servants or a passing lunatic who preyed on maids. Which would make this elabo-rate affair a waste of time.

"And so I've asked you here to dine on Cook's succulent roast duck and now to test the game for ourselves. No pranks, just"—she paused, gave one of those half shrugs that the French were partial to—"scientific inquiry."

She took the corner of the cloth between two fingers and whisked it from the table, leaving a wooden game board. The letters of the alphabet lined up in two arches across the top. *A* through *M* in the first line and *N* through *Z* on the second. Below that was a row of ten numbers, 1–0. In the right corner was the word "No," and in the left corner, the word "Yes."

"Ouija," Cassie squealed. "I love this game."

"I'm so glad." Gran Gwen sat down on one side of the table. "Who would like to be the first to ask the board a question?"

"I will," said Cokey.

"You will not," said Herbert. "You'll cheat and make it say the things you want it to say."

"Why don't we have one of our new friends give it a whirl. Madeline? Lord David?"

Lord David threw up his hands in mock horror. "Not I. I'm afraid of what it might say."

All the men laughed. Gran Gwen gave him an arch smile.

"How about you, Madeline? Would you care to participate?"

Madeline shook her head and took a step back.

"Oh, come on, Maddie," Cassie urged. "It's easy and great fun. We've all played before." Cassie nudged her toward the table.

"I don't know how."

"Why don't you go first and show her?" Vlady suggested.

Cassie lifted her shoulder. "I will." She sat in the chair across from Gran Gwen. "You just let your fingers rest lightly on the planchette and the game will do the rest." They both put their fingers on the planchette.

"What shall we ask it?" Cassie asked.

Vlady leaned close to her ear but said, loud enough for them all to hear, "Ask it to name your boyfriend." He winked at Cassie.

Mrs. Woodruff raised her eyebrows.

Cassie giggled. "See if I don't. Ready, Gran Gwen?"

Gwen nodded.

"Who loves me most?" Cassie asked the board loudly.

Everyone laughed. "She's got you there, Vlady."

"Hush," Gwen said. "You must concentrate."

Everyone obeyed and leaned closer to the board to watch.

For a second nothing happened, then slowly the planchette moved across the board, first to the left, then to the right, then it swung all the way to the bottom of the alphabet.

V.

Everyone leaned in a little closer. The planchette moved again.

L.

The planchette made a slow sweeping circle and ended at the far side of the board.

A.

Madeline laughed. "You're doing that on purpose."

"No, I'm not."

"Well, I think you've asked it enough, miss," Mrs. Woodruff said, laughing.

Cassie stood and gave her mother a saucy look.

Deanna couldn't imagine being that close and confidential with her own mother.

"Now, who's next?" Cassie looked around the room. "Dee?"

"Not me."

"Then it must be Maddie."

Madeline shook her head.

"Mad-die," Vlady chanted. "Mad-die," he repeated, and this time Cokey joined in. Soon everyone was urging Madeline to give it a try.

"Very well," Madeline said looking her most charming. "But we won't be asking it about boyfriends."

Everyone laughed except Deanna and, as she saw after a quick glance, Charles Woodruff.

Madeline sat in the chair across from Gran Gwen.

"I just put my fingers on that wooden thing?"

"Yes. Barely touching it."

Gran Gwen and Madeline both put their fingers on the planchette.

"I don't know what to ask."

"Ask if you'll be staying in Newport." Cassie suggested.

Once again, the planchette began to move. Straight to the left corner.

"Yes!" squealed Cassie. "I knew it. We'll have such fun."

Madeline looked over her shoulder at her brother. He smiled and shrugged.

"Ask it why," Deanna suggested.

"Okay. Why?"

The planchette began to move, straight to the middle of the board.

S.

Then straight to the end.

W.

The room became so quiet that Deanna could hear someone's adenoidal breathing.

A.

"Swan!" Herbert exclaimed.

"But Swan is dead," Vlady said.

Madeline started to rise.

"Put your fingers back, Maddie." Cassie pressed her back into the chair.

"Swan is the reason?" Gran Gwen asked.

The planchette swung to the left again.

Yes.

"Why?"

They all crowded so close to the table that Madeline couldn't get up if she'd wanted to, and it looked to Deanna like she would love to flee. And why was that?

The planchette moved.

P.

It moved downward and shot upward.

O.

I.

The planchette swung wildly now.

S.

"No!" Madeline's fingers recoiled from the planchette as if it had become hot. Gran's fingers left the planchette, too, but the little heart-shaped piece of wood continued to move without them.

O.

A wild circle, and back to . . .

N.

"Poison!" cried Vlady and Herbert at the same time.

"He took poison," Vlady said.

Madeline attempted to put her fingers back on the planchette, but it jerked away.

M.

"This isn't possible," Herbert said, almost to himself.

U.

"Make it stop!" Madeline cried.

"Yes, do," said Mrs. Woodruff. "Gwen, you're scaring the young people."

Gwen held up both her hands in a helpless gesture. No one was moving the board.

Olivia whimpered and clung to Cokey.

R.

The last letters came in rapid succession, the planchette sliding across the board of its own accord.

The guests stood mesmerized. No one moved or stepped back but kept their eyes on the board.

D.

E.

R.

The lights flickered and went out just as the French doors flew open and fog rolled into the room.

Cassie screamed and hid her eyes. Vlady pushed her behind him for protection.

Before anyone recovered, a figure stepped out of the mist. Tall, large, with yellow slashes floating in the air, moving closer.

Deanna had seen it before, knew what it was, and still it shot chills up her back.

"No-o-o-o!" Madeline stood so fast that her chair toppled backward.

Then the turban and the feathers came to view.

"It's Swan," Cassie said feebly, peering around Vlady's shoulder.

Mrs. Woodruff sat down abruptly on the nearest chair.

Gwen's expression didn't change; she didn't turn around or acknowledge the apparition in any way.

It was unnerving to behold.

Then from the hall the long clock began to gong. Everyone huddled closer together, as an arm rose from the robe, pointing at the group. First at one, then another, until it stopped on one in particular: Lord David Manchester.

"Mur-der," it intoned in such a low voice that the planchette and crystal sconces shook.

Lord David staggered back.

"No!" cried Maddie. "You're dead. Leave us."

"Maddie," Lord David said, "get ahold of yourself. It's a trick."

The apparition's arm rose. Turned to Lady Madeline. "Murdered. All of us. Murdered."

"All of who?" Cokey whispered, and edged toward the door.

Vlady grasped his sleeve. "Wait."

Maddie shook her head. "You're dead. Do you hear me? Dead."

The arm reared back and everyone cowered together, afraid of what it might unleash.

All but Madeline. "Leave us, I say! I killed you once, and I'll kill you again if I have to! Go to hell, fiend!"

Swan stepped forward, larger than life as the mist swirled around him, both arms outstretched as if to strangle her.

"No!" Madeline flung herself around and pushed Cassie aside.

An unearthly hiss echoed around them and the entire room as fog engulfed Swan, and he was gone.

The lights came on, and through the retreating mist, Deanna saw Madeline throw open the door and run, Lord David on her heels.

"Good Lord," Vlady cried, and started after them.

Deanna was just a step behind him.

But when they reached the hall, there was no sign of Madeline or her brother.

Vlady turned in a circle. "Where'd they go?"

They could see Carlisle standing by the front door, hands open. They hadn't come that way.

"They must have gone out through the conservatory," Deanna said just as Herbert, followed by several others, burst into the hallway.

They ran toward the back of the house to the conservatory. The door to the lawn and ultimately to the cliff walk was slightly ajar.

"Do you see them? I can't see anything in this dark."

"There!" Herbert yelled and pointed to two figures, fog curl-ing around them as they ran across the lawn to the sea. "They must be heading for Seacrest along the cliff walk."

They were being followed by two men, and another figure who was shedding turban and flowing robes as he ran. And behind them followed Elspeth, hiking up her skirts and trying to keep up.

Deanna stopped to unclasp her shoes. Cassie ran up beside her. "What's going on?"

"Come and see," and Deanna. She kicked off her shoes and sped across the grass.

"Wait for me!" Cassie called and ran after her.

Deanna cut over to the walk. The wind was stronger near the cliff; beneath them the waves were crashing loud against the rocks. Out of the fog, Deanna thought she caught a glimpse of a ship before it disappeared again.

Ahead of her, the figures seemed to have slowed down. And when she at last reached them, she saw that Lord David had grabbed his sister . . . and was holding a gun to her head.

"She's crazy," he said. "I've tried to help her, but there's nothing to be done."

"Put the gun down, Manchester. It was Swan, who wasn't Swan at all, but Will finally divested of turban and robe, though his face and hands were still covered in black.

Will stood alert. Joe moved in beside him, and Orrin next to Joe.

"Stay back," Will ordered Deanna. Deanna stopped. Elspeth stood rigidly nearby. Slowly she began inching her way toward Deanna. Across the lawn, the other guests crowded together in the open doorway. But Deanna was focused only on the two Manchesters.

"He's lying," Madeline cried. "*He* killed the maids and made me poison Swan. He said he would kill me if I didn't do it."

Lord David laughed. Turned her around and kissed her savagely. "Adieu, sister dear."

He pushed her toward the trio of men. She fell into Joe, who staggered back from the force of the impact.

"David!" she screamed.

"He's getting away!" Elspeth yelled as Lord David turned and ran.

Madeline squirmed, then rammed her head into Joe's stomach.

He looked down as if he couldn't believe it.

She clawed at his face.

"Joe, do something!" Deanna yelled.

Joe tried to grab hold of Madeline's hands to restrain her, but she thrashed wildly.

"Now he decides to be a gentleman," Deanna muttered. "Come on." She and Elspeth ran to either side of Madeline and pulled her away. But she twisted and wrenched out of their hands and ran.

Straight at the cliff.

She was there and then she was gone. Not hidden by the fog this time. But into darkness. All that was left was her scream.

After a stunned moment, they ran as one to the edge of the cliff. At first they could see nothing. Then, through the mist, they saw the body of Madeline Manchester lying unmoving on the rocks, until she was again swallowed by the fog.

"Six feet away she would have fallen into the water and had a chance of survival," Joe said.

"Serves her right," Elspeth muttered.

Deanna nodded and turned to Joe, only he was no longer there. He was running after Will and Orrin in pursuit of Lord David.

From the north, circles of light appeared, followed by the shrill of whistles. Reinforcements would cut off his escape.

Lord David stopped, realized he was surrounded, and turned abruptly to run back the way he had come.

And ran straight into Joe, who tackled him at the knees. Lord David went down hard.

But a quick movement of his feet upended Joe, and he fell beside him. Lord David staggered to his feet and started off again, but Joe launched himself at the man's back, and both men went down. They rolled along the walk, locked together in combat.

And awfully close to the edge of the cliff.

From out on the sea, a foghorn sounded, then the blowing of a ship's horn, but Deanna hardly noticed it. Every nerve was taut as she watched the two men inch closer and closer to the edge. Then, suddenly, both men were on their feet.

Lord David pushed Joe away and, in the moment they were parted, he turned enough to smile at Deanna, then stepped over the edge. Joe grabbed for him, but he was too late to save Lord David . . . or himself.

Both men disappeared over the cliff.

Chapter
28

D eanna screamed and rushed to the place where the
two men had been. She knew it was a straight drop
from there to the water. They could be drenched but alive.

"Down there," she cried to Will, who motioned to his men,
and they spread out, some shining lights straight out into the
water, others finding places nearby where they could climb
down. If only one of those lanterns would find them. Deanna
wanted to go look but knew she would be in the way.

So she and Elspeth stood on the walk and stared down into
the dark sea until it hurt.

There was no sign of either man.

From out at sea, they heard the steam whistle of a passing
yacht.

"That's coming closer," Orrin said. "Listen."

Deanna and Elspeth held each other and listened.

"The whistle is getting higher," Deanna said.

"That's because sound shifts to a higher frequency when it's coming closer."

"How do you know that?" Elspeth asked, her voice trembling.

"Mr. Joseph told me." His voice broke. "I sure hope they find him alive."

Deanna squeezed her eyes shut and prayed.

It was cold, and someone brought them blankets to wrap around their shoulders. Gran Gwen came out to stand beside them.

Deanna looked up. "He went over the side with Lord David."

Gran Gwen nodded. "He's jumped off that cliff hundreds of times as a boy."

"But—"

"Hush, child."

Will dispatched four men to retrieve Madeline's body and sent the rest to spread out searching closer to the rocks in case they had washed ashore. The wayward lights became smaller, fainter.

"They won't give up looking, will they?" Elspeth asked.

"They'd better not," said Orrin.

Gran Gwen just looked out to sea.

The night drew on; Will climbed back up to where they were standing. What Deanna could see of his face looked grim.

"Will?" Gran Gwen said.

"Nothing yet. But we'll find him."

Find him, thought Deanna. She wanted to shout. *You have to find him alive.* "Why did the Manchesters have to come here? Why did we trust them?"

No one answered. Only Gran Gwen, Will, and she still stood

on the cliff. Vlady, Cassie, and the others had gone to watch the policemen carry Madeline's body across the rocks and up the steps that led from the beach.

Orrin was taking Elspeth back inside, but they stopped to watch with the others. "I think she's dead, Miss Deanna," Orrin called out.

Good, Deanna thought, but her throat wouldn't let the word escape. She didn't care. She hoped Madeline was dead. She hoped Lord David was dead. *Just please save Joe.*

Finally, Will took them both by the arm. "Let me take you inside. I'll let you know as soon as there's any word."

But Gran Gwen wouldn't budge. Deanna moved closer to her. "They'll find him." But she was beginning to lose hope.

Hours had passed, or so it seemed, when out of the mist arose a ship. Like a phantom boat. For the briefest second, Deanna thought maybe this had all been a part of the plan, but she knew it wasn't so.

Then she heard voices and the sound of a boat docking in the distance.

"The yacht," Gran Gwen said, as if in a dream. "Lionel and your father were coming up in the yacht tonight."

"My father?" Deanna asked.

"Yes, and to come home to this."

"No," Deanna said, and began to cry.

Gran Gwen took her by the shoulders. "We must meet them. Tell them what has transpired."

"No."

"Come, Deanna, we must be brave."

They walked south, past the rocks where Madeline had fallen. Past the wooden staircase that led to their private beach, where she and Joe had been friends again, if only for a little while. Down the sloping path to where Mr. Ballard's yacht, the *Laurette*, had docked. Deanna could see it through the clearing fog. The activity of the deck hands was so normal that she couldn't believe that things were not.

She heard Gran Gwen's intake of breath and saw Lionel Ballard walking down the gangplank with—she looked more closely—her own father. And between them another man, wrapped in a blanket.

Deanna grabbed Gran Gwen's hand and squeezed it as they both watched the men step onto the dock and begin the ascent up to the lawn until they were in full view.

Deanna wanted to run just to put them out of their worry, but Gran Gwen moved slowly, stately. They were still several yards away when Gran Gwen whispered, "*Mon Dieu. Gloire à Dieu.*"

And then Deanna saw. It was Joe, wet and huddled in the blanket. Deanna ran and didn't stop until she was standing in front of them. "That was so stupid! You could be dead!"

"But I'm not," Joe said, taken aback.

"But you could be! And you worried Gran Gwen. Idiot!"

Her father interceded. "Yes, yes, Deanna. But let's wait until Joe has dry clothes and a brandy before you tell him so."

Then she noticed a fourth man walking a foot behind them. Lord David?

She would scratch his eyes out. She stepped in front of him, but even in the dark she realized she'd never seen him before.

"Who are you?" she demanded.

"Deanna!" her father warned, but Lionel Ballard laughed.

"Miss Deanna Randolph, meet Lord David Manchester."

————•◦◦❈◦◦•————

I
t was a good hour later, the guests had departed, and Joe was finally dry and sipping brandy like it was any other night at home.

Whenever he looked up and saw Deanna glaring at him, he looked sheepish and went back to studying his brandy snifter.

Introductions had been made, and Will and Joe explained their plan to catch a murderer; they didn't even mention Deanna and Elspeth's part in at all.

Elspeth was out of earshot because she and Orrin were eating leftovers in the kitchen with Cook, but Deanna heard every pompous word. When she couldn't stand Will and Joe's bravado any longer, she blurted out, "If you're the real Lord Manchester, who were those other two?"

"I haven't the foggiest," said new Lord David. He did have blue eyes and a drooping mustache, but those were the only features that were even close to the former Lord David. He was shorter than average height, had a high forehead and a slightly receding chin. "I began to be concerned when Mr. Woodruff never arrived at my plantation last month. So I sent a telegram to Lionel here, and when I learned that I was already in Newport, I immediately boarded my yacht and came to see what I was doing here."

Deanna started to smile. This new Lord David was certainly an odd creature. But she already liked him more than she'd ever like the old Lord David, despite that one's good looks.

"I missed Lionel's telegram to my bank, but fortunately, I landed in New York Harbor this morning and went to R and

W just in time to catch these gentlemen preparing to leave for
Newport. So I hopped a ride."

"I don't understand," Deanna said.

"Nor I," Joe added. "I mean, I get that those two were
imposters, some kind of swindlers. But the only people who knew
what they were about are dead or missing."

"The hospital rang earlier to say that Madeline, or the woman
who called herself Madeline, succumbed to her injuries shortly
after being admitted."

"Did she suffer?" Deanna asked.

"Yes, Madame Guillotine, she did."

"Good."

"Deanna . . ." her father began.

"Yes, good," Gran Gwen said.

"A couple of avenging angels," Mr. Randolph said.

"Nothing angelic about either of them," Joe mumbled.

"You, young man," said his father, "keep your opinions to
yourself."

"My men are still looking for Lord—the other Lord David's
body. So far, nothing. He might never be found, depending on
the tides."

"But he *is* dead," Gran Gwen said.

"Most probably," Will said. He'd wiped most of the burnt
cork off his face and hands, leaving only a streak at his neck
and around his eyes.

"I lost hold of him," Joe said. "I called to him, but he swam
away. As if he didn't want to be saved. Then I was being grap-
pled out of the water by the *Laurette*. I don't think I thanked
you properly, sir."

"You will, son. You will."

Joe sank down into his chair.

Mr. Randolph put his glass down. "Well, if Francis revives, he'll tell us what happened, by God."

"Indeed," Mr. Ballard agreed.

"Unfortunately, the prognosis isn't good," Joe said.

Will cleared his throat. "Thanks to your daughter, Mr. Randolph, we were able to obtain a specimen of the medicine being administered to him. It was laced with a potent depressant. It would surely have killed him eventually, but we would never have guessed how he died."

"That must have been what Daisy saw," Deanna said. Tears sprang to her eyes; she couldn't help it.

Joe leaned forward, his elbows resting on his knees. "And I prevented her from going to tell Orrin what she knew. She might be alive if I hadn't been so chivalrous."

"Deanna and Elspeth were right," Will added. "And I didn't believe them. I thought they'd been reading too many dime novels."

Deanna saw her father cut her a quick look and smother a smile.

"What about Swan?" Deanna asked. "Will he recover? He must know what happened or have been a part of it." She got up to pour herself and Gran Gwen more tea. "I hope he wasn't in on it. He warned us to get away."

"We'll have to wait and see; the doctor believes Elspeth got to him in time, and he has a good chance of recovering," Will said.

Deanna handed Gran Gwen her cup and went back to her seat.

"Deanna?" Her father asked. "Where are your shoes?"

She looked down at her feet. She'd taken off her wet hose when they'd first come back into the house and had forgotten about her shoes in the excitement that followed.

"I don't know. Somewhere outside."

Her father put his hand to his forehead. "Thank heaven your mother isn't here."

"Is she coming?"

"Not anytime soon. The doctor has recommended she take Adelaide to Switzerland to one of those nice spas for the cure. She's arranging the trip now."

"Mama wrote to say she was sending Aunt Harriet to me."

"So she told me. But once your mother and sister are gone to Switzerland, I think we can dispense with Aunt Harriet. You'll stay in the city with me or here with Gran Gwen during the week, if she'll have you."

Gran Gwen nodded. "I'd be delighted, George."

"Thank you. But, Gwen, try not to make an anarchist out of her before we return to New York for the fall."

Gran Gwen just smiled.

Chapter
29

On the day Swan, the obeah man, awoke to consciousness, Francis Woodruff breathed his last.

Will picked Joe and Deanna up in a hansom on his way to the hospital.

"I probably shouldn't let you in on my conversation with Swan, but since you were both so involved in the outcome, you may listen." He gave Deanna a pointed look. "Listen."

She nodded.

Will showed his badge first at the front desk and then to the officer assigned to sit outside the door of Swan's private room.

Swan was sitting up in bed in a white hospital robe, which made his complexion seem even darker. His eyes were nearly black until he looked up.

Then his eyes widened and flashed, and he seemed to shrink a bit beneath sheet. But he didn't look away as he watched Will approach.

And he didn't hesitate when Will asked his first question.

He told them that Lord David and Madeline, whose names were really Harry and Mary Osbourne, had in fact been brother and sister, but not plantation owners. They were actors.

"Two actors whose company had been stranded by their manager when the money ran out. They found me by the road. I was an obeah man in Barbados, but my people beat me, drove me from my village, and left me to die by the road because the chief's son died and I could not bring him back to life. Harry and Mary found me and took me in. We became . . ."

"Swindlers," Joe interjected.

"Yes, swindlers. Harry was very good at it. It was the way he and Mary survived, by trickery, when they could not find an acting job.

"We are on the same steamer to Barbados with Mr. Woodruff. He gambles—not very well—and consorts with the ladies, Mary included. He loses. Every night he loses and takes Mary off to his bed."

Deanna reeled on her feet. Father and son. Madeline had seduced both. It was horrifying.

"We get close to Barbados; he is more reckless. He loses all the money he is to pay for sugar, then he gives Harry stocks so he can lose some more."

"When we dock and he realizes what he has done, he begs my master to hold on to the stocks until he can buy them back. The three of them concoct a plan for my master to be this Lord David and come to Newport for more money.

"Mr. Woodruff, he thinks he can raise more money, then return to Barbados for the sugar." Swan tapped his temple with a long finger. "But Harry, he is very clever. He don't tell Mr. Woodruff, but he plans to sell those stocks to the big sugar man in New York."

"Havemeyer," Joe said in disgust.

"Yes, that is him. He pays very much for them, much more than they're worth, my master says. Now Harry has much money."

"Except that he drowned in the ocean."

"Perhaps. You have found him?"

"Not yet," Will admitted. "We may never recover his body. The currents are swift there."

"Or perhaps that is because he doesn't wish to be found."

"If he sets foot on American soil, he'll be arrested and sent to prison."

Swan shrugged. Not smug, or triumphant, just accepting.

"Did this Harry Osbourne kill Daisy and Claire, the servant girls?"

"He did not."

"Did you?"

"I do not kill."

Will looked incredulous. "What about your suicide note?"

"Not written by me. That maid saves me. I am grateful."

"I'll tell her," Deanna said.

Swan nodded.

"Then who killed them?" Will asked, impatience lacing his words.

"She-devil."

"That would be Mary?"

"Mary," Swan said.

"Why?" Deanna asked.

"Because the first saw her pour poison into medicine. The second, because she was afraid of what the girl might know."

"Madeline—Mary saw her talking to me and Elspeth."

"Deanna," Will warned.

Swan was looking steadily at Deanna. He nodded solemnly. "She would have killed you next. I told your Elspeth to leave, but she is a stubborn woman."

Deanna nodded.

Will scoffed. "I'm having a hard time believing that a woman of her size and stature could've overpowered them and then carried their bodies out to the cliff and thrown them over the side. Can you explain how she managed that?"

A slash of a smile from Swan, then he was expressionless again. "She strangled the first one, pushed the second one down the steps. I, Swan, took them to the cliffs."

"That makes you an accessory after the fact."

"That makes me a man whose life she held in her hands. Is she really dead?"

"Yes."

"We shall see."

"You're not really afraid her spirit will come back to haunt you?"

"To punish me for telling her that I would not do more, no more. I would not do that again. She try to kill me, too. She puts poison in my drink. She doesn't like weak."

"Is that why she put poison in Mr. Woodruff's medicine?"

"Like me, he begin to feel bad about what he has done, especially when he sees her with his son. He wants to confess, to tell his son to leave her alone. He rages, he begs, he goes a little crazy. She don't like him no more. She puts him out of the way. But she can't kill him right away." Swan closed his eyes.

"Why?" Will asked.

Swan's eyelids fluttered. "She need him until Harry collects all the money and they can disappear."

"Why was it necessary to destroy so many lives?" Will asked.

"To Harry, it was a game to be played for money. But she— she was insatiable."

"So she didn't really fall in love with Charles, like she said?" Deanna asked.

Swan coughed a laugh. "Not that one. First the father, then the son. She was insatiable in this, too. Her own brother. She took them all. And all were powerless against her desire."

Deanna shuddered, as did the others. She didn't want to hear more.

"Okay, that's it," Joe said. "I'm taking Deanna outside."

For once, Deanna didn't protest. She was more than ready to go.

They waited for Will on the steps of the hospital. It was only a few minutes before he joined them.

"I shouldn't have let you come."

"You couldn't stop me. I would have come on my own."

"Bob would kill us both for subjecting you to that."

"Perhaps, but if you recall, I was the one who told you about seeing those two kissing on the landing." Something she would not forget for a long time. And wished she'd never seen in the first place.

She'd have to ask Gran Gwen about women like that. Were they fiends? Or was it the way most women outside of society were? She couldn't ask Joe or Will.

"At least now it's over," Joe said. "Did they really think they could get away with it?"

Will passed his hand over his face. "According to Swan, they always did before. I believe this wasn't even the first time that Mary resorted to murder."

Deanna shuddered. "What will happen to Swan? Will he go to jail?"

Will shrugged. "That isn't up to me. But it doesn't look like he has much of a future. Jail or sending him back to Barbados, where it doesn't sound like he'll be welcomed. He may be a victim of circumstance, but we can't just set him free to roam the streets of Newport."

"It's all so sad," Deanna said.

"It's life," said Will.

———⊶⊷———

Within a fortnight of the announcement of Francis Woodruff's death, Charles learned the full extent of his father's debt. Not only had he gone through Mrs. Woodruff's millions as well as his own, he also owed vast amounts to his gambling companions.

Charles was obliged to put Seacrest up for sale, including the furnishings and stables, and the family made plans to move to Nevada, where they hoped Mrs. Woodruff's father would take them in and help the family start over again.

On their last day in town, Charles drove his mother and sister to Randolph House to say good-bye. Cassie and her mother only came in for a few short minutes. Charles waited at the curb.

Deanna and her father walked them to the street, and Mr. Randolph helped Mrs. Woodruff into the carriage.

Deanna gave her friend a heartfelt hug.

Cassie clung to her. "I'll miss you."

"I'll miss you, too. I wish I were going with you."

"How can you say that? No more Newport. No more life. I'll never marry Vlady now."

Deanna was afraid that was true. "Perhaps not. But think

of all the adventures awaiting you, instead of being stuck here and strangled by society."

"But I want to be strangled by society! I want to marry Vlady."

"Come, dear, it's time to say good-bye." Mrs. Woodruff smiled, but it trembled on her lips. She gave her hand to Mr. Randolph. "Thank you. I'll send you the money for our trip as soon as I can. But I'm afraid there might not be anything we can do about the business for a long, long time."

"Don't you worry about either. I'm sure with Charles's business sense you'll recover quickly. I just wished things had turned out differently for you."

"Oh, don't mind me. I've never been afraid of hard work. That's where I started before Papa discovered the silver lode. I only hope he'll forgive my marrying a scoundrel and take us in." She sniffed. "That's what Papa called Francis then and I'm afraid he was right. Maybe he'll help us get started again."

"I'm sure he must."

"We'll take Tillie with us, of course. That might make things a little more difficult. They never have made up. It's time they did." She straightened. "And it won't be bad for Charles and Cassie to work; that way they'll appreciate success all the more."

"But I don't want to do hard work," Cassie wailed. "I want things to go back to the way they were!"

Which was something that none of them could give her.

The last Deanna saw of her lifelong friend was Cassie leaning out of the carriage and waving, the pink ostrich plumes of her hat swaying in the breeze.

"Poor Cassie. Poor Mrs. Woodruff." Deanna sighed.

"Not poor Charles?" asked her father.

"I guess, but he wasn't faithful to Adelaide."

"It's a blessing we found that out before she married him."

"Yes, I guess. Is she disappointed?"

"More humiliated than disappointed, I think. But a nice long trip to Geneva will go a long way to helping her forget. And how about you, my dear? Are you contemplating any more adventures more appropriate to dime novels than to a young lady of fashion?"

"Not me. I've had enough of that kind of excitement to last me a lifetime."

"I hope so, because your mother is certain you'll cause a scandal if I let you stay in Newport without her. Promise me you'll behave."

"Yes, Papa. I'll do absolutely everything Gran Gwen tells me to do."

"I shudder to think." He reached over and kissed her forehead. They walked back into the house arm in arm.

She didn't know what her father was thinking, but Deanna was thinking that as soon as she got to Gran Gwen's, she would take off her corset and order a tennis outfit and one of those new bathing costumes.

And then she was going out to buy herself a bicycle.

The Gilded Age, named by Mark Twain because of its conspicuous consumption, lasted from the 1880s until after the turn of the twentieth century. It was a time of outrageous spending, ruthless business practices, and the rise of monopolies, but it also saw a blossoming of scientific progress, political unrest, and women's rights.

At the height of this turbulent era Newport, Rhode Island, was known as the "Queen of Resorts."

The Newport Season during the Gilded Age lasted six to eight weeks, from the middle of July through August. During that time exorbitant amounts were spent on entertainment and outdoing everyone else on the social ladder—a very exclusive ladder.

No expense was spared for the building and outfitting of the "cottages" where the Astors, Belmonts, Vanderbilts, and their peers displayed their wealth and partied for a few weeks a year. The best of European art and architecture was utilized, the most talented craftsmen employed for these edifices, whose constructions ran to millions of dollars: Marble House, Belcourt, Rosecliff, The Elms. The largest and most expensive of all, The Breakers, built for Alice Vanderbilt and finished just in time for the 1895 season when *A Gilded Grave* takes place, cost $12 million (about $315 million today).

Entertainment was lavish and closed to all but the best families. Dinners often cost many thousands of dollars, balls even more. Entertainment budgets for the few weeks could run into the hundreds of thousands.

While the men spent their weekdays in the city, the women's days were carefully scheduled, with time allotted for visiting, the beach, tennis, afternoon teas, evening soirees. Participation in society required changing dresses six to eight times a day, up to ninety new gowns a season, mostly from Parisian designers. Designer dresses cost from $100 to $500 (approximately $3,000 to $13,000 today) and most were worn only once.

On the weekends the men would return aboard luxurious ferries to attend their wives' extravaganzas and spend time on their yachts or at the several men's clubs in town. One such club was the Reading Room, a frame house in the center of Newport, used less as a place of reading and more as a retreat where the men drank and smoked, and where talk and gossip ran from business to racier subjects.

The staffs of the cottages were made up largely of local Newporters who might take a dim view of the summer people but depended on them for their livelihood. Local shopkeepers overcharged them during the summer months so they could live for the rest of the year. The townspeople had their own entertainments and never mingled with the cottagers.

In the 1890s, American dime novels—cheap paper-covered novels with bold cover pictures of bloodshed, Western adventures, heroes in action, as well as those geared toward young women, often innocent maidens under the power of dastardly villains—were inexpensive enough to be popular with the working classes. The era also saw the rise of female detectives like Kate Goelet, Loveday Brookes, and Cad Metti, who inspired Deanna and Elspeth with their daring deeds and even more so by their ingenuity at outsmarting criminals.

The story in the magazine Elspeth and Deanna find in Daisy's room is based on Dr. William Pritchard, a Glasgow physician convicted in 1865 of poisoning his mother-in-law, his wife, and possibly a household maid. Pritchard was a popular subject for these lurid tales. The actual cover I used was inspired by a 1913 copy of *Pritchard the Poisoner* by H. L. Adam. But it was so perfect I appropriated it for my 1895 story.

I likewise appropriated on Joe's behalf the inventions of John Arbuckle, a Philadelphia coffee merchant and wholesale grocer who in 1898 introduced automated packaging of his coffee beans and also began to repackage sugar. In *A Gilded Grave*, Joe is working on a series of inventions that would make sugar refining safer and more efficient, including a bagging machine.

Until that time, sugar was sold in large cones of hard compact sugar. The grocer would break off the amount requested with a pair of heavy pinchers and wrap it in paper for the customer to take home and store. In real life, Arbuckle was no match for the tactics of Havemeyer's Sugar Trust and, after a lengthy battle, was put out of business.

When the trust was declared illegal in 1891, Havemeyer and partners reopened as the American Sugar Refining Company. In 1900 the name was changed to Domino Sugar, and Havemeyer became the undisputed supplier of sugar in the United States. (I thought it was only right that R and W Sugar in *A Gilded Grave* should try to beat the trust as its own game.)

For more about life in Gilded Age Newport, visit shelley freydont.com.

Shelley Freydont is the author of several mystery series, including the Celebration Bay Mysteries (*Independence Slay*, *Silent Knife*, *Foul Play at the Fair*) and the novels featuring Lindy Haggerty and Katie McDonald. Under the name Shelley Noble, she is the author of *Beach Colors*, *Stargazey Point*, and *Whisper Beach*, among others. Her books have been translated into seven languages. Visit her online at shelleyfreydont.com.